MW01377622

THE SECRETS OF SHADOWCREST

THE SECRETS OF SHADOWCREST

LANCE MCCOLGAN

Cabalian Games

While some historical events are referenced to in *The Secrets of Shadowcrest*, this book is a work of fiction. Characters, dialogue, and the vast majority of names, places, and incidents are products of the author's imagination. Any resemblance to actual persons, living or dead, places, or incidents is entirely coincidental.

Copyright © 2023 by Lance Ian McColgan.
All rights reserved.

A Cabalian Games book
PO Box 911, Lanesborough, MA 01237
www.cabalian.games.com

First edition
ISBN 979-8-9896315-0-6

Cover Graphics and Map by Melanie "Zeragii" Griffith

10 9 8 7 6 5 4 3 2   // IS //   24 25 26 27 28 29

For the God who gave me life, breath, and a love of words. To You be the glory.

And for my grandfather, Marty, whose long life ended all too shortly before this tale could be finished. I made the hero after you, Papa.

Contents

PART II

THE HEART OF SHADOWCREST

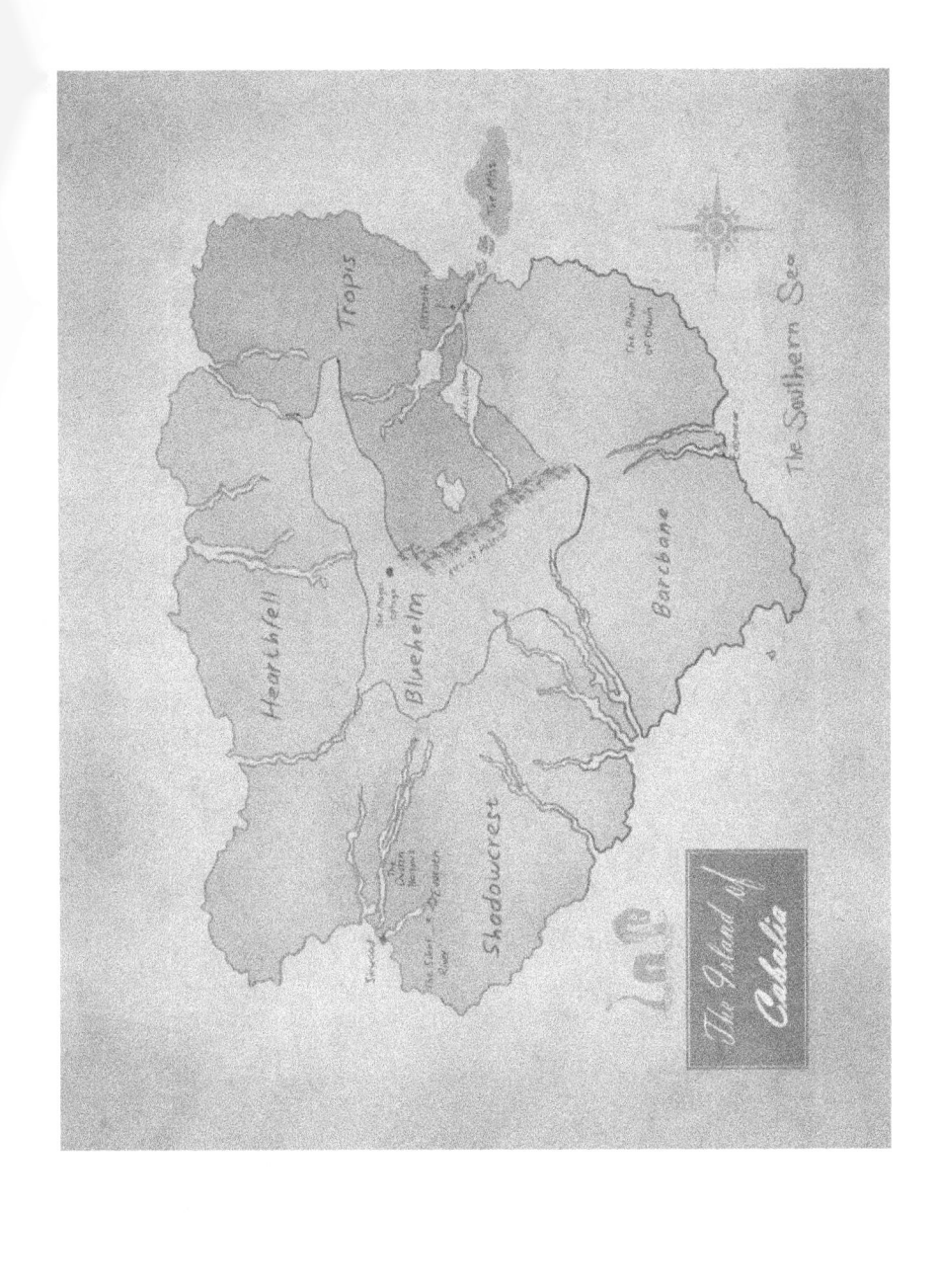

PART I

The Essari Shores

Prologue

A Fate Unknown

The flickering glow of a candle's flame illuminated an assortment of parchments, scrolls, charts, and codices strewn across a weathered table. A thick, musty smell that whispered of years long gone by permeated the air while the timbers of a room creaked from the ocean waves battering them from the other side. As the room rose and fell with the ship to which it belonged, a man sat stooped over his collections of antiquity. The lateness of the evening only served to encourage the man's musings.

"Cabalia..." he murmured. *The Island of Magic.* He reached forth his hand to a tattered map of the land that would have remained unknown to the civilized world—if the Mist had not appeared.

Ancient accounts spoke of a luminous blue mist that appeared off the west coast of Britain in the days of Julius Caesar. Most every man and child since that time knew the story of what happened thereafter. Mankind has always been curious, even if too much for its own good. First scouts, and then the armies of the Roman Empire traveled into the Mist. What they found was nothing short of extraordinary. A massive island with rich resources and stunning scenery beckoned for the arrival of civilization and culture. It would have seemed the paradise of

Eden itself had been rediscovered. That is, until one stayed long enough to realize the island was not deserted.

Fantastic creatures of fearsome abilities roamed those lands, many of which did not have a liking for the sons and daughters of Adam. Barbarians lived there also: people of a strange tongue and even stranger abilities. One tome described warriors with glowing eyes that could call fire from the very air. Other scrolls mentioned a prevailing culture of demon worship.

All of this taken together would have deterred most normal people from settling there, but the Romans were certainly not a normal people. So said Rome, after all.

The man gazed upon a sketching of a four-legged monstrosity with talons that were probably exaggerated in size. But not by much. Depictions of men running away from it in all directions served as a perfect summary of what happened during the reign of Emperor Vespasian. The colonies the Romans had worked so hard to establish for decades were all but abandoned by the end of AD 77. For hundreds of years since that time, no one had dared to attempt settling there again. Not until the Ships arrived.

The man rubbed his temples as he recalled the first time he had seen the merchant ships of Cabalia come into port. "Ah yes... the Ships," he sighed. They were magnificent vessels — lumbering behemoths of vibrant brown and rich black, far superior in size and quality than any other nation could build at the time. As wondrous as they were to behold from the outside, the treasures that lay within were truly stunning. Every variety of precious metal and gemstones without number were laden within, just waiting to find a new home with the owners-to-be that could afford them.

The chronicles of the sixth century described the occupants of these ships as friendly, cultured, and savvy in the art of commerce — hardly the savages feared by the Romans centuries earlier. They claimed their land had just emerged from a dark age of tyranny and perverse magic, and that they sought aid from the nations of the known world to help rebuild theirs. The island was supposedly rid of the monsters that had plagued it from antiquity, and the demon-worshiping had long since been disbanded. They offered their exotic treasures in exchange for food and the services of skilled craftsmen.

The man brushed his fingers over the stack of parchments detailing the experiences of those days. *What would it have been like to live then,* he wondered. *If only it could have lasted.*

For a time, this trade arrangement worked well. The nobility of the ancient world obtained shiny relics to prove their superiority over the rest of mankind, and the Cabalians obtained resources to build their world anew. People traveled freely between the realms in a spirit of peace and goodwill.

But peace bred familiarity. And familiarity drifted into complacency. And complacency gave room for stupidity. And stupidity, when it matured, married greed. And greed found a willing accomplice in violence. And so it was that in AD 712, the major powers of Europe allied themselves to invade Cabalia to have all its resources for naught the cost.

The man's jaw clenched, and he shook his head. "Fools!" he spat.

Unfortunately for Europe, none of the Roman colonists remained alive to warn of just what it was getting itself into. The old legends were laughed off as old wives' tales, certainly nothing worthy of standing in the way of literal mountains of jewels and gold. While it was true that the monsters and demon worshipers were (mostly) gone, it was also true that the Cabalians still had their unique abilities to practice magic. Magic that could, incidentally, *still* call fire from the very air. The sole reason the invasion stood a chance of success was that Cabalia had just spent many lives and resources in a great war to defeat an ancient and powerful foe. Weakened as they were, magic ultimately proved to be the trump card that drove the world's nations from the shores of Cabalia.

A depiction of a masked face glared back stoically at the man from the chart he held. *I can only imagine what they are like at home,* he pondered.

The betrayal of Cabalia at its time of need led to an acute souring of relations with Europe. Cabalia neither forgot nor forgave the "civilized world" for its covetous aggression. All foreigners, peaceful or not, were driven off the island, and Cabalia withdrew its people from foreign lands. They then used their curious arts to enchant the Mist, making it such that only Cabalians could find their way back home through it. All others who tried to follow would enter the Mist only to find themselves back at the home port from which they first left. Silence ensued for almost three hundred years.

And then the ships returned. The same magnificent ships, carrying the same magnificent cargo. The people who sailed those ships, however, had changed remarkably. There was no friendliness to be found in their behavior and little warmth to be felt in their business dealings. All of them were covered from head to toe in new regalia designed to protect and to intimidate. Most disturbing of all were their masks. Cold. Soulless. Indiscernible. This was the new face of the Cabalian traveler. And it was this face that gave Lord William Steele a most uneasy feeling as he sailed west to an unknown fate.

I

The King's Mission

William reached into a pocket of his cloak, wishing to focus his mind away from the unsettling images that swelled in his consciousness. His fingers rummaged until they found the worn leather journal he never traveled without. After pulling the candle on the table closer to him, he made quick work of setting up his quill and ink. He inhaled deeply and tried to gather his thoughts even as the tempest outside rattled the room around him. As best he could manage under the circumstances, he began to write:

December 28th, A.D. 1153

There truly is no rest for the weary. I was summoned by Geoffrey ere the break of dawn Christmas eve — urgent matters Henry wished to discuss. The snow was so deep it took me twice as long as it should have to arrive at the court.

Being the right-hand man of an up-and-coming king was never supposed to be an easy job. William knew this. Still, it was always a painful experience when the excitement of adventure and intrigue gave way to the gritty realities of duty and sacrifice.

When I finally arrived, he was overjoyed to see me. "Ah, William, my friend!" he said. "Thank God Geoffrey could find you in time! Another hour, and I dare say it would have been too late!"

He beckoned with great eagerness to a table with some curious-looking artifacts on it. After dismissing all other company from the room, he turned to me and spoke with a hushed tone. "Can you believe it's been a month already since we sealed the treaty? The majority of my advisors think it's solved all our problems." Henry's eyes narrowed in disgust that I couldn't blame him for. "But you and I know better. My claim to the throne is never fully sure while Stephen and his son roam England."

It was true. Years of civil war in England had stalemated into a treaty that technically assured Henry II the throne... eventually. The terms stipulated that Stephen's oldest remaining son would abdicate his claim to the throne and that Henry would succeed Stephen upon his death. Much could happen before that event occurred, though, and both sides knew it.

"Rumors have it they're already planning my assassination. We must strike first."

"My liege, you need only say the word, and I will assemble my best men to deal with them both," I assured him.

"No," he insisted. "We can't do this the conventional way, my friend. While I don't doubt the abilities of your men, my position with the Church is mediocre at best, and the clergy have already expressed their support for Stephen over me. If they die by a clear assassination, everyone will know who to blame, and the treaty will be nullified. No, we will need to handle this in a much more... subtle manner." I saw a glint in his eyes that foreshadowed the secret he was about to divulge. "You are familiar with the legends of Cabalia, are you not?"

"Of course, sire. I would be a poor advisor if I were not."

"Good. Tell me what you know about House Shadowcrest."

I stroked my chin as I searched my recollections.

"A sinister house, that lot," I said. "Descended from a patriarch of pure

shadow, they say. Infamous for their spies, assassins, and cutthroats. Rumored to be skilled in dark magic and forbidden alchemy. Even the other Cabalians fear them."

I didn't like where this conversation was going. Why was my king so interested in these people?

"A fair synopsis," he said. "What in particular is known of their 'dark magic?'"

I furrowed my brow. "Very little. People either don't know what they do or are promptly killed for what they somehow find out."

Henry leaned in closer. "Correct. The only one knowledgeable of Shadowcrest's secrets would be a Shadowcrest himself."

"Sire…. what are you getting at?" I asked. It may have been foolish for me to be so blunt with His Highness, but the satisfaction in his smile assured me that he took no offense. At least not yet.

"When we captured Montsoreau last year, we made a most unexpected discovery," he explained as he brought his palms to rest on the table. "There was a rather pale-looking fellow in the dungeons—much paler than the other prisoners. It turns out he was, in fact, a Shadowcrest fugitive. He was willing to divulge some rather fascinating details of his homeland in return for his freedom."

A mix of emotions filled me: Roused curiosity. Wonder. Foreboding dread. And a little hurt that Henry only now took the time to tell his supposed right-hand man of this monumental event. My disappointment must have shown through.

"I see that look on your face. Please don't take it personally, William," he said. "If you had been there at the siege, you no doubt would have made the discovery yourself. But, in your absence, I had to make a decision at the moment. And there are some secrets only a king should know."

Until now, I ruefully mused. "I completely understand, my lord."

A smile played across his lips. "No… Not yet, you don't. But you will soon." His hand beckoned toward the table. "Look over here. What do you see?"

I tilted my head and swept my eyes across the length of it, squinting to make out the shapes that lay inert on the table's surface. "Rather curious things, sire," I replied.

To the left was an amulet with a strange red symbol on a black background, fastened on a black neck chain. To the right, there rested a map of Cabalia. In the center, there lay a sack that glowed from the inside. I approached the sack and unloosed the drawstring that kept its contents sealed within.

When I reached in my hand, I felt a solitary object: hard, smooth, and cool to the touch, that left my fingers with the strangest sensation I'd ever felt in my life. It felt as if I'd brushed against some primordial power of the cosmos, hiding itself behind the faintest of pulsing tremors. When I withdrew the object, I found myself staring into a brilliant blue stone the size of my fist. Its glow was mesmerizing and only reinforced the sense I got from touching it — that it was something otherworldly and very powerful.

"What is this?" I gasped.

He slowly drew up alongside me. "This will be what grants us what we seek from Cabalia. The Cabalians call it a Danuri stone. As it happens, a stone of this color and brightness is considered highly valuable."

"But what does it do?" I asked.

"They say it amplifies the results of their magic and alchemy to a considerable degree. With this in hand, even a child could level a fortress."

The information was much to take in, and I had yet to investigate the other objects on the table. I motioned to the amulet. "And this? I can only assume it has some kind of powerful magic, too."

"Indeed it does. This trinket is going to be your ticket into Cabalia itself."

My mouth dropped.

"Yes, you will be going to Cabalia personally to facilitate the transaction I desire with House Shadowcrest. With this around your neck, you and your ship will enter the Mist and successfully emerge at the Island itself, just like in olden days."

My eyes glanced over the map, whose subject and purpose were easy to discern.

"You got all these from the man in the dungeons?" I asked, my curiosity deepening at a pace only matched by my offense at how much the king had kept secret from me for so long.

"Actually, no. He was a fugitive with nothing but the clothes on his back, in no place to facilitate trade with his people. He was on the run from them

for reasons I didn't pay much attention to. Something about forbidden love and traditions and whatnot." He waved his hand dismissively. "The important thing is that he told me both where to find an actual representative from his house and what I should attempt to gain from them."

"Which is...?"

"Shadesteel, they call it. I've arranged to purchase two sets of armor made of the stuff." He turned to look me directly in the eyes. "Now, William, it's important that you be careful when you obtain the armor. The two sets will look identical but will serve two different functions entirely. One will protect me in all my future campaigns against Stephen's ilk, while the other will be a Trojan Horse that sucks away the life of any close by it. To err on the side of caution, do not stay near either set once you have them. I would hate to lose my finest compatriot."

I nodded gravely as I braced myself for this quest of a lifetime sprung on me. "When do I depart?" I asked.

"Tonight."

"That soon?"

"I'm sorry, old friend. You won't be spending Christmas here on these shores. Trust me that it's absolutely essential you leave as soon as possible. It pains me to do this, but I can't reveal all the cards in my hand just yet."

Cards: a painful reference to games I would not be enjoying, around a fire I would not be sitting around, for the holiday I would not be at home celebrating. Nothing but this blasted squall and—

A rapping on the door startled William from his flow of thoughts.

"We've spotted the Mist, sir!" a deckhand called out.

William scrambled to put away his journal and writing utensils, then tightened his cloak in preparation for the tempest that awaited him on deck. With a final deep breath, he fingered the amulet that hung around his neck and opened the door.

2

Into the Mist

The wind howled in anger, biting the faces of everyone above deck as William stepped out from his cabin. He had little time to shield his face from the frigid brine that crashed over the railings and drenched everything in sight. More than one sailor lost their footing as the ship lurched forward into a monstrosity of a wave. Barrels of supplies not properly secured spilled their contents into a sea of chaos.

"Over there, sir! Dead ahead!" a shivering sailor rasped as he pointed a purple finger into the recesses of the sea. William could barely discern the tell-tale glow of a blue haze over the crests of the waves that battered the ship.

"How long until we reach it?" he asked.

"At this rate, sir—" The ship lurched forward again, nearly knocking the men off their feet again.

"God knows. Maybe half an hour."

If we can even make it that long, thought William to himself. "Stay the course and do whatever necessary to speed us along," he commanded.

The sailor saluted and hurried off. For minutes that seemed an eternity, the ship's captain hollered out orders that were promptly obeyed. Masts were adjusted, cargo was tossed overboard, and men trampled in desperation to complete their errands.

Amid the hustle of the crew and the tumult of the sea, William found a vantage point on deck and fastened his eyes on the target that slowly but surely drew closer. Even in the middle of a starless night, the Mist glowed with enough light to make out the waves that frothed around it. The men could only hope that whatever waited on the other side of its unearthly glow would be better than the maelstrom wreaking havoc on them.

As the travelers approached their destination, it seemed nature itself was enraged at their near success and doubled down its efforts to prevent any outsiders from setting eye on Cabalia again. When the ship's bow entered the Mist, one final wave rose above the others and crashed down with indignation, soaking everything on board to its core.

And then there was stillness. The roar of the waves subsided, and the wind exchanged its howling for a placid murmuring. The sea below lapped gently at the sides of the boat, almost as if in apology for its foul temper just moments ago. The half-frozen men could only stare dumbfounded as the cerulean haze grew thicker around them. Many questions drifted into their numbed stream of consciousness. Had they all perished at sea and now entered some form of afterlife? Had they been knocked unconscious and now saw a dream? Had this whole voyage just been a dream they were about to wake up from? How long would this last?

Those of quicker wits shook themselves from their daze and took stock of the situation. Many supplies were either lost to sea or too waterlogged to be of much use. Structural damage could be seen anywhere one dared to look. Far too many men were at the point of frostbite, with no practical way to produce heat any time soon.

None of this was supposed to be happening. The night had been clear when the sun set last evening, and while everyone had been prepared for the chance of a winter storm at some point, the chaos that unleashed itself in the dead of night took them all by surprise. Something had to be done soon, or death would not be far behind.

Yet nothing could be done. Visibility remained obscure, with nothing to be seen but the Mist glowing in every direction. Time slid onward at an unknown pace while the scenery remained unchanging. Each passing moment sent any hope of survival drifting further into obscurity.

William slumped back against a damaged mast and put his head in his hands. *"So much for finding Cabalia,"* he sighed. *"Here I thought I'd make the discovery of a lifetime. Now all I'll be is a frozen corpse lost at sea."*

Painful memories surged before him as an all-too-familiar string of failures and misfortunes replayed themselves: the look of pain in his father's eyes as he explained Mother's death was because of *his* untimely birth; the rawness of the gashes and bruises from the bullying his most unsightly birthmark earned him; the snickering of his cohorts he was not supposed to catch but overheard anyway; the shame of missing major battles because of that stupid injury he got while drunk, mourning the death of his beloved wife.

Images of his soon-to-be orphaned boy glared at him. He drew his coat around himself to shield from view the tears that trickled down his numbed face. So distraught was he that he failed to notice the peculiar warmth the others began to feel.

What began as a barely noticeable flicker of light from underneath the door of William's cabin gradually swelled into a pulsing sequence of soft-colored light that radiated outward to all corners of the ship. Each pulse of light that reached the frozen sailors soothed them with a deeper and deeper warmth. The rhythmic hum accompanying these pulses intensified until they jarred William out of his remorse.

When he looked up, an incoming wave of light forced him to squint. He blinked a time or two before regaining the composure needed to investigate this altogether unexpected occurrence. Rising to his feet, he stole a glance around the deck. The men who had been on the brink of death just minutes ago already had ruddiness returning to their faces and limbs. For some men, the light seemed to invigorate them. Others appeared mesmerized by it, drifting into a deep and comfortable sleep.

Whatever was going on, William could not decide whether this was a dearly needed godsend or a new danger about to unmask itself. He raced toward his cabin as rapidly intensifying pulses of light, sound, and heat bombarded his senses. A handful of men clattered on behind him as eager to make out the source of the spectacle as he was. When he reached the door, he flung it open without hesitation. His eyes were adequately adjusted by then to pick out the source of the anomaly: The locked chest that stored the Danuri stone blazed with light and rattled with each new vibration that raced outward. In moments he acquired the necessary key from his now almost-dry coat. The rest of the men arrived just in time to see him twist the key into the lock and clank the massive chest open.

Every eye could now see the energy that crackled across the stone's surface in dazzling array. William paused as his mind raced. With no better plan he could think of at the moment, he thrust his hand down to envelop the stone and yelled in desperation:

"*STOP!*"

And to everyone's amazement, that is precisely what the stone did. With a final, violent tremor, the stone ceased pulsing and blazing. Bright white faded into warm yellow, then morphed into its original blue glow. The cacophony of noise died off until nothing but stunned silence filled the room. The men stood there trembling, speechless at what they witnessed, half expecting something to set it all off again.

When moments passed by and nothing else happened, William lowered the stone back into the chest with shaking hands. The stone's luminescence filled the room until the chest clinked shut and left them all in darkness.

"What the bloody hell was that?!" a man finally spat out. All eyes fastened on the still speechless Lord Steele. William had to think quickly, as he could feel the mutinous intents rising within the shocked and angered sailors.

"Yeah, what *was* that?" another sailor rumbled. "First we almost freeze to death, and then you almost burn us up and blind us with that... thing!"

Beads of cold sweat trickled upon William's brow as he realized the full extent of his predicament. He was not at leave to discuss the nature of the Danuri stone, but the men would surely mutiny if not given some explanation. It seemed clear to him the only path forward would involve some deception. Straightening his posture and regaining command of his tone, William replied with the calm authority he had learned over the years to use even when he felt neither calm nor in authority.

"*That*, gentlemen, is the only reason you are not currently a block of ice keeping the Kraken's spirits nice and cold. As it is, I'm under strict orders not to reveal the identity of this artifact." He paused just long enough to give his next sentence an air of deliberation. "But, given the circumstances, I think you have all earned the right to know. That item you saw comes from the very land we sail to. The Cabalians call it a Hearthstone. It's a magical item used to bring light and heat to their land in seasons of extreme winter. I expected it to act as a safeguard if a storm like this happened, but I didn't realize it needed time to charge in the Mist before it could be used.

"When it didn't work for us before we entered the Mist, I stashed it away as a hopeless cause. Though it appears that all the time we've spent in the Mist overcharged it—a miscalculation, but a happy one at that. Given the squall we just went through, we needed to have as much heat as possible. I apologize for the scare, but as I said, I was not at liberty to share my knowledge of this item."

William impressed himself with how well he was doing under so much pressure. The tale he wove on the spur of the moment seemed to satisfy the disgruntled crew members. He could feel the tension dissipating from the room, so he decided it was safe to seal up his ruse.

"You have proven both your bravery and your abilities through this ordeal. Our king is in your debt for the success of this mission, so I have no regrets sharing this with you all. I have full confidence you can keep a secret of the king. I must, however, caution you that if, God forbid, I have misjudged you and word of this slips out to anyone off this ship, I will have the whole lot of you punished to the *fullest extent* allowed by our sovereign. Am I clear?" The men nodded their assent, and thus satisfied, William led them back to join the others on the main deck.

The men lulled to slumber by the Danuri stone were now fully awake and quite confused at how warm and dry they all were. Once again, many pairs of eyes turned to William for an explanation. As he opened his mouth to reiterate the story he had just shared, he perceived something the others had not yet seemed to notice. The Mist was thinning, but there was still plenty of light to see with, which could only mean one thing: They were about to exit the Mist in broad daylight. What were the odds that Cabalia was just moments away from being unveiled? Good enough in William's mind to aim for some dramatic flair.

"I understand, men, you have many questions about what's happened in the last several hours," he said as he paced to the front of the ship. "How such a ferocious squall could appear from thin air with not a moment's warning. How long it's been and how far we've gone since we first entered the Mist. The display of light we experienced just now. How we survived the full rage of the sea, fully warm and dry, to boot."

Having reached the ship's prow, he turned to face his audience. "By all accounts, we should be dead men. Yet here we stand. I cannot explain everything that has befallen us, but what I *do* know, I share with you now.

"When we left the shores of Europe, you were told only that our destination was Cabalia. What you were not told is that we carry an artifact of great price that comes from the shores of that land itself. This artifact was powerless to aid us while we remained in our own land. But we are no longer in our own land." As he said this, the first shafts of golden sunlight streamed through the thinning Mist. William smiled as he continued. "The lights you saw and the warmth you felt were the effects of the Hearthstone: the item we now return to its rightful place... to Cabalia."

He beckoned behind him to the front of the ship. The men's gaze extended past their leader's hand to see the prow as it broke through the Mist. The full glory of a summer day's sun burst forth upon them, vibrant with a fullness one would not have thought possible outside a dream. Yet for all its brilliance, the light did not overpower their eyes so much as invite them onward to see what lay ahead.

Waters as blue as the cloudless sky above them stretched on toward a sight that truly was a marvel to behold. From the depths of a sea clearer than crystal, there rose a tower, if it could indeed be called such. At first impression, it was of solid silver, and it rose hundreds of feet into the air. When the men craned their necks to find its peak, they found the massive edifice ended in five spires that rotated steadily. A single orb of light hung above each spire, each of a different color: one blue, one green, one red, one yellow, and one gray.

Upon further scrutiny, the men realized that the tower's trunk was not solid at all, but composed of five separate strands that rotated around each other and culminated in the spires on top. Water churned at the base of the structure, creating the continuous roar of a waterfall that only reached their ears as a distant rumble.

Off to the side rose a smaller but still gigantic monument that bore the shape of a man. The man depicted was old but did not look frail in the slightest. His eyes were keen, peering as it were into the souls of all who emerged from the recesses of the Mist. Long hair hung down loosely, flowing well past his shoulders. One hand gripped the simple staff he carried while the other rested at his side as if ready for action at a moment's notice. His overall expression preserved in metallurgy was a look of great wisdom, experience, and patience blended together. It looked as if this sage had kept a calm and watchful guard over his tower for centuries untold.

As the men looked onward, a great flock of brightly colored birds darted past the tip of the sage's staff and dove hundreds of feet head-first to the ocean below. A breathtaking array of emerald, cobalt, violet, gold, and flaming red interwove itself as the birds fell in a crisscrossing pattern. Rather than break off to skim the top of the water as the men expected, they continued onward and plunged deep below the sea's glassy surface. The men could only stare awestruck as they waited to see what would happen next.

Whether it was seconds or minutes that passed by, no one could tell, until all at once the water erupted into a geyser of living rainbows as the birds ascended once again, freshly caught food still hanging out their mouths. The men's eyes followed the course of the departing formation to see the unmistakable shape of a coastline directly ahead of them. There was no question in anyone's mind that these were the shores of Cabalia itself, finally seen by the outside world once more.

William allowed the crew a minute more of awed reverence before he broke the silence.

"We won't get any closer just staring at it, men. Get to your posts and bring us to shore!"

The sailors complied readily, and soon the ship bustled with activity once again. Although most of the structural damage remained from the squall, it seemed the magic of the Danuri stone saw fit to repair the rigging ever so slightly to render it just barely usable. Progress toward the island was slower than anyone would have liked, but at least allowed everyone additional time to take in the view. As they first passed the statue and then the massive tower, they were even more impressed to see them up close. The roaring at the tower's base was so deafening no one could hear themselves so much as think. By the time the booming dropped off to a low rumble again, everyone was relieved to have a return to tranquility.

In time, the once-distant silhouette of the coastline took on colors and detail. A vast tree line stretched farther than the eye could see, broken only by the beginnings of an exceedingly great city. Upon further approach, immense ports and docks could be distinguished. Countless ships of different colors and sizes drifted along with the wind, some heading to port and others breaking off to follow the endless tree line. Two enormous outcroppings of rock formed a natural bay that the ships entered and exited.

Not long after entering this bay, William saw a few of his men pointing to the water in excitement. When he drew near to investigate, he had trouble at first finding what had them so thrilled. There was nothing unusual on the surface of the water, and nothing approached them from the depths. He then saw the glimmering that had caught their eyes.

Focusing his gaze below the waves, he was surprised just how far down he could look into the depths. At the bottom of the ocean floor, there sparkled in clear view a variety of precious gemstones. Sapphires, amethysts, rubies, emeralds, topazes, diamonds, and more all reflected the sun's light back up at the gawking men. It was a painfully alluring sight to witness: a king's ransom many times over, able to be seen but not retrieved. He shook his head as he sympathized with the longing looks of his men who had never seen so much wealth in their lives. *"I see where the Cabalians got all their gemstones,"* he thought.

Brushing aside the urge to continue staring, he turned around and made his way back to his cabin. He retrieved the map of Cabalia that King Henry had given him, then returned to the main deck to consult with the captain and the helmsman. Stretching the map before them, he pointed to a spot in the bottom corner. "Right now, we appear to be in the midst of Glimmerstone Bay," he explained. "There will be two great ports up ahead that we can enter. We'll want to land at the rightmost one, here." The helmsman nodded and made the necessary adjustments to the ship's course.

Turning to face the captain directly, William continued: "The men must be kept to the ship as much as possible, Captain. There is much we don't know about this land, and venturing out unnecessarily will only invite disaster. However tempted your men may be to explore this island, you must keep them here and ready to depart at a moment's notice. The king's business should only take until the evening to complete, and I expect to be sailing home as soon as the ship is in good enough repair." William paused briefly. "If anything should delay me, you are to stay put here and continue making as many repairs as you can."

"Understood, sir," the captain replied. "But what if, God forbid, something happens to you out there and you don't make it back?"

It was a question that William dreaded to think about, but it was a possibility of dealing with House Shadowcrest.

"If I don't return by the time our ship is repaired, you're to return home without me and inform the king of everything that's transpired."

The captain gave a solemn nod. "At this rate, it'll be a couple of hours before we make it to port," he said. "Perhaps you should get some rest."

The very mention of the word "rest" provoked a sudden wave of exhaustion for William. He began to notice just how sorely his muscles ached and how hard his head throbbed. The physical and emotional turbulence of the past several hours had started to take its toll.

"An excellent idea, Captain. If you need me, you know where to find me." Glancing one more time around the ship, he strode to his chamber and locked the door behind him. As he settled down on his cot, he drew a mostly dried-out blanket over him and let gravity bring his head to rest. A weary sigh escaped him as he finally allowed himself to rest for the first time since his voyage began. Setting aside a myriad of questions to ponder and plans to make, he closed his eyes and murmured faintly before he sank into a deep and tranquil sleep.

3

The Streets of Elkreath

A pounding on the door roused William from his slumber. He groaned as recollections of the past day flooded his mind and clamored for attention. Apparently, he did not respond fast enough to his summoning, so the pounding grew harder. Stirring out of bed and muttering a curse under his breath, he rubbed his eyes as he cleared his throat. "Yes, what is it?" he croaked out.

"The captain sent me to fetch you, sir. We've made it to port," came back a reply. William chided himself for knowing better than to take a nap before he would be needed. He cleared his throat again.

"Tell him I'll be there shortly," he said firmly this time.

"Yes, sir!" the voice snapped back. The thumping of boots on timber gradually faded into the distance, and William was left alone in silence. He rubbed his still-aching muscles and mentally braced himself for what lay ahead. He shuffled over to the chest still housing the Danuri stone and transferred it to a sack thick enough to hide its glow. After slipping it into a deep pocket in his coat, he drew his hand to his neck to feel the Cabalian amulet still hanging where it was supposed to be.

Everything appeared in order, so he turned his attention to the map resting on the center of his table. The outline of Cabalia's eastern shores stared back at him, along with a sketch of the city he was about to enter. A note with instructions hung attached to the map, though he could still recall its details from when he last talked with Henry.

It all seemed straightforward enough: He was to enter the city of Elkreath at the rightmost of two great ports. From there, it was a three-mile walk to the Yohati Inn, clearly marked on the map. He was to enter any time after sundown, and a representative from House Shadowcrest would detect his amulet and approach him to finish the deal. Two sets of shadesteel armor for one strangely glowing stone. Simple enough.

William folded up the map and made his way to rejoin the crew. Orange light streamed upon the deck as he went, announcing the approach of sunset and making it apparent that the warm temperatures of Cabalia did not spare it from the short daylight of winter.

As he strode about the deck, the captain failed to notice William's arrival until he was nearly within arm's reach. He jerked around to face William, startled at the sudden appearance so close to him.

"Ah!" he exclaimed. "There you are! I was beginning to worry." He eyed William in brief scrutiny. "Did you have a good rest?"

"While it lasted," sighed William with a weary smile. Changing the topic back to business, he then queried, "How long has it been since we arrived?"

"Not too long. Maybe fifteen minutes or so."

"And no one has approached us yet?"

"Other than mooring the ship, not a soul."

William peered down at the quay their vessel docked at. A number of dockworkers busied themselves in mooring the ship, while a handful of men milled around waiting for its occupants to disembark. One of them was somewhat taller and better dressed than the others. Judging by the official-looking book he carried, one could only assume he was in charge of collecting the docking fee. William turned back to face the captain. "Wait here while I deal with them."

"With all due respect, sir," his compatriot protested, "I *am* the captain of this ship, and I have loads more experience than you with bringing a ship to port."

William reluctantly ceded the point. "Fine then, but I need to be the one to present our credentials for being here in the first place."

The two men disembarked from the boat without further discussion and stepped onto the dock. The better-dressed dockworker approached them as the others finished securing the ship. The blur of sounds with which he spoke made it quite clear that English was not the language of choice in Cabalia.

William fingered the amulet that hung around his neck as he said, "I'm sorry, sir, but we only speak English." At this, the man's eyes and mouth widened before he caught himself. He shouted something to one of the dockworkers before turning to face them. He spoke slowly in broken sentences.

"My sorries. Not know much English the best. Valdwin know more."

A middle-aged man of short stature and even shorter black hair stepped forward and shook William's hand. His copper brown eyes shone with a friendliness as warm as the sun's setting light.

"Welcome to Cabalia, Englishmen," he said. "My name is Valdwin. Please forgive my friend here — it is very unusual for us to have visitors from other lands. I see you are here on business of...Shadowcrest." He frowned momentarily before recovering his warm composure. "I see that your ship needs repair, and I'm sure your men are quite tired from their journey. We must, of course, still collect the docking fee for your ship. We normally do not accept foreign coin here, but gold is gold," he said with a wink. "Let's see what you have."

William nodded and opened the moneybag Henry had given him. After counting out three rather large gold coins, he held them out for inspection. "I think these should suffice."

Valdwin's eyes narrowed as he evaluated the currency. Both William and the captain knew how easy it would be for the Cabalians to charge a grossly inflated price for foreigners to dock in their lands. They could see a number of thoughts crossing Valdwin's mind as his eyes narrowed and he turned to look at his boss. They held their breath to see if their already overpriced offer would be accepted. When his gaze focused back on them, he smiled.

With a nod that brought great relief, he stated, "Yes, that should do just fine. Let's get your custom papers squared away." Valdwin motioned to his superior, who then approached the captain and began to fill out official records. As William stood gazing at his ship and the sunset behind it, Valdwin cleared his throat.

"It really is rare to see a foreigner here," he said. "I've already introduced myself, but what is your name?"

"William," Lord Steele replied as he turned to face the Cabalian. The final rays of the setting sun accentuated the already burnished nature of Valdwin's eyes. If this is what Cabalians looked like without their masks on, it was a shame Europe never got to see their faces anymore, he mused.

The jovial nature of Valdwin's eyes appeared just as clearly in his voice when he replied, "Well, William, I know plenty of good inns and taverns to refresh your men not too far from here. Elkreath is quite the sight to see at nighttime, you know."

William could not help but smile for a moment before he sighed. "I appreciate your friendliness, Valdwin. I really didn't expect to find that here. But I'm afraid my men must remain at the ship. I'm here on important business, and I can't risk any delays. We must be able to leave as soon as possible."

The dockworker's smile dampened slightly but held up quite well as he replied: "I understand. Duty's call is a hard master, but quite necessary for us all."

William raised an eyebrow. "You seem a little too well-spoken to be a mere dockworker. Unless all of you are like that here..."

"Goodness no!" Valdwin laughed. "It's the same here as in Europe. But you are right. I haven't always worked the docks. I was a bard, actually, down in Edomear."

William's head tilted slightly in confusion.

"Ah, that's right," chuckled Valdwin. "You wouldn't know where that is. It's the capital city of House Barcbane, on the far south of the island. We're here in the far east. But anyway, I come from a long line of bards, all the way back to my great-great-grandfather."

Now William was intrigued. "How then does a fifth-generation bard end up working a dock on a different corner of the island?" he asked.

Valdwin looked down in embarrassment. "Ah, it would be a lot to explain. But the short story is, my father got in trouble with the Church down there. He called them hypocrites, and they called us heretics. We couldn't make a living down there anymore, so he moved us up here to Elkreath. There's always work to be found, even if it has nothing to do with song." Most men would have said this with bitterness, but William noticed only a quiet sadness that lingered on Valdwin's words.

"Is that how you can speak English so well?" asked William. "From being a bard, I mean?"

Valdwin paused for a moment, then smiled. "Partly, I suppose. I was raised in a world of language and culture, so yes, that was a foundation. And I did find some old English books in the libraries from the olden days. But it was working the docks that I learned from the traders. Even went with them several times to Europe. That's mainly how I got to practice speaking it."

The sun had now set below the horizon, leaving only ambient light to see with. William opened his mouth to ask another question when a shrill bark from the dock's foreman suddenly called Valdwin to attention. "Ah... sorry, William," Valdwin apologized. "Duty's call, and all that. *Sita!*"

William's eyes lingered on the bard-turned-dockworker as he hurried off. "Interesting," he muttered as he stroked his chin.

The sound of approaching footsteps roused William from his pondering. He turned to see the captain coming toward him. "These Cabalians are a difficult bunch if you ask me," he grumbled as he stopped within arm's reach. "You wouldn't believe the hassle it was to handle customs. I've had easier times in Spain!"

"Is everything taken care of, then?"

The captain guffawed. "Yeah, we're all set. They're going to charge us an arm and a leg for repairing the ship, but we already knew that."

"Good enough. We have the gold to handle ourselves." William turned to eye the ship's silhouette. "How long will it take to fix?"

"If I heard them right, five days."

"Really? That soon? Well, that's not bad news at all. Are all the men accounted for?"

"Yes, sir. Followed your orders to the letter."

"Good. Keep it that way. I'm going into town tonight, and I expect the same report when I return in the morning."

At this, the captain snapped a salute. "Aye, sir. You needn't worry 'bout a thing."

William knew better than to take that phrase to heart. *There's always something to worry about,* his cynicism groused.

"Very well, Captain. I'll take my leave, then. Fare you well."

With a final salute of his own, William set off. An ample supply of torches lit the pier's wooden walkways, even as the freshly risen moon provided enough light to navigate the still-bustling shipyards. The evening air was crisp with starlight and invigorated his steps going forward. The distance from the docks to the city proper was not especially long at the pace he went, perhaps fifteen to twenty minutes at the most. When he arrived at the edge of the shipyards, William found the division between the two areas to be abrupt. Plain walkways and weathered timber ended where a most curious scenery began.

Buildings rose from the ground as far as the eye could see, and what buildings they were! Many ascended seven or eight stories into the air, though a number of simple two-floor dwellings huddled together at the bases of these goliaths as if in fear. Regardless of its size, every structure in sight was made of wood. The wood of the city proper was altogether unlike the shipyard, though. The shipyard was made of plain wood: wood that everyone has seen in their life, wood that people walk on and creak over and don't give a second thought about except how old it is and how soon it needs to be replaced. The wood of the city Elkreath was not that kind of wood.

Its wood was ancient but still going strong. Its colors were earthen brown and charcoal mingled with blue, violet, and green. And while the city lay in the darkness of night, it glowed brightly—that is, the grain of it did. Fine patterns of cobalt, amethyst, and emerald branched along the uncovered sides of the buildings, leaving the edges of every dwelling completely visible from the public streets. Many houses still had torches and lanterns hanging outside to illuminate the streets that ran by them.

The streets themselves were wide and appeared to be of solid stone. Their surface was smoothed off with no clear distinction of where one stone ended and another began. Perhaps it was only the lack of daylight, but it looked as if the entire road was but a single stone chiseled to perfection. But that could not be possible, could it?

The light gray of the pavement was interrupted by a deep green line — the width of a man — that ran directly through the center of the road. Staring at it, one could see sparks of prismatic light shimmering to and fro, rising gently into the night sky before fading from view.

Vast crowds of people traveled along the roads. The flickering of torchlight and the strange glow of the Cabalian wood cast an ever-changing flow of light upon men and women alike as they weaved between buildings. Many went inside the buildings for one thing or another, but even more stayed on the streets to conduct their business. Makeshift markets with goods strewn about them peppered the thoroughfare for miles into the distance. The din of thousands upon thousands of people bustling along almost reminded William of home, except there were far more people here than there ever were in England.

Every variety of person imaginable roamed the streets. Merchants in expensive clothing haggled over the price of their wares, while vagrants with nothing but the clothes on their backs drifted around in search of a free meal to grab. Wandering minstrels entertained impromptu audiences with instruments William had never seen before, and those drunk with one too many spirits staggered about slurring the words of a language he would never have understood anyway. Hooded figures with sharp eyes and even sharper blades drifted through the rabble on business known only to themselves. Men in long robes guided a caravan through the bustling roads, looking ready to either kill or be killed to get their shipment to its destination. Scattered throughout them all, armored enforcers patrolled the streets with axes as big as themselves, casting a gaze as tangible as the steel they wielded. All this and more William observed as he walked the streets of Elkreath.

Realizing there would be no quiet place to gather his thoughts, he retrieved his map and scanned it again for directions. By the look of it, he only had a mile to go straight ahead. He was to enter the Yohati Inn at the intersection of two main roads. It would be a yellow building three floors tall with a red lantern hanging outside the front door. It shouldn't be too hard to miss — unlike the scowling hulk of a brute he suddenly bumped into. William chided himself for overlooking such a sizable obstacle as the man turned and glowered at him. How could he have not noticed the spawn of Goliath brooding there before him?

He returned the glare he received with one of his own, signaling with his body language that he knew perfectly well how to ruin someone's night. He did not break eye contact until he saw the goon defer to his unspoken threat. With a final grunt, William turned to find a large intersection at the edge of his sight. This had to be it, he thought. Just one more bridge to cross, and he would be there. Muscles tensed with anticipation, he covered the remaining ground, intent on reaching his target. So intent he was, that he almost did not notice when a man just off to his left burst into flames with a loud cry.

The reaction of the people in front of him signaled him to look around. When he did, all he saw were the smoldering remains of who had walked within arm's length of him just moments ago. He could only stare dumbfounded with a furrowed brow as he tried to wrap his mind around what could possibly have happened. When he finally turned his head away from the freak spectacle, he was even more perplexed to find no one in a hurry to do anything about it. It seemed that everyone had already returned to their business as usual. *Unbelievable*, he thought. Was this just a common occurrence in Cabalia?

William shook himself and hurried his pace. All he wanted was to make it a thousand more feet without something else going awry. He noticed that people took extra care to move out of his way and avoided anything close to eye contact with him. He could not understand

Cabalian, but he could detect a murmuring of the crowd when he heard it. Things did not feel right at all.

A distant peal of thunder sounded when he finally reached the intersection. *Perfect,* he thought. *Just what I need: an omen of doom.* Looking up and around, he noticed a sign with bold, black letters illuminated by a reddish-orange lantern that read:

YOHATI

The building's fresh coat of pale yellow paint was the last confirmation he needed. This was it. Without so much as a second glance, Lord William Steele strode forward for the glory of England.

4

Another Bargain Struck

It was a decrepit sight when the door creaked open. A bare earthen floor supported tables and chairs too rotted to be used in any respectable establishment. Cobwebs obscured most of the light from the few lanterns that hung, but not even the dimness of the inn's poor lighting could hide the grime that layered everything in sight. William could have sworn he saw rats scamper across a table and onto the floor just to his left.

To make matters worse, the clientele which occupied the tavern looked even more barbaric than its surroundings. It must have been a requirement of entry that one have either rotting teeth, gaping scars, or clothing that had not been washed in thirty years.

It was a tempting thought to step right back outside. Any normal person would have. But William was not a normal person. So he told himself, at least, as he let bravado propel him past the threshold. Even before the door creaked back shut, he could feel the stares attempting to skewer him alive. Many patrons kept staring at him even after his gaze broke away from theirs, but he knew better than to get involved with this shady of a crowd.

Who knew which of these ruffians was the Shadowcrest agent he was to meet with? Better for him to find as quiet a corner as possible and wait. An empty table by a cracked window in the corner seemed to fit the bill, so William sat there. Before his back even made contact with the chair, he actively scanned the environment. Years of experience had taught him to always examine his surroundings, and what he saw did not look good.

The only entrance in sight was where he had just entered. Between him and that entrance were four dozen or so of the shadiest characters he had ever seen in his life. There were not many windows accessible, but the one next to him could be used as an escape if necessary. The wood was rotted enough that he could probably just bash his way through the walls if he needed to.

Everyone there seemed to be armed. Some did an adequate job of hiding their weapons, but most not well enough to escape his sight. Many of them had stopped staring by the time he sat down, but a few still did. The most disturbing one was the behemoth of a man who sat in the corner closest to him. A mask concealed his lower face, and the hood covering the top of his head did little to hide the glowing red tattoo on his forehead. He sat alone, and he was not drunk like most of the others. His hazel eyes were deliberate, calculating, and clearly focused on the newcomer.

William's attention broke when a scantily clad barmaid approached his table. She cursed as she staggered over a pile on the floor that William did not dare to identify. Her voice was hoarse and thick with a strange accent. He could not understand a word of what she said, so he waited until she finished speaking and then displayed his amulet to her. This had the opposite effect of what he intended, however. Her eyes widened, and her speech grew faster and more agitated. At this rate, William feared the whole tavern would have its eyes focused on him again.

Before he could decide how to react, the large man with the tattoo closed the distance between them and pulled the barmaid aside.

Whatever he then said to her seemed to calm her. When he had sent her away, he turned his gaze to William.

"You iss Wil-yim, from Ing-lend?" His fine-grained accent sounded out of place for a man who stood well over six feet tall and looked straight out of a nightmare. It finally clicked for William that this must be the agent he searched for.

"Yes."

The man pulled up a chair and sat down directly across from him. He extended an arm of pure muscle toward him and opened his clenched fist to reveal a silver ring that sparkled against the backdrop of his dirtied skin. Engravings that matched the patterns on the man's cloak covered its length.

"Put on," he ordered.

Not willing to question such a formidable man to his face, William complied.

"What is it for?" he asked once it was securely on his finger.

When the man replied, his accent was muted, and he no longer spoke in broken English. "We can talk freely now. You can understand me, and I can understand you. No one speaks English here, and you don't know Cabalian. But with some magic, we can close the gap."

William looked around the room. What had once been a blur of incoherent sounds around him melted into recognizable speech. He could hear the barmaid arguing with the bartender about her wages. He could understand that the fat man screaming two tables down was furious about losing a bet. The profanities pouring out of the men at the center tables would have been better left untranslated.

"Does this mean I can speak Cabalian now?"

"Correct. You speak like a native."

"Impressive!" William gasped. Such an item would revolutionize the world back home. Kings, diplomats, soldiers — who wouldn't find a use for this? It took every ounce of discipline not to daydream about the possibilities. Turning his attention back to the matter at hand, he looked the man full in the eyes. The resoluteness in the man's gaze suggested little room for small talk.

"I suppose this is the part where we seal the deal?" guessed William.

The man's eyes narrowed. "Indeed."

William reached into his coat and retrieved the sack which held the Danuri stone. He undid the drawstring and slid the stone out into the palm of his hand.

"Here you are, then. One blue Danuri stone in exchange for Shadesteel."

The man's eyes widened as he leaned back in his chair, stunned. He stared at the stone, lost in thought, awkward moments passing by before he came to his senses and cleared his throat. Extending his arm, he finally found his voice. "Ah, very well then. Rules are rules. All risks notwithstanding, you have yourself a deal with Azkalah."

After taking the stone, the man shook William's hand, then proceeded to beat his hand to his chest, clenched it, and brought it to touch the strangely glowing tattoo on his forehead while he closed his eyes. A rather odd ritual, William thought.

"Now... for the shadesteel?"

The man's eyes bolted open, and he leaned forward.

"Ah, yes. To be honest, I didn't expect you would actually make it here with the payment. For obvious reasons, I wouldn't bring my items with me for a no-show. We'll need to make a stop first to pick them up."

Indignation surged within William. He didn't care if this was a foreign land with different customs. He didn't even care if he was dealing with the fearsome House Shadowcrest. A deal was a deal, and he had nearly frozen to death trying to get there.

The man pulled out a small flask from his cloak. "Unfortunately, where we are going has a strict policy. If I am to take you there, you will need to drink this first. It will knock you out long enough for us to get there without you learning its location."

It was all too much for William to take.

"Absolutely not!" he exclaimed. "If you didn't expect me to make it here, why did you even cut the deal in the first place? I know what this is. I already gave you the stone, so now you'll just do me in like the Shadowcrest blackguard you are!"

The man looked bewildered. He was about to reply when a hooded figure pulled up alongside him. William could barely discern the hushed voice of a woman.

"A dozen of them," she murmured.

"How long?" the man replied.

"Two minutes. Tops."

The man turned to face William and relaxed his posture. He pulled away the mask from the bottom of his face to reveal a handsome growth of sandy brown stubble and a calm expression.

"Let me put it this way, Wil-yim. That stunt you pulled on the bridge didn't go unnoticed. No one at the scene had the guts to interfere with Shadowcrest business, but the authorities can't simply overlook an open murder on their streets."

"If you mean the man that just exploded out of the blue, I had nothing to do with that!"

"Oh, I believe you. But I don't think the Councilors of Elkreath will see it that way. They've already sent their elites to round you up. And once they arrest you, they'll either try you in their courts or turn you over to Shadowcrest for them to deal with you. Either way, I guarantee you they won't deal favorably with a foreigner. If you want to stay a free man, you had better drink this." The man extended the vial to William and nudged his head toward the window.

When William looked out from where he sat, he could see the crowds of Elkreath thronging by on the streets. He could also see *them:* men in brown robes forming a perimeter around the tavern—the same perimeter he and his men would form in England when sent to arrest a high-priority target.

He turned and stared at the vial offered to him. Fleeing was out of the question, and to fight with such formidable people would be suicide. To refuse the offer would land him in a legal nightmare in a faraway land. To accept would be to place himself in the hands of a stranger. Neither option was appealing, but at least one had a remote chance of ending well.

"Fine then. I suppose I don't have much of a choice." He reached for the vial and undid the cork. "I never caught your name, by the way," he said after forcing himself to swallow the bitter contents.

The man smiled before pulling his mask back up.

"My name is Brinwin."

And that was the last thing William recalled before the world went black.

5

A Bargain Struck

Silence hung in the air when the first traces of blue appeared in the sky. Dawn was not far behind, and King Stephen of Blois knew he was running out of time. He chided himself as he slipped out of bed, trying not to wake the woman still passed out from last evening's festivities. He should have known better than to stay late at the banquet, and now he would have to hurry.

It was difficult work fitting on his black cloak in the dark. The boots were just as difficult, but at least they provided a muffled step when they were finally on. He eyed the dagger lying on the chest by the door before he slipped it on and stole outside the bedchamber.

The hallways were empty, which meant his men had carried out their orders well. He trod softly down the upper flights of stairs that led to street level. Even before he took his first step out a side door onto the frozen cobblestone outside, Stephen was already playing out in his mind's eye what the next fifteen minutes would involve. The path to St. Matthew's Cathedral was not long, but it was exposed to plain view. Staying close to the edges of buildings along the way would be crucial. He had observed how the general populace walked and carried themselves, and he was determined not to reveal his identity through his gait.

Even as the eastern sky brightened, few were willing to brave the frigid winter air before sunrise.

Good, thought Stephen. *It would be a shame having to use this dagger the day before Christmas Eve.*

He wound his way through the city streets without incident, with nothing but the soft crunch of snow beneath his feet to keep him company. When he approached the walls of the old stone cathedral, he scanned his surroundings for any sign of life. Finding none, he slunk to the back corner he had visited many times before. The lack of sunlight proved no hindrance as muscle memory guided his hands to just the crevice he searched for. The faint click of a lever was all the confirmation he needed to begin pushing his shoulder against the side of the building. It was being stubborn, but a secret door did eventually budge open to reveal a staircase that descended into darkness.

Stephen stood on the threshold when a loud screech rang out behind him. He spun around with his dagger in a ready position before realizing it was only a rooster crowing in the field behind the church. If his nerves were not so tightly drawn, it would have been comical: Stephen of Blois, King Proper of England, Lord and Defender of the Realm, fully poised to gut a rooster. To think, what songs would be written of that legendary encounter? But Stephen was in no such jovial mood. With nothing but a scowl, he disappeared into the depths of the hidden passage and closed the door behind him.

The sheer darkness and musty air that permeated the corridor would have disturbed most. Stephen, however, showed no signs of concern as he inhaled as much of the stale air as his lungs could handle. "*Ize Gaiyeem!*" he uttered.

Light sprang into existence from seemingly nowhere and illuminated the corridor. Engravings of a foreign script stretched downward at eye level along the length of the staircase, while the remains of long faded frescoes stretched out in the ceiling above. Tatters of a purple carpet provided slightly better cushioning than the cracked stone on which it lay. The hall would have been an architectural marvel at its construction, but the passage of time had well taken its toll.

Stephen traced his fingers along the lines of text as he descended the staircase. "It really is a pity no one here can read you anymore," he sighed with a shake of his head. "If only they'd left some books behind when they all vanished."

The corridor opened into a broad chamber at the bottom of the stairs. At its far end, there stood a massive pair of stone doors. A brazier on either side of the doors blazed with a deep purple flame. Stephen retrieved the dagger from his cloak and pressed the tip into the flame on his right. When he withdrew the weapon, its tip remained on fire. He brought the makeshift torch to touch the centerline of the doors, and a hissing sound escaped from behind it as the doors slid open.

Thick vapors billowed out with a pungent odor that made his lips curl. Stephen coughed as he strode past the doors and into the chamber beyond. No matter how often he visited this place, he never could get fully used to those fumes. *Ah well*, he reasoned. *A small price to pay for the power that lay within.*

The vapors soon melted into oblivion, and Stephen had a clear view of the room in which he now stood. Tattered banners spanned the length of the walls in a full circle. Each had the same insignia emblazoned on it, though most were too damaged to form a complete image. In ages past, Stephen would have been able to gaze around the room to see a score of grinning ebony skulls staring back at him from the banners, each resting on a purple background surrounded by black flowers.

Bookshelves that once housed various tomes now lay bare with nothing but layers of cobwebs to grace their surface, while a solitary stone table stood in the center of the room. What its original purpose was, anyone could only guess. At present, its sole use was to store what few artifacts had been gleaned from the room upon its discovery.

The weariness of forgotten centuries weighed heavily in the room, forcing a sigh from Stephen as he stepped forward and reached his hand into the earthen vessel that stood on a corner of the table. A few moments later, he retrieved a handful of the black flowers once so clearly depicted on the banners. He arranged them carefully in a circle on the bare stone floor. After several close inspections, he appeared to be satisfied with the arrangement, and he then stooped down to touch the circle with the tip of his still-flaming dagger.

The instant his dagger touched the first flower, the whole circle blazed into flames. As the fire grew and soared into the air, the ground within the circle rippled into a translucent glow. Moments later, the apparition of a shrouded figure rose from the circle's depths. Violet pinpricks of light shone from its eyes, fully transfixed on the now trembling King Stephen. When the phantasm spoke, its voice was like the distant rumble of a landslide mingled with the echoes of a thousand deep caves.

"You're late."

Stephen choked back the fear that held his tongue in place as he sheathed his dagger. "Even so, I have the payment."

Silence ensued as the being held its piercing stare.

"Is that right?" it finally hissed.

"Yes. Twenty thousand pounds of gold, ready for dispatch."

"Twenty-five thousand, for your tardiness."

"Of course." Stephen inwardly cursed that bloody festival for the hundredth time. There was only so much gold he could squeeze out of England through taxes and borrowing. Another slip-up like this, and he might as well plant a sign on the cliffs of Dover saying, "Sorry gentlemen, we're all broke here. Best go on somewhere else if you need to use money." Stephen's attention snapped to reality when the visage rumbled another terse question.

"And the stone?"

Stephen reached into his cloak and pulled out a luminous blue stone the size of his fist. He held it openly for inspection. "Also ready for dispatch," he said.

The light from the specter's eyes went dark as it began to chant a most unsettling melody. The stone glowed brighter, rising in temperature until Stephen's hand began to burn. He was about to scream in pain when the chanting suddenly ceased, and the stone reverted to its original state. The circle of flames grew dimmer as the apparition faded back into darkness.

"Very well," it said, its voice now more of an echo than a rumble. "You'll have your deal with Azkalah. This should be all your agent needs to make the journey. Don't be late this time..."

A gush of wind blew through the chamber and extinguished the flames, leaving the room in stillness once more. Where the flames had been just moments ago, the border of a circle lay charred into the floor. In its center lay a small wooden box.

Stephen knelt over the box to see a grinning skull surrounded by black flowers gazing up from its cover. Staring at that skull, a horrible feeling lodged itself in the pit of his stomach that warned him he was making a grave mistake. But it was too late to turn back now. With trembling hands, he reached out to finish what he had started for the glory of England.

* * *

When Stephen closed the secret door, the first light of dawn had already broken over the horizon. On any other day, the scenery would have been beautiful to him. The winter air offered no obstruction to the golden light that gleamed off the snow-covered fields. But Stephen's mind was too preoccupied with the darkness of man's scheming to appreciate the beauty of nature's light.

As he stepped forward to begin his trek back into the city, he suddenly noticed the man who stood three paces off to his left watching him. Stephen gave a start before he recognized the man.

"What the... Geoffrey, how did you find me?" he sputtered.

The man replied with a carefully concealed smirk.

"I'm your spymaster, sire. It's my job to know where everyone of importance is."

"How long have you been here? And what did you see?" Stephen demanded with a fresh wave of indignation.

"Long enough to not feel my fingers... or my face. And just enough to know that His Highness is preoccupied with something important.

Aside from you ascending from the depths of an old church, I can't say I saw much else."

"And what are you doing here?"

"To bring you word on Henry. He's planning something serious."

"Tell me about it back at the hold. I have a mission for you of higher importance."

The spymaster bowed as much as his frozen back would allow him.

"Of course. I'm at your disposal, my lord."

"Go and fetch me William Belston. Tomorrow he leaves for Cabalia."

6

Fur and Fireworks

When William opened his eyes, he was not expecting to find himself settled comfortably in bed with a lakefront view of the noonday sun. Yet the sun continued to shine, and the waves of an endless sea continued to splash against the shore regardless of his disbelief. Even after rubbing his eyes and squinting, the scenery refused to relinquish its existence. Seabirds circled about in the heavens while crabs scurried about on white sand that stretched in either direction as far as the eye could see.

For having such a fine view of the scenery, he was not actually amid the great outdoors. Faint reflections in front of him betrayed the enormous glass window he looked through.

"How is this even possible?" thought William in amazement. In all his travels across Europe, he could not recall ever seeing a window as large and clear. What few windows of glass he had seen could only be found in the wealthiest of nobles' homes, and even then, they were never a solid sheet of clear glass. At best, they were composed of small sections of opaque material fitted together in an elaborate frame. Something like this would have been beyond opulent — and quite impossible.

Turning over on his side, he was amazed at how soft the bed beneath him was. Not that he had ever spent time on a monarch's mattress, but he was certain even kings did not have beds this comfortable to sleep in. It was tempting to fall back asleep right there on his side. Perhaps he would have, had he not noticed movement out of the corner of his eye.

Fearing the worst, William spun his head to find a small creature meandering toward the base of the bed. Even with a clear view of the approaching animal, it was difficult to determine what exactly it was, other than *cute*. It looked like some mammal, with a lush coat of chestnut fur and soft, green eyes. Its overall appearance suggested a docile nature, which he found reassuring. Its thickly padded paws made no sound as it drew closer and hopped onto the corner of the bed, peering with curiosity at the stranger who sat staring at it.

William chuckled to himself and extended his hand to the creature. "Well hello there, little one. Whatever might you be?"

It tilted its head and squinted its eyes in response, as if to say, "I could ask the same of you too, 'big one,'" before it crept closer with caution. It paused as it sniffed William's outstretched fingers. Once satisfied with this, it looked at William with an approval that said, "Yes, go ahead. You can touch me now." He smiled as he put his hand out to stroke the beast's fur. Nothing could have prepared him for what followed next.

The moment his hand would have touched the animal, its fur exploded into a sea of colors. He squinted in time to see the creature's nose swell to three times its previous size and burst into an avalanche of pine cones that scattered across the bed. Its two front legs shot off from its body and flew in zigzags around the room before erupting into a shower of confetti. In the meantime, its tongue unfolded two feet outward and flapped about wildly, almost hitting William in the face.

He ducked his head and rolled off the bed in shock. When he found his footing, he looked up to see the spectacle of the animal-thing floating to the center of the room. Before he could do anything to stop it, the creature blazed into a ball of light that bathed the room before bursting into oblivion. The entire mess that seconds ago had cluttered the bed all but vanished, leaving the room once more in pristine condition.

Laughter rang out from the entrance to the room as a woman fell to her knees, barely able to breathe from laughing so hard. It was all William could do to stand there flabbergasted at it all. The form before his sight was of an adult in her prime, but one could easily confuse the mirth pouring out from her to be that of a schoolgirl. When she looked up at William, his confusion only made her double over again in laughter.

"Look at his face!" she finally exclaimed. "I don't care what Brin says! That was *so* worth it!"

Her laughter continued, even after the sound of footsteps in the hallway behind her gave way to the lumbering form of the man called Brinwin. He ducked his head to enter past the doorway, and once inside the room, he scanned it quizzically. His eyes flashed from William, who remained at a loss, to the woman still on the floor laughing. His gaze was quick, precise, and torn between exasperation and amusement.

"Zala... what did you do?" The familiarity in his voice sounded more like a father scolding his child than a warrior interrogating a comrade.

The woman's laughter tapered off as she clambered to her feet. "Oh relax, Brin. I didn't hurt him. Just practiced some illusion magic on him."

Brinwin continued to interrogate her with his eyes, clearly unsatisfied with her answer.

"It was only Mr. Floofles and the pine cone party! Nothing you haven't seen before."

"But certainly something *he's* never seen before," he gestured toward William. "The first chance you get to interact with an outsider, *on official business,* and this is what you do? I wish I was surprised, but you never can resist acting like a child around here, now *can* you, Sister?"

The woman put on a mock pout. "Forgive me for the intrusion into 'official business,' oh serious one. If I'm going to work with him, I need to know whether these outsiders have a sense of humor or not."

Brinwin shook his head and turned to face William. "For whatever it's worth, she probably messed with you because she thinks you're 'cute.'"

"Brin!" the woman exclaimed with indignation.

"What? That's what you said when we brought him in here, is it not?"

William buried his head in his hands. This could not be happening right now. This was a strange... no, *very* strange dream he was about to wake up from.

While the brother and sister continued to argue, he wandered back to the bed and crawled under the covers, cramming his eyes shut and hoping against hope he would be jarred back into reality any second now. There came a pause of silence, and he tensed in anticipation of finally waking up. Such hopes were dashed by the muffled comments he heard through the bed sheets.

"What's he doing?" the woman called Zala asked.

"I think you broke him," came Brinwin's reply.

"If only all men broke so easily," Zala snickered back.

William groaned as he ruffled the bed sheets to sit upright. It was no dream, and reality had rapidly turned stranger than fiction. He stared speechless at the pair of strangers before him until the distant cawing of a seabird filled the silence between them — a poor attempt by nature at breaking the awkwardness of the moment.

Brinwin finally cleared his throat. "I apologize for this rather un-professional turn of events, Wil-yim. When I saw how... ah... *eager* you outsiders are at conducting business so quickly, I intended to keep you comfortably unconscious until everything was ready to go. But it appears a certain *someone* had already helped herself to my spare stocks of sleeping solution."

Zala opened her mouth in protest but did not get the chance to counter Brinwin's glare before he continued to speak. "And of course, the Essari don't have any spare alchemy ingredients on hand. That, unfortunately, means it will be another three days of waiting before everything is ready for you. What your king requires of us is no small feat to prepare, even with access to the best of equipment."

William's heart sank in his chest. By this point, he resigned himself to the fact that he was at the mercy of these strangers to fulfill their end of the bargain, if they even would at all. Protesting would be useless, and with everything else that had gone wrong, what would three more days be?

Things could be much worse, he tried to reassure himself. *Surely, this is all just a misunderstanding. We didn't realize they were going to make the suits from scratch. What's three more days if that's what it takes to craft them? It's still another five days before my ship is repaired anyway... plenty of time to return before it leaves.*

The peculiar sound of Brinwin's firm yet subtle voice coaxed William's thoughts back to the conversation. "As much as it may trouble you, three days is the best I can do. I'm afraid I cannot under any circumstances be interrupted from my endeavors during this time."

Brinwin paused and glanced at his sister before gazing back at William. "Zala will look after you in the meantime. Feel free to explore the grounds or interact with our hosts, but please do not put yourself into any *risky* situations."

Something inside William shuddered at the end of Brinwin's instructions. More so than his appearance, something about his voice suggested he meant business and was in no case someone to cross. Even more unsettling was the awareness with which his eyes searched William's. He could see Brinwin detect his fear and ever so subtly nod in approval that there was an understanding of who was in charge.

"I'll come to fetch you when everything is ready," he said as he turned to exit the room. It only took a couple of strides for his massive legs to reach the threshold of the hallway beyond. "Oh, and Zala," he called back. "Please don't break him again."

7

The Hunt Begins

Inquestor Telnis Raiko was not having a good day. Last night's sleep was as elusive as the criminals he sought to catch in the city of Elkreath, and his coordination was paying for it. While changing his clothes, he stubbed his toes against his mother-in-law's dresser: an ugly piece of furniture he had despised owning for the last eight years. No matter how much he begged his wife to let him get rid of the blasted thing, she just could not bring herself to part with the family heirloom. It belonged to her grandfather, after all. Even if the man's relationship with his granddaughter was as wooden as the antique he left behind, that in no way changed the sacred status of the artifact.

As he carried on ranting at the mental image of his unreasonable wife, he failed to notice himself apply the warming enchantment to his tea for a tad too long. When he absentmindedly gulped down the beverage, he scalded the better part of his mouth and throat. The yelp of pain that followed managed to wake the infant boy who had quieted down only an hour ago. It was all he could do not to join in crying with the agitated baby. Even if he were not able to partially read minds, he would have still been able to discern how displeased his wife was at waking up to such a commotion.

If he was honest with himself, he could not blame her for being on the edge of her patience. Raising a newborn was far from easy work, and he had been of little help lately. The job of an inquestor was never easy in a large city, and Elkreath was by far the largest city in Cabalia. It alone could boast of two million souls walking its streets. And of those two million souls, any number could be engaged in mischief and crime.

The enforcers could handle the cut-and-dry duties of apprehending criminals identified as such, but many were not so easily caught. So it was of necessity that Elkreath's Council of Inquest employed men of talent and dedication to investigate crime wherever it reared its ugly head. That was how things were supposed to work, anyway.

Telnis would have been relieved when his wife took the screaming child from his hands were it not for the dirty look and less-than-amicable thoughts she did not even try to hide from him. He knew better than to say anything, so he stepped into his workroom with little more than a sigh. Maps of Elkreath hung about the walls, most covered with notes and geometric shapes scrawled over this region or that. He sat at his desk and stared blankly at the dossiers piled before him. A clock ticked on somewhere behind him, counting its way ever so slowly toward infinity.

When he finally came to himself, Telnis rubbed his eyes and glanced over each of the documents in reach. Criminal activity was higher than usual this year, and there were many options he could focus on. He fingered one pile and rifled through its pages.

Breaking and entering at an alchemy supply warehouse. *No,* he thought. *Not enough leads to prioritize this.* He scooped up another pile.

Disappearance of a gem merchant's daughter. *Interesting, but better handled by someone more familiar with the district.* Setting it down, he examined a third bundle.

Murder of a dockworker, possible connections to Azkalah. *Aha,* he thought. *Now we've got something!* Anything even remotely tied to the island's most infamous criminal organization was worth investigating.

Telnis leaned back in his chair to examine the report in depth. He only made it through a page and a half of details when he felt his desk vibrate and heard a low-pitched hum overpower the monotony of the clock's ticking. Even before glancing up from the report, he knew what he would see. The dull green amulet he was supposed to be wearing but had left on the surface of his desk now shone with a verdant glow that meant only one thing: He was being summoned to the field. Whatever was going on, it was urgent, given how strongly the amulet vibrated.

He picked up the amulet and rotated it to its back. The address of his destination shimmered in bold letters. "The Tafrik Bridge, hmmm?" he murmured as he rose from his desk. "I wonder what's got them all in a tizzy." He stretched groggily and yawned before he grabbed the amulet in one hand and his street cloak in another. He closed the door to his study carefully enough not to make any noise and then trod as softly as he could toward the exit of his house.

His wife stood by the dining table holding their child, and a glance at her was enough to convey what was happening. He could see in her eyes that she had resigned herself yet again to being married to a workaholic inquestor. He just hoped she could see in his eyes that he was truly sorry his duties had once more called him away from the loves of his life.

* * *

The early morning sun greeted Telnis when he stepped outside to the streets of Elkreath. Cool, fresh air invigorated him and offered a moment's reprieve from the troubles in his life. He paused to take a deep breath, then strode onto the perfectly carved stone road that ran by him, already crowded with the new day's foot traffic.

When he reached the emerald strip that ran through the middle of the street, he called out his name and destination. He then kept walking as usual down the center line—that's how it appeared from his perspective, at least. To anyone else traveling the thoroughfare, he was but a blur that whizzed by them and vanished in a flash. After a minute's "walk," he arrived at his destination and stepped off to the side of the line.

A small crowd had already gathered in the middle of the Tafrik Bridge, peering over the edges of a barricade guarded by a dozen or so enforcers. Beyond them, Telnis could see a group of men wearing garments similar to his own that were deeply engaged in discussion. As he surveyed the scene, he recognized several inquestors in plainclothes that mingled with the rabble surging by on either side of the barricade.

This is more serious than I thought, he pondered as he approached the nearest sentry and flashed his amulet. The guard stepped aside with a grunt and allowed him to pass by.

An inquestor with a grizzled beard and pale blue eyes was the first to notice Telnis's arrival. "Ahh, Raiko. Welcome to the mess," he said. The gruffness in the man's voice was something Telnis had learned not to take personally.

"Morning, Tilthrir," he replied to his boss in like fashion. "What are we dealing with?"

"A right hot mess," another inquestor answered. The man gestured to the center of the blocked-off area, where a ring of scorch marks and ashes blackened the otherwise flawless surface of the stone pavement. When Telnis stepped closer to investigate, he could see the charred remains of a human body scattered among the ashes. Off to the side, small veins of cobalt blue branched out toward the edge of the bridge.

"Barely an hour after sunset last night, witnesses say a man spontaneously combusts. No warning, no previous altercations. One minute, business as usual, and the next — *boom!* The man screams as he burns to a crisp before their eyes."

Telnis tilted his head. "And?"

Tilthrir spoke up. "And they say a man with a Shadowcrest badge stone on his neck was standing right next to him until he fully burnt to the ground, then took off in a rush. The bystanders got a good look at the man, so we have a physical description."

"And you'll be *shocked* where our Shadowcrest agent scurries off to," an inquestor named Galfrik chimed in with sarcasm.

Telnis raised his eyebrow. "The nearest brothel?"

"Ha! You're not half wrong. The guy just strides right into the Kozheithy."

Telnis could not keep back the disgust that creased his face. How he wished they could shutter that abominable tavern for good! It was an open secret that the place was a cesspool swarming with felons and hoodlums. By all rights, it should have been closed years ago, but unfortunately, political favors had a way of circumventing common sense. Not that the general public would ever know it, but the son of an influential councilman was a prime patron of the establishment. A deal had been cut where the authorities would not snoop in so long as the riff-raff did not bring their troubles outside or use the place as a safe house on the heels of a crime. Whatever possessed the inn to break their end of the bargain was mystifying, but Telnis welcomed the turn of events.

"So, I take it we finally sent our men into the place?" he asked.

"Oh, yes... and that's where things get interesting," replied Galfrik.

Tilthrir cleared his throat. "It's actually why we called you in, Telnis. We wanted you on the scene before the adjudicators show up."

"Adjudicators?!" Telnis exclaimed. Whatever his colleagues were about to explain had to be huge if *they* were getting called in. The Mages College only loaned their top-of-the-line peacekeepers for the most crucial situations. Having almost become one himself, Telnis knew this all too well.

"Well, out with it! What happened?" he demanded.

Galfrik spoke up. "The enforcers raided the place and apprehended our man. Except he wasn't actually our man. Someone used some darn good illusion magic to make someone else *look* like our man. He had the badge stone on him and fit the physical description, so we had no reason to question it. But then the place broke out into a brawl. They got all up in arms we entered the joint, as if *we* were the ones who broke the deal. When we finally got the man out of the ruckus, his appearance changed before our eyes, and our actual target was gone without a trace. It took all night to question the witnesses, but—"

Tilthrir could see the impatience in Telnis's eyes and cut in.

"A large man with a glowing red tattoo on his forehead talked with the man just before the raid."

Time came to a stop for Telnis. It made perfect sense now. A man of that description, accompanied by illusion magic, on the heels of a highly unusual murder, sitting in the shadiest haven of crime...

"It's Brinwin, Telnis."

Of course it was. Who else could it be but Brinwin Zikennig? The last decade had seen nothing but caper after unsolved caper headed by Azkalah's Best. No other mercenary had caused more grief for law and order, and no other alchemist had worked more wonders in the past two centuries than Brinwin Zikennig. If there was ever a man the Adjudicators wanted to catch, it was him. And through ten years of utter failure of Cabalia's finest to do so, it was the lowly inquestor Telnis Raiko of Elkreath who had *almost* caught him. Now fate stood before Telnis, offering a second chance to prove himself. His countenance was nothing but resolve when he looked up at his superior.

"Take me to the tavern, Tilthrir. We have some work to do."

8

Enter the Essari

When Brinwin left the room, William was determined not to let awkwardness have free reign again. He cleared his throat and turned to look at the woman who observed him with amusement in her eyes. She stood the same height as William, making her taller than the average woman. The majority of her dirty-blonde hair was dyed a deep red and drawn into a ponytail that came down to her waist. Her hazel eyes matched her brother's, except they did not exude the same level of austere preciseness. They were softer, complemented with far more laughter than Brinwin's ever were. Though relaxed at the moment, her lithe figure spoke to years of physical training that William would have been thrilled to have seen in his men. Not that he would ever admit to it under the circumstances, but she was certainly an attractive woman.

"Right then," he said with as much composure as he could muster. "I suppose we should have a proper introduction." William then bowed as he would have addressed a noble back in England. "Lord William Steele, at your service."

Zala smiled and replied with a voice as graceful as her appearance, "And I am Zala. Zala Zikennig, mercenary mage at your service... quite literally. Let me show you how we greet each other here in Cabalia."

She brought her right hand across her chest with fingers extended to touch her left shoulder, then waited for William to repeat the gesture. "Very good, just like that."

She then brought her hands behind her back and bowed at a moderate angle. "And this is how you should greet someone if they look scary to you. The scarier they look, the deeper the bow, unless you plan on me having to rescue you from Yahos-knows-who."

William nodded, making sure to pay close attention.

Zala then bent backward in a full circle to bring her head up from between her legs.

"And this is how you greet someone if you want to throw your back out and look like a fool in the process."

William's jaw dropped as he stared in confusion and disbelief. Zala laughed as she snapped her fingers and instantly reverted to a normal standing position.

"Relax, William. Rule number one when you're dealing with a light mage: Nothing is as it seems."

She then patted him firmly on the back. "Now come on. You've had more than enough sleep, and there's plenty to see around here. I can't wait to see the look on your face when you see the Essari."

William crossed his arms in protest. Beautiful as she was, Zala's assertiveness and liberal use of practical jokes were getting on his nerves.

"Now just a moment," he said. "I'm not going anywhere with you until we get a few things settled. I don't know what customs you Cabalians are used to, but where I come from, it is quite improper to prank someone you've just met. I've had an *incredibly* stressful time of it till now, so you really need to tone down the magic, if you could. I've also a thousand questions flying around my head right now, so some straightforward answers would be appreciated."

The exasperation in William's voice might have come off more forcefully than he had intended, but he was in little mood to be diplomatic.

"You might find it humorous to watch the outsider gawking at everything, but enough is enough. I'm not some joke here to amuse you at will, and I won't stand for being treated as such. Am I clear?"

Zala's eyes fell as she straightened her posture. She stood silent for a time, searching for the right words.

"I'm sorry, William. I suppose I did get a little carried away," she sighed. "It may surprise you, but I'm not usually this way with people. I'm used to living a very... regimented life. This is one of the few places that feels enough like home for me not to worry about being too playful or too careless. It's not every day we get to deal with an outsider, so it's pretty exciting to show them around. But Brinwin is right: This is official business. I suppose I should act as such."

William's anger abated at this, and he regretted having snapped at her. He could sympathize with living a regimented life, having served in Henry's army for years on end. It was not easy having to always live one's life on some mission or another — he could understand wanting to let down one's guard at home.

"It's alright," he said. "I didn't mean to come across so hard. So long as we can scale things down a bit, we'll be fine. Fair enough?" He offered her a bow as a gesture of encouragement. "If you're alright with that, I'd be happy to see what you have to show me. From what little I've seen, this really is an amazing place."

Zala's eyes met his with a fresh spark of enthusiasm. She smiled once more and let her gaze linger a few moments longer before she twirled around to face the room's exit. "Well then, Sir Steele," she spoke softly, "prepare to be amazed even more. The wonders of the Essari await us."

* * *

The first thing William noticed when he took his first steps out the door was the light. Neither window nor flame lit the corridor he walked, yet he could see Zala in front of him as clear as day. He looked up to see an unbroken line of whitish light stretching onward above him. On further inspection, the light appeared to come from bulbous contraptions that ran in regularly spaced strips along the ceiling. Looking too long at them hurt William's eyes, so he tried to observe them in short intervals.

When William's attention shifted back to Zala, he realized he had fallen behind. He quickened his pace to catch up, all while trying to look as if he were not having difficulty in doing so. When he regained a respectable position next to her, he decided it was time to start asking the questions that inundated his mind. "So who exactly are the Essari, Lady Zikennig? Brinwin said they're our hosts?"

"Yes. The Essari own this vicinity and are graciously letting us stay as guests while Brinwin does whatever he needs to do. They're normally a reclusive people who try their best to keep prying eyes out, but my brother did them a big favor some years ago. They've been partial to him ever since. You're actually pretty lucky to be seeing this right now."

Zala paused as she leaned against a metal railing that separated her from an open shaft extending down to a depth one could only guess at. William peered over the edge to see the movement of gigantic metal cogs that faded into the darkness of the abyss below them. Deep clanking sounds reverberated up the shaft as the gears ground steadily on.

"As you'll see, the Essari are masters of invention," Zala continued. "They're an ancient people who predate the five kingdoms that rule the island today. If you believe the legends, they're actually the ones who created our writing system for the founders of Cabalia."

"Fascinating..." mused William as he stroked his chin. "Do *you* believe the legends?"

Zala remained silent as she stared off into the distance below. She eventually shrugged her shoulders and looked back at William. "It's a possibility. I wouldn't put it past them, that's for sure."

Before William could probe further, the arrival of footsteps echoed from farther down the hall. He turned his gaze to see two hooded figures emerge from around a bend at the end of the walkway. They wore evergreen robes and were equipped with a brown mask-like apparatus that covered the lower half of their faces. Each of them held a thick tome in one hand and gestured freely with the other.

The newcomers were so engaged in talking to each other that they failed to notice the man and woman who leaned against the railing and looked straight at them. When they finally did notice, they gave a violent start. In a single smooth motion, they slipped their books away and drew swords from the sheaths at their sides.

William instinctively reached for his sword before realizing he did not have it with him. He cast a frantic look at Zala. Her smile disappeared, but she remained motionless even as the armed men approached them in a sprint. William stepped forward, intending to position himself in front of Zala, but she extended her arm to hold him back.

William did not know how to respond to this. Every muscle in his body wanted to face the attackers head-on, but reason cautioned that he should trust the native who knew better of this land than he did.

The men nearly reached striking distance before one of them shot out a hand to stop his companion. "Wait!" rang out a garbled voice. "It only Zala Zikennig is!"

The other man squinted after he skidded to a halt. "Ahh. You correct are," his equally garbled voice replied.

"Lady Zikennig!" the first man scolded. "What are doing you leaning against that railing? Do not know you that it unsafe is?"

"Is that you, Garthis?" Zala responded.

"Yes, I it is." The man's tone shifted into one of respect. "You getting better at recognition are."

Zala's face beamed with pride. "No one else has a blade better engraved than yours. An eagle with *three* stars under his feet."

Even with a mask obstructing half the man's face, William could see the smile glowing from behind it.

"You right are, my lady."

A mischievous smile spread across Zala's face before she carried on: "Of course, it does also help that you still haven't cleaned that stain off the bottom right corner of your mask."

Garthis gave an embarrassed start. "I... what?"

Zala stifled a laugh as the other man gave him a hearty pat on the back.

"Alright it is, friend. It nothing is little cleaning solution not can fix," he said with encouragement.

"Knew you?" Garthis bemoaned indignantly. "Why not did... oh never mind."

The humiliated man turned to face Zala and William. "Please, if you would, just go outside and enjoy the fair sun before you over the railing fall."

Zala bowed with her hands behind her back. "Yes, sirs. As you wish." She turned her head toward William and nudged him to do the same. William's compliance seemed to satisfy the men, who stood and watched them until they moved beyond sight.

William cleared his throat once he was sure they were beyond earshot. "I take it those are..."

"Yes, William. Those are the Essari. Once you get used to their Old Speak, they're actually pleasant to talk to." Zala then gave a wink. "And Garthis is right. The sun is quite fair today. Let's go for a walk around Lake Iddeah. I think some warm sunlight and fresh air would do you some good."

Zala led William down a flight of stairs until they came to a plated metal door not much bigger than they were. Wishing to be chivalrous, William reached out to open the door for Zala, only to find it locked and completely unwilling to budge. The amusement in her eyes was plain when she moved him aside to access a small panel next to the door. It had a number of buttons on it, covered in what William could only guess was writing of some kind. Each button she pressed gave a small beep as it flashed blue. Five beeps later, the door gave a loud click. Zala then pushed the door open and led a bewildered Sir Steele outside.

9

The Mage's Tale

The waters of Lake Iddeah stretched southeast beyond the horizon. Any child in Cabalia who went to school and knew anything about geography could have told William that the lake he now saw was the largest on the island. They could have also told him the legends of sea monsters and ghosts that haunted the parts no one dared to settle or explore yet — parts such as he and Zala now sauntered around. But, for better or worse, no such schoolchildren were present to tell of such superstitions.

The afternoon sun waxed strong, with only a handful of billowing white clouds to offer the occasional shade. Water splashed against long patches of fine white sand, while at other points, it crashed against jagged rocks that covered the rest of the coastline. Zala walked alongside William on a stretch of sand she chose not far from the compound they had just exited. They walked in silence at first, taking in the beauty of the scenery before Zala spoke up.

"I'm sure you weren't exaggerating about having a thousand questions," she said. "Ask anything you'd like. There shouldn't be anything extraordinary here to raise more of them while you talk."

Except for you, perhaps, an uninvited thought flashed through William's mind. Brushing it off, William laughed. "I certainly hope so, for my sake. Another question, and I dare say my head would explode." He leaned against a small outcropping of rock next to him and rubbed his temples. "Where do I even begin?" he sighed. "So much has happened in the last... well, *there's* a question: How long have we been here? The last thing I remember was your brother drugging me at the tavern and then waking up here not even an hour ago."

"It hasn't been long at all," she replied. "That all happened last night. I still have the bruises from a stray fist or two."

"So that *was* you next to Brinwin."

"Yes," affirmed Zala with a smile. "He always prefers having a look-out in case anything unexpected happens."

"And what did happen? As in... what happened after you drugged me? Brinwin said there were some sort of elites coming to round me up. How did we get out of there?"

Zala's eyes fluttered in recollection.

"I'll admit it wasn't easy. The enforcers burst in seconds after you conked out, but we know how to think on our feet. Before your head had a chance to hit the table, Brin yanked off the amulet you were wearing and whipped it onto someone else at the table next to us. I used my light magic to make the poor sap look like you and vice versa. Oh, and I had to change Brin's appearance too. Every enforcer and their third cousin know his tattoo from anywhere. I told him he was a fool for getting it in the first place, but the blasted thing's a badge of honor for him. He'd rather die than get rid of it." Zala caught herself before she rambled on further.

"Anyways, it wasn't easy, but it worked. The authorities moved in and grabbed the fake you while we slipped off quietly — at least until everything broke into a brawl and I got these nasty things." She grimaced as she rubbed the bruises on the back of her shoulder. "Though I guess it worked out to our advantage. With the fight going on, it was easy to explain why you were unconscious. We got out of there before they arrested the whole place, and from that point, it was pretty simple getting you here in the middle of the night."

William's head spun to consider what he heard. The sheer speed of mind needed to improvise and execute a plan that flawlessly on a moment's notice would have put anyone he knew back in Europe to shame. He stretched his muscles and stepped away from where he leaned. "Let's go on a bit farther," he proposed.

Zala found the idea agreeable, and they continued their walk down the coastline. Brightly colored crabs scurried off in front of them as they went, retreating into the water before the seagulls circling overhead swooped down for a bite to eat. At one point, a long eel-like creature with blue scales darted out of the water and dragged a full-sized crab back into the depths it came from. The water around it sloshed a few moments longer, then returned to the usual rise and fall of the waves approaching land.

"Now how about you?" William asked. "If you don't mind my asking, what's your story?"

"My story?" Zala chuckled. "What do you mean by that?"

William blushed, not expecting that kind of response.

"I mean, well... where are you and Brinwin from, and how did you get to be so good at what you do?"

Zala brushed her hair to one side. "So, you want our general life history?"

William nodded, feeling more self-conscious than he would have liked.

"Well, alright," she said after a moment's deliberation. "I'll tell you what I can. But you owe me a story of your own afterward."

William paused for a moment as he weighed her offer. He was not sure how much he could trust this new acquaintance, but he was too curious about her history to turn down her terms. "Fair enough. You have a deal," he said.

Zala sat down on a rock that rose above the sand and focused her eyes on the horizon as she gathered her thoughts. William stood by her awkwardly before deciding to sit down next to her. Once he stopped shifting around, Zala began to speak.

"Brin and I were born to a wealthy family of House Hearthfell. We Zikennigs have been influential in the affairs of state ever since our greatest-grandfather Kennig killed a dragon single-handedly, you see. They made him king, of course, but his dynasty only lasted for a time. Even after his bloodline lost claim to the throne, we've been active in politics. Every generation expects greatness of us, and Father made it clear we were no exception. He wanted us to be warriors and chieftains like him, but Brin was never like that. I see that look on your face, but believe me, my brother wasn't always the intimidating man you've seen. He was actually really thin. Tall, thin, and *clean*. He was always obsessed with being clean, physically and philosophically. I honestly can't tell to this day which was more annoying. Whether he intended to or not, he came across as a know-it-all.

"Then again, when it came to alchemy, he did kind of know it all. It fascinated him the moment he learned of it, and he always had a knack for it. Even when Father would smash up his alchemy station and try to 'beat some sense' into him, he would always just build a new one and continue his experiments. I think Father came to respect his resilience and eventually left off trying to stop him.

"He was completely, and I mean *completely*, enamored with the work of Tanwin Xhamul: the greatest alchemist ever. If the man hadn't already been dead for a millennium, Brin would've married him if he could. He'd never shut up about this tenet of Tanwin's teaching or another, so it was no surprise to anyone when he wanted to join the Keepers of Alchemy: the society Tanwin founded over a thousand years ago to 'practice and perfect' the most highly noble and holy art in the whole wide world.

"He made it into the organization with flying colors, the youngest initiate they ever accepted. Even Father was impressed. And for five years, he was the darling prodigy of the Keepers. Probably would have been that way for life if it hadn't all got to his head. He never knew when to let off bragging, showing people up, or lecturing them on the true meaning of Tanwin's teachings. Strangely enough, that's an excellent way to make enemies of your cohorts. If he wasn't the best alchemist they had, they would have removed him sooner than they did. But eventually enough was enough, and the less scrupulous members of the order found something to frame him for. No one was eager to defend him, so they ended up expelling him from the order.

"It broke him, especially not being allowed to practice alchemy anymore. You see, when they expel you, they brand you. Half of that tattoo on his forehead is from that, and when you have it, you can't legally buy or use ingredients anymore. He returned to Father's estate a complete failure, and everyone pretended he didn't exist for two years. I was pretty much the only one who visited him then when I could. He didn't have it in him to carry on a conversation, but I know he appreciated it.

"Meanwhile, I was going down a very different path. Unlike Brin, I trained to be a warrior. Before I was ten years old, I knew how to wield a blade, ride a horse, and put on my own armor. Father was quite pleased with me until I wanted to learn magic. Mother eventually convinced him it would make me a better warrior and bring the family more honor, so he reluctantly agreed to send me to the Mages College.

"Turns out I had a knack for magic. I passed my exams with no difficulties. And then I made my mistake: I chose to study light magic. Father wasn't too happy about that. 'Light magic isn't direct enough, it's the weakest of all the elements,' and so on. But that made me want to study it all the more. I already knew how to be direct and swing a sword at your face, but how much more interesting would it be if I could make you think my horse was a dragon? And besides, just think of how embarrassing it would be to lose to a light mage. I couldn't resist.

"I joined the military when I graduated from the College, full of hopes I would be the best warrior mage in the land. So long as Father was watching, they gave me opportunities to prove myself. But he couldn't always watch, so they didn't always treat me as an actual warrior. They used me for menial tasks and treated me as their inferior. If I dared report them to Father, they would just find ways to make my life even more miserable. And it only got worse.

"A few years after Brin was expelled from the Keepers, my commanding officer thought he could get away with forcing me to sleep with him. The poor fool didn't know what he was getting himself into. I could've slit his throat on the spot, but I knew that wouldn't turn out well. So I used some light magic to blind him and walked the other way. I didn't think the scumbag would try to catch me anyways. He tripped and fell on his own sword, which everyone blamed on you-know-who, of course. I had to flee for my life before they executed me, so I rode away. Far away.

"I kept riding until I found myself on the shores of a lake not much different than this one. That's where I met Toff. He was a mage of the oldest order, older even than the College. He taught me so much I would have never learned back home — showed me things my professors would have hidden for fear of misuse. I'd probably still be there learning from him had fate not taken an unexpected twist."

The wistfulness that strayed into Zala's eyes at the mention of Toff melted away as her lips curled into a smile.

"The last time I'd visited Brin, I made him promise to go outside regularly, not just sit there in his room and rot away. He kept his promise, and one day he took a stroll through the adjoining village. That's when he saw the wanted posters for an agent of Azkalah. You see, William, there's more than one organization dedicated to practicing alchemy. While the Keepers have all their rules and restrictions and hypocritical ethics, Azkalah is founded on one principle: Anything is possible — for the right price. Having been declared an illegal association, there were no barriers to entry for outcasts like my brother. As long as you were good at alchemy and could keep your contracts, you could have access to the best the black market had to offer.

"My brother was intrigued. Let's just say he burned a few flowers, and within the month he was an agent himself. He was thrilled to be practicing alchemy again, with a new sense of purpose in his life. The work was exciting, kept his mind busy and his body employed. He rose through the ranks about as quickly as he did through the Keepers, but this time he knew enough not to make enemies of his new employers.

"Time went by, and he received a most unusual contract. A leader of the Hearthfell military was willing — illegally, mind you — to use Azkalah to hunt down a fugitive they lost: a treacherous light mage with high honors from the College who murdered her commanding officer and fled into the night. Turns out, getting high marks in school puts a large bounty on your head if you go rogue. My brother accepted the contract, and imagine his surprise when he finally tracked down the fugitive to find it was none other but his beloved sister, the one soul who pitied him when he was at his lowest.

"He knew full well what they'd do to me once he brought me back, so he came up with a crazy idea. We talked it out and agreed to follow it through. He brought me back with him to House Hearthfell, collected the bounty, and then proceeded to eradicate every last official who wanted me executed. He technically fulfilled all his duties and saved me in the process: win-win. We've been a team from then on, him with his alchemy and me with my magic.

"Thankfully, he saw the sense in bulking up. It took him a bit, but you've seen what he's grown into. He'll never admit it, but I taught him everything he knows with the sword and hand-to-hand combat. Don't tell him I said so, but between you and me, I think he's gotten good enough even to take me on."

Zala then turned to look at William and leaned closer. "So now you've heard my story, Outsider. What's yours?"

10

Horse Dancer

The fresh wave that crashed against the seashore gave William just a few fleeting moments to plan his response. It was difficult to focus on how to match the story he had just heard, especially with the charming figure who sat next to him, eager to hear his every word. Finding it difficult to improvise a grandiose story on the spur of the moment, William decided to start with simple honesty.

"I fear my story will be nowhere near as interesting as yours just now, Lady Zikennig," he said. "I'm an English noble, which means I was born to a long line of people who were nobles themselves — something you understand quite well. My great-grandfather served under a mighty conqueror named William. He's my namesake, you see, along with every third man-child born under the sun back home. This William ruled our land for decades, as did his son. Under their reign, my forebearers were diplomats and warriors who built a reputation for themselves through years of faithful service.

"Things went swimmingly until tragedy struck the royal family about thirty years ago. Some three hundred souls — mostly nobles — boarded a vessel known as the White Ship. Drunk out of their minds, they thought they had good fortune on their side..." William shook his head with a sigh. "But the ship struck a rock and they perished at sea —

including the only male heir of William's son. When the time came for a new monarch to be chosen, war broke out.

"My parents supported the wishes of William's son, who declared his daughter Matilda to be his successor. But a cousin of the King, Stephen of Blois, usurped the throne and drove Matilda from England. This same Matilda gave birth to the master I now serve: Henry II.

"Since I could first wield a sword, I've done whatever it takes to ensure Henry occupies the throne that should have belonged to the Queen Mother. Duty alone would require this of me, but beyond that, I've always looked after him as an older brother. I've been with him wherever he's gone, whether to make sure he attended his lessons on time, rubbed the right elbows at court, or didn't get a sword to the throat when he attempted to take back his kingdom. He can be impulsive sometimes, but he's a fine young man who will make for a good king."

At this point in William's discourse, a wave slammed against the base of the rock below, shooting a spray of cold water into their faces. When Zala looked back to William after wiping her face dry, a curious combination of admiration and dissatisfaction lay in her gaze.

"That's very noble of you, my fine sir, but that's not quite what I asked you. I want to know *your* story, not your king's. Tell me more about... how did you say it? 'Where you are from, and how you got to be so good at what you do?'"

William blushed, feeling a surge of warmth drive off the cold from his face. Were it not for the embarrassment at the moment, it would have felt refreshing. But as it was, he did not quite know how to handle Zala's prompting. It was rare for anyone to care more about his personal life than the services of his duty — especially someone this good-looking.

"Oh... right. My apologies, my lady," he faltered. "Well, I was born to my parents in a place called London, the most important city in England. I'm afraid I was both their first and only child. My mother died in childbirth."

William shifted in discomfort as a bitter taste rose in his mouth. He pulled back the curls of black hair from his head to reveal the beginning of the scar that ran down to the corner of his lip. "The doctor tried to save us both but only ended up giving me this. It's funny, you know. Most scars come from living a life to the full, but this one came from taking a life away."

William did not intend for his voice to break, yet it did anyway. The sympathy in Zala's eyes and the press of her hand on his shoulder did not help with keeping his cool. When William regained his composure, he continued: "With neither a wife nor other children to shoulder the family responsibilities, my father came to expect a lot from me. I'd often joke with the few friends I had that my father actually had three sons, but they were all just forced into one body — a body, it so happened, my peers thought deserved a thrashing or two for being so ugly."

His face contorted as he raised the pitch of his voice in mocking imitation: "That's a nice scar you got there, Willy! Let's give you a matching one on the other side!"

Such memories were unpleasant for him to recall, yet he also could not resist feeling some pleasure at the look of pity and then indignation that flashed across Zala in rapid succession. The result was a half-smile that he hoped was not too noticeable.

"The beatings hurt," he admitted, "but I suppose some good came of it —I learned early on how to fight for myself. In time, they didn't dare pick a fight with me."

An approving smile from Zala encouraged him to share the details of his life he would have otherwise kept to himself.

"My father was quite active in political affairs, so whenever I wasn't accompanying him, I learned how to conduct myself as the man of the house while he was away. I excelled both at my academic studies and martial training, so they considered me a useful asset by the time Henry came of age. Ever since he mounted his first invasion force at fourteen years old, I've been a key leader in his army. Yet for all my successful ambitions, I remained a lonely man. My charm never improved since childhood, and my family was so wrapped up with the war that I never thought I would find a woman to marry—until I met Adelaide."

At this point, William wished his face was still dripping wet to hide the tears threatening to gather in his eyes, while Zala attempted her best to maintain a neutral expression at the mention of another woman.

"She didn't find me repulsive like all the other noblewomen did. She would talk with me whenever she got the chance, and her mind was so sharp! It was never a dull conversation with her, and her convictions were just as strong as her intellect. Stubborn as a mule sometimes, but then again, I'm sure she thought the same of me. She was beautiful, too, which made it all the more confusing why she found me so interesting.

"But I was happy to accept her love, just as she was happy to accept my proposal. We were wed within the year, and our joy only grew when she gave us a bouncing baby boy. But I suppose it was too much temptation for fate to resist. Just as Henry's army made headway on the mainland, my poor Addy fell ill of the fever, and... she never recovered."

William looked down, his eyes fixated on the numb expanse of nothingness between his mind's eye and his feet.

"And just like that, the love of my life was gone. One day breathing, joking about the doctor's funny wig, and then the next... still as the grave. I couldn't fathom it. Couldn't accept it. So I left my son in the care of my father's estate, and I drank. Drank until the pain stopped, and the memories quit stabbing me, and I couldn't remember she was gone anymore.

"But, alas, it turns out that being drunk out of your mind leaves you vulnerable to other woes. The bystanders said I tried dancing with another man's horse on the thoroughfare after I fell off mine. I don't remember a moment of it, only waking up to a broken leg and a pair of black eyes. Whatever happened, I was bedridden for weeks — ones filled with important battles I couldn't fight. It took a while for my reputation to recover, but I did eventually work myself back into the King's favor. Enough for me to be sent here on his urgent business." William's lips then drew tight in resolve. "It's something I dare not fail."

A somber silence ensued as another wave smashed into the rock face below. Both onlookers remained still as they processed what had been said, oblivious to the dark clouds that massed at the horizon. A distant peal of thunder sounded, and Zala was the first to stir from her musings.

"I, for one, think your king is lucky to have as devoted a knight as you, William. Even with your drinking, I've seen plenty of men who would have never recovered from such circumstances. And besides that," she said with a smirk, "it's not every day someone trifles with a horse like that and lives to tell the tale."

The mirth in Zala's face dampened somewhat as she looked up and scanned the horizon.

"Though we should head back before the storm blows in," she insisted. "They can be pretty fierce around here." A gust of wind blew past them as if on cue, followed by the perfect stillness only an impending storm can bring. Before William had a chance to grow too concerned, the care in Zala's countenance flashed into a mischievous smile.

"Let's go, Horse Dancer," she said as she stood and offered William a hand. Torn between embarrassment and amusement, William took her hand. Within moments, he was by her side as they trudged back through the white sands that shifted into gray.

William noticed on their way back some human silhouettes in the distance wading into the waves. On closer approach, he recognized the evergreen tunics these people wore as identical to the robes of the Essari he had last encountered. He turned his gaze to Zala, not even needing to voice the obvious question before she replied: "The Essari often come out here right before a storm. It's the best time to harvest the shells they value so highly. In the olden days, the whole island used those shells as currency, but now they mostly just make for trinkets and decorations."

The scavenging party was composed entirely of women and children, except for a few men scattered in their midst with some fishing spears in tow. By their posture, William could not tell if they used the spears to help collect the shells or to protect the others from an unseen threat. William's observation was interrupted when Zala nudged his shoulder.

"They often return to finish scavenging after a storm ends," she explained. "By the look of it, this storm won't break until sometime tomorrow. I'm sure if you came back then, you could strike up a good conversation with them if you wanted to."

William was not sure how she could tell the length of a storm just by looking at the clouds on the horizon, but he resigned his doubts to the fact that things just did not work normally in Cabalia. His mind then toyed with the not-so-subtle suggestion posed by Zala. Would he be able to hold a conversation with these people even other Cabalians thought were odd?

An even better question was if he would *want* to do that. They did, after all, almost run him through with swords the first time he saw them. But then again, this was a rare opportunity even by Cabalian standards. Who knew what he could learn by talking to the Essari? He decided it was worth a try, at least.

Zala and William stopped at the door they had exited from earlier. Zala paused in thought as she struggled to recall something important. Moments later, she gasped in recollection. "Thilmarin," she spoke firmly in a low tone. The exterior beside the door rippled to reveal a camouflaged panel with buttons similar to what William had first seen inside the building. Zala leaned in and pushed a combination of buttons that beeped and blinked green until the door cracked open a sliver. She then slipped her fingers into a crevice and pried it wide enough for them to enter.

"There's so much to remember about this place, it's hard to keep it all straight sometimes," she chuckled half to herself as she disappeared behind the door. William looked back at the lake shore to see the first drops of rain descending on the open waters. The sound of sprinkling grew into a steady patter on the sand as he closed the door behind him with a clank.

Zala set a brisk pace, and it only took a few minutes to lead William back to his room.

"I think you've had a full enough day," she said as she lingered by the entrance. "So I'll leave you to yourself. I'm sure the Essari have left you ample resources to amuse yourself with. They may be hermits, but they're pretty generous to the few guests they let visit."

A cursory glance around the room proved Zala's words true. Platters with a colorful array of food lay ready for consumption by William's bedside, and a bookshelf on the opposite side of the room stood well-stocked with books of different sizes and subjects. A pile of trinkets lay neatly arranged in the center of the room, looking quite like a vendor's front window display of goods. Dozens of artifacts and curios beckoned for further investigation, more than enough to pass the hours away.

"I'll be down the hall, in the second room on the left. If you need me, just give a knock or two," said Zala with a smile and a small bow. "Enjoy the rest of your evening, William. It really was a pleasure to hear your story."

William returned the bow with a smile no less sincere. "And you as well, Lady Zikennig. The pleasure was all mine."

Zala rolled her eyes with a light chuckle. "Please, William, I've used your first name this whole time. You can just call me Zala."

Something inside William's heart fluttered as he found himself giving a second bow. "Very well, Zala. I truly hope you enjoy your evening."

The smile in her eyes betrayed the warmth behind the reserved smile on her face.

"Thank you, William. I'll see you tomorrow." With a gentle turn, she wandered down the hall in no great hurry.

William stood transfixed as he watched her disappear into the distance. Half of him was minded to call after her, but the sudden appearance of Essari in the corridor pushed the other half of his mind to the forefront: namely, it had been another full day, and a comfortable bed was calling his name. There would be plenty of time tomorrow, he reasoned, to visit with the red-haired warrior mage that so intrigued him.

William surveyed the table by his bedside and helped himself to a scrumptious dinner. Much of the food he had never seen before in his life, which was a pity — it was tastier than anything he had eaten back in England. After picking the last morsels clean from his teeth, he scooped up a trinket in the center of the room and toyed with it while he reclined on the bed.

A flash of lightning illuminated the room as he watched the thunderstorm in progress outside his window. Moments after the lightning retreated into darkness, a boom of thunder arrived, furious to have been so narrowly outpaced by the lightning. The thunder's rumbling gave way to the constant patter of rainfall, and William's eyes grew heavy while his mind wandered through a labyrinth of new memories to process.

With each twist and turn his recollections took him, he found it more difficult to believe everything that had happened. Just a few days ago, he had been warming himself by a fireside in England, knowing Cabalia as little more than a distant legend. Now, it felt like he could write a whole book on the subject! Would anyone even believe it if he told them?

William sighed as he set down the trinket and resigned himself to sleeping away another uncertain night on the Island of Magic.

I I

Two Bridges

Back in the city of Elkreath, a thick fog rolled in from the sea. Lanterns on the sides of buildings remained visible at a distance, yet only by offering a distorted glow that made for an altogether eerie impression. Many people still traveled the streets, carrying their own sources of light with them. Those of reputable business were either closing up their shops or already traveling home for dinner, while those of less reputable business were just hitting their stride. Nightlife was never dull in Cabalia's largest city, and there was always some money to be made. Or spent.

One bridge in particular on the west side of the city was a favorite haunt of those who feared nothing of the "dangers of the flesh," as the Church would call it. The Nightside Bridge, as it was named, lacked most of the lighting that benefited other regions in the city. What little light it held came from the windows of rooms built around the edges of the bridge to house certain "pleasurable activities." So long as the sun was down, soft echoes of giggling mingled with the grating of jeers. No respectable person would pass by that way. And yet, when the bell tolled an hour before midnight, the footsteps of Inquestor Telnis Raiko fell squarely upon it.

His day had been long, unfruitful, and thoroughly exhausting. The only place he wanted to be was at home, preferably in bed, even more preferably in the arms of his wife. But as it happened, that godforsaken bridge represented the quickest way home. So it was that with reluctance he strode down it, intent on crossing as soon as possible. He made eye contact with no one, even as a number of beautiful young women approached to proposition him. Even with the worry lines that creased his face, he was a handsome man still in his prime. A man with less scruples would have taken a detour to a pleasurable evening. But no detour did Telnis make. He passed straight through, quite possibly setting a record for the least amount of time ever spent crossing the bridge.

It was frustrating for him, actually. So many crimes being committed in front of him, yet he was powerless to do anything about it. Money was being made — money that seeped its way into the Councils of Elkreath, including the Council of Inquest. Even if he were naive enough to pursue an investigation there, the end of such labors would be the inevitable turning of a blind eye at court. As long as business was kept on the bridge, it would stay on the bridge. Such was the way of things, however corrupt they were.

Telnis hated every bit of it. When he failed to make the cut as an adjudicator for the Mages College, he took the inquestor position in Elkreath as a distant second-best. It was an insult added to injury to experience firsthand as often as he did the effects of city corruption. *Why couldn't he have been an adjudicator?* The question yanked at his heart for the thousandth time as he cleared the end of the bridge.

At his first step past the edge, the atmosphere grew noticeably lighter, and he could breathe easier at last. He uttered a brief prayer of thanks to Yahos before turning onto the lane that traveled by his house.

When he drew near to the door of his home, he paused in surprise. He had not expected to see the light of a lamp shining through the window at that hour. Upon twisting the door handle open, it was even more of a shock to find his wife sitting at the dining table, waiting for him. The lamp she held spared him the need to use light magic to read her emotions. Her face was tired, stretched thin with longing, but she was not angry.

"Eris! How long have you been waiting for me?" his voice quivered with shock and concern. She merely shrugged and continued to look at him. The lamp's light danced across her hair, leaving soft flickers of yellow across a field of chestnut brown. Weary as her eyes were, the gleam they held proved them as still not lifeless.

Telnis gaped at her before coming to his senses. He took off his coat and wrapped it snugly around her before sitting down beside her. "My poor wife," he said as he wrapped his arm around her. "You could have been warm and cozy in bed. How long have you been sitting here in the cold?"

Her voice, while feeble, held a spark that reminded him of when they first met. "As long as it took."

Telnis buried his head in her neck. "You didn't have to do that."

Gently, she lifted his head to look into her eyes. "I did if I wanted to see you." His heart pulled forward within him, and he leaned in to kiss her. She drew him into her arms, and for a few brief moments, the cares of life melted away behind their lips. The stars passed by on their celestial courses while the lamp flickered further into the night.

After some time, Telnis breathed a heavy sigh.

"Long day at work?" Eris asked. He nodded as she stroked his hair.

"Incredibly so. This case is going to be a big one."

"Am I allowed to know what it is?" she queried.

It was only after a long pause of silence that he answered. "It's Brinwin. They want me to hunt down Brinwin Zikennig."

At this, she gave a start. "What?! He's back in Elkreath? What's he done now?"

Telnis groaned. "We don't fully know yet. All we know is that someone randomly exploded on the Tafrik Bridge. Yes, that's right — spontaneously combusted," he said on feeling her incredulous look. "And then someone connected with Shadowcrest ran from the scene, only to meet up with Zikennig himself. They both slipped away into the night, but we made some progress tracking them. I followed the trail as far as Lake Iddeah before it went cold. Where they are now, I think only Yahos knows for sure!"

Eris said nothing as she waited to hear more, her husband clearly not done with his rant of the day's goings.

"It wasn't easy, getting as far as we did. And still, it was all for nothing! He could be clear over to the Mountains of Haldvar by this point."

"And?"

Telnis blinked. "How do you mean, 'and?'"

"I know you, Telnis," she said. "There's something else troubling you. What is it?"

He looked down and grunted. Even after eight years of marriage, he found her perceptiveness uncanny. Had he not known any better, he would have sworn she practiced some light magic herself.

"I had to trudge miles to get back here," he said. "It was so late, and I just wanted to get home. I took the Nightside to save extra time." Eris said nothing until he finally spat out, "And I just can't stand it! Every night! Every night those hoodlums get off with their shenanigans, and we can't do a blessed thing to stop them! What's the point of being in law enforcement if you can't enforce the laws that are broken right in front of your eyes? We know where they're doing it! When, too! If this blasted city just had a backbone, we could put an end to it! But why don't we? Because we're corrupt. All of us! Enforcers, Inquestors, Councilors, the whole rotten lump of us!"

At this point, Eris interrupted her husband. Putting her fingers to his lips, she spoke softly. "Quiet now, love," she said. "You're going to wake the child at this rate." She held his face in her hands as she attempted to soothe him. "You've had plenty enough action for one day. You should rest. You can worry about this tomorrow with a level head."

Telnis nodded wearily and took his wife's hand as she helped him stand. Once firmly on their feet, they shuffled past the dining room and made toward their bedroom. It would have taken less than a minute to reach their destination had Telnis not caught a glimpse of his son sleeping peacefully in his crib. The sight stopped him in his tracks, prompting him to draw closer. Eris offered no objections, and the two of them stepped quietly to the cradle's edge.

"How long has he been sleeping?" he whispered while he watched the infant's chest rise and fall.

"Only a couple hours," came her reply.

Despite the responsibilities and cares the infant introduced into their lives, little Davin Raiko lived every inch up to his name: *One who is a gift*. Seven years of barrenness, broken by an unexpected blessing of Yahos. The realization settled in their hearts as they stood gazing at their child that every sleepless night had been worth it. The pain, the hassle, the frustration — it had all been worth it to be standing there at that moment. No further words were spoken between them, and neither did there need to be.

They closed the door behind them and retired to bed at last. As soon as Eris extinguished the lamp, the house settled into the stillness of night. Telnis's head hit the pillow, and no sooner did he feel the warmth of his wife's arms around him than he sank into a deeply needed slumber. He snored as the hours passed, but neither his child nor his wife was awake enough to notice. They were all too exhausted in their own right to notice when Telnis's dreams caused him to toss and turn, moaning at the sight that flashed uninvited across his mind's eye.

As he dreamed, he saw himself standing on the Tafrik Bridge. It was evening, and a thick mist swirled about him with not a soul in sight. He opened his mouth to call out, but no sound could come from him no matter how hard he tried.

All at once, the mist blew to his right and tumbled off the bridge to reveal a patchwork of glowing blue cracks in the pavement. Telnis remembered seeing the cracks from earlier in the day, and he drew near to investigate. When he got close to them, they grew brighter and began to hum in a low tone. He suddenly felt a presence behind him, and he wheeled about to find Brinwin Zikennig towering over him, his red tattoo twice its usual size. He turned to run, but the cracks spread to his feet and glued him in place as Brinwin drew a sword from its sheath. He opened his mouth to scream, but still no sound came out. Time came to a crawl as the sword swung toward his face.

It was merely inches away when Telnis jolted awake, nearly rolling off the bed. He gasped in shock first, then in relief when he realized it was only a dream. Brinwin's presence was easy enough to rationalize, but he stood at a loss as to the cracks on the bridge. He had seen them on the Tafrik Bridge at the investigation last morning but had paid them little attention. Now, he could not shake them from his mind. *What were they?* Telnis shook his head and vowed to prioritize it for the upcoming day's investigation. With a final sigh, he rolled over and clung tightly to the last few hours of sleep that he could.

12

Trouble Brewing

Brinwin cursed as the lights went out in his laboratory. Essari technology was wonderful to work with, but the storms that often blew in from the east across Lake Iddeah always found a way to disrupt power at the most inopportune times. At least with a torch, he would not have to worry about losing light in the middle of his research, but far be it from these masters of invention to use something so primitive.

He sighed in frustration as he withdrew a vial the size of his ring finger from his cloak. After giving it a firm shake, he set it on the table beside him and unstopped the cork. Moments later, a thin strand of gold gleamed in the vial, which twirled about several times before expanding to fill the vessel with a radiant light.

With his work visible once again, Brinwin directed his focus back to the notes he had been poring over. He scanned the handwritten data, hoping against hope something new would jump out at him, perhaps something he missed the first twenty times he read it. Were it possible, his gaze would have pierced a hole clean through the parchment he held and maybe even the table beneath it.

At length, he set down the parchments. "*Nothing!*" he hissed in frustration. No matter how many angles he tried, he could not get his experiment to succeed. It was beyond late, and Brinwin knew he would pay the price for depriving himself of sleep. But he could not sleep now. Not while he had so little time to work with. He told the Englishman three days, and in three days he would be ready to go.

Not that he needed three days to assemble everything for the mission. He had already done that before setting out for the Kozheithy Tavern. What he truly needed was time to answer the question that stood as the focus of his life's work: Could a master of alchemy successfully transmute a Danuri stone to a higher level?

Brinwin reached into the chest by his feet and pulled out the stone William had offered him in payment for his services. He turned it over in his hands, its brilliant blue glow pulsing with untapped power. Rare indeed was it to find a virgin stone no one had ever used for magic — rarer still to find a blue one. A stone of this quality could grant him the luxury of a king or the power to rival the sorcerers of old. But Brinwin cared for neither riches nor power. Knowledge was most important of all, and he was going to uncover it. Could he turn this stone violet?

Those versed in either the arcane or alchemical arts in Cabalia knew the basics of Danuri stones, how they were the result of ordinary rocks being too close to an unstable discharge of magic. Such rocks would absorb Kyne: the very essence of magic that mages would channel from a dimension beyond the physical world, known in their tongue as the Eldanu. As a rule, mages would take the utmost care while channeling Kyne to keep the connection between their world and the Eldanu stable. But if, whether through inexperience or sudden interruption, such connection was not kept stable, Kyne could discharge itself into anything nearby.

For living things, such a discharge would be catastrophic; for inanimate objects, the Kyne would make them glow. The brightness of their glow would show how much Kyne the object had absorbed, while the color revealed the quality. Red sat as the lowest quality, followed by yellow, orange, green, blue, and then purple as the highest. Regardless of their color, such objects had limited use; any use of the Kyne within would deplete them, causing them to grow duller and duller until they were no longer usable for magic.

All of this was basic knowledge that Brinwin knew well. What was far less basic was his theory that such objects could be modified to grow stronger. His trials with lesser stones over the years led him to one conclusion: only blue stones were both powerful enough and unstable enough to be successfully transformed.

Brinwin stared at the Danuri stone in his hands. "So many years of work... so much effort," he mused. "And only you can prove me right. You have to." He tucked the stone back into its container with a longing sigh. The lights had still not come on, which could only mean the power outage was a serious one. Time was drawing to a close, and he could not afford to end his research in failure.

No, he resolved. He would do whatever it took to complete his work. Sleep or no sleep, three days would be enough to prove to the world that he was right. Whatever misgivings the academics had with his past, Brinwin Zikennig would not go down as a failure.

His hand trembled only slightly when he gripped the glowing vial in front of him. Cramming his eyes shut, he swallowed its contents in one gulp. No sooner had the last drop of liquid left the bottle than a searing pain ripped through his stomach, forcing him to recoil. He fought the urge to convulse as best he could. He knew the pain would be over soon.

The vial dropped to the floor and shattered into pieces as a fresh clap of thunder rattled the room. Darkness filled the laboratory and overshadowed the gasp that escaped from Brinwin's contorted face.

"Let's... get down... to business."

* * *

The heavens remained shrouded in gray when William awoke the next day. The rain had diminished to a steady sprinkling, giving the air a thoroughly damp feel. Thunder could just barely be heard in the distance above the swishing of the waves outside the window. It was difficult at first to make anything out in the early morning light, but it was clear someone had already visited the room: The trinkets and food from last night had disappeared, and a small fireplace in the corner of the room had been lit. William straightened up to find a fresh pile of clothes at the end of his bed. He rubbed his eyes and brought the clothes to the fireplace for further inspection.

There was a complete set of bright green tunic, leggings, and socks made of a sturdy yet surprisingly comfortable material that smelled of fresh pine. He peered in caution around the room before changing into the new garb, half expecting some newfangled trick of Zala's to startle him. As seconds passed by into minutes, the lack of Zala's surprises became itself something of a surprise, and a pleasant one at that. Nothing but the peaceful silence of a new morning greeted him.

Once fully clothed and satisfied with how everything fit, he set his mind toward his plans for the day. It would be at least another day until Brinwin finished with the shadesteel, and the storm had not yet subsided. As best he could figure, there were three options for him at the moment: He could either stay in his room and enjoy some time in solitude; *or* he could go to Zala's quarters, who would no doubt guide him through another day of surprises and wonders; *or* he could wander off on his own to see what he could discover for himself. He weighed the options in his mind until a soft knocking came on the door. Fully expecting it to be Zala, William answered with an eager, "Come in!"

What came through the doors, however, was anything but Zala, or even a human, for that matter. Whatever it was that strode toward William was unlike any creature he had seen before. It stood on two legs and was two-thirds the height of an average man. Its dark skin was smooth and glossy, reflecting the light of the fireplace back at William. Large, beady eyes, each the size of William's fist, stared unblinking at him as it carried a platter of fresh food to the side of the bed with its two arms. Each hand had six fingers, much like a human's hand would look with a second thumb directly opposite its counterpart. Two protruding nubs stood where the ears on a human head would be, while a mouth drawn into a perpetual straight line remained motionless on a rectangular head. It thumped around softly as it walked barefoot, clothed in a simple garment of the Essari's characteristic green.

William could not tell if this was another of Zala's tricks of the light, but he was too intimidated by what he saw to try finding out. After it set the food down on his bedside, it turned toward William and offered him a full bow. It then turned and strode out of the room as purposefully as it arrived, shutting the door softly behind it.

Any desire William might have had to go adventuring on his own faltered on the heels of this unexpected visitor. Who knew what else lay beyond the door? There did not seem to be an end to the surprises this land held, and it was only a matter of time before one of these surprises was not a friendly one. And yet, it would be cowardice to stay locked in his room like a child afraid of monsters outside.

Best to go forward with a guide, William reasoned. Fully resolved in his mind, he pushed the door open with as much swagger as he could muster and stepped out into the hallway.

The lights overhead were dim but still enough to make his way to Zala's quarters. No one could be seen in any direction as he walked down the hallway, something William found both chilling and comforting at the same time. He paused when he arrived at the door Zala gave him directions to last evening. Not sure what he was about to get himself into, he clung to a final few seconds of stillness before rapping on the door.

Nothing but silence replied to his knocking, and William waited for another few seconds before trying again. The last rap of his knuckles reverberated off the door when a voice came from behind him.

"Good morning, William."

The gentleness of Zala's voice did little to prevent William from startling. He jerked around to find her standing a few feet away with a cup of steaming liquid in her hands. She gazed at him with a bemused look that William was aggravated to see directed at him yet again. He sputtered, but Zala spoke before he could spit out his first words of surprise or indignation.

"I know, I know... but believe it or not, I didn't plan on surprising you first thing in the morning. I just went down to fetch something to drink and came back to find you knocking on my door. If I really wanted to surprise you, you already know I could've done *much* worse."

It was annoying that she was right. Zala continued to sip her beverage while William's tongue remained tied, unable to find an adequate comeback despite his best efforts. He finally gave up and forced himself to swallow his indignation.

"I suppose. The thing that brought me breakfast wasn't your work, then?"

"Not at all," she replied. "That would be a thilmig. A backbender, to be precise." Zala finished the rest of her drink before attempting to satisfy William's curiosity. "You must not have them in Europe, then, do you?"

"Ah... no. We most certainly do not."

"I'm surprised they haven't been exported to you by now. But then again, House Tropis never did like them, and they control the ports. Can't say I blame them. It *would* be hard for the great cities of timber to accept a creature that eats wood like there's no tomorrow."

"I beg your pardon? They eat *wood*?" William could not keep the disbelief out of his tone.

"Oh, yes. That's what they prefer the most. Though if there's none of that on hand, they're fine enough with eating rocks. Or dirt."

Now William knew she was joking. He implored Zala with his eyes to stop teasing him, but she only shrugged in response.

"What? They do actually eat dirt," she insisted. "If you don't train them right, they'll literally *eat* your house and home. And don't even get me started on the stench."

A soft thudding came from behind them as a thilmig shuffled by, similar in appearance to the one William saw earlier, except much frailer. It paused to stare at Zala as if it knew she was talking about it. Zala softened her tone as she reached out to grab the creature's hand and drew it to their midst.

"There are different breeds of them. This one's called a backbender because they're the ones best trained to serve in the house and bow to company. Yes, lots of bowing you do, don't you little one?"

The creature seemed caught off guard, not knowing how to respond other than with a series of quick and timid bows that made William feel sorry for it. Zala sat down and pulled it onto her lap, stroking the nubs on its head while she turned to face William. She nodded her head toward the creature as it suddenly grew still. "They physically can't eat anything while in their human-like form, which is why their owners often keep them employed like this. They eventually need to eat, though, and this one looks starved. I may not fancy them as much as other creatures, but an animal starving in the home is unacceptable. Go into your room and grab some ashes from the fireplace," she instructed, motioning to the cup she had set down.

William grabbed the mug and set off at once. He returned before long with a pile of ashes that still smoldered inside the cup. Zala took it with a free hand as she continued stroking one of the thilmig's nubs.

"I know you wouldn't believe me unless I showed you," she said. "Normally, I wouldn't be able to do this since they're trained to transform only on the command of their masters. But I've learned a trick or two." With a wink, she turned the comatose backbender upside down and pressed her thumbs against the nubs on either side of its head.

Zala was right. William would *not* have believed it if he had not seen it himself. The backbender's skin lost its glossy sheen and morphed into a chestnut color before sprouting over three inches of fur. Its eyes shrunk to nearly the size of a cat's while their edges filled with emerald green until their irises resembled that of any other mammal in nature. The fingers on each hand folded together to form thickly padded paws, and the topmost arms relocated themselves until Zala was left holding a creature that looked exactly like a larger version of the "Mr. Floofles" she had pranked William with the day before.

The beast stirred when Zala turned it back upright and set it on her lap. It wobbled as it gained its bearings, then sniffed the air intently. A moment later, it swung its head toward the ash-laden mug Zala held. No sooner had she lowered the cup to its mouth than it gobbled up the ash with a voracity that William found unsettling. After picking the cup clean, it gave a contented sound that fell between a chirp and a meow before attempting to scuffle off Zala's lap.

"Oh no you don't, little guy. Let's get you back on two feet before they have a heart attack." Zala held it in her arms as she stood up, just as an Essari man turned the corner and came upon them. For the first time since William had arrived in Cabalia, he saw a look of fear cross Zala's face.

The Essari's eyes first widened in shock before they contracted in fury. "Zala Zikennig! You a thilmig dare transform?!" The man snatched the frightened creature from Zala and bellowed, "Get out! Now! Before I you throw out!"

Zala grabbed William's hand and fled without a word. William glanced behind him as they went, searing into his memory the image of four emerald eyes gaping at him: two overflowing with rage and two with fear. Such fear he no doubt would have seen in his own eyes were he able to view them.

13

Into the Depths

Zala's pace was beyond brisk, and it did not let up even as she and William struggled to catch their breath. "What just happened there?" William gasped in between breaths as they descended a flight of stairs. The rattling of their footsteps off the metal grating set them further on edge as they hurried forward.

"Well," she huffed back, "it's kind of forbidden to transform someone else's thilmig without their permission... especially a backbender."

"Then why'd you do it?!" William spat out, almost stumbling over his own feet.

"Because the Essari are nothing but clockwork! They *never* deviate from their schedules. And I know their schedules for that hall — he wasn't supposed to be there!" she yelled with a yank on his hand as she rounded the corner of a corridor. "And you saw that thing! I couldn't just let it starve! Ten more seconds, and I would've had it back to standing again!"

"Why are we still running?! I think he's quite behind us," William panted.

"Because when an Essari says to get out of his home, you get out as fast as your precious little feet can carry you!" Zala shouted back before narrowly avoiding a collision with the wall as they shot around another turn. She did not even stop to glance behind her when she stumbled upon an exit.

With trembling fingers, she punched a quick combination into the keypad by the door. The keypad flashed red, and Zala let loose a curse as strong as the door that still barred their way. She wiped the sweat from her forehead and attempted the combination again. William saw no one pursuing them when he spun his head around, but that did little to calm his fear as Zala worked herself into a frenzy fussing with the door. The moment the keypad flared green in success, Zala propelled them outside to the hardened surface of Lake Iddeah's dampened sand. As it happened, William's foot caught on the threshold and sent them both sprawling face-first to the ground.

William was the first to look up as a seabird cawed in laughter overhead. The clouds that had dominated the sky since the previous day were breaking up, allowing bright streaks of silver light to reflect off the grit that caked Zala's face. It was a comical figure she struck, and the jolt William received from his fall broke his panic enough to notice. It further dawned on him that nothing but silence had emerged from the door behind them. There were still no pursuers.

Perhaps the only danger they had to fear was what they would inflict on themselves. William's mouth stretched into a quivering smile as he tried to hold back from laughing at it all, but when he glanced at the mortified expression on Zala's sand-covered face, he could no longer restrain himself. A hearty laugh escaped from him while Zala stared at him, flabbergasted.

"Forgive me, Lady Zikennig!" he implored between laughs. "I think I now understand how you feel looking at me half the time!"

Zala's eyes narrowed. She clenched her fist to scoop up a clod of sand, which she then threw straight at William's face. Her mark was impeccable, and the sand-ball gave a satisfying thud as it walloped his still-laughing face.

"William Steele!" she called. Her voice was ominous. Perhaps too ominous. She glared at him as his face dripped with wet sand. "I told you to call me Zala!"

She made as if to lunge at him, which led him to roll backward straight into a rock. He blinked stupidly with a dazed look when his back bumped against the unyielding surface of the stone, prompting Zala to break down into an uncontrollable laugh of her own. Tears of laughter and pent-up stress poured down her face while William sat upright and tried to make sense of the world. Failing to do that, he joined in with the laughter that rang across the otherwise quiet beachfront.

Their laughter eventually died down, and with the silence came a return of reason to them both. Zala's cheeks flushed nearly as red as the dye in her hair when she spoke. "I might have overreacted. It must have felt like our lives were on the line..."

"You think so?" William replied.

"I'm sorry," she faltered. "It's not that I thought they'd kill us... it's just that they could throw me out of here for good if they wanted to, and the last thing I needed was for them to think I was being flippant about it. I've seen people do that before, where they don't follow their demands to the letter. It didn't go well."

"It sounds like quite the story," he probed as she rose to her feet.

"Sorry, William," she said with a weary half-smile. "I'm nowhere near in the mood to tell that story."

Waves drawn by the changing tide lapped close to where Zala stood and William sat. She motioned farther down the shore and said, "Let's go farther on. With any luck, I might be able to have a final conversation with some Essari before they all find out what I did."

She waited while he rose to his feet before setting off down the coast at a not-quite-but-almost-leisurely pace. The clouds above them continued to disperse as they walked until cracks of blue sky opened to pour light across their path. The lake's wildlife seemed to take its cue from the sun and returned in full array. The splashing of the waves and the chirping and the cawing made it all sound as if there were not a care in the world; as if nature itself attempted to compensate the wearied pair for their troubles.

At length, they came upon a group of Essari that had resumed gathering shells. It appeared as though Zala's hopes were fulfilled when none of them seemed to mind her arrival. Some of the women gave her a friendly nod, while most of the others remained focused on their tasks. Once within talking distance, Zala called to them, "How blow the winds?"

One of the men holding a fishing spear turned to face her. "Poorly," he answered with a grim expression. "It long time has been since so few shells our way have come. Something in the deep them all is eating."

"Have you any idea what it could be?" William chimed in, much to Zala's approval.

"Hard with certainty to say." The man wiped his brow of the perspiration brought on by the fully unveiled sun. "Many things in the deep reside — things not even we know about."

"Is that what your spears are for?" William queried.

"Indeed, they are. One never too careful can be."

"Let us hope your people never actually have to use them," said Zala with concern.

The resolve in the man's reply reminded William of the bravest men he had commanded before riding into battle. "Hope or not, any threat us prepared will find, Lady Zikennig." He then turned his gaze back to the water and tightened the grip on his spear. "Work we must go back to. If you us wish to help, you welcome to us join are. Otherwise, please excuse us."

William glanced at Zala and shrugged as he rolled up his sleeves and leggings. "What can we do to help?" he said.

The ghost of a smile played across the man's face before he replied, "We no extra spears have. You and the Lady the searchers can join. They you what to do will tell."

William and Zala waded over to the group of women and children that scoured the nearby shallows. One of the women held up a green shell the size of her hand that flashed a prism of light back toward the sky. "These the most valuable are," she said. "Try to find as much of them as you can."

A child beside her bent over and pulled up a plain brown shell with red stripes. "And these worthless are. Don't bother them picking up. Everything else good is."

"Here!" another child yelled before tossing them each an empty sack. "Put them in here!"

With no further instructions, William and Zala set to work. The job was tedious and painstaking at times, but at least the coolness of the water offered refreshment from the sun's heat.

What felt like hours went by with little success, although William did manage to find a small fragment of a green shell that brought the congratulations of those next to him. Zala had no such success, however, and she grew more irritated with each passing hour at still having nothing to show for her efforts. She longed to have some tangible proof of having helped the Essari before returning to their compound by the day's end, but each second spent bending over in vain put that hope farther away from her.

The sun had risen well past noon when a small girl came running up along the beachfront calling out for her mother.

"Mada! Mada!" she wailed. "Liddy ran off, and now I him can't find!"

The girl's mother stood up from collecting shells and called two of the older children in the group. "Boys! Help your sister her thilmig find."

Zala's eyes gleamed as she spoke up. "William and I can help. We were about to head back to the Enclave anyways." She could tell the boys did not want to be dragged into helping their sister, and the mother seemed relieved to have someone else willing to complete the errand.

"That very kind of you is, Zala. Much thanks," she sighed in relief before calling back to her daughter. "Uma dear, show Lady Zikennig where you Liddy last saw. We right here will be when you him find."

William raised his eyebrows before following Zala, who practically skipped out of the lake. Within a minute, Uma was leading the pair down the beach as fast as her little legs could wobble. They went until they came to an outcropping of rocks that led away from the water's edge. The openings to many small caves could be seen as they came closer.

"Liddy there ran off," the child said as she pointed to one of the caves. "I him called, but he didn't come back, and I too scared am to him go find."

The cave receded into a darkness that neither of the adults would blame the child for being afraid of.

"It's alright, Uma," said Zala with the soothing voice of a mother. "We'll find Liddy. You wait here with William, and I'll be right back, ok?"

The child gave a timid nod and held William's hand as Zala disappeared into the cave. They could hear her voice at first echoing off the walls as she called for the creature, but it soon grew quieter and more distant until it vanished altogether.

Minutes passed by in silence while Uma fidgeted at William's side. Zala's absence was beginning to concern William, and he started planning what to do next. He was about to bring the girl back to her mother and search for Zala himself when they heard footsteps ring out from the cave. Zala appeared at the entrance and stepped toward them with a smile.

"Well, Uma, I found Liddy, but he's a little stuck. I'll need William's help for this, but there's no way I'm leaving you here alone while we get him. Let's get you back to your parents, and then we'll get Liddy, alright?"

"Oh please! Please get Liddy unstuck now! I here can wait!" the child pleaded.

"Don't worry, dear, we'll get him safe. But your parents will kill me if we leave you alone. It'll just be a few more minutes."

Zala scooped the child in her arms, then turned to face William. "I'll be right back. Wait for me to return — we'll need my light magic to see where we're going in there."

William nodded, and Zala jogged back to the gathering party.

While he waited, William stepped to the edge of the cave and peered into its depths. He could only see a dozen paces in front of him before darkness obscured the rest of the cavern. Streams of cold air drifted by him as he stared into its depths, and he pondered the wisdom of entering the cave. He was certain Brinwin had something like this in mind when he said to avoid "risky situations." If a thilmig got stuck in there, what would keep them from getting stuck as well?

William's thoughts were interrupted by the thumping of sand when Zala returned with a pack slung over her shoulder.

"Ready to go?" she asked when she reached his side.

William's brow furrowed as he stroked his chin. "I suppose. You said this would only take a minute, yes?"

"Yeah, he's right at the back of the cave." Her eyes twinkled as she raised her eyebrows. "Why? Are you scared?"

"Well... no, but Brinwin said to avoid risky situations."

"I really doubt Brinwin would count this as a risk. Unless you're scared you'll bump your toe and need me to carry you all the way back...."

William waved his hand dismissively. "Oh, enough! Let's just get this over with."

Zala shrugged as she took the first steps into the cave. She waited for William to follow before continuing to the edge of the darkness. She paused for a moment as she raised her hand, concentrating before a ball of light flashed into existence and hovered in place over her hand. Content with its illumination, she pressed onward to the back of the cave.

William followed suit, taking care not to give her the satisfaction of actually stubbing his toes while they navigated the cave. Such a task proved to be more difficult than anticipated, however. Stalagmites littered the floor, each sturdy enough to hurt his feet if he was not careful. Zala's light was bright, but not bright enough to give him perfect vision of the obstacle field before him.

Weaving their way to the back of the cave proved to be something of a dance: one that Zala breezed through as effortlessly as a butterfly on the spring's wind. William did his best to keep pace and follow her lead. By the time they reached the back of the cave, he had only stubbed his foot twice, and both times it had happened so softly that he was certain she had not noticed it. Whatever pride he felt at the accomplishment soon dissipated when they arrived at their destination.

The floor ended at the bottom of a slope, where he could make out the feet and hindquarters of a bipedal thilmig as it flailed about from a hole in the ground. William shook his head as he took in the spectacle. "How do you propose we handle this?" his voice echoed off the walls.

Zala shut her eyes in concentration and flicked her wrist toward the trapped creature. The ball of light hovering over her hand flew toward the thilmig before coming to rest on the wall just in front of it. Within moments, a new orb flashed above her hand to replace it.

"Carefully," she replied before pointing at the incline that stretched before them. "If you look closely, you'll see that slope is covered in slime. The poor thing must not have noticed and slipped headfirst into that hole. If we're not careful, we'll take a tumble of our own."

She let down the pack from her shoulder and retrieved a coil of rope. Once she had tied the rope around her waist, she threw the other end to William. "Tie this to the firmest rock you can find. I'll go down and get him unstuck, then you can use those big muscles of yours to pull us back up. Simple as that. Now stand still," she ordered before launching her light orb straight at him.

William flinched as he fought the urge to duck from the incoming projectile, which came to a stop above his head. The orb remained above him as he wandered in search of a suitable anchor point. "Simple as that," he muttered under his breath. "Easy to say when you're not doing all the pulling." He continued his search until a spire as thick as his waist caught his eye. He made short work of tying a knot around it thick enough to support the weight that would soon be required of it. He returned to Zala and gave a curt nod that everything was ready.

"Alright then," she exhaled. "Here we go."

William let down the rope at a cautious pace while Zala descended to the edge of the slope. Her weight was easy enough to handle, but as she went, her boots stirred up the bluish-gray slime coating the surface and caused it to release a rancid odor that forced William to gag. The rope nearly slipped from his hands as his stomach heaved, prompting a shrill gasp from Zala. William fought to regain control of the rope as she plummeted down the slope, and he burned his hands in the process.

Without a second to spare, the rope pulled taut and jerked her to a halt just inches away from the thrashing thilmig.

William could feel the stab of Zala's glare from where he stood. No small number of grumblings and comebacks simmered in his mind as he braced himself for the difficult work of hauling up even more weight than he had let down. "Do you have him yet?" he called down in frustration.

"I've almost got him..." Zala's reply echoed back. Seconds later, the rope's burden grew heavier than he expected, and the walls rang out once more: "Got him! Pull us up!"

William's muscles shook with exertion as he heaved with all his might. His grunts did nothing to stop the sweat that poured down his face and across his hands, making it all the more difficult to maintain his grip on the rope. Pain burned out from the blisters on his hands until he cried in agony, "How much longer?!"

"Almost there!" came Zala's response. Her voice was close.

When the tip of her head appeared in view, William gave a final cry and pulled with all his might. The rope raced forward, driven by his desperation, until a jagged outcropping of rock snagged it on the precipice. The rope frayed with a snap, and Zala and the thilmig plunged back down the slope with a scream. William dove after them, but he managed only to send himself hurdling alongside them. The light above the hole enlarged as they tumbled toward it, then diminished into nothing but a pinprick when their combined weight crashed through the hole and they fell into darkness.

14

Saphrathah

Shafts of flaming orange reflected off the waters as the sun set on Lake Iddeah. The surface of the lake rippled in concert with the evening breeze that swept the region, setting a million topazes of light to gleam their way across the horizon. While the last of the seabirds sang their evening song, groups of Essari gathered to watch the scenery of their beloved home unfold before their eyes. Mothers held their infants close in their arms while children swam, ran, and splashed about in celebration that another week's work had come to a close. It was now time to play.

The men set down the implements of their trade and gathered into clusters along the beach as they created bonfires along the shore. Those so inclined took up their instruments of music, while others gathered a captive audience to hear again the stories of days gone by. Kings and monsters, nature and magic, acts of valor and the betrayal of lovers all made their entrances and exits in the imaginations of those gathered to hear them.

Some groups were larger than others and had more elaborate festivities. Those with the best attire congregated in the largest groups, while those of lesser status met in small groups of their close relations. Large or small, the common factor among them all was the entourage that toured between them, following the lead of the best-dressed of all the Essari.

Twenty-five winters had marked the tenure of Thilmarin the Grand Savant. For every gathering throughout that time, without fail as the weather permitted, the leader would visit every group he could find along the shores of his realm. He sincerely cared for all he encountered, but the groups that delighted him the most were those teeming with children. The fondness of his own childhood he poured into the lives of the children he met, as much as time and duties allowed him. Though no longer in the prime of his life, he relished trading waves in a splash fight as equally as telling stories around a fireside.

This evening in no ways differed from any other before it. From the first note of music played, Thilmarin began his rounds through the people. It took the better part of the evening, but he lent his presence to each cloister he found. The people began dispersing to their homes around midnight, but by the time Thilmarin concluded his final story, it was well past that. The bonfires had been extinguished, leaving just the stars and moon to illuminate the beachfront. Yet when the Grand Savant gazed toward his quarters, another light flickered on from above.

It was the light of a room. Brinwin's room.

Thilmarin deliberated in silence as the waves lapped against the shoreline. *Time our assiduous alchemist to visit,* he determined.

* * *

The door to Brinwin's laboratory creaked open louder than the Savant had anticipated. *Another thing for the thilmigs to fix,* he sighed within himself. Brinwin ceased pacing in the corner of the room and called out in irritation, too occupied to turn his head toward the distraction: "I said I was to have no disturbances!"

"Of utmost importance it must be, to count jikat as a disturbance," came the Savant's reply. He set down a bowlful of the Cabalian treat, knowing full well that not even an irate alchemist could long resist his favorite dish.

Brinwin turned in surprise and spoke in a more respectful tone. "Ah... forgive me, Grand Savant. I wasn't expecting the honor of a visit while the moon still shone on a Saphrathah."

"That's because the Saphrathah has already ended, my boy. Much later it is than you think."

Brinwin rubbed his temples in exhaustion. "I lost track of time, it seems. My head still hurts from the vial of Shimmerbrew I drank last night..."

Thilmarin beckoned to the table he settled at. "Sit," he commanded with a gentle firmness that could not be refused. Brinwin acquiesced after a moment's hesitation and sat down across from him. He made little attempt of polite restraint as he yanked the dish of jikat toward him. The Essari chief nearly smiled in amusement while he waited for Brinwin to finish stuffing his face with the delicacy. Only after he had emptied the bowl and wiped his mouth clean did Thilmarin put forward the question on his mind.

"Tell me, *Melir*, what great project has so occupied you?"

Had it been anyone else, Brinwin would have refused to answer any questions until his research was complete. Such a reply had already formed in his mind before he checked himself. It was a rare honor to be addressed as friend by the most powerful Essari on the island. Rebuffing his request for information would be foolishness.

"I'm trying to prove my theory of Danuri stone transmutation," he answered candidly. "I obtained a perfect specimen from the Englishman, and I'm within inches of a breakthrough."

"Fascinating." The glowing green of Thilmarin's eyes diminished as they narrowed in thought. "How did you manage such an acquisition? I doubt the first outsider to visit our island in centuries just gave it to you of his own goodwill."

"It's the final price of contract with Azkalah."

"Is that so?" Thilmarin mused as he stroked his chin. "Dynasties have been overthrown for less payment than that. Whatever on earth has he contracted you to do?"

"He's an agent of an English king," replied Brinwin. "Stephen of

Blois, I think his name is." Brinwin then paused as he weighed the ramifications of what he was about to share. "He wants the recipe for shadesteel."

Thilmarin's eyes widened. "But Brinwin..." his voice dropped. "That's a suicide mission."

Brinwin bit his lip. This was the news he had not wanted to share with anyone. "Most likely, yes," he answered. "But a contract is a contract. You know what happens if I refuse one already paid for. I'd rather die with honor."

Thilmarin's lips drew tight in recognition of Brinwin's resolve. "So that's why the feverish work? Experimenting like there's no tomorrow?"

Brinwin turned his eyes away. "Something like that." The seat below him creaked as he leaned back in resignation. "Not that I'd bring it with me, even if I did succeed in transforming it. The last thing those Duskbloods need is another Danuri stone when they catch us."

The two of them sat in silence before Thilmarin put a hand on Brinwin's shoulder. "I'm so sorry, my boy. I knew something like this was bound to happen eventually, but that makes it none the easier to bear. Know that we are ever grateful for what you've done for us. Our mourning will be deep if you don't survive."

Brinwin could not fend off the bittersweet smile that lingered on his lips. "Thank you, Melir. Our friendship has truly been a blessing of Yahos."

Thilmarin raised an eyebrow. "I never thought you were the religious type, Brin. Have you been spending more time with your brother than I was aware?"

Brinwin laughed. "Not necessarily. But I'll admit his words take on more interest in the face of death."

"Better late than never, I suppose," the old man murmured half to himself. He rose from his seat and stepped toward the door, but before reaching the threshold, he stopped and turned around. "I'm sorry for the poor timing of this all, but on second thought, I think it would be better for you to know this now. I received word today from an Assembly member that we caught your sister transforming a thilmig within the Enclave. I tried to keep the report from circulating, but it seems word has gotten out."

Brinwin rose from his seat with a start. "She what?! I am beyond sorry, sir!" he stammered. "Whatever possessed her to do such a stupid thing, I assure you I will rectify it myself—"

Thilmarin raised a hand. "I appreciate the gesture, my friend, but that won't be necessary. It'll be difficult, but I can smooth the feathers she's ruffled. I know how much she cares for our home, and reports have trickled in of her helping our people today, too. No doubt she's attempting to balance the scales in her favor, and as long as she doesn't do anything else colossally foolish, it may just work. Keep her low-key, and I'll handle the rest." He then stroked his chin with an air of speculation.

"As for her sudden propensity for risk, it seems she's taken quite a fancy to this Englishman of yours. The past two days they've ever been at each other's side. Perhaps she desires to impress this man."

Brinwin put his head in his hands. "That would be like my sister," he groaned. "She's always dreamed of traveling beyond the island, and now a golden opportunity is dropped in front of her."

"You don't think she'd grow bored beyond Cabalia? My reports indicate magic is still not practiced in the outside world."

"That's precisely why she'd revel in it. Here, it's a level playing field. There? She'd be free to mess with anyone and everyone's head. She'd have a blast. Literally."

"And this doesn't bother you?"

"Not as much as you'd think. Sure, it would be a massive change in how I complete my contracts. But don't forget, I made a name for myself just fine before we teamed up. I knew I couldn't expect it to last forever, either. I've kept my options open. If we somehow survive the mission, she can take off with him if she likes. She's more than earned a life of her choosing."

Thilmarin nodded before he turned once more toward the door. "A pleasure as always, Brinwin. I look forward to seeing you before your departure." With that, he opened the door.

He would have taken his first step outside, but before he could pass the threshold, a flaming ball of light raced by him into the room. It left a glowing trail in its wake as it zigzagged, before exploding into an arrangement of letters, each the size of a hand.

The two men gaped in shock as a message unfolded before their eyes. It hovered in place, suspended perfectly in thin air. Brinwin then cursed and scrambled about the room in search of supplies while Thilmarin rushed down the hall to raise the alarm. Little sleep would the Essari have that night.

15

The Waters Below

Zala clasped her hand to her chest as she fell. The touch of her fingers upon her necklace triggered a spell saved solely for emergencies. Her clothes blazed with light, revealing the surface of the subterranean pool she rushed toward. The imminent collision left no time to think, only to react. She maneuvered herself to break the surface and filled her lungs with as much air as possible. She could only hope William did the same.

Pangs of coldness shot through her as she plunged beneath the surface. She sank deep into the water until she hung suspended in place. After a moment of shock, the realization struck her: She could feel pain. And if she could feel pain, then she was still alive. She swam upwards for her life, even while her lungs buckled on the verge of collapse. The light from her clothes did little to penetrate the murkiness around her until she broke the surface not a moment too soon. It was all she could do to keep herself afloat as she gasped for breath.

Had her lungs not been so desperate, she would have choked at the stench that permeated the area. The air was squalid but still enough to preserve her life. Barely. Her head spun, and her vision blurred so much she could not find a shore to swim toward, if there even was one.

Her anxiety grew as the moments passed until a small splash came from beside her. A pressure enveloped her hand, and before she knew it, the six strong fingers of a thilmig were pulling her forward. "Liddy!" she rasped. Relief flooded over her as the backbender swam ahead, guiding them toward some semblance of safety.

They paddled on until they came upon a shallows. No sooner did Zala's feet light upon solid ground than Liddy release his grip and swim back into the darkness behind him. Too exhausted to protest, she continued forward. The water receded until it rose just to her ankles. Only then did she collapse to her knees on the ground. Her mind spun in circles as she lay there panting until a single thought pierced her mental fog. *William!* Her eyes strained toward the water, and she called his name in desperation.

She would never forgive herself if she were the cause of his demise. But what could she do? Her strength was all but spent, and her mind was far too exhausted to practice magic. Her only hope lay in the backbender that had just saved her life.

She stared across the darkness, hoping for something — anything — to appear in her line of sight. Time crawled by in agony as she waited, and the rippling of the waves taunted her senses. Was that the splash of a paddle she heard? Did she see the edge of a limb just over there? No… it was only a wave.

Zala cradled her head in her hands. "Where are you?" she moaned in despair.

Nothing but the sloshing of water answered her in reply.

Tears spilled down her face, each drop mingling with the water she sat in. Sobs she could no longer contain echoed in the chamber so deeply buried beneath the ground. A multitude of thoughts condemned her, merciless in their accusations. Were it not for her foolhardiness, none of this would have happened. Foolish she was. Reckless. Her pride was the death of an innocent man and the stain of a community. Brinwin was right about her: she was just a child. A sad, scared little child who tried so hard to prove herself, only to make life worse for everyone involved. Every disappointment in life she had more than earned, because it was her fault. Even the abuse was her fault. From her father. From her commander. From all of them. *They were all right...*

The train of thought broke with a splash when Liddy deposited William in the shallows beside her. The Englishman lay unconscious on his back, his mouth just inches above the waterline. Zala sat beside herself in shock, not able to believe her eyes. It wasn't until the back-bender reached out its hand and tugged on Zala's sleeve that she came to her senses.

Frantic, she scooped William into her arms. Every attempt to revive him was unsuccessful, and she cursed at not having learned the Essari's medical procedures. She had nearly given up hope when Liddy tugged on her sleeve again. "What? What is it, Liddy?" Zala asked in confusion. The thilmig stared and pointed at William, then pointed at itself. "I don't understand..." she trailed off before her face lit up in excitement. "Of course! You'd know how to save him, wouldn't you? Here you go then, take him," she said as she slid William over to the thilmig.

The backbender wasted no time as it took him into its muscular arms and compressed his chest in a series of rounds. By the third round, water began to sputter from his mouth. Liddy paused and evaluated William. Turning his head, he pointed from Zala's mouth to William's, striking a comical pose as he imitated breathing out.

"Oh... yes," she mumbled. It was all coming back to her. She had watched the Essari do this once. It was not a pleasant image, watching an ugly man save an equally ugly boy in this way, but at least William was better looking. She was thankful no one else was around to see this. She would have never heard the end of it.

* * *

When William opened his eyes, he was acutely aware of three things. First, he was coughing, and it hurt; second, he was cold and wet, and it hurt; third, he was staring up into Zala's face, and that was the only thing that did not hurt. Objectively speaking, she looked as poorly as he felt. But as far as he was concerned, the joy that radiated from her more than compensated, leaving a most stunning impression on him. Even while a dripping mess, her beauty shone through.

"Simple as that, hmmm?" he murmured.

* * *

Once outside the water, Zala's clothes provided enough light to observe their surroundings. They stood in a chamber hundreds of feet long, covered in water and devoid of natural light. Openings to smaller caverns lay scattered around the pool, the largest of which lay directly behind them. On further examination, they noticed a thin bluish-gray film that layered the water. William skimmed it with the tip of his boot and brought it to his fingertips to smell. He nearly choked, confirming it as the source of the stench which made coherent thinking difficult.

The hole they had fallen through still glowed faintly with Zala's light orb. By William's estimation, it hung at least sixty feet over their heads. *No chance of getting back up that way,* he thought. He pursed his lips and shook his head before turning back to Zala. "What are we to do now?" he asked.

Zala narrowed her eyes in thought. "Well," she replied, "the first thing we should do is get away from this reeking lake. I can't concentrate enough to use my magic with the air like this." She then pointed to the opening behind them. "With any luck, we can find some cleaner water and get this muck off us."

Common sense told William they should wait in place until help arrived, but his nose pleaded for relief. Another whiff of the foul air was all the convincing he needed. "An excellent idea," he agreed. He grabbed Liddy's arm, and the three of them set off.

The first cavern they entered was smaller than they had expected. Stalactites with razor-sharp points hung just above their heads, forcing William and Zala to duck as they went forward. No traces of water could be seen, but as they approached the end of the cavern, a faint echo of running water reached their ears. Two openings branched out before them. The one on the right ascended at a slight incline, while the other on the left descended farther into the depths. William nudged his head toward the ascending exit, and Zala nodded in agreement. Before they could proceed, however, Liddy yanked William's hand toward the other entrance. The force nearly sent William tumbling, and he narrowly avoided smashing his head against a stalactite.

"Liddy! What the blazes are you doing?" he spat out once he had regained his balance. The thilmig merely responded with another yank. For whatever reason, the matter was not open for negotiation.

William frowned, but he reminded himself that the creature had just saved his life. *Perhaps it could sense something they couldn't*, he reasoned with himself. "Alright. Left it is, then," he sighed.

With Liddy leading the way, they entered a narrow corridor that descended at a steep angle. Even with the ground as dry as it was, the descent proved treacherous. Both William and Zala nearly slipped when their still-dripping boots lost traction for a fraction of a second. They seriously questioned the wisdom of following the backbender's guidance until the sound of rushing water grew louder. The corridor ended a small distance farther, opening into a spacious cavern through which flowed a stream of fresh water.

"Way to go, Liddy!" Zala called out before racing toward the water. William followed close behind, and neither of them lost time rinsing the putrid gunk off their clothes. At last, they could breathe without their noses stinging!

Liddy stood off to the side, not minding the stench on him. He likely would not have bathed at all if William had not dragged him into the river by force. Handling the thilmig was not easy, but there was no way they could allow the creature to continue smelling like that. Only after the last residue of slime had been scoured off did he release it to scamper over to Zala's side. It threw a shaking fist in the air as it went, thoroughly displeased with the involuntary bath.

"Well then. Now that's settled, what's our next move?" William asked as he approached Zala.

Liddy glared at William while Zala replied, "I think a good nap is in order."

"I'm sorry, I don't think I heard you rightly," said William. "Did you just say to take a nap?"

"Yep. That's exactly what I said."

"But shouldn't we, I don't know... try to find our way back to the surface? Or at least go back and wait for help? We've been missing long enough. There should be people looking for us by now, don't you think?"

Zala blushed. "Well... ah, actually, no. When I brought Uma back, I told her family we'd just return Liddy to their house. That way they could get as much work done as possible before the Saphrathah celebration the Essari hold every week. They won't notice we're missing until well after midnight, probably."

William stared blankly at her. "And why did you do that?"

Zala shrugged. "Because they appreciated the gesture, and I didn't think we'd fall through a hole in the ground?"

William put his head in his hands. "Right."

"Look, William, I know this isn't ideal, but I need some rest to bring my concentration back up. I can't use my magic effectively when I'm this exhausted, and if we're going to make it out of here, we need my magic. So... nap time."

Zala sat down and leaned up against a wall of the cave. "I only need an hour or so. If you can't bring yourself to rest, you've seen how to transform a thilmig. I'm sure Liddy would appreciate munching on a few rocks. Just make sure that if he needs to do his business, it's far away from us. If you thought the lake smelled bad," she paused with a yawn, "thilmig droppings are so much worse."

She then settled into as comfortable a position as she could manage and closed her eyes. Within seconds, she had fallen fast asleep. William glanced from Zala to Liddy, who only glared back at him. He shook his head as he considered handling the irritated creature.

"No... I think not."

16

Rise and Shine

If Zala had slept for only an hour, then William was pregnant. While he had no way to prove how long it had been, his instincts screamed that it was far longer than "just an hour or so." He was half-minded to wake her up. His growing impatience made the thought tempting enough. But he knew she needed as much rest as she could get if they were to make it back to the surface. That, and Liddy had apparently decided Zala was worthy of his favor while William was not. He eyed William aggressively whenever it looked like he was about to wake her. So it was that unknown minutes slipped by into hours until Zala stirred from her slumber at last.

She stretched her arms and yawned, and when she noticed Liddy keeping a guard over her, she smiled and gave him an appreciative pat on his back. "No wonder I had such a good rest," she said, her voice filled with a renewed vigor. "I had nothing to fear while having such strong protectors watching out for me."

William blushed, half from flattery and half from shame. "Ah... Yes. Indeed," he mumbled. Clearing his throat, he then spoke firmly. "How are you feeling, Lady Ziken — er, Zala?"

She rolled her eyes before shooting back a question of her own.

"Do you always return a compliment with formality, William, or just with me?"

William stood at a loss for words. Her audacity had returned, which at least meant she was feeling well. She reveled in his lack of response just a moment longer before breaking into a smile and softening her tone. "At least you caught yourself." She gave him a playful nudge and then turned to scout out the rest of the cavern.

"Looks like this chamber's a dead end. We should head back up and hope for the best with the other passage." William offered no objections, and the three of them set off through the corridor. It was trickier ascending than it had been descending, but they managed to climb back up without incident. Before long, they stood at the entrance of the gradually sloping incline they had passed earlier. The path was wider than the one they had just come from, with no significant obstacles to be wary of. The farther they went, the more it leveled out to become perfectly flat.

"How long will those clothes of yours keep glowing, Zala?" William asked as they walked.

"For as long as I want them to," she replied. "There's no time limit. It's just that if I extinguish the light, it would take a new enchantment to start it back up again."

"I see."

"Well, thank Yahos for that," Zala bantered. "You have to admit, this would all be much harder if you were blind."

William rolled his eyes at the terrible joke. "How droll," he muttered before then tilting his head. "Though in all seriousness, I've heard you use that term several times. What is Yahos?"

Zala appeared puzzled. "That's odd. I would have figured your ring would translate it for you. Yahos is the deity the Church worships. I believe the word you Europeans would use is 'God?' Of course, the name existed before the Church came over with the Founders. In the older religions, Yahos was the chief deity that ruled over all the lesser ones. So naturally, when the Christians wanted to explain their religion to the locals, that's the name they chose for the so-called God above all gods."

"Oh. I see," said William. They continued in silence until William gathered the courage to ask Zala another question. "I hope you don't find this too personal a question, but from the way you talk about it, it's not entirely clear to me. Do you not believe in Yahos?"

Zala said nothing for a moment as she continued to walk. When she answered, her voice was quiet. "I don't know. I do think there has to be someone behind all of this. Hang around the Essari long enough, and they'll make a pretty convincing case for it. I just don't understand how someone wise enough to make the world could be so careless to let evil run rampant through it. I've seen far too much death and heartache to accept what my brother Gaimis keeps spouting off."

"You have another brother?" William probed, unable to keep the surprise out of his voice.

"Oh, yes. Gaimis is my father's youngest son. He 'felt the call' early in his life and went down south to Edomear to train as a cleric as soon as he could. Father viewed it all as a waste, and we rarely keep in touch. He's a nice man, but his enthusiasm for the Church can be aggravating at times."

Zala paused when the pathway led into a well-carved chamber. The perfectly chiseled geometric shapes made it clear this cave was not purely natural. Zala motioned for William to remain quiet, and she stepped forward cautiously. After a dozen or so paces, she gasped in delight.

"Look, William! Those are support beams! We're in an Essari mine! All we have to do is follow it to the surface, and no one will even know we've been gone!"

William smiled, pleased to have some good news at last. Even Liddy grew more animated, grabbing Zala's hand and setting off at a sprint. William jogged behind them as they navigated the mine shafts. While not quite abandoned, the tunnels showed signs of infrequent use as they hurried along. At one point, the tunnels diverged into three paths, at which Liddy barreled down the center path without missing a beat.

The others followed along, knowing by this point to trust the animal's instincts.

The path sloped downward as they went and became even less maintained than the rest of the mine. The support beams grew farther apart, and the rocks less artfully chiseled until the passage assumed a completely natural form.

"Ahh... Liddy? You sure this is the way to go?" Zala called out as she started to lose her breath while keeping pace with him. Liddy only plunged ahead, increasing his speed even further.

"You need to slow down!" William's voice rang off the walls.

Zala filled with panic as she realized the thilmig's grip on her wrist was too tight to break. "Liddy, stop!" she yelled. Yet her command was to no avail. They raced onward, even as the air grew rancid with the smell of the cave scum she wished she could forget. The floor and walls oozed with the familiar blue-gray slime, and the stench intensified.

William threw everything he had into catching up to Zala, ready to take down the backbender if necessary. He gained ground and was just a few feet behind her when the ground suddenly sloped downward. The angle was steep enough to send all three of them tumbling. They slid through the slime, picking up speed until they splashed into a shallow pool of water.

Liddy slid headfirst into the base of a stalagmite, cracking the stone and knocking himself unconscious. William slammed his side against a boulder before continuing to slide for another few yards, while Zala narrowly avoided a collision with any dangerous objects. When she stumbled to her feet, her face was coated with the slime she detested more than ever. She wiped off as much as she could in disgust before searching for the others. She did not need to travel far before she heard William moaning off to her right. By the time she reached him, he had lifted himself to a sitting position.

"Are you alright?" she asked.

William groaned as he clutched his side and rose to his feet. "Yes, I'll be fine. My side is sore, but I don't think it's anything serious. Where's that blasted thilmig?"

"I don't know," Zala said as she put her arm around William's shoulder and helped him limp on while they searched. "What do you think caused him to run off like that?"

"Hell if I know," William grunted back. "All I know is I'm tired of falling inside caves. If we ever escape this godforsaken place, I could go my whole life without stepping inside another cave again!"

Zala smirked. "You outsiders aren't that good at staying on your feet, are you?"

"And what is that supposed to mean, pray tell?" pressed William.

"Well, it's just that from the time I first met you, you've somehow managed to slip, trip, or otherwise wind up off your two feet."

"Such as when?" he demanded.

"Such as... when we had to drug you and cart you off here in the first place. *And* when I pranked you with Mr. Floofles. *And* when you tripped us out onto the beach. *And* when you let the rope slip and tried to catch us. *And* just now, even though your hand wasn't in the grip of a runaway thilmig..."

"I hardly think that's a fair assessment," William protested, "given that in half of those cases, I was trying to save you, and in two of them, *you* directly caused me to fall."

"All the same, five times in two days is a bit much, don't you think, Horse Dancer?"

Little could have brought William more satisfaction than when, moments later, Zala herself slipped and fell face forward into the water. Such satisfaction was a double-edged sword, however, as Zala's sudden tumble also dragged him along to the ground.

It came as a surprise when, instead of hitting the unforgiving surface of stone, their faces squished against a fleshy surface. The momentum of their fall made them slip off to the side of it and land on their sides. They scrambled to their feet in time to see what resembled a blue tentacle recede into the darkness away from them.

They stood still as if by instinct, straining their eyes in curiosity and dread. Neither of them dared to so much as breathe when a dark form twisted beyond the edge of Zala's light. A hiss swelled above them, its intensity rising as a column of darkness lumbered into the air. Fear shoved their hearts into their throats as the column slithered into their line of vision.

The light revealed a sea serpent, over twenty feet tall and as wide as a fully grown man. Its slime-covered skin was smooth, almost translucent, with wisps of inky black whirling about under a surface of sapphire blue. Its eyes were small compared to its overall size, its mouth even more so at only half the size of William's fist. Teeth filed to a razor's edge reflected Zala's light as it slid closer and poised itself to strike.

Zala slipped William a dagger and mouthed a final instruction before all hell broke loose: "Hit as it comes." No sooner had William nodded his acknowledgment than the serpent lunged its head at him, air whistling around it. Zala drew a dagger for herself as William thrust his weapon straight toward the incoming array of teeth. It hit one tooth squarely before deflecting off it and scraping into the gum line above.

The creature shrieked in pain as its bottom teeth clamped down on the base of the dagger, inflicting deep cuts on William's hand. He released his grip on the dagger and rolled to the side, giving Zala a clear shot at the monster's head. She sent a well-aimed slice just below it, but the creature's reaction was quicker. It turned its head downward, receiving merely a scratch at the top. It then shot its mouth toward Zala's face. Her hands blurred as she thrust them up, knocking the serpent's mouth off course enough to miss her face. She felt its teeth bury into her hair before she swung again, this time at its underside. The blade met with limited success as it only delivered a surface wound.

William leaped onto the creature's back and attempted to pound its head with his elbow, but he failed to land a strike before it flung him off. Its tail whipped around, driving Zala backward. Her dagger dropped from her hands and landed with a splash.

"Run!" called Zala before she dove behind an outcropping of rock. William turned to run but felt a chunk of flesh torn from his back as he fled. His cry of pain echoed throughout the chamber, which seemed to distract the beast long enough for him to jump onto a ledge that ascended farther into darkness.

"Hide, William!" Zala's voice echoed faintly as her light extinguished, leaving the cave in utter darkness. William hunkered down to remain as silent as possible, yet every fresh pounding of his heart convinced him he was done for. Surely it could hear him! He offered in his desperation a silent prayer that the creature would somehow lose them.

Moments passed by, and it appeared his prayer had been answered. He could hear the serpent slithering aimlessly through the cave in search of its prey, failing to find them. The cave reverberated with a hiss of fury as the serpent's pace quickened, determined not to give up the hunt. William could only guess how much stamina the beast had, but he was certain it would outlast theirs. With neither fight nor flight being a viable option, the situation was desperate indeed.

The only thing that can save us now is a miracle, he thought in despair. His eyes crammed shut in fear when the slithering passed too close for comfort. *No,* he chided himself. *Face your death with your eyes open.* He forced his eyes open in time to see a fiery ball of light rocket past him out of the chamber. A stream of ambient light followed behind and lingered in place, leaving a glowing trail in the projectile's wake.

Zala watched as her distress signal vanished, bearing with it a final hope of deliverance. *Please,* she thought in desperation. *Find your mark!*

17

The Kumuzhkan

Brinwin shoved a cork into the final bottle he needed with a loud pop. The concoction was not ideal, but it would have to do. Time was of the essence, which gave little opportunity to be fussy with his materials. The words of the distress message still blazing in midair caught his eye as he raced out of his laboratory to rendezvous with the Essari warriors on the beachfront. In the Cabalian tongue, it read: "*Kumuzhkan. Follow the trail. Need help now. Zala.*"

This was beyond bad news. The *Kumuzhkans* were not supposed to exist anymore — not since the founders of Cabalia had eliminated all the great monsters of old over a thousand years ago. How his sister had managed to find and unleash the wrath of an *Ezith Baal*, Brinwin did not want to know. Whatever had happened, she had gone places she had no business going to. Even if the rescue attempt were successful, there would be repercussions.

But then was not the time to be concerned with such things. A challenge of monstrous proportions was afoot, and it required complete attention. For whatever comfort it was, Brinwin had been in riskier situations with Zala before. Not much riskier, but that was beside the point.

By the time he arrived on the lake shore, Thilmarin had managed to rally several dozen warriors armed to the teeth with fishing spears and long swords. They stood at the ready, their torches flickering in the dark of night. Many had been roused from sleep just minutes earlier, but the nature of the emergency filled them with plenty of adrenaline to energize them for the task ahead. Upon Brinwin's arrival, they fell into formation behind him and followed Zala's trail. Warning sirens blared throughout the compound as they went, and a garbled voice announced that all those unable to fight should shelter in place until further notice.

Brinwin shook his head when the trail turned aside from the beach and into a cave. "Zala, you fool!" he muttered under his breath. The stalagmites slowed their advance as they navigated to the back of the cave, their torches nowhere near as powerful as Zala's light had been hours earlier.

When they reached the end, they found a spire of rock with a rope still attached. Their eyes followed the rope as it descended toward a gaping hole, still illuminated by the glowing orb Zala had put there. The Essari muttered to themselves at the sight, and the cave buzzed with activity as they fastened new ropes in preparation for their descent.

Brinwin tossed a stone down the hole and listened as it fell. The sound of a distant splash confirmed his fears. "Send for rafts!" he called to the others. "We have some water to deal with."

* * *

The cold sank deeply into William's bones as he crouched on the ledge. His skin froze against the stone below him, but he dared not move. It was everything he could do to hold back the shivers threatening to reveal his position. The *Kumuzhkan* was relentless even while it blundered about failing to find its prey above the water's surface.

Zala remained motionless behind a stalagmite, knowing better than to move while water rose to her ankles. Any vibration she sent through the water would immediately alert the serpent of her location. She could do nothing more but stand there and hope Brinwin received her message in time. The monster may have been outside its preferred environment, but such fortune would not spare her the fate of being torn apart chunk-by-chunk were she discovered.

Come on, Brin, her thoughts pleaded. *We need you.*

* * *

Precious moments slipped by attempting to cross the subterranean pool. The rafts took longer than expected to arrive, and they moved slowly through the mire that layered the surface. The delay was unacceptable, but Brinwin made the most of it. He briefed the warriors on the best plans of attack when facing a *Kumuzhkan*: what to do above water and what to do underwater if it could not be avoided. It was fortunate for the Essari that he and his sister shared a passion for ancient lore that left them well-versed with the monsters of old. From how they could talk about them, one might have thought they had been there to see the beasts in person.

When Brinwin's raft had nearly reached the pool's edge, he jumped the remaining distance and set off at a full sprint along the trail. There was no time to wait for the Essari formation; they would know what to do when they finally arrived. He could only hope it was not too late. He weaved, ducked, and slipped his way through corridor after corridor, the distance seeming endless. *Hang in there, Zala,* he begged. *Just a little longer!*

* * *

Zala's heart filled with dread when she heard the splash. Liddy had regained consciousness and disturbed the water as he rose to his feet. Any second, the *Kumuzhkan* would come barreling down on the hapless backbender, and the whole point of their excursion in the first place would have been in vain. Zala was torn, knowing that if she acted to save its life, hers would most likely be forfeit. Once done with her, the Kumuzhkan would still proceed to eat Liddy. If she just kept quiet, Brinwin would eventually come along and save the rest of them from this mess. But, she remembered, the thilmig had saved both her life and

William's. Then again, it had also led them to the *Kumuzhkan* in the first place.

Her memories flashed to her years in the Hearthfell military, where only a coward would abandon their comrade in the heat of battle. She could not just stand by and let their companion die. Surely, she reasoned, William had been trained the same in his army. If she survived this ordeal, how could she explain to Liddy's owners — to little Uma — that she stood hiding behind a rock while the family thilmig was torn to pieces? *No,* she decided. Death would be more tolerable than that fate.

She leaped out with a scream from behind the rock and kicked the water as she landed. It was not a moment too soon, as the monster had already begun its rush from the other end of the cavern. It momentarily paused its rush on Liddy as it processed the disturbance Zala had created. Changing its course, it went straight for Zala.

William heard the scream and shuffled off the ledge from which he hung. His hand brushed against a jagged rock as he descended, and finding that he could pick it up, he kept it close in hand as he rushed toward Zala's cry. If she was to die, he was determined to die with her. The cave still hung in darkness, so he remained at a loss how to land a hit on the blasted thing even if he made it there in time. The dilemma was unexpectedly answered for him when a sudden flash from Zala filled the cave with light. The monster was closer than he had thought, the tip of its tail just a few yards in front of him.

William set off with a running start and leaped with all his might, dashing the tip of the stone into the center of the beast's tail. It released a pained hiss, but not before it struck Zala to the ground. Liddy ran toward William, his hand clenched into a fist. He had nearly reached his destination when the tail shot up and whipped William back into the water. It swooshed through the air before spraying a burst of black ink directly into Liddy's face. The backbender fell to the ground with a spasm, the waves frothing about it being the last things its eyes would ever see.

Zala cried out in despair as she saw the scene unfold. It was the end of the line for them. A few moments longer, and they would be torn into pieces. She would then pay the ultimate price for her foolishness.

She locked her eyes on the *Kumuzhkan*, intent on looking her vanquisher full in the eyes. It coiled its head back, face contorted in rage. It wanted far more than a meal by this point — it wanted *vengeance*.

Such vengeance proved harder than expected when a lone figure splashed down in front of it. The newcomer held a sword in his right hand and a glowing vial in his left. The rage in his eyes matched that of the monster he stood glaring at. Raising his sword, he cursed the beast in a tongue known only by the beast itself. Its eyes flashed crimson in fury, and the man unstopped the vial he held. Tilting his head back, he consumed the vial's contents in one swig.

"Your move," rumbled Brinwin with a voice deeper than William had ever recalled hearing before.

The serpent lashed out at him, quick as lightning. What followed next was difficult for William to comprehend. The glow of Brinwin's tattoo barely registered as a blur when he dodged the strike and sped to the side of the beast. His sword advanced so rapidly it could not be followed, except for the air that whistled in its wake. The serpent's blood poured out from multiple wounds inflicted in but a second.

It lunged again, but once more Brinwin proved too fast to catch. He whipped open his cloak to gather many small vials, then flung them at the serpent. Dozens of explosions erupted across its back with a bang, causing it to double over in pain and lower its head to exactly where Brinwin wanted it to be.

With a flip as graceful as it was efficient, he leaped onto it and plunged his sword deep into the beast's skull. The *Kumuzhkan* sank into the water with a convulsion, and with a final gurgling hiss, it breathed no more. Brinwin then stepped off from his vanquished foe to stand before Zala.

"Brin! You made it!" she gasped in relief.

Though pleased that she still lived, his expression was far from happy. "I'm afraid your troubles aren't over yet, Sister," he murmured. "It'll be hell to pay for this one."

Dozens of torches flickered by the entrance to the cavern, and the clattering footsteps of the Essari rescue party resounded off the walls. One look at the Essari's faces when they arrived was enough to confirm the certainty of his words. William dragged Liddy's limp body over to where Brinwin and Zala stood, and he held Zala's hand as they braced themselves for a reckoning.

18

A Reckoning

"The Special Assembly is now in session," a voice rumbled.

For hundreds of years, the Essari maintained the tradition of never closing the door to a legal proceeding. Such tradition, however, did not prevent the leadership from taking any other measure possible to ensure privacy if they so desired. The session then in progress was supposed to have been secret, but word of it had somehow leaked to the general populace. So it was that bystanders jostled for position at the entryway of a chamber known as the Bleakwatch while armed guards kept them from entering past the threshold.

The inside of the room was bare, illuminated sparsely with harsh white lights that flashed into focus upon the opening announcement. Rows of metal benches were packed with members of the Assembly of Savants, while an elevated platform at the far end of the room seated the highest-ranking Assembly members. At the very center of the platform, Thilmarin the Grand Savant rose to his feet and began his address. His voice was resolute, centered in professional formality. He spoke first after the manner of the Essari, then in Cabalian.

"Be it known for our records that in this the twenty-third day of the fourth month of the one thousand seventy-sixth year of Haldvar's Dominion, the Scholarship stands summoned at Special Assembly to consider the complaint of Savant Keltarin against Zala Zikennig, a sojourner. Whereas the matter in question involves the actions of a sojourner in our midst, the following proceedings do not fall under the purview of the General Policies of the Scholarship, including the protections afforded therein. Neither yet do they qualify as criminal investigations as defined in our Policies, and therefore can no criminal punishments be delivered at this time. Zala Zikennig, do you understand the terms of these proceedings?"

Thilmarin peered down at where Zala sat on the bench nearest the platform. She stood and answered with deference, "Yes, Grand Savant. I do."

"Very well," he replied. "Then let the proceedings continue. As a matter of courtesy, I shall moderate in the Cabalian mode of speech."

Zala took her seat next to William and Brinwin, composing herself with great care. The weight of the attention centered on her was enormous, and William was impressed with how well she handled it. The Essari had given them little time to prepare for the proceedings after their rescue — only a few hours to tend to their wounds — but she had made the most of it. She wore a simple dress, carefully chosen to accentuate her beauty but also project an air of humility.

Thilmarin carried on with an elegance that fostered an atmosphere of awe within the room. He struck an impressive figure, his eyes the only pair in attendance to glow a brilliant hue of green. "Lady Zikennig, it has been reported that you transformed a backbender to bestial form while it was on duty within the Enclave. Do you deny the truth of this report?"

"No, Grand Savant, I do not."

"Are there any elaborations you wish to make on the matter?"

"Yes, sir, there are."

"Then speak further on what transpired."

Zala rose again, offering a bow first to Thilmarin and then to all the other Assembly members. "Members of the Assembly, I offer to your scrutiny the following facts: Two days ago, it was early in the morning when I rose from bed. As is my custom, I visited the common breakfast hall in the West Wing to prepare a morning tea." She then motioned to William. "When I returned to my room, I found Lord Steele waiting for me. The thilmig in question passed by us as we talked. Its hands were empty at that moment, and it was in no other way employed. It walked west, away from the feeding trough in that wing, even as it was emaciated from hunger. I have seen backbenders enough to know the signs of starvation, and this thilmig was starving. Some of you present know that I am not especially fond of thilmigs, but to see a creature of service starving in its own house moved me with compassion. I instructed Lord Steele to—"

"Watch your words, Outsider! You us of being negligent accuse!" came the voice of the Essari that stood to Thilmarin's left. William recognized him as the man who encountered them in the hallway after Zala transformed the backbender.

The green of Thilmarin's eyes flashed brightly even as his voice held steady. "Hold your peace, Keltarin. To a defendant mid-sentence interrupt, an equal amount of disrespect upon us brings." He turned his gaze back down toward Zala. "Proceed with your explanation, Lady Zikennig."

Zala bowed in gratitude. "As I was saying, Grand Savant, I instructed Lord Steele to fetch some ashes from the fireside in his room and bring them to me. I have handled many a thilmig in my line of work, and I knew the most efficient way to transform and feed it without it slipping away. Once it had eaten its fill, I was about to transform it back to bipedal form when Savant Keltarin chanced upon us in the hallway. I was given no opportunity to explain the situation but was ordered to immediately depart from the Enclave. William and I did so promptly. Even without an explanation from me, surely he could see in bestial form how malnourished it was."

Thilmarin's eyes narrowed before his voice then rumbled. "Keltarin, is this true?"

The Grand Savant's question turned the gaze of the Assembly to the agitated Savant. Keltarin's response was flustered before it rose in condescension. "Well, I... How would know I the minutia of a backbender's physiology? I much too busy with important work am to my time on such things waste."

Thilmarin's voice cut as a sharpened blade. "That perhaps would explain why your servants starving are." He turned his eyes to the Assembly and projected his voice for all to hear clearly. "No society greater than its weakest link is. Failure to our servants nourish even us for the worse will impact. By my estimation, Lady Zikennig nothing wrong has done. No, she a favor to us has done, and to evil for her good repay, the wrath of the Maker surely on us will bring."

Murmurs of assent rose from many in the room, and William noticed the trace of a smile light upon Brinwin and Zala. Such a trace vanished when another Assembly member rose to speak.

"A wise admonition, Grand Savant," his voice rang out. "But you something are forgetting." The room hushed to silence as every eye turned to focus on the new speaker. "Transforming a thilmig not the only act of recklessness on her part is. Have forgotten we the danger we this Saphrathah have faced? A *Kumuzhkan* she unearthed, and even to it gave a glowing trail of light to our homes follow back. My wife and children terrified in the middle of the night were, as most of yours were too, I sure am."

Thilmarin frowned. He should have known. Savant Gazfir had both a silver tongue and a dark mind. His political activity of late was especially troubling. The results of an alliance with Keltarin unfolded before the Grand Savant's eyes, and he knew that it did not bode well for Zala. How many others of the Assembly were in on this? He could only hope his ploy of tipping off the general public to appear would bring enough support in the background to sway their minds. For him to speak up and answer every objection would paint him as unduly biased in her favor. There had to be some other Savant willing to point out the obvious.

To his relief, a young Assembly member rose to speak. "Yes, Gazfir, I of this well aware am. I among the men sent to fight the beast was, unlike yourself. Brinwin Zikennig single-handedly the monster quelled, with not a drop of our own blood spilt. No harm of it came."

Thilmarin made a mental note to remember that man's name and seek his acquaintance afterward.

Gazfir shot a scowl the young man's way before recovering himself. "If you down to the caves went, then surely you the *other* thilmig saw. The one that now maimed and blinded is, yes? How can claim we justice in this matter when the servant of one of our families disabled lies? Ever since these outsiders on the edge of our doorstep showed, this lady has nothing done but havoc cause wherever she goes. Three offenses in two days too much is, even by our generous standards."

The room buzzed with murmurs as the Savants debated among themselves in low tones. Many heads shook, and a sense of discontent swelled across their ranks. The tide, it seemed, had turned for the worse.

William rose to his feet, prompting Brinwin to shoot him a mortified glance in protest. Ignoring him, he addressed Thilmarin boldly enough for everyone to hear. "I wish to speak, Grand Savant."

The room fell silent once more, many jaws having dropped in suspense. Thilmarin's eyes narrowed, but the curiosity of far too many had been piqued for him to refuse the request. "Then speak, Lord Steele. We await your address."

William's eyes darted toward Zala and met her eyes for a brief moment. He then gazed upon the Special Assembly and spoke with as much courage as he could muster.

"My esteemed lords of the Essari, I plead with you to suffer, just for a minute, the words of a traveler far from home. The hospitality you have shown me these last several days has far exceeded what I expected to find in this land. You live in a truly amazing world, and the blessings of Yahos are evident upon your people. No one could rightly blame you for wishing to protect such blessings from harm. Despite the events of late that have threatened your blessings, I urge you not to threaten another this day.

"I have seen proven time and again since my arrival here the care that Lady Zikennig holds for both your land and your people. I have been by her side from the start of it, and I can assure you on my honor as a nobleman that none of these dreadful events occurred with malicious intent. For many of them, I wager any man here would have done the same were they unfortunate enough to find themselves in the same position. Who here would not have attempted to rescue their friend's beast in time of need? How could one have possibly foreseen the results that transpired from such aid? Shall one be held accountable for circumstances beyond their control?"

Zala's eyes filled with tears as William spoke, overwhelmed that he would still defend her after all they had been through. It was all she could do not to cry as he continued his speech.

"I was there in the thick of it, seeing what none of you had to. I saw Lady Zikennig risk her life to save the very thilmig now used as a bargaining chip against her. That her attempts ultimately failed should in no way be held against her when she did everything in her power to ensure otherwise. I therefore urge you to discern wisely. A woman now sits in your midst that cherishes this place as she would her own home. To harbor this complaint against her would threaten the loss of yet another blessing. Even now, I see your people thronging the door. I'm sure that if you ask them, they could tell you more than I ever could."

At this, the crowd by the entrance erupted into chaos. Some chanted in Zala's favor, while others screamed against her. Many of the Savants' faces were troubled, unsure how to handle this new development. Thilmarin's spirit fell even as his shoulders straightened.

He knew all too well that the stirring of a mob was the worst possible thing to happen. Even if the passion behind William's address was powerful, it lacked any knowledge of Essari culture. He sensed Keltarin scrambling to speak first, more than willing to make the most of the situation. Thilmarin would beat him to the punch, even if only to deliver a slightly less powerful blow.

"Lord Steele, given that you are a foreigner to these lands, we will forgive you this once of the ignorance that has propelled your most motivational of speeches. We are a government of rules, not chaos. Wisdom is what guides our decisions here, not a mob. You will do well to remember that as we determine the fate of this matter. All discussions are now closed." He then slammed his staff against the floor, sending a clank to reverberate throughout the chamber. "Guards! Escort the sojourners to their quarters and bar the doors. You are to allow them no visitors in the meantime."

The guards moved briskly, and within moments they stood at William's side. They laid hands on neither him nor Zala, but their posture demanded immediate compliance. Brinwin refused to look at the others as they were all escorted out of the room. A tumult surrounded them when they reached the threshold, forcing security to clear a path ahead of them as they walked to their chambers. William exchanged a final anxious glance with Zala before they were shoved into separate rooms and the doors barred behind them.

Zala collapsed beside her bed and wept. In her heart, she knew their stay with the Essari had concluded. Whatever judgment lay in store for them, there would be no avoiding it now. A foolish question rose suddenly in her heart, but her strength was too far spent to prevent it from reaching her lips.

"*How could things get any worse?*" she asked herself.

19

The Departure

William lifted his head when the door to his chambers opened. He had seen no one since the Essari escorted him there earlier in the day, and he did not know what to expect now. Even though his accommodations had been well-furnished for him, the fact remained that he was being held in custody until further notice. The morning's trial had ended poorly for both him and Zala, and for all he knew, the guards had come to throw him out of the Enclave.

A wave of relief flooded over him when Zala emerged over the threshold. With a faint smile, her eyes met his and reciprocated his satisfaction at seeing her again. Brinwin followed behind his sister with his gaze turned downward. Despite his lumbering stature and formidable features, his demeanor resembled a pup scolded by its master. Thilmarin the Grand Savant came last of all, shoulders drooping at a slight angle. His eyes glowed a dull green, affected by a burden he did not wish to shoulder. He shut the door behind them and waited for the others to gather around him.

"The Assembly has agreed to forgo any disciplinary hearings," he said as he gazed upon them. "Though you certainly made it difficult for me to accomplish that." The others looked down in shame, and a silence filled the room. Only the crackling of a fireplace somewhere in the corner broke the silence as they waited for the Grand Savant to continue.

"No official action will be taken against you. However, I'm afraid your stay with us has reached its end. One more misstep, no matter how small it is, will have you officially banished — or worse. Given your sudden propensity for calamity, we had best not push your luck." The sage's reasoning rang hollow as he focused on Brinwin and addressed him directly. "I'm sorry, my friend, but you will have to complete your work elsewhere. You have until sundown to gather your belongings. By the stars' first twinkling, you must all be gone from here."

He looked down in grief before he faced Zala next. "And Zala, it pains me to say this, but the Assembly would prefer that you not return." The sympathy in his tone failed to lessen the impact of his words, each one tearing deep into her heart as a sharpened blade. The conclusion of his pronouncement unleashed a torrent of heartache in her that rivaled the force of a landslide, yet the pain trickled through to the outside world as nothing but a blank stare.

A flurry of fear swept through William when Thilmarin then trained his eyes upon him. "As for you, Lord Steele, the Assembly believes it too dangerous for an outsider who has shown such contempt of our customs to roam this world freely with knowledge of our home. As you were drugged upon your arrival here, you will be drugged when you leave, but I must further instruct Brinwin to erase your memories of this place as well. I will ensure he has the proper ingredients."

William's head spun as numbness spread through his stomach. "Erase my memories?" he faltered. "Will I have any recollection of Brinwin or Zala?" Not that he cared much to remember Brinwin, but the thought of forgetting Zala was painful to bear.

Thilmarin's reply was grim. "The ingredients we provide would wipe away everything since your arrival here, I'm afraid. I apologize for the loss, but I can guarantee that the alternative is much worse." The edge to the Savant's voice cut off any further pleas of resistance William had. One look at Brinwin made clear the certainty of his compliance.

The fireplace continued to crackle as all four stared dismally at the floor, lost in thought. Thilmarin stirred first and opened the door for the others. "I am truly sorry, all of you. There are but a couple of hours left until sundown. I suggest you prepare for your departure as soon as possible."

No one else moved, not even to acknowledge his speech. Thilmarin pursed his lips, then nodded before leaving the room. He shook his head with a deep sigh as he traveled down a corridor beyond sight. Far be it from him to rush them through their grief. He just hoped they could prepare everything in time.

As he walked the corridor, the soft clomping of his feet on the stones beneath was his only companion to break the silence. A host of cares and worries swam about in his mind, each demanding a solution he felt inadequate to provide. The sheer improbability of the whole affair stung him as a freshly opened wound. *How could this have happened?*

He grimaced as he reflected on the sheer amount of political capital he had spent to lessen the sentence of his friends. His position in the Assembly would suffer for it, a fact his opponents would take full advantage of. He would need to tap into deeper reserves of political power than he felt comfortable with, but he had little choice. Surrendering control to the likes of Keltarin and Gazfir was out of the question. He would rather be exiled himself than see those arrogant fools drag his people further into the ground.

His deliberations were cut short by the two hooded figures who approached him at the end of the corridor. The light was too dim to recognize their faces, but their posture revealed their identities before they even spoke. "I surprised am, that you had it in you after all, Thilmarin," came the pompous tone of Savant Keltarin. "You to just smuggle them out of here, I fully expected."

Thilmarin groaned within himself. *Oh, what rotten luck!* He drew a tight breath and narrowed his eyes in resolve. "The surprise mine is, Keltarin, that you thought I the orders of the Assembly would not keep. My duties I have ever kept."

"Yet you still too soft with them are," Gazfir chimed in. "You soft in your old age have gone. Our people a stronger hand of guidance need, one that the outsiders in their place keeps."

Thilmarin frowned, and his eyes flared a brilliant hue of green. The ease with which his opponents shrank back disgusted him and gave a fresh edge to his voice. "Watch your tongues, the both of you. I old may be, but I no less sharp am. I your petty attempts at alliances and scheming have seen. If you to replace me wish, you better men must be, not rats in your own filth cowering."

Thilmarin leaned close to Gazfir and rumbled in a low tone, "It a shame would be if your wife about the fisherman's daughter knew. How many others have you seen in that hut, I wonder? It would to find out a trifle be." Gazfir's mouth dropped in shock, and he remained speechless as the Grand Savant turned his head. "And you, Keltarin, knowledge-able as you on the Policies are, the penalties for greenflowing know better than me. Three offenses in two days too much might be, even by our generous standards."

The two men stepped away from him and avoided his gaze. "Yes, I what you two have done know. If like rats you wish to behave, then in the gutters stay. Anywhere else, traps there are." Thilmarin then smiled and drew his cloak about him. "Farewell for now, gentlemen. We before the star's first twinkling shall again meet."

* * *

Hours passed by while Brinwin and Zala gathered up their belong-ings. William accompanied Zala to pack the few chests of items she had while Brinwin stayed behind in his laboratory to deconstruct his equip-ment. He insisted that no one else enter the area while he worked — an arrangement the others found to be agreeable. He had done nothing but brood since the trial ended, exuding the social charm of a wet porcupine. He would pack massive chests and crates to the brim and leave them by the entrance for William and Zala to carry out. William wished he had more free time to spend alone with Zala, but the ap-proach of sunset left little time to lug all of Brinwin's equipment to the shores where their boat lay. It was not until the sun cast red streaks across the sky that Brinwin closed the lid to the last chest and brought it to the doorway.

They spoke nothing to each other as they departed from the Enclave, each taking in the view of Essari technology one last time. The Assembly of Savants had gathered outside by their ship, and many onlookers stood along the edges of the shore. No one spoke, and no one smiled, even as the sun set and the waves lapped against the coast in the most picturesque of ways. Brinwin boarded the ship with the last bundles of luggage while Zala and William lingered behind on the beach. The stares of the Essari were unsettling, but William was determined to savor his final moments with Zala.

He turned to look at her, and his heart broke when he saw the tears that spilled down her cheeks. She stood with her hands at her side, staring down into the sand as the sun behind her illuminated her dress. A breeze swept by and ruffled her hair, causing her to look up as she brushed it away from her face. Her gaze met William's, and time froze between them. He saw in Zala a beauty deeper than the sunset mixed with a pain deeper than the sea, and it held him speechless. Zala held his gaze as he reached out his hands to envelop hers.

"Zala," he said at last, "you are the bravest woman I have ever known. It truly has been a pleasure to adventure with you."

"And almost drown and get eaten by a sea monster?" she asked with a rueful smile.

William paused, but it only took a moment for what lay on his heart to bypass his reason.

"If that's what fate required to journey with you, then yes. Even that."

Zala bit her lip and fought back a fresh supply of tears. With reluctance, she pulled back her hands from him. "Please, William," she said softly. "Don't make this harder than it has to be. A few more minutes, and you won't even remember who I am anymore."

"Which is precisely why I must speak my mind. I won't have the chance to do it again." He pleaded with his eyes for a final chance to do more than just speak his mind. Zala took his hands in hers again and squeezed them.

"I can't," she whispered. "Not when the first is also the last."

William nodded. It hurt, but he understood. "Then do me a favor, please. Keep holding my hand, and let you be the last thing I see before it happens."

Zala smiled through her tears and squeezed his hand again. "Of course! I think I can manage that."

Now it was William's turn to fight back tears. What he would have given to stop time!

Thilmarin's voice rose above the waves and drew the attention of all gathered. "Brinwin, come forward and receive the elixir." Brinwin disembarked the ship and strode toward the Assembly of Savants. Several closest to the front of their formation shrunk back, frightened by the scowling behemoth that drew near them. If looks could kill, more than one Savant would have met their end in those moments.

Only Thilmarin was brave enough to close the distance between them and extend a small vial with a pouch attached to it. He clapped his hands to that of the giant and shook them with conviction. He then said loudly enough for all to hear, "Everything has been prepared under the Assembly's supervision, the Savants as my witnesses. Administer the whole vial to him once you've added the catalyst, and be on your way." Thilmarin then drew his head close to Brinwin and whispered a final farewell.

Brinwin nodded and wasted little time in fulfilling his instructions. He stopped before the Englishman, towering above him into the twilit sky. "I'm sorry, Wil-yim," he said as he uncorked the bottle and sprinkled a powdered substance into the vial. Some of the powder failed to dissolve, leaving clumps that looked like blackened tea leaves. The concoction looked disgusting, and it smelled as unappealing as its appearance.

"You must drink all of it. Your well-being depends on it," he said with such firm conviction that William dared not doubt it.

William took the vial into his hands as he looked up into the evening sky, then back toward the Essari compound. He took in the sight of it all one final time, meeting eyes with the incredible race of people he knew he would never see again. Many of the Essari appeared likewise to savor their last look on an outsider, an oddity that would never again roam their shores. Lastly, William looked upon Zala and fixed his gaze on her. She nodded with a resolve that eased his pain if only a little.

With a final squeeze of her hand, he swallowed the entirety of the vial's contents. He looked at Zala for a few moments longer until his vision blurred and his head swam. The tears in her eyes were the last thing he saw before darkness seized his recollections.

Brinwin caught him as he collapsed and lowered him gently to the ground. After examining him for signs of any complications, he then slung him over his shoulder and boarded the ship with Zala. Minutes later, they departed into the night. The first star in the sky served as their guide, its twinkling beauty leading forever away from the shores of the Essari.

Interlude

The Black Book

The skies were dark when King Stephen slammed the doors to his chamber shut. It had been a long day, and the duties of ruling a kingdom were never-ending. He felt exhausted, yet something else important weighed on his mind. Free at last from prying eyes, he lit a candle and unlocked the chest by his bedside. He retrieved a tattered book from its depths and brought it to bed.

Of all the souls in England, he alone knew its contents. It had been unearthed when he discovered the secret passage below Saint Matthew's Cathedral, and it remained his most closely guarded secret. If anyone else knew of its existence, there was no telling what would come of it. At best, he would decline a thousand offers of payment for it. At worst, he would be even more of an assassination target than he already was.

He carefully opened the front cover to see the familiar shape of English calligraphy blazoned across its pages. The blackness of the ink matched the evening sky, refusing to disintegrate with the rest of the book. Its pages were weathered, yet intricate illustrations still depicted the features of an era long since forgotten by most.

Stephen turned its pages until he reached the most relevant section to him. The illustration of an army riding into battle soon spread before his view. The riders wore identical sets of armor, forged of metal as black as midnight and mingled with strains of deep blue. Below the riders, a band of assassins crept along the page clad in the same material as the riders.

Shadesteel, read the inscription at the top of the page. Stephen scanned further down to read the description that followed:

"The chief alloy of House Shadowcrest. Lighter than cloth, stronger than steel, and darker than night, none who wear it are heard before they strike. Coveted by soldiers and assassins alike since the days of King Rastegar of Tropis. Wrought by the arts of dark alchemy, its origin and craft remain secret to all outside that dire Family."

Stephen stared once more at the armies of horsemen, and he saw in his mind's eye the banner of a united England flying above their ranks. None could oppose him once the secret was his. He was sure of it. All that remained was for William Belston to bring him the recipe. His last communications with Azkalah had been promising. They assured him his agent had arrived on schedule and provided the necessary payment. Their best agent was working with William as they spoke to fulfill the contract. Now, all he could do was wait. He gazed onward, lost in thought until he came to himself and turned the page.

A solitary figure glowered up at him from the new entry. It bore the likeness of a man, with an ashen exterior that somehow seemed darker than black. Its eyes shone an iridescent purple, and it wielded a sword as wicked-looking as itself. Stephen shuddered at the thought of William encountering such a fiend. He hoped the support of Azkalah would be enough to overcome it if their paths crossed. Its description was brief, but it caused even the flame of his candle to tremble with a sense of foreboding.

Azgari, its title read. "Guardians of the Western Wastes and keepers of Shadowcrest's secrets. Once mortal men, corrupted by infernal alchemy to become the 'Soulless Ones.' Without fatigue they defend the Seat of the City Everoth in loyalty absolute, yet are unable to pass beyond their masters' dark domain. None who cross them survive to tell the tale."

PART II

The Heart of Shadowcrest

20

The Hunt Continues

The sun shone brilliantly through the clouds as it rose upon the city of Elkreath, yet did little to alleviate the chill that hung in the air. Sporadic gusts of wind whipped about, stirring up clouds of dust and other debris that stung anyone exposed to them. Those traveling the streets wore thick clothing to protect themselves and kept their heads down as much as possible. Under such circumstances, few noticed the hastening form of Inquestor Telnis Raiko as he weaved through a maze of streets and alleyways.

He tightened his coat about him as he hurried, hoping he could make it to the ports before the roads became too congested. He had been summoned to headquarters before sunrise and had no intentions of running behind. Had it been an emergency, he could use the emerald lane in the center of the streets to arrive in seconds. But, alas, his appointment was not *that* urgent. Fortunately for him, the weather's poor condition ensured that fewer than usual traveled that morning. Before long, his destination lumbered into view amid the bustling thoroughfare.

The headquarters of the Council of Inquest was a simple yet elegant building positioned squarely in the center of Elkreath's harbor district. It stood many stories tall, with a black wooden exterior that loomed high above the ships coming to port. The location had been strategically chosen to send a message to the hundreds of thousands conducting business in Cabalia's busiest seaport.

Vigilant in knowledge, its motto read, etched into an elaborate placard that hung above its entrance. Those who failed to take those words into account would discover just how quickly their secrets could be exposed; such was the fact many a criminal could attest to throughout the Council's five hundred years of existence. All in all, it was a respected, if not feared, institution. Holding a position there was no laughing matter, as Telnis often reminded himself.

The placard flew about with the wind as he drew near the entrance, sparing him from having to read the Council's motto for the thousandth time. As he ascended the front steps, a lengthy array of slits peered down on him from the upper levels of the building. There were no windows to gaze through, as that would run contrary to the building's purpose. Secrets came in, never out. It was thus fitting that anyone outside could be observed from within, but not the opposite. The architecture was chilling, but effective. Just as the Council liked it.

Telnis showed his amulet at the entrance before slogging through a cluster of security measures. Upon clearing the last checkpoint, he finally reached the office of his overseer, Tilthrir Frostmane. The door was closed, but he knew the expectation was to help himself inside without wasting time on the pleasantries of knocking and announcing himself. If he was not supposed to enter, the door would be locked. His boss was a no-nonsense man, and every practice of his showed it. The office was maximized for work down to the last inch. As such, *nothing* was out of place. If not pertinent to a case, it simply did not exist there.

Most inquestors were intimidated by Tilthrir, and Telnis was no exception. Upon entering the room, he cleared his throat and stood at attention. Tilthrir's eyes flashed up from the report he read before immediately looking back down. "Raiko," he acknowledged gruffly. "What took you so long?"

Telnis knew better than to dispute the claim that he was late. He had made *fantastic* time on his way in, but if Tilthrir said he was late, then he was late. He also knew better than to waste time offering an apology. "Poor winds," he answered. "What's the job for today, sir?"

The words had no sooner left his mouth than Tilthrir fired off a question of his own. "You tracked Zikennig to Lake Iddeah yesterday?"

Telnis nodded. "Yes, sir."

"It was a fine job you did, but you still lost the trail." Telnis's mouth dropped before he caught himself. No one outside the Council's employ would understand how significant a compliment his boss had just paid him in that he offered one at all.

Tilthrir continued, "An adjudicator's been sent to the lake and will handle everything there. In the meantime, I have some business for you here in Elkreath." He pulled a slip of paper from a drawer in his desk and handed it to Telnis. "Go to this address and speak with the head alchemist there. The Council thinks he may know something about those blue cracks we found on the Tafrik."

This time, Telnis could not keep his mouth from dropping. What were the odds he would be assigned to investigate the very evidence he wanted to see?

"Take a visioning orb if you can remember the scene well enough," instructed Tilthrir. "I want a report on my desk by sundown." Telnis snapped a salute, then withdrew from the office without another word spoken.

"Another quality conversation," he muttered with a shake of his head as he made his way to the equipment room. He signed out for the last visioning orb in stock, then set out at once. The address was on the opposite side of the city, but he knew how to make good time there. Five years of working in Elkreath had taught him a trick or two. By the time he arrived at his destination, the sun was still well shy of noon.

Telnis checked the address on the paper with the sign on the building before him. *The Crimson Crucible* the sign read as it hung above a modestly adorned alchemy supply store. A variety of vials, cauldrons, and recipe books were displayed with pride in its front window while a small but steady stream of customers entered and exited the shop. Most of them were well-dressed and dignified in posture, but a few were of more modest means. The address matched his directions, so he entered with no further delay.

A glance around the interior confirmed it to be of superior quality. Everything was tidy, from the tools arranged on well-polished shelves to the carpeted floor without a smudge on it. Attendants in red uniforms traveled about, assisting customers and stocking the shelves with new supplies. More so than their appearance, how they conducted themselves spoke to a climate of professional dignity rarely seen in Elkreath. They moved and talked with a confidence born from experience, yet also lacking in the arrogance Telnis had found in many other high-end stores. It was difficult for him to describe, but the atmosphere just felt different from other places: top-notch quality, but comfortably down to earth at the same time.

A front desk stood in the center of the spacious area, giving him time to observe his surroundings as he strode forward. Upon reaching the desk, the attendant on duty offered him a warm smile. "Good morning, sir. Is there anything I can assist you with?"

Telnis flashed his amulet and spoke discreetly. "Yes, I would like to speak with your chief alchemist. Official business for the Council of Inquest."

The attendant's smile dropped into a frown. "Of course," he replied. "Right this way, please." The attendant rose from his seat and led him to the far side of the building. He paused at an elaborately carved wooden door, on which he knocked with a series of short raps. "Dr. Komazis? A gentleman to see you from the Council of Inquest," he announced. A moment of silence followed.

"Ah, very well then. Send him in, Ferrel," came the hesitant reply. The attendant slid open the door and held it for Telnis. "Step right in, sir," he said with a nod. Telnis offered a slight bow and stepped into the office before the door closed with a firm click.

While not quite *messy*, the room was less tidy than the rest of the store. Elaborate contraptions filled with exotic materials snaked across a row of tables, smoking and bubbling from the flames kindled beneath them. Dr. Komazis sat behind his desk, peering apprehensively at Telnis as he approached. His appearance suggested a man in his early sixties, thinner than average, with a silver beard that transitioned to white. When he spoke, his voice was stronger than one might first expect.

"Good morning, Inquestor. What brings you to the Crimson Crucible today?"

Telnis offered a bow suitable for addressing an elder of superior rank. "Good morning, Dr. Komazis. Unfortunate business, I'm afraid." The alchemist shifted in discomfort but said nothing as he waited for Telnis to elaborate. "I'm sure you've heard by now what happened on the Tafrik Bridge?" Telnis probed.

At this, Komazis frowned. "Ah, just vaguely from the word on the street. A most unusual murder of some kind, yes?"

Telnis used his light magic to peer into the man's thoughts and emotions as he talked. He could not read exact thoughts, but he *could* sense a paraphrase of one's intent. He perceived that Komazis was unsettled, fearful of being suspected of the crime. He was not hiding any guilt, though. It was time to relieve the man of his worries.

"Indeed. I obviously can't discuss all the details of an ongoing investigation, but the Council believes your expertise could be of service to us in solving this case."

The alchemist's posture immediately relaxed, and his tone took on a warmer ring. "But of course. Whatever services the Crucible can offer, we are more than willing to help."

Telnis smiled as he pulled the visioning orb from his cloak. "Excellent. I'm glad to hear it." He projected his memories of the Tafrik Bridge onto the orb as he held it, causing its surface to ripple into a vivid image of the blue cracks glowing on the bridge's pavement. "We found this on the bridge the morning after the incident. Are you able to identify it?"

The alchemist's eyes gleamed as his professional curiosity was aroused. "Fascinating," he murmured. He stared deep in thought before coming back to himself with a start. "I have an idea, but I'll need to see it in person to be certain."

While not pleased at the prospect of waiting longer for an answer, Telnis was not surprised. "I understand, Doctor," he said. "But I'm afraid there's a bit of a time constraint. I'll need you to come with me at once to investigate."

Komazis's brow furrowed, and he looked ready to protest. Telnis held his gaze, making it clear he would not take no for an answer. The alchemist sighed, then composed himself in resolve. "Very well then, I can be ready to leave in twenty minutes if that's agreeable." Even if it were not "agreeable," he would plainly move no faster.

"Alright," said Telnis. "I can help you pack up if that would make things any quicker."

Komazis shook his head. "I appreciate the offer, Inquestor, but it really would be best if I handled all the preparations. Alchemy is nothing if not finicky, and we wouldn't want my observations to be skewed. Why don't you wait for me at the front desk, and we can set off once I'm ready?"

"Of course," Telnis nodded. "I'll wait for you there." Strolling past the door, he made his way to the front desk. The attendants stared at him in concern but promptly busied themselves whenever he turned to meet their gaze. Telnis leaned against the desk with a nonchalant stretch. *This'll be fun,* he thought with a grin.

True to his word, Dr. Komazis emerged from his office twenty minutes later. With nothing but a cane in hand, he limped over to the front desk where Telnis stood waiting. "I'm ready to go, Inquestor," he said.

Telnis raised an eyebrow in confusion. "Ahh... where's your equipment, Doctor? Weren't you bringing tools of some kind?"

Before Telnis could finish his sentence, the door to the office opened again. An attendant staggered through with a heavy trunk in tow, and Komazis grinned in reply. "Why yes, of course. Talkrin here is carrying it with him."

One look at the lad made it clear he did not relish the idea of carrying his load across Elkreath. Telnis shook his head. With Komazis's limp and Talkrin's burden, it would take hours of extra time to cross the city. This would simply not do.

"Come along, then," Telnis sighed. "I'll call for a carter."

* * *

Even with a horse-drawn cart, progress to the Tafrik Bridge was slower than Telnis would have liked. The winds had died down, and the direct light of the noonday sun had driven off the morning chill. Crowds filled the streets, conditions once again ideal for commerce and sightseeing. By the time they reached the crime scene, it was already the middle of the afternoon.

Telnis wasted no time helping the doctor's assistant unload the trunk after they secured passage into the restricted area. Several enforcers looked on in curiosity as the alchemist unpacked the trunk's contents and set up an elaborate array of tools and curios around the cracks still glowing in the pavement. He fussed with the equipment for what felt like an eternity, tweaking nobs and turning valves back and forth ever so slightly.

It was all Telnis could do to keep his patience through the process. Time was ticking by, and he only had so much of it to prepare a report for Tilthrir. Even veteran inquestors feared failing him, and Telnis was far from being a veteran. How much longer could this possibly take?

When Dr. Komazis finally appeared satisfied with the arrangement of his tools, he withdrew a stick-like apparatus from his sleeve. He scraped the instrument along the ground as he traced the surface of the cracks. Sparks began to fly about in all directions, causing Telnis and the other onlookers to flinch away. When their gaze returned, they found that the sparks had assumed a bright blue color and the tip of the stick glowed the same hue as the cracks.

The doctor then drew the stick away from the ground and plunged it into a device shaped like a hollowed-out drum. The device rotated in place, letting off a low-pitched hum as it began to vibrate. The vibrations spread within moments to the other devices around it until they all hummed and vibrated at the same frequency. The chorus of hums intensified until a green light flashed on the side of the drum. Komazis then flicked a valve shut, and the humming dropped into silence. The stick ceased glowing, even as the drum continued rotating around it.

The alchemist turned to face Telnis, his expression brimming with confidence. "My suspicions have been confirmed, Inquestor. These cracks are the direct result of a Danuri stone exploding. And not just any Danuri stone, but a blue one that has seen very little use."

A nearby enforcer whistled in amazement, and Telnis stroked his chin. "A blue Danuri stone? You're certain of this, Dr. Komazis?"

The doctor's gaze remained as fixed as the stones beneath his feet. "I could bet my life on it. And for whatever it's worth, I'd also wager this exploding stone has a twin that came in close proximity to it."

Telnis furrowed his brow. "A twin?"

"Yes, a twin. It's not common knowledge, but there have been accounts throughout history. When a blue Danuri forms, the Kyne often splits off into a second object. Whenever you find one, there's bound to be another nearby." The doctor's eyes then glimmered with a knowing look. "What's more, the Kyne in the twin objects seems to have something of a... memory, if you will, of its other half. It's not as well documented, but I've seen some rather suggestive reports. The circumstances are all different, but they share a common thread: Fate always finds a way of bringing the separated siblings back together. And, like siblings, they often fight with each other."

"How do you mean they fight with each other?" Telnis pressed.

An amused grin spread across the doctor's face before he responded, "Well, mind you, Inquestor, this is not a scientifically established fact, just the opinion of one who's spent more time than most looking at ancient lore. Typically, one of the objects is slightly more powerful than its twin, and the shared magic in them can exhibit a fierce competition. For whatever reason, the objects by themselves cannot harm each other, but when they're both possessed by living beings close at hand..." Komazis spread his arms to encompass the bridge. "Things get interesting. The stronger one overpowers the weaker one, and soon the world is down one more Danuri stone."

Telnis stared down at the cracks as he processed what he heard. "So you're telling me that two people walked this bridge with sibling Danuri stones in their pockets, and the stronger one nixed the weaker one?"

"Correct. And I wouldn't be surprised if it was unintentional on the part of the people walking the bridge. As I said, such reunions are usually orchestrated by fate, not the design of men."

Telnis again stared off into the distance. *Now that complicates things,* he thought to himself. *If it wasn't an intentional murder, then why did he run off to meet Zikennig at the Kozheithy? And what does Shadowcrest have to do with this?* He rubbed his temples in frustration. It just was not fair. The more he learned, the less he knew what was going on. He cringed at the thought of the report he still had to write.

Things only got worse for him when another inquestor burst his way into the area and startled him from his thoughts. "Telnis! I thought that looked like you!" the man shouted. Telnis groaned. It was Galfrik. The only thing worse than his coworker's big mouth was his tendency to butt in at the worst possible times.

"What is it, Galfrik?" he called back. "I'm in the middle of something here." He knew by now the annoyance in his tone would fail to register with the man, but he still held on to the faint hope his point might get across.

"You're gonna want to see this! We've got a major lead on the docks." Galfrik's voice was insistent, like a puppy dog that had to play *right now.* Telnis sighed. If he hurried, he would still have enough time to write his report. Probably.

He turned to face Dr. Komazis. "Thank you for your help, Doctor. I'm afraid I have to go, but I'll make sure you're compensated for your efforts. The carter will see you and your assistant back to the Crucible." He flipped the assistant a coin to cover the cost of travel, then turned and trotted off to follow Galfrik, unsure what awaited him at the docks.

As annoying as his coworker was, he had to give him credit that he was fast. They would reach the docks in no time at the pace he set.

"What's this all about, Galfrik?" Telnis panted as they ran, weaving through a sea of people and buildings.

"I'll tell ya when we get there, you impatient jackrabbit!" he called back.

Telnis resented that Galfrik bantered with him like a younger sibling just because he had served for three years longer. If he tried that with anyone else — with Tilthrir, perhaps...

Telnis could not keep the grin off his face at the picture of his boss responding to such a situation. It was probably for the best that Galfrik was too far ahead to notice his smirk.

A few minutes later, their pace slowed to a walk as they reached the limits of the city proper. Galfrik led Telnis across the weathered planks of the shipyard, and only then did he begin to explain himself. The hefty boots he always wore thudded on the wood beneath them as he spoke, forcing Telnis to pay extra attention.

"While you were off tracking Zikennig, Tilthrir sent me to the docks to search for anything I could find. So I did a bit of searching. And what do I find? *Two* — not one, but *two* — ships from England docked here on the night of the murder. Did a bit more searching, and what do you know? *Both* of them are here on 'official Shadowcrest business.' What do ya make of that, huh?"

Telnis shrugged. "I mean... interesting, I suppose. Plenty of ships from Shadowcrest stop by here on their trade runs, so..."

Galfrik stopped and stared at Telnis. "No, Telnis, I don't think ya heard me right. Not two of *our* ships coming back from England. I mean two ships *from* England. As in, outsider ships, filled with Englishmen, speaking English but claiming to work for Shadowcrest."

Telnis gave a start. "Outsiders?! Here? How are we only hearing about this now?"

"I'm still lookin' into that," Galfrik replied. "Best guess is they paid the dockhands extra well to keep it all hush-hush."

Something then clicked inside Telnis's brain. "Wait, hold on. You said there were *two* of them? On Shadowcrest business?"

Galfrik burst into a smile and clapped his hands on Telnis's back.

"That's right, now you've got it! I found the ships, too, but kinda figured you'd be better at handling interrogations, you with your light magic and all." Logical enough, Telnis had to admit. Still, a question niggled at the back of his mind.

"Shouldn't you have told Tilthrir first before you came to me, though?"

Galfrik laughed and responded with a wink. "You're not the only one with reports to write, my friend. I just took the opportunity for extra help to make sure it's a good one."

Telnis rolled his eyes. Of course.

They came at length to a battered ship in the middle of repairs. "This here's the first one," Galfrik said. He looked around as if searching for someone, then whistled loudly and waved his hands. "Ey, Valdwin! Over here!" He nudged Telnis as the dockworker approached them. "This here is Valdwin. Turns out, he knows English better than anyone on the docks. Not sure how a dockhand learns English that good, but we'll take it. He'll translate for us."

Upon reaching them, Valdwin gave a deep bow. "Inquestor Galfrik, I see you've returned."

Galfrik nudged Telnis again. "Very polite fella, too," he said as he attempted to talk under his breath but failed utterly. Telnis just groaned as Galfrik continued, "Indeed I have. Me and my friend are here to talk to the outsiders."

Valdwin bowed again. "Of course, sirs. I'm ready whenever you are." The inquestors nodded, and he led them to the ship.

As they approached, the men on board glared at them with suspicion. Many of them paused their repair work and muttered to each other in low tones. One turned toward the stern and shouted something in English. Telnis could not understand a word, but he perceived that the man sounded a warning to the rest of his fellows. They were anxious over the disappearance of someone important. A superior of some sort. The ship's captain, perhaps? No, that was the man striding toward them now. Then who could it be?

Telnis steeled his mind in preparation for extensive use of his magic.

He would be reading a lot of people this day, it seemed. *Oh well*, he thought. At least he would sleep well that night.

The ship's captain drew near and stopped a couple of paces before them. His face was weathered and stretched thin in worry, but tightened in resolve. He stared in silence, waiting for them to speak first.

"Good evening, Captain," Valdwin said. "These men are from the government of Elkreath, and they wish to ask you a few questions." The captain grunted a reply, and the inquestors glanced back to Valdwin. "He wants to know if they're in trouble," he explained.

Galfrik spoke up before Telnis had the chance to reply with more tact. "Tell 'em that all depends on how cooperative they are."

The captain said nothing but merely nodded for them to continue.

Telnis asked the first question. "Tell me, Captain, what are you doing here from England?" Even before Valdwin offered his translation, Telnis discerned the man was not lying to them.

"He says they were sent by their king to deliver a... Hearthstone to our people."

Galfrik and Telnis exchanged glances. "A what?" came Galfrik's incredulous response.

"A Hearthstone," he insisted again.

Upon being informed that no such item existed in Cabalia, the captain broke into a cold sweat. "I wasn't aware of this," he insisted. "All I know is that my superior told us we were under secret orders of our king to deliver an item called a hearthstone. He left two nights ago to deliver the blasted thing and hasn't returned since."

Telnis murmured, half to himself and half to Galfrik. "He's not lying."

Galfrik merely snorted. "Well, he ain't tellin' the truth either. Ask him some more questions."

Telnis fought the urge to roll his eyes. "What did this hearthstone look like?" he asked.

The captain stroked his chin in recollection. "I only saw it for a few seconds, but it was a stone about the size of your fist. One moment, it was glowing bright white, and then it was a deep blue."

Telnis's mind raced. *A blue Danuri stone!* Now they were getting somewhere. "You said that your superior's been gone for two days. Tell us more about him."

Upon hearing the translation from Valdwin, the captain's eyes searched Telnis's soul as intently as Telnis searched his. "Is he in trouble?" he asked.

Telnis gave a candid response. "We don't know yet. Right now, he's the prime suspect in an open murder, but we're still gathering evidence. Anything you have to tell us will be useful."

The man was torn. Telnis could tangibly feel the struggle in the captain's mind between loyalty to his leader and pragmatism to cooperate with the authorities. The harsh lines of experience etched into his face suggested he would err on the side of pragmatism. Such proved to be the case as the sailor sighed and rubbed his temples. Telnis almost felt sorry for him, even if he was an outsider.

"His name is William Steele," he said in resignation. "He's the right-hand man of our King Henry. Good with a blade and just as good with his words. Whatever duty's required of him, he's done it, but he's also a principled man. I don't believe he'd ever murder someone pointlessly. We have no quarrel with your people, so I doubt he's the man you're looking for. He told me when he left that he planned to be back by morning, but it's been nearly two days. Whatever happened to him, I'm sure it was unexpected."

Galfrik guffawed while Telnis furrowed his brow in contemplation. Had it not been for the perception his magic afforded him, Telnis would have been as skeptical as his cohort. "Is there anything else you wish to tell us?" he asked.

The captain shook his head. "Only that he instructed us to return home if he didn't come back from his errand. Are we free to follow our orders?"

Telnis glanced at Galfrik, who shook his head slowly. "I'm sorry, Captain. As long as William Steele remains a suspect, we cannot allow you to leave port. You are to remain here until we sort through all of this. We'll be in contact with you."

The inquestors then turned to disembark from the ship. The despair of the crew hung so thickly that even Galfrik could feel it. Before he reached the base of the pier, Telnis turned and called back over his shoulder, "Don't worry, Captain. If William is truly innocent, we'll find out sooner than later. It's what we're good at." The captain only stared back down at them, his face burdened with the same unyielding worry it carried at the beginning of their encounter. Telnis turned again and trudged back to the docks.

"What was that all about?" Galfrik asked once they were beyond earshot.

Telnis's eyes gleamed before he replied, "You can read about it in my report. Speaking of which..." He stared in the direction of headquarters. "I need to get busy writing it."

"But what about the other ship?" Galfrik protested.

Telnis laughed and patted his compatriot's back harder than necessary. "Come now, my friend. You can surely handle an interview on your own. I'll see you back at Tilthrir's before sundown." With a satisfied grin, Telnis then turned and trotted off to headquarters, thoroughly enjoying the dumbfounded look he felt from behind him.

* * *

Sunset came faster than Telnis would have liked, but he still completed his report before the deadline. Even as his eyes burned and his head throbbed, he prided himself in how much he had accomplished in a day's work — much more than anyone else would have, he was sure. He tidied the stray edges of his report and scooped it into his hands as he hurried out of his office. The orange light of a setting sun filtered through the slits in the walls as he went, an uneasy reminder of how little time he had left. He increased his pace to something shy of a jog as he wove through a labyrinth of stairways and corridors. Security details eyed him with suspicion but did nothing to interfere with his progress.

When he arrived at the entrance to Tilthrir's office, the sun hovered on the verge of the horizon. He swung the door open without breaking his stride to find Galfrik sitting in front of his boss with a report in hand. Their gaze flashed to Telnis, then back to each other.

"Raiko," Tilthrir grunted. "Pushing the limits, as always."

Telnis scuffled into the seat next to Galfrik and tried to ignore the smugness brimming from his coworker's eyes. "As good quality often does, sir," he quipped as he turned his report in. Tilthrir said nothing in reply and remained silent as he scrutinized the paperwork. He motioned Galfrik to share his findings with Telnis while he kept reading the report.

Galfrik took care to avoid distracting his boss with loud speech. "Beyond what you already know," he explained, "it turns out the captain from the other ship also went missing two nights ago. The crew said he was guarding some mysterious object he wouldn't even talk about. The only thing he told them was that he was heading to the Kozheithy Tavern. He instructed them to wait until he returned, which he never did. Fascinating, right? But it just gets better.

"As it so happens, his name is William, too: William Belston, trusted agent of the right honorable King Stephen of England. You know what that means, Telnis? Two English kings at odds with themselves each sent a man named William to do Yahos-knows-what over here. They come to the same port, and both of them go missing. I'd bet you my left foot the man who blew up on the bridge was one of those Williams, knocked off by his rival. A political assassination, cut and dry."

Tilthrir held up his hand abruptly, and Galfrik took the cue to silence himself. "Actually, Galfrik, it's less cut and dry than you think. Raiko's report throws a twist into the matter." Tilthrir rose from his desk and paced over to the far side of the room, where he paused to gaze through a slit in the wall. The setting sun still shone brightly enough to cast its light through the slit onto his face. No one dared to speak as he looked out in silence over Glimmerstone Bay and the thousands of ships that found refuge in its harbor for the evening.

When he finally spoke, even the air seemed to still itself in anticipation of his verdict. "The intents of men can be difficult to uncover, but this much is certain: Whichever William survived the explosion is guilty of manslaughter, voluntary or otherwise. Should he be foolish enough to set foot in Elkreath, the Council stands ready to apprehend him."

Tilthrir turned from the slit and fastened his gaze on the two inquestors. "Azkalah is involved in this, and it will require our best effort. Put the enforcers on high alert and notify the seekers to shift priorities. Whatever happens, we will be vigilant. Justice will be served, and we will uncover the truth... one way or another."

21

Golems

The rattling of wheels on a dirt road and a heavy jolt startled William to consciousness. "Watch it, Brin!" Zala's voice rang out as another jolt flung William clear across the carriage in which he found himself. His impact was softened considerably when he landed straight into Zala's arms. She looked down on him in delight, relishing the moment with a mischievous grin. "On second thought, never mind!" she called out again.

William heard Brinwin groan from somewhere in front of him. "Show some restraint, Sister. We need to be alert," came his stiff reply.

Zala rolled her eyes and looked back down at William. "Hi there," she said sweetly. William furrowed his brow in confusion. The darkened interior of the carriage provided a stark contrast to Zala's beaming eyes. A blur of green and blue raced past the windows on either side, and a sudden beam of sunlight fell upon his face, almost blinding him. He covered his eyes and scrambled upright as he searched for his bearings. He could not for the life of him recall how he had found himself in such a strange position.

"What in the…" he trailed off as a sudden realization hit him. "Zala?" he gasped in disbelief.

She laughed in response and batted her eyelashes. "Yes, William?"

"You… I remember who you are! How do I remember you?" he stammered.

"Because I'm just that awesome," came her reply.

"I beg to differ!" Brinwin called back as he hid a rare smile from view. Zala only shook her head as he continued to speak. "What actually happened is that our friend the Grand Savant did us a favor. When he handed me the vial of sleeping solution, he also slipped me some Ninferen leaves, which, as any skilled alchemist knows, negates all memory-erasing properties of a solution. A stroke of genius, really."

"And you knew all this beforehand?" William probed.

"Well… actually, no. I have to hand it to Thilmarin that he played it up well. I had no clue until he whispered in my ear before I gave it to you. The fewer people who knew, the more believable it was. Even had poor Zala fooled. You should have seen how much she cried and wailed—"

"And you were no picture of joy and happiness either, Brother," Zala cut in, eager to change the subject.

"As anyone would be in my situation. Do you have any idea how close I was to finishing my work? He couldn't have given us just one more day?" lamented Brinwin with a shake of his head.

William straightened himself and leaned forward. "Now that you mention it, Brinwin, what will we do now? Will it be much longer until I get the shadesteel? I do have some business to complete for my king, after all, and a deal's a deal."

Brinwin merely waved his hand. "Don't worry, Englishman. You'll get your shadesteel soon enough. We just need to make a quick stop in Elkreath, and then we can finish what we've started."

At this, Zala chimed in with hesitance. "Yeah, about that, Brin. You realize the whole Council of Inquest is looking for us, right? All of their assets are on high alert, according to my sources. Do you really want to go up to their front doorstep? We have other ways to—"

"Yes, Zala, we must go to Elkreath. I have some unfinished business to attend to." Brinwin was adamant, and it was clear the discussion would go no further.

"I just hope you know what you're doing," Zala said before she trailed off to a mutter. "That Inquestor Raiko almost tracked us to the lake."

At this, Brinwin's face lit up with glee. "So they did put him on the case! Splendid!" he exclaimed. "I was hoping they would. It'll make all of this much more enjoyable."

His sudden exuberance caught everyone else off guard. Zala stared at her brother as if he were crazy, and William could only guess what he was talking about.

Upon noticing his confusion, Zala leaned in toward William. "Inquestors are people that work for the royal government by investigating crime. There's a particular one by the name of Telnis Raiko who almost caught my brother and me a few years back. Brin's been obsessed with the man ever since, views him as a noble archrival or something."

"Because he is quite a remarkable man," Brinwin cut in. His eyes focused ahead as he spoke, directing the horses that drove their carriage. Having passed the edge of an open pasture, they took a trail straight into the depths of a forest that sprawled before them. "All the rest of them are either arrogant *gunuhs* with limited skill or imbeciles who wallow in their complacency and corruption." The horses swerved to avoid an outcropping of rock in the center of the path, causing William to slide and crash into Zala again. The impact was far less comfortable than the previous one, and William rubbed his head as he strained to make out the rest of Brinwin's ramblings.

"He's a good man with respectable talent, but beyond that, he's *frustrated*. Frustrated with the corruption, frustrated with the incompetence, frustrated with having his talents overlooked. And this frustration pushes him to do the unconventional. And yet... for all his frustration, he doesn't leave for greener pastures. He sticks it out in a place he knows will never change, just so he can do what he thinks is right. If the Keepers of Alchemy had men like him, I'd probably have stayed with them."

William braced himself as the carriage raced around a bend faster than it should have. The whole right side of the carriage rose into the air before it landed back down with a creaking thud. Freshly damaged wheels gouged a rut into the trail behind them as they raced on. William stared in dismay through the back window.

"Sounds like quite the fellow," he said after he recovered himself. "You said he almost caught you?"

"Oh yes! And quite the tale that is. Once we leave Elkreath, you'll have to remind me of it. Now Zala, you said the adjudicator is somewhere past this forest, yes?"

"Yes," she called out. "If we're going to avoid him, we'll want to take the left at the waterfall up ahead."

"And where would be the fun in that? You said he's an earth mage, yes?"

Zala groaned. Whether it was in reaction to Brinwin's speech or from hitting her head against the roof as they went over a bump, William could not tell. Whatever the case, the displeasure in her voice was unmistakable. "Yeah, I think so. What does it matter?"

"What do you mean, 'what does it matter?' It's the only element we haven't bested yet! We take him out, and we'll have beat old Kaloran himself!"

Zala put her head in her hands. When she met William's quizzical look, she merely shook her head. "I'll explain it later. Whatever happens, just stay in the carriage and stay hidden." She then stared out the window and shook her head again. "And people think *I'm* the foolhardy one."

She murmured further to herself, but the crashing of the waterfall in front of them rendered it all but indecipherable. The horses charged forward to the right of the falls and followed the trail as it wound through the remainder of the forest.

An uneasy feeling settled in William's stomach as the others fell silent, preparing themselves for he had no idea what. In time, the dark green of the canopy above them gave way to the solid blue of the open sky, and only then did Brinwin bring the horses to rest. They stopped beside a pool of water at the far side of a field, and Zala exited the carriage to attend to the horses. She spoke to the exhausted animals in hushed tones while scanning the surrounding area intensely. Her brother, meanwhile, settled himself by the pool with such nonchalance that William found himself baffled. Could these siblings be any further opposite from each other?

"Relax, friend," Brinwin called out to Zala with a yawn. "This place is so remote, not even an adjudicator could find it. A bit of rest would do you some good." Zala continued her search for a moment longer before giving up with a shrug and sitting beside him. From his vantage point in the carriage, William caught the flash of a hand signal Zala gave to Brinwin before she loosened her posture.

"I suppose you have a point, comrade," she said. "The place seems secure enough. Perhaps a little rest wouldn't hurt."

"Finally, now you're talking some sense!" said Brinwin as he planted a firm clap on his "comrade's" back. William did not know what was going on, but something was off. The atmosphere he felt inside himself contrasted sharply with that on display before his eyes. By all appearances, he and his companions sat alone in a meadow, surrounded by a vast expanse of nature. Patches of tall grass and wildflowers stretched before them and rustled in the wind while songbirds called out their melodies from the trees behind them. The mid-morning sun was full of warmth, but not oppressively so. It should have been a scene of serenity. And yet it was not.

The hair on William's neck stood on end with anticipation, aware of an unseen presence. Zala and Brinwin maintained their postures of ease, but William knew they felt it too. They sat a minute longer in tranquility, prolonging their game of charades for as long as their opponent would allow. Such games ended with the abrupt arrival of a boulder as it flew through the air. It sounded no warning as it raced toward them, but the looming shadow that darkened the grass beneath it was all the warning necessary.

Brinwin and Zala dove in opposite directions before the projectile splashed into the center of the pool. Water sprayed out in all directions, dousing them both. No sooner had they wiped their eyes dry than the ground shook with a fearsome rumble. From the edges of the field, there emerged towering figures of stone and dirt crudely shaped in the form of men. They lumbered forward, slowly at first, but gained speed with each step they took. Particles of earth scattered about them as they charged ahead, forging a cloud of debris that raced forward like an avalanche.

"The boulder, Brin!" Zala called out before sprinting toward it. Brinwin nodded and likewise sped forward. He retrieved a vial of glowing red liquid as he went and handed it to Zala at the base of the boulder.

"These aren't normal golems, so make it count," he instructed. "And take this," he added as he whisked her a pair of thick goggles. Within moments, Brinwin had fastened on his own pair and hoisted Zala to the top of the boulder. She, in turn, pulled him up to join her, and they stood side-by-side as the golems closed the remaining distance.

William watched on in dread, knowing there was little he could do to help. Zala had ordered him to stay hidden, and he fully intended to do just that. He could only hope these adversaries were as easy for them to slay as a sea serpent, but the longer he stared at them, the emptier that hope seemed. Their eyes and the center of their chests both glowed a vibrant green, pulsing with an unknown power that struck fear deeper into his heart than even the *Kumuzhkan* had. At least then, there had only been one fiend to worry about. Yahos help them, there were now at least five bearing down on them.

The golems came within a few yards of the boulder when Brinwin and Zala leaped from their perch. Their precision was flawless, each landing on the head of a different golem. Brinwin drew two daggers and used them as picks to maneuver the body of the golem he landed on as they barreled past the boulder. He scurried about in a blur of motion, spinning, turning, twisting, and twirling as the other golems attempted to pound the life out of him.

Zala drew a dagger of her own and soaked its tip in the vial's solution before plunging it into the eyes of the golem she hung on to. A horrendous roar erupted from the creature, the force of it nearly knocking her off her mount. The light of the golem's eyes flickered, and Zala leaped off onto the closest golem nearby before it collapsed and crumbled back into the dust it came from. She repeated the process with similar success, her target far too focused on smashing Brinwin to notice her in time.

William looked on in awe, captivated by the acrobatics that seemed to defy reality. It was not until the second golem collapsed into dust that he noticed by chance the figure of a man standing at the base of the remaining golems, shrouded from the others' view by the dust storm raging about them. The man stood there patiently, eyeing his prey as a cat would an unsuspecting mouse. William opened his mouth to yell a warning, but he checked himself. Not only would his friends fail to hear him over the chaos of the battle, but the adjudicator might be alerted to his presence. *No*, he decided. He must remain hidden, at least for the moment.

He searched the inside of the carriage for anything he could use as a weapon. To his unexpected relief, he found a chest on the floor stocked with an assortment of small weapons. Most were suitable only for melee combat, but he picked through the cache until he found a throwing knife. The size and balance felt strange, but he did not have much time to be picky.

While he had been searching the carriage, the situation had taken a turn for the worse. Before Zala could safely leap from the third golem she destroyed, the adjudicator conjured a stone from thin air and hurled it at her with all his might. The projectile found its mark and knocked Zala to the ground unconscious. She landed with a sickening thud, and in moments the adjudicator was upon her. He summoned an iron chain into being, with which he bound her. Having blindfolded her, he turned his attention back to Brinwin, who had felled all but the last remaining golem.

As before, he summoned a stone and sent it flying at Brinwin's head. Unlike his sister, however, Brinwin perceived the projectile in time to dodge it. He glanced down at his assailant with a look of scorn, then carried out the remainder of his maneuvers without missing a beat.

He swung around the head of the last golem and slid down its chest, stabbing its core with his remaining dagger. The golem disintegrated into dust, and before he hit the ground, Brinwin had his sword drawn and ready.

The adjudicator rushed to him and unleashed a volley of cuts and slashes that would have ended the life of an average swordsman. Brinwin kept pace with the onslaught, if but barely. They traded blows back and forth, each strike whizzing as a blur and ending with a clang.

Neither side made much progress until the adjudicator landed a blow on the strap of Brinwin's goggles. As they fell to the ground, the adjudicator launched a spray of dust into Brinwin's face that caused him to stumble backward and trip to the ground, unable to stop his eyes from stinging or his lungs from coughing. With a decisive blow, the adjudicator sent his opponent's sword flying into the distance. Chains as thick as his neck wrapped themselves around Brinwin's arms and legs, and the adjudicator pressed the tip of his sword against his captive's throat.

Brinwin turned his gaze downward as he panted. "Beacon's light, you're stronger than the others," he said between gasps.

The adjudicator tipped his sword up to force Brinwin to look at him. "My orders were to bring you in alive, but I've studied you enough, Brinwin Zikennig. You're too dangerous to be left alive. If I say that I killed you in self-defense in the heat of the fight, no one would question it." He then turned his head to look at Zala as she stirred to consciousness. "Though I'm not sure yet how to handle your sister — yes, I know who she is. I know about every course she took at the College, the grade of every assignment she ever completed, and the extent of every campaign she served in the Hearthfell guard. I know what she's capable of. Her magic is all show and no bite. Now with a sword, she's nowhere near the legend you are, but she is quite powerful. Too powerful to be left alive, I think." He drew back his blade and readied it for execution. "I'll finish you first and then deal with her. Do you have any last words, you arrogant piece of scum?"

Brinwin smiled and spoke with serenity as he held his gaze. "With all due respect, sir, you really are an arrogant piece of scum yourself. And quite an incompetent one, too, given the glaring error of what you overlooked. If I have any last words for you, it would be... duck?"

Before the adjudicator could react to Brinwin's speech, a throwing knife shot through the air and landed firmly in his back. He fell to his knees with a gasp, clutching his sword tightly.

Zala's voice then called out softly from behind him. "I know this is a bad moment for you, Mr. Adjudicator, sir, but you were actually wrong about me. You *don't* know what I'm capable of. I hope you don't mind if I set the record straight."

The adjudicator turned around to face Zala in time to see a ball of fire rocketing toward him. The missile struck him squarely in the chest and knocked him onto his back, driving the knife deeper into him. He roared in pain as the flames swelled to engulf him. He rolled over and turned to flee, only to meet the swift end of William's blade as the Englishman put him out of his misery.

"It really is a pity you blocked up that pool of water. Might have done you some good, poor chap," said William as he stepped away and cleaned his blade. He then made his way over to Zala and removed the blindfold from her. "Well hello there, beautiful," he said. "I guess I'm not the only one who's good at falling nowadays."

Zala smirked and bit her lip. "Gloating doesn't become you, good sir. Either do something useful or do something fun."

William's heart raced, and he grinned with a mischievous smile. The second option was quite appealing, and he would have chosen it had Brinwin not ruined the mood.

"You know I'm still here, right?" he called out as he rattled his chains. The incessant clinking of it nearly drove William and Zala mad. "These things are quite uncomfortable. Could you please free me before you two have any fun?"

William's eyes rolled in annoyance before they gleamed with mischief once more. "You know, we could just leave him here," he murmured to Zala. The suggestion prompted a burst of laughter from her.

"Now that would be useful!"

Brinwin's chains clinked onward with a growing intensity. "If you don't hurry up, I'll drug you so hard even your grandchildren will feel it."

William shrugged before he set about releasing Zala first. "Alright, you crotchety bear, just hold on. We're on our way."

Brinwin's chains proved harder to pry off than Zala's, even with the extra help. Regardless of their assertions to the contrary, he was convinced it took longer on purpose. "You know, I could give your children two left feet," he mused half in jest. "Or turn their skin purple."

"Oh knock it off, Brin, we've just about got it," Zala huffed before the chains sprung loose at last.

Brinwin rose to his full height and stretched his arms. "Finally!" he blurted before stooping down to pick up the still-smoking cloak of the fallen adjudicator. He waved it teasingly in front of his sister. "See? I knew I could handle it."

Zala merely snorted. "You? Looks more like *we*, to me. If William hadn't sunk a knife in his back and bought me some time to fling a fireball at his face, you'd have been a dead man."

Brinwin just shrugged. "A minor detail of a major accomplishment."

Zala rolled her eyes as none but a sibling could, while William shook his head at the hubris behind Brinwin's smile. The moment soon passed, and William turned his gaze to Zala as he stroked his chin.

"Now that you mention it, Zala... if you've been able to use fire magic this whole time, then why the blazes didn't you use it on the *Kumuzhkan?* That would have been a tad handy, don't you think?"

Brinwin and Zala glanced at each other, then back at William. "Well, actually, no," she said. "Fire's a pretty poor choice to fight water with. According to the legends, they're remarkably fireproof."

William squinted, still not convinced. "If you say so, I suppose." He looked back at the carriage and then at the adjudicator's cloak in Brinwin's hand. "So now what?" he asked.

Brinwin surveyed the heavens, then trudged back to the carriage. "Now, we make it to Elkreath after sunset," he replied.

"And then?"

Brinwin retrieved his sword from the ground and polished it. His voice was pensive when he replied, and it sent shivers down William's spine.

"And then we have some more fun."

22

A Night to Remember

Telnis leaned forward in his chair and rubbed his temples. Freshly melted wax trickled down the side of the candle on his desk while the clock on his mantelpiece ticked on at the same relentless pace it always did. It was not especially late, but his wife had gone to bed early and left him to his research. Even his child had fallen fast asleep, leaving him the only one awake. Though, perhaps "awake" would have been too strong a word to use. His eyes may have been open, but his brain felt dead.

It had been weeks since he slept well, and the importance of the case before him left little prospect of that changing anytime soon. He could not afford beauty sleep while Brinwin Zikennig ran amok, doing who knew what. Nothing had been heard of the scoundrel in days, and even the adjudicator sent to track him had failed to turn in a report that evening. Things had been silent. Too silent. Just thinking about it made his stomach turn. Or perhaps it was the tea.

His wife had brewed him his favorite tea for dinner, which was not a simple process. Even if it had not been his favorite beverage, he would have felt obligated to drink it out of sheer appreciation for his spouse. But, alas, she was just as exhausted as he was, and something about the drink tasted a little off. But far be it from him to let that thwart his wife's sacrifice.

His stomach gurgled in protest for the dozenth time and forced out a belch. Telnis groaned and stared at the bottom of his empty mug. "I suppose that's what's got you upset, hmm?" he asked himself. His stomach growled an unhappy response back at him. Rising from his seat, he went to retrieve his coat. Perhaps some fresh air would do him some good, he thought. He shook his head and muttered as he went, "Good grief! What was in that tea?"

Before he made it to the other side of the room, the fireplace abruptly flickered out. Darkness filled the room, and a fine-grained voice rose from its depths. "An excellent question, Inquestor Raiko." The fireplace flashed back to life but failed to quell the panic that shot through Telnis. The flames blazed an unnatural purple as they revealed the hulking form of Azkalah's Best that stood to his right. He stared in shock, caught in what he assumed to be another nightmare.

Brinwin chuckled to himself and spoke with amusement. "Now that I'm actually standing here, I think this is a bit of overkill. It wouldn't do us any good to have you frightened out of your mind." With a glance at the hearth and a clap of his hands, the fireplace flickered out again before flaring back up in its natural color. "Ah, now that's better." Brinwin turned his attention back to the inquestor and offered a bow. "Good evening, Telnis."

Telnis stood dumbfounded, first in shock and then in confusion. This could not be happening, could it? Surely, the city's most wanted criminal would not just up and reveal himself in the middle of an inquestor's home.

As if in response to his thoughts, Brinwin spoke up to reassure him. "Yes, this is actually happening. You aren't sleeping. Though it looks like you could use it."

The clock ticked on behind him until the reality of the situation finally registered with Telnis. His mind sprang into action with a start, and he concentrated all his effort on blinding his opponent with his magic. Yet, despite his efforts, nothing happened. For the first time since attending the Mages College, he could not access the Eldanu.

Stuck without his magic, a tidal wave of panic threatened to overwhelm him. He cast his gaze for anything he could use as a weapon.

Brinwin stepped forward but kept himself out of arm's reach. "Don't bother. I spiked your tea with Virilium extract. It'll be another twenty minutes at least until you can use your magic again, and I think we both know how a battle of arms will end."

Telnis assessed the behemoth of the man before him, and he grappled with the hopelessness of the situation. He would die there in his own home, murdered in cold blood while his wife and child slept. The least he could do was face his death without cowardice. "If you're here to kill me, then get it over with," he said.

"Kill you?" Brinwin exclaimed in dismay. "Beacon's light, no! I'd rather cut my own hand off!"

Telnis blinked. "Then... what are you doing here?"

Brinwin smiled and folded his hands behind his back. "I'm here to pay my respects." He turned and paced to the fireplace, where he stared into the flames. "You see, Telnis, I've taken on a contract that, frankly, I don't expect to survive. This may very well be the last you ever see of me, and I've been meaning for a while to tell you just how impressed I am with you."

Telnis's brow furrowed in confusion. "You're here to compliment me?"

"Yes, that's right. A little slow on the uptake, but then again, I did drug you."

A sudden realization hit Telnis. "Did you also drug my family?"

"Indeed I did," he confirmed with a nod. "I didn't want any interruptions... those can get complicated. But don't worry. I made sure their sleep is a restful one. They'll wake up the most refreshed they've felt in weeks, judging by the circles under their eyes. You know, you really should find a way to reduce the stress in your life before it kills you."

Telnis crossed his arms and shrugged. "A little difficult to do when you and your friends cause so much trouble in this city."

"My dear inquestor," Brinwin replied, "there will never be a shortage of crime on these streets so long as men are permitted to walk on them.

If you won't rest until it's all eradicated, then you will simply never rest. And after you've run yourself into the ground, the city will have one less man able to do something about it. Take my advice, and just be content to do your part with a decent day's work."

"I'm sorry, since when did you start offering life advice to law enforcement?" Telnis demanded.

Brinwin laughed as he turned from the fireplace. "I only offer it to you, Telnis. I'd hate to see you burn out before your time."

"Oh? And why is that? I *am* trying to arrest you, if you haven't forgotten."

"Because you're a good man. Truth be told, this city needs more people like you — men who actually believe in the ideals of their service and don't abandon them even when everyone else does. It's something I envy about you, actually, how you manage to stay loyal to an organization that's the epitome of hypocrisy. I never had it in me."

Telnis inched his way toward his desk as Brinwin talked, hoping against hope he had left his amulet inside one of its drawers. He may have been deprived of his magic, but perhaps he could send a distress signal. If he could just keep his unexpected visitor distracted, maybe he could pull it off.

"Yes... I recall you once served with the Keepers of Alchemy, didn't you? Until things went a little sour."

Brinwin smiled as if he knew precisely what the inquestor was attempting to do. "Smart man. I see you've done your research. It's a pity I'm not much of a biographer, as that would be quite the story to tell. But I'm afraid I'm short on time."

As if on cue, the clock on the mantelpiece struck a new hour and filled the house with its chiming.

"That tea's going to wear off soon, and we'll have quite the evening ahead of us. But before I go, let me just say this: Keep up the good work. With your character and talent, I can already see you'll become an important person. Just don't forget to rest when you can." Brinwin approached a window beside Telnis and slid it open. "I suppose I owe you a favor for all the headaches I've caused you in the past. Before I say farewell, do you have any questions for me about our past encounters? Any at all?"

Telnis scratched his head, dumbfounded. Here was the opportunity of a lifetime dropped in front of him, and now his brain pulled a complete blank! All he could do was stand there speechless with his mouth slightly gaping.

Brinwin chuckled. "I understand. I truly am sorry for drugging you, but it was the best option. Please be more careful in the future about what you drink — it was far too easy for me to do. Perhaps a taste tester would be a good idea..." Brinwin trailed off, then shook his head. "Anyway. Farewell, Inquestor. I wish you all the best." He then hopped onto the window sill and prepared himself to jump.

"Brinwin, wait!" Telnis called.

Brinwin turned and raised an eyebrow. "Yes, Telnis?"

The inquestor paused, then dropped his voice to a murmur. "At the Vetelis Fair... was that actually you in a dress?"

Brinwin grinned as he met Telnis's gaze for the final time. "Guilty as charged." With a snap of his fingers, the fireplace flickered out once more. When it blazed to life moments later, Brinwin had vanished, and the window had been pulled back down. The room looked exactly as it did before as if nothing had happened.

Inquestor Raiko paused a moment longer as he processed everything that had transpired. He did not know what to make of it. He just hoped Brinwin was ready for the chase of his life because that's what he was about to get. He rummaged through his desk drawers until he found his amulet, and with no further hesitation, he sounded the alarm.

* * *

Brinwin landed from his jump and trotted to the edge of the road. William and Zala waited for him in the shadows, saying nothing until he reached them. "Dare I ask what that was all about?" William asked.

"Had to catch up with an acquaintance of mine and arrange some business for tonight."

"And what business is this?" asked Zala. She made little effort to conceal the irritation in her voice.

"If I told you beforehand, you'd have never come. Just stay by my side and do as I tell you, and you'll be fine."

Brinwin knelt and placed a cube-like contraption onto the green center line that ran through the road. With the push of a button, the machine began to hum. The humming intensified until he pressed a second button and a discharge of raw energy shot into the ground. The center line crackled with an overload of power and then fell dim as far as the eye could see.

Zala gasped in dismay. "Brinwin... what have you done?"

"Making it a fair chase," he said as he straightened up. He stared into the sky and breathed in the crisp evening air. He stood content and relaxed, much as one would while on vacation in a beautiful park.

"Brinwin? What are you doing?" asked William in confusion.

Brinwin stretched as he exhaled. "It really is a beautiful night, Wil-yim. I've always found it best to relish the calm before the storm. No good in getting anxious *before* your troubles begin."

William cast a nervous glance behind him. "What do you mean, troubles?"

"As in, Inquestor Raiko's alarm will have reached the Council of Inquest any moment now, and the entire city will pursue us for the chase of our lives."

William and Zala's mouths dropped. "And why would you have done that?" William challenged. Fury rose within him at how difficult this would make his efforts to rendezvous with his crew. What good would having shadesteel be if he could never leave port?

Before Brinwin could answer, the pealing of alarm bells broke out from the city center. Within seconds, smaller bells clinked through the streets, and the lights inside many buildings flared to life. Urgent shouts soon filled the air and collided with each other, and the clattering of armored boots on pavement rang out in the distance.

Brinwin smiled and winked at William. "For fun." He then sprinted straight ahead toward the chaos. William and Zala exchanged mortified glances, then followed suit as much as their adrenaline would allow. They raced together side by side, yet were unable to match Brinwin's pace. A line of enforcers blocked the road ahead, each brandishing poleaxes as large as themselves.

"Hurry up, you two!" Brinwin called back. "We can't afford to dawdle."

Zala refused to be scolded. "You have longer legs than us, numb-skull!" she shouted.

"Then get longer legs!" Brinwin called back before he drew his longsword and barreled into the enforcers with an ear-splitting roar. For all their brawn, nothing could have prepared them for the ferocity with which he unleashed his blows. Two of the men fell in seconds before the remaining ones dove for cover. Zala spread her arms toward them, and spheres of thick darkness settled over their heads. They stumbled off in a blind panic as a fresh wave of enforcers rushed forward to replace them.

"This is madness, Brinwin!" William yelled. "We'll never clear them all!"

Even the side streets and alleyways around them filled with enforcers, dozens upon dozens of them.

"Nonsense! Let them come!" Brinwin roared back. He stood his ground as the horde descended on them, waiting until they were only a few yards away. He then swung around and clapped his hands over William's eyes. "Now, Zala!" he breathed in a hush. No sooner had he buried his face into his arm than the air flashed about them with a blinding light. Even with his eyes covered, William winced at the intensity that seared his eyes. It felt as if he had stared at the sun for several seconds.

As much as his eyes hurt, his ears hurt even more when their pursuers collided with each other in their blindness. A cacophony of clangs, scuffles, and shouts of pain rang out as they trampled themselves onto the pavement. "Come on!" Brinwin shouted as he clambered over them and yanked William and Zala forward.

The last remnants of the usual night traffic cleared the streets as they fled, most finding refuge indoors. Those left in the streets participated in the manhunt, both officials and vigilantes alike. More than one met their end after getting too close to the escaping trio as they sprinted toward the city center.

After rounding the corner of an intersection, a volley of arrows whizzed past William's shoulder and nearly sank themselves into Brinwin's backside.

"Arrows!" cried Zala as she yanked the others in her direction.

"I heard them!" Brinwin yelled back. He stopped at the entrance of a culvert just long enough to kick in the grating that covered it. "This way!" he called as he slid feet-first through the opening. William and Zala ignored the stench that rose toward them and dove in after him just in time to avoid a fresh volley of arrows.

They fell a short distance before landing in a slime-covered cesspool that rose to their shins. No sooner had they found their footing than Brinwin led the way onward with a glowing vial in his hand for a lamp. They carried on slowly at first, the passage too cramped to fully stand, but soon it emptied into a tunnel just tall enough for them to stand at full height. William could not tell whether it smelled worse than the *Kumuzhkan's* lair, but by that point, it did not matter. He was again running for his life in a cold, stinking tunnel, and he hated it. God help him, he'd never set foot beneath the ground again if he survived this nightmare.

The tunnel increased in both size and stench as they went, with an increasing number of sewer lines emptying themselves into the passage they traveled along.

"I really hope you know where we're going," said Zala before nearly gagging.

The confidence in Brinwin's reply was about the only positive thing going for them. "As a matter of fact, I do." He paused and scrutinized the sides of the tunnel. "We don't have much farther to go. Just another fifteen minutes or so—"

The racing of footsteps behind them cut Brinwin off mid-sentence. The others turned in time to see the razor point of an icicle flying through the tunnel toward Brinwin's side. Zala unleashed a stream of flames from her hands to melt the projectile before it found its mark. Nothing but a splash of tepid water reached Brinwin's tunic to draw his attention to the oncoming threat. "Blast it!" he cursed. "They weren't supposed to reach us this quickly."

A further barrage of icicles flew from the arriving pursuers, forcing them to duck. Zala gained her footing first and launched a flaming salvo at their attackers. Brinwin followed up with a fistful of small vials that exploded on impact. A pause ensued as the smoke cleared, and William thought that perhaps their pursuers had been deterred.

Such hopes were dashed when a purple bolt of energy flew through the air and struck the ground beside him. The impact shattered the stones beneath his feet and knocked him backward into the air. He landed with a splash into the passing stream of sewage as another beam of energy flashed overhead and struck the ceiling above him. Before he could rise to his feet, Brinwin scooped him into his arms and fled with all his might. Zala followed behind them, casting intermittent fireballs behind her as she ran.

"Chaos magic? These guys aren't fooling around!" she panted.

A third blast of energy nearly knocked her off her feet before Brinwin yelled back, "Just drop it, Zala! Stop with the fire and run!"

Zala followed his instructions without another word, and the three of them fled farther into the depths of the sewers. Every corner they rounded gave a few seconds of respite from incoming projectiles, and the sound of pursuing footsteps grew distant. Yet even after the sound of pursuit had dropped off completely, they dared not slow their pace. They kept running until the tunnel opened into a spacious, rectangular chamber. Strange markings covered the walls, some etched directly into the stone and others written in a green chalky material.

Brinwin sighed in relief. "Finally! We've just about made it. Our exit should be somewhere right around here..." He ran his hands along the wall and followed a trail that apparently only he could see. He had gone about twenty paces when the walls reverberated with a spine-chilling echo. Brinwin stopped in his tracks and strained his eyes into the darkness beyond him. He shook the vial he held to increase its brightness, motioning for Zala and William to stay back. For a few tense moments, they heard nothing but the rushing flow of sewage beneath them.

The darkness beyond them then shifted as a shadow loomed in the distance. The shadow grew as it shuffled toward them, and the walls rang out with a gurgling growl. Brinwin's sword flew from its sheath not a moment too soon as the mangled hand of a monster tore at his face from the edge of the darkness, its talons dripping with raw sewage. Brinwin lurched backward to avoid the strike, then followed with a well-aimed thrust at the monster's hand. The blade found its mark, but to no avail, as it lodged itself in the armored hide of the creature that stepped into view.

Never had William seen a nightmare more hideous than what he now stared at in horror. It stood an amalgamation of rotting flesh and iron bone, with bloodshot eyes whose gaze wandered around the chamber. Its frame was thick and sturdy like a rhinoceros, but it shambled about as an ape when it moved. Everything about the creature, from its appearance to its mannerisms, felt inexplicably unnatural, and the speed with which it moved caught everyone off guard.

For all his experience with horrifying creatures, even Brinwin stood petrified in shock. Had Zala not recovered herself first and knocked the monster backward with a ball of fire, it would have made quick work of an easy target. The flames, however, only made their problems worse by angering the creature even further. It unleashed a howl of pain and fell upon them with renewed fury, its skin flaming as the spawn of hell.

Things quickly degenerated into a free-for-all as everyone dodged about on the verge of panic. Claws flew out and weapons slashed back in a blur of motion, one person ducking and another weaving. Time lost its grip in the thick of the chaos as moments felt like minutes and minutes felt like moments. At one point, Zala found herself backed into a corner at the same time Brinwin lay pinned on his back, exerting every ounce of strength he had to keep the talons above him from sinking into his chest.

William glanced at the chamber's entrance and spun a plan on the spur of the moment. He wrapped his hand around the throwing knife secured to his thigh before maneuvering himself to the front of the creature. Inhaling deeply, he took aim. After exhaling, he let loose the weapon straight toward the creature's eyes. The knife missed its target only slightly and buried itself into the beast's nostrils, causing it to release its grip on Brinwin with a fresh screech of pain. It then looked up and trained all three of its eyes squarely on William.

It was too late to reconsider his plan, so William made the most of it. He turned and fled toward the entrance, fully expecting it to chase him down. What he did not expect was the purple beam of energy that flew straight at him and forced him to duck before he reached his destination.

The beam hit the monster squarely in the groin and knocked it a step backward. If looks could kill, all ten inquestors that stepped into the room would have been slain on the spot by the fully enraged beast. It let loose its loudest roar yet and stampeded toward them. William dove out of the way, but looked up in time to see the inquestors flee in terror back through the tunnels. The beast charged after them, and soon the chamber was left in silence once more.

Brinwin, Zala, and William all sat in shock. No one stirred for several minutes, each processing in their own way the horrors they had just survived. Zala sat with her head between her knees, stifling back the tears that welled in her eyes. William and Brinwin sat staring into the distance as they trembled. Eventually, Brinwin mustered the strength to stand and look upon his companions.

"Well... I guess that works," he said with a feeble laugh that failed to amuse anyone. He then moved toward William and Zala and cleared his throat. "We'd better get moving before that thing makes its way back here." He offered his hand to Zala and helped her to her feet.

William stood on his own and glared at Brinwin. "How much more of this insanity do we have left?" he demanded. "I don't think we can handle another encounter like this, Brinwin."

Brinwin sighed. "I am sorry, Wil-yim. And you too, Zala. I didn't expect things to go so horribly down here," he said. "I've scouted these tunnels dozens of times. Not once have I seen anything like that. Once we get above ground, there shouldn't be any more surprises."

"And how long until we get above ground?" William asked.

Brinwin glanced around the chamber with a faint smile. "Forty seconds if my explosives work as they should."

Zala laid a reassuring hand on William's shoulder. "Which means it'll be forty seconds," she said with a gleam of hope in her eyes. She understood just how badly he wanted to be aboveground and could not blame him in the slightest. She just wished she could have offered him more comfort in the meantime.

William forced a smile and braced himself. "Right," he said. "Well, let's get on with it. I'm tired of this stinking cesspit." Brinwin nodded and strode over to the strange markings on the wall. He ran his hand along its edge until he stopped and tapped the stones above him with his knuckles. Satisfied with whatever result he was looking for, he retrieved a small cube from his pocket. He flicked back an opening to the contraption, then poured a tiny vial of blue liquid into it. He shut the cube again before shaking it firmly. He stuck it to the ceiling above him and stepped back to join the others. "Now stand back," he instructed, "and cover your ears."

William knew enough to take Brinwin's command seriously. He plugged his ears and, for good measure, covered his eyes too. Seconds later, the ground rumbled, and a muffled explosion reached his ears. When he opened his eyes, light from the city streets filtered through the hole toward him. The closer he stepped to the opening, the more the city's light mingled with the moonlight. Taken together with the fresh evening air, it raised his spirits as little else could.

Brinwin led the way and exited the sewers first. Zala went next and offered a hand back down to William. Once back on street level, the first thing William noticed was how empty the streets were. Roads designed for crowds of hundreds lay vacant, except for small bands of patrolling enforcers and vigilantes. Guarded blockades rose high into the sky at every intersection, with spotlights that shone far too power-fully to be anything less than the result of magic.

Zala cast a camouflage enchantment to avoid detection, and the three of them ducked into a lightly patrolled alleyway. "We're close to our target," Brinwin whispered to Zala. "How long can we avoid detection with that enchantment?"

Zala shrugged in response. "For as long as we need, so long as we don't get too close to those lights."

Brinwin peeked around the corner, then turned to face Zala again. "Fair enough. Keep us covered."

They crept back onto the main street, staying huddled as they went. Zala kept her focus behind them as she projected what she saw to in front of them. They made as little noise as possible as they managed to sneak past a blockade and around a corner.

Brinwin motioned them to stop behind a formidable-looking build-ing layered with thick gray bricks. He rapped softly on one of the bricks, and to the others' surprise, it slid back and to the side. A pair of milky white eyes gazed down on them in silence. "It's time, Vestis," said Brinwin softly. "Serve their eggs sunny-side up." The eyes stared down at them until, without warning, the brick slid back into place without a sound. Brinwin then led his companions farther down the street.

"What was that all about?" asked Zala.

Brinwin did not reply until they reached another sparsely searched alleyway. "You don't honestly expect us to reach the docks with the entire city focused on catching us, do you?" he said. "We'll need a diversion."

William beat Zala to the next question. "And what diversion have you planned?"

Brinwin's eyes twinkled with a mischievous gleam. "You wouldn't know what building that was we stopped at. That's the Grand Dungeon of Elkreath. My good friend Vestis and I have spent years lacing that place with explosives—"

"You can't be serious!" Zala cut in.

"Why not?" Brinwin replied. "The Council was able to catch them once. Surely they can do it again..."

Before he could say more, a series of explosions rang out from behind them. William glanced over his shoulder to see the dungeon engulfed in flame, with gaping holes strewn throughout. Chunks of stone flew in all directions, leaving craters in whatever was unlucky enough to be struck by them. In the course of a few minutes, dark and bloodstained figures rose from the ruins and leaped out onto the streets. Many organized into gangs, while others fled alone into the night.

Brinwin pulled his companions to the side of a tower that soared above the city's skyline. He reached up and gripped the rungs of a ladder built into the structure's side. "Best not to be on the streets right now," he said. "Follow me." He began his ascent up the ladder, and the others wasted no time following behind.

Though William was not necessarily *afraid* of heights, he was still uncomfortable with the concept as he pulled himself further into the reaches of the night sky. He knew better than to look down, so he fastened his gaze on Zala as she climbed above him. Covered in sewage as she was, she was still a better view than any of the alternatives. Surprisingly, the stench was bearable enough. Whether this was due to the length of exposure to it or the urgency of the situation at hand, such concerns shrunk in relevance as the once-distant peak of the tower loomed closer into view.

For a brief moment, William experienced a sense of relief when his boots were once more planted on a level surface. Zala smiled to see him at ease, even if such ease lasted for just a moment. He returned the smile as Brinwin hurried to a chimney and knelt at its base.

It took a couple of minutes for Brinwin to pry open a hidden hatchway and retrieve a cache of bundled equipment from its depths, but when he turned to address his cohorts, Zala and William still stood gazing at each other. Brinwin cleared his throat. "If you two are done having a moment, we need to keep moving." They both gave him an evil eye as he divvied the equipment between them and shoved it into their arms.

"You two lovebirds will have plenty of time to ogle each other soon enough," he said with annoyance. "We're almost at the end of our adventure for tonight, so I need you to focus. In each of your bundles, you will find a green potion. We'll be traveling by rooftop for a while, and you'll need the potion to make that possible. Now would be a good time to drink it."

Zala set straight to work digging through her bundle while William paused and furrowed his brow. "Pardon the skepticism," he said, "but every potion of yours I've had to drink so far has both knocked me out *and* tasted terrible. What exactly is this supposed to do to me?"

Brinwin narrowed his eyes in further annoyance. "It's a bottle of Caecilian Brew. It lets you jump."

William raised his eyebrows. "Jump?"

Brinwin rolled his eyes and gave an exasperated huff. "Beacon's light! Yes, that's what I said. Do you outsiders just have bad hearing, or do you always ask stupid questions?" At this, Zala shot Brinwin a look that could have curdled milk. He then checked himself and returned to his customary detached tone. "Caecilian Brew lets one jump many times farther than normal and cushions the impact of such jumps."

William squinted. "And what does it taste like? Frog legs?"

Brinwin bit his tongue. *If only,* he thought. "No, Wil-yim. It tastes quite sweet, actually."

Zala unearthed her bottle and downed it with a swig. A look of pleasant surprise spread across her face. "He's right," she said with a smack of her lips. "It tastes like fruit, almost."

William retrieved the potion from his bag and eyed it warily, but after another glance at Zala, he willed himself to consume its contents. Not that he would ever admit it to Brinwin, but it *did* taste sweet. Had he known what a watermelon was, he would have likened the taste as similar. He flashed a smile at Zala before he caught himself and wrinkled his nose. "Eh...I've tasted better."

Zala rolled her eyes. Brinwin ignored the comment and downed his vial. "Now then. Let's be off," he said as he slung his share of the equipment over his shoulders. With a running start, he leaped off the building's edge and soared dozens of feet into the air. He then landed on the nearest roof as effortlessly as a cat. Had William not seen it with his own eyes, he would have struggled to believe it. He hesitated as he felt torn between bravado and fear. Should he jump next, or should he let Zala do it?

Zala sensed his dilemma and offered him a nudge. "Come on, William," she said. "It'll be fun! Why don't you go first?"

William nodded. *Right then,* he thought. *Bravado it is.* He focused on the roof next to him and tightened his grip on the bundle he shouldered. A final deep breath, and off he went as Brinwin had. His instincts screamed in protest as the edge of the building rushed closer, but he sprinted on anyway. The urge to look down was tempting, but he kept his gaze steady as he crouched his legs and leaped with all his might.

He shot into the air as if a puppeteer had yanked him upward with an invisible string only to guide his way back down with the grace of a master. When he landed beside Brinwin safe and sound without even a smidgen of pain, he gasped in disbelief and stared at his legs, half certain it had all been a dream. He would have stared much longer had Zala not bounded into him with a crash from behind. They both nearly fell to their faces but recovered their balance at the last second. Zala muttered a curse, then gave William a sheepish shrug. "Sorry about that! I've never tried this potion before. It takes a little getting used to..."

"I don't know," Brinwin quipped with a mischievous grin. "Even the outsider got the hang of it on the first try."

"No one asked for your opinion!" she retorted as she dusted herself off. The others waited for her to collect herself before Brinwin led them onward. Their nerves were tense, and they spoke little among themselves as they leaped from one rooftop to the next. Even if they had wanted to talk, the commotion on the streets below would have made hearing difficult. The noise of intense conflict could be heard across the city as every effort of the Elkreath guard turned toward containing the jailbreak. To add further confusion to the chaos, a number of buildings exploded at random and burst into flames, each sounding like the blast of a cannon.

William glanced down to see a group of citizens flee from a burning building, only to find themselves caught in the middle of a fight between law enforcement and a gang of fugitives. Their screams cut deeply into his soul, and he shook his head in dismay as he jumped forward. Brinwin had gone too far. This was not a diversion — this was an act of terror.

When will this nightmare end? William asked himself once more. Little did he know that Brinwin was asking himself the same question at that very moment. A single tear trickled unseen from both their faces before Brinwin stopped at the center of a circular rooftop. He pointed east toward the open waters of Glimmerstone Bay. A single building rose above the rest, and Zala recognized it immediately. "This is it, friends," Brinwin said. "One final errand on that rooftop, and we'll be out of here."

Zala looked ready to strangle her brother.

"Absolutely not!" she protested with a hiss. "You're not taking us to their *literal* doorstep! I refuse!"

Brinwin's eyes narrowed, and his voice dropped to a low rumble. "We've come too far to back out now. If we don't stay together, then we perish."

Zala cut Brinwin off with a curse. The redness of her face rivaled that of her hair as she scolded him. "If we follow you, we'll perish! Whatever business you have on their *roof,* you can finish by yourself, and we'll wait for you."

Brinwin's demeanor darkened. "I'm not asking you again, Zala. Not when we're this close," he replied with an ominous growl.

William's insides lurched in fear. Things had soured quickly, and he did not know why. What he *did* know was that open conflict between the brother and sister could only end in disaster. A sense of urgency coiled about him. Time was short, and the longer they argued with each other, the worse their chances of survival were.

Without time to think, he opened his mouth and spoke with

split-second reactions to instinct. "We need to go with him, Zala," he said. Zala's eyes bulged in shock, then glared at him as he continued. "Neither of us asked for this, but like it or not, the whole city's after us. He's the only one with a plan right now, and we've made it this far. I may want to strangle him too, but he's the best chance we've got right now."

She stared at him with an intensity that could have pierced bone, but he held her gaze firm. Tension gathered in the air between them until she grumbled at last, "Fine." She turned and strode forward with her back to William. With a final glare at Brinwin, she leaped off the building without another word.

Brinwin saw the anger in William's eyes, and he knew better than to patronize him with his thanks. "For what it's worth," he said, "you're the only other man to survive that look from her. I see why she likes you." William shook his head in disgust and followed after Zala with a jump. Brinwin shrugged before catching up to the others with a single bound.

A series of spikes surrounded the summit of the Council of Inquest's headquarters to ward off any ambitious climbers. Fortunately for Brinwin and his companions, they were not climbing. They avoided the spikes with ease and landed securely on the open roof. A few small pillars rose intermittently across the area, but they proved easy enough to avoid. Brinwin made his way to the center of the roof before he whipped out a cylindrical contraption and tinkered with it.

"How long is this going to take?" Zala called out. "I have a really bad feeling about this."

"As well you should, lass," came the frigid voice of Tilthrir Frostmane from behind them. With a burst of speed, he struck Zala with the pommel of his sword and knocked her to the ground in a daze. He held his sword above her head and motioned for William to stay put. He then turned slightly to face Brinwin while still keeping a watchful eye on William.

"I have to hand it to you, Brinwin Zikennig," he said. "You are a ballsy pile of *gunnuh*. All these years of coming after you, and now you come straight to us. To what do we owe the pleasure of this surprise?"

Brinwin continued to fuss with his device without even lifting his head in response. "You'll see in a couple of minutes if you idiots just leave me the hell alone," he muttered loudly enough to be heard.

Tilthrir raised his hand and disposed of any last vestiges of banter. "Drop the device, Brinwin. This is your last chance to surrender peacefully." Brinwin remained hunched over his contraption and continued tinkering with it as if no one were with him.

Tilthrir stared on for only a couple moments longer. "So be it," he muttered as he struck Zala down with his pommel again, then raised his sword and charged forward. Brinwin scooped up his device and dove to the side while William dashed toward Zala. Brinwin's sword flew forth as ferocious as ever, but it found its equal in Tilthrir's swordsmanship.

While they exchanged blows, William attended to Zala's injuries. She stirred in and out of consciousness as he sought to quell the flow of blood from her head. He had just managed to staunch the bleeding when he heard a sword clatter to the ground. He turned to see Tilthrir knocked to his knees, disarmed.

Before Brinwin could execute his final blow, Tilthrir opened the palms of both hands and unleashed a torrent of wind from them. Brinwin flew backward and slammed against a pillar as Tilthrir rose to his feet and continued to direct a stream of wind in their direction. William gazed at Brinwin in panic when he began to slide backward himself.

"Your legs, Wil-yim! Grip with your legs!" called Brinwin as he wrapped his legs around the pillar behind him and clung for dear life. William grabbed hold of Zala and followed Brinwin's example as the winds bore down on him. Despite his fears, the strength remaining from the Caecilian Brew proved enough to withstand the force of Tilthrir's storm.

A nearby building exploded with a gigantic boom, and the screams of more displaced refugees rose to their ears soon after. Tilthrir scowled and ceased the use of his magic. The flames from the mayhem below illuminated his face, accentuating the fury that burned beneath it. "I've had enough of this!" he rasped.

A hatchway in the rooftop opened up as he spoke, and a group of inquestors ascended into view. Leading the formation was Telnis Raiko. "We made it, sir!" he shouted with a salute. "We're ready to take them into custody."

"That won't be necessary, Raiko," Tilthrir grunted. "I'm finishing this." He stretched forth his hands toward Brinwin and the others. At first, nothing seemed to happen. Then, the faint outlines of spheres surrounded the heads of William, Brinwin, and Zala. They fell to their knees and clutched their throats, unable to breathe.

Telnis's eyes widened in dismay. "But sir!" he spoke up. "Suffocation spheres are only authorized for public executions after a due trial. This is illegal!"

"Look around you, Telnis!" Tilthrir snapped. "Our city's on fire, and public order is all but gone! Now isn't the time for formalities! They're too dangerous to be kept alive."

Telnis gazed on in dismay as the three fugitives suffocated before him. His conscience screamed that this was unjust, but he was in no position to intervene. He resigned himself to fate and looked on in shame.

Perhaps it was from the angle he stood at, but only he seemed to notice when Brinwin slipped his hand into his pocket. The faintest sparkle of a glowing blue stone hid behind his clenched fist as he withdrew it. Telnis could have drawn attention to it, but something within prompted him to silence. Perhaps whatever followed would be fate's attempt at balancing the scales of justice. He watched on in curiosity and held his breath for something to happen.

He gasped when that something proved to be a bolt of blue energy that blasted itself into Tilthrir's chest. In the blink of an eye, it reduced his boss to nothing but a pile of ashes. It also released a shock wave that knocked the perimeter spikes and the remaining inquestors over the edge of the building. Only Telnis was fortunate enough to catch a grip on the building's brink. He hung by both hands, straining with all his might to keep his hold.

Brinwin and the others wheezed for air as the spheres dissolved from around their heads. Once their strength had returned, Brinwin barred the hatchway shut and returned to working on his contraption. "Wil-yim!" he called out. "Inside your bundles are what we need to get off this building."

"Can't we just jump?" William called back.

"No!" Brinwin shouted. "There isn't a Caecilian Brew strong enough to let you survive that fall. You won't reach the water, either."

William nodded and fumbled through his bag. He eventually freed a bulky contraption from its confinement. "What is it?" he called out as he examined it with his hands. Whatever it was, it was large, and it consisted of a metal frame covered with a durable black cloth.

"It's an Essari invention," Brinwin replied. "They call it a wind glider. I'll show you how to use it in just a few moments."

With a final few twists and turns, he set his cylindrical contraption down on the center of the rooftop. "All set," he said. He turned around with a smile, but his smile faded as he glanced to the side of William. "How is Zala doing?" he asked.

"I'll live," she responded weakly. She tottered to her feet, and William helped her recover her balance. "Just need a minute," she groaned. William released his grip to allow her to stand on her own. She faltered at first but gained some strength the longer she stood.

William then heard a sound from the edge of the building. He drew cautiously toward it to find Inquestor Raiko hanging on for dear life. Their eyes met, and Telnis froze in fear. William weighed his options as he gazed down on the helpless form before him. Given the chance, this man would either arrest them all on the spot or try to kill them, more likely. If he wanted to escape this nightmare, reason held he should either ignore the man or help send him on his way.

Yet the screams from below reminded William of the needless bloodshed that had already transpired. So many lives extinguished for no good reason he could see. This inquestor probably had a family and was just trying to do his job. William looked closer, and he saw the same desperation in the man's eyes that he felt himself back in the Mist —

the hopelessness of leaving behind a child he could no longer care for. *Yes*, he realized. *This man was a father.* Like him.

He reached down his hand and grabbed the man's arm. With great effort, he heaved him back up to the safety of the rooftop.

"Are you alright?" William asked him.

Telnis looked at him with surprise. "Yes... but why did you—"

He never finished his sentence, for William brought the sheath of his sword down upon the inquestor's head and knocked him out cold.

"Good," said William. "I'm sorry about that, friend, but we can't have you arresting us. You can just take a nice nap here and wait for your friends to fetch you. Fair enough?" He paused for the courtesy of a reply, and finding none, he shrugged and then rejoined the others.

Zala stood ready with the wind glider on her back, and Brinwin had fastened on his as well. It took but a minute longer to equip William with a glider and instruct him how to release himself when required. "Alright then. We're finally ready for our getaway," said Brinwin. He scanned the horizon of the open bay and pointed his finger into its depths. "Over there. Do you see that green light?" William and Zala nodded. "That's our target. It's attached to a ship manned by the best wind mages money can hire. We make it to that ship, and we'll be out of here before you know it. You do know how to swim, right?" William and Zala looked at each other with apprehension, then nodded again. "Good," said Brinwin with a smile.

The barred hatchway behind them began to pound from the other side, and the sound of splintering wood reached their ears. Brinwin turned to look back, then shrugged. "No time like the present, I suppose. Let's get going."

The three of them took off with a running start, and with a final leap, they soared into the night sky. By the time the hatchway erupted into a shower of debris, only the faint silhouettes of the wind gliders' wings could be seen hovering over the bay.

The rushing air upon his face invigorated William, and he relished the feeling of weightlessness as the city fell farther behind them. Even the coldness of the water was a welcome relief when they splashed down in the middle of Glimmerstone Bay. The filth of the sewers melted away from their bodies with each stroke of their paddles, cleansing them even further. In what felt like no time, they reached the vessel waiting for them. Once they had clambered on board, they draped themselves with an ample supply of dry towels.

Brinwin beckoned the others with glee to the edge of the deck after they had dried themselves off. "You won't want to miss this," he said. His hands trembled as he withdrew a small sphere and held it with anticipation as they gazed upon the City of Elkreath, lit ablaze with fire and chaos. Brinwin then raised the sphere above his head, and with a loud click, he pressed a button.

Everyone held their breath when a flare shot up from the top of the Council of Inquest's headquarters. It exploded into a dazzling array of red orbs that danced and weaved about until they aligned into the same pattern as Brinwin's tattoo. The image hung there, suspended above the city for every eye within miles to see. William wrapped his arm across Zala's shoulder while she leaned against his chest. Tears fell from Brinwin's eyes as he stood with his hands behind his back. With a hush barely heard, he bowed his head and whispered into the night, "Rest easy, Elkreath. Your debt is now paid."

23

Fairy Tales?

At Brinwin's command, the ship set sail into the darkness beyond. William and Zala remained at its edge, gazing at the turmoil of Elkreath as it sank farther into the distance. Few bothered to pursue them amid the chaos; of those that did, none could match their speed as they plowed through the waters, guided by the masterful arts of the ship's air mages.

William watched in curiosity as a team of hooded men stood beneath their sails and summoned a steady wind to propel them along. Others stood off to the side, charting the course forward with strange instruments that gleamed in the moonlight. He would have watched longer had he not felt Zala slip further into exhaustion beside him. She insisted she was fine yet could barely raise her voice above a murmur. Another minute, and he feared she would not have the strength to make it to her bed.

Against her protests, he led her below deck to her quarters, where he tucked her into a cot. Her efforts to stave off the inevitable were admirable, but the moment her head reached the pillow, she could not resist sinking deeply into the quicksand of slumber. William watched as she lay in bed, her pale and weakened form suddenly still, punctuated solely by the rise and fall of her breathing. He felt the same level of exhaustion weighing on himself, fogging his mind and burdening his muscles the longer he stood. His cabin was just a short walk away, and he knew he needed the rest desperately. Yet he still found himself unable to pull his gaze away from her.

Memories of his poor Adelaide returned unbidden, forcing his mind to rewatch the spectacle of his beloved wife as she lay on her death-bed, eyes closed and struggling to breathe. Her hair was unkempt, her skin pale, and her lips just barely parted — much as Zala's were now. A sudden pang of sorrow thrust his focus from the past to rest once more on the woman now before him: a woman so different and yet so similar to the one his soul had loved.

Emotions too complex for description filled William's heart and tangled with thoughts too incomplete to voice. From this chaos, a co-herent thought eventually coalesced.

What would I do if I could go back to that moment?

He pondered this question for untold minutes as he watched the steady rise and fall of Zala's breathing until a single ray of clarity shone through the storm within him. Fate was going to be different this time. Zala was not ill with fever. She would awake once more.

A warmth unexpected but by no means unwanted spread through his heart as he found the answer to his question. Laying a tender hand on Zala's shoulder, he stooped down and kissed her forehead. "Sleep well, milady," he whispered. "I'll see you in the morning." He then rose to spend the last of his strength scuffling off to find his own share of slumber.

Brinwin, meanwhile, remained above deck well into the night, issuing orders and consulting with the crew on the next stage of their journey. Where it would all end, William had no idea. His strength was too far spent to care anymore. Tomorrow would just have to sort itself out as far as he was concerned. He and Zala were safe for the time being, which was all that mattered. He dimmed the lamp by his bedside and closed his eyes. Sleep came quickly, and it remained unbroken as they sailed away to the south.

When William awoke the next day, it was well into the afternoon. To say he felt "sore" would have been an understatement that every muscle in his body would have objected to. A burning ache accompanied his every move, and an ever-present headache refused to forgive him for last evening's abuse. He sought to rise from bed, but the weight of his blankets felt like a cast-iron prison. No matter how hard he tried to escape them, his efforts were in vain. He relented with a final groan, and his head sank back into his pillow.

He stared at the ceiling as his mind turned onward, replaying the events that had brought him to this point. Henry, Brinwin, the Essari, Zala — they all flashed into view. Especially Zala. The more he thought about her, the less sense it made to him. By all standards of English decency, she was improper, impulsive, and insubordinate. Not that long ago, he would have characterized her as annoying, overbearing, and impudent — hardly someone he would have found appealing.

And yet, he had shared more adventures with her in just a few days than with men he had served with for years. Even with her recklessness, he had seen in her a depth of determination and honor he wished more of his soldiers back home possessed, to say nothing of her skill. He hated to admit it, but even her snarky sense of humor had grown endearing to him. And beneath her abrasive exterior, he sensed a genuine concern for the well-being of others. Her similarities to Adelaide only impressed him more the longer he thought about them.

Perhaps the most impressive similarity was that she genuinely found him... interesting. No one else except Addy had cared to know his story and spend time with him as she did. She had little need for money or title that an English noble could offer, yet for whatever reason she found him attractive, even with his lack of magic and good looks. That was the mystery he could not figure out. Why was she so interested in him?

His thoughts were interrupted when the door swung open with a creak. William tilted his head to suddenly find Brinwin peering down on him with eyes as sharp as a blade. He instinctively recoiled with a gasp and shrank back into the bed sheets. Brinwin, however, seemed oblivious to his imposing figure.

"Ah, good! You're awake," he said. "I was beginning to worry you'd never get up."

William recovered himself and crammed his eyes shut with an indignant huff. "Do you Cabalians ever sleep? How the bloody hell do you people have so much energy?" he muttered.

Brinwin shrugged his shoulders. "It helps when you're the world's best alchemist alive," he said.

William's brow furrowed. "Touché, I suppose," he mumbled back. *I can see how you got yourself in trouble with the Keepers*, he thought privately.

"Don't feel too bad about it. Even Zala slept through the morning."

At the mention of Zala, William perked his head up. "Is she awake now?" he asked.

"Oh, yes," said Brinwin with a chuckle. "If she had her way, she'd already be here hanging by your side. But she needs time to recover, so I made her stay in bed. I promised to check on you and bring her word again."

William stirred and struggled against his bed sheets with a renewed vigor. His muscles still ached, but he was determined not to let that stop him. "No need!" he said. "I'll bring her word myself." He attempted to roll out of the bed, but in his haste, he tangled himself in a fold of the blanket and tumbled onto the floor. His face flushed red as Brinwin broke out into laughter.

"Stubborn as a mule, the both of you!" he exclaimed. "No wonder you like each other."

He offered William a hand, but William squirmed and brushed him away. "No no, I'm fine, thank you." Brinwin shrugged again, then turned to exit the room.

"Suit yourself," he said. "If you absolutely must, you can visit her for a little while. But then she needs to rest. She's taken even more of a beating than you have."

William grunted an acknowledgment, then followed him to Zala's quarters. Upon entering her room, they found that she had fallen back to sleep. With a slight nod from Brinwin, William stepped carefully to her bedside for a closer view. Even upon a cursory examination, he could see the level of care Brinwin had arranged for her. She lay clothed in clean raiment, fresh bandages wrapped around her head. An array of vials and ointments lay on the table beside her, no doubt the best remedies Brinwin could offer.

William watched intently as her chest rose and fell in regular intervals. Her breathing may have been faint, but it was nonetheless stable and restful. Her eyelids fluttered lightly as one in the middle of a dream. William could have stayed with her for hours as she slept, but Brinwin soon insisted she be left to herself. With great reluctance he acquiesced, perceiving her to be in good hands and on the mend.

Taking his leave, he stepped out to the corridor between their rooms and paused in thought. He had slept for long enough, and even if he wanted more rest, his mind was far too active to afford him that. *No*, he figured, the open air and warmth of the sun would do him some good. He had yet to explore the ship, and that would keep him occupied until Zala woke.

His mind thus determined, he ascended the stairs to the main deck. He went slowly at first, stopping to lean against the walls from time to time until enough of his strength had returned. Crisp ocean air filled his lungs with each step he took, invigorating him such that when he reached the top of the stairway, he could stand without aid.

A smile spread across his face as a view of the open sea greeted him, bright shades of blue stretching above and beyond him as far as the eye could see. The sun shone upon him in full glory from a cloudless sky, its rays beaming with a warmth no blanket could ever match. Seagulls squawked above and competed with the waves below to see which could make the most noise as he approached the ship's edge.

William leaned against the deck's railing to take in the view, then closed his eyes and breathed deeply. The soreness of his muscles slipped to the background of his mind, and for a precious few moments, his headache ceased throbbing. When he opened his eyes, his mind felt clear, ready to explore his new surroundings.

At a closer look, a faint outline of land could be seen far in the distance. One could only assume they followed the coastline of Cabalia, but in which direction was not immediately clear. There were no other ships in sight, which he took for a blessing. With all the events of last night, he was more than willing to keep a distance from any other group of Cabalians. Perhaps Brinwin planned to lay low for a few days until it was safe for them to smuggle William and his crew out of Cabalia. With Elkreath in disarray, he was certain his ship would not be leaving any time soon. He would have to ask Brinwin about it the next time he saw him. If only he had remembered earlier....

Once he had taken his fill of the view beyond, he turned to inspect the ship on which he stood. While not quite the caliber of the trade ships seen in England, it was still sturdier than any other ship he had seen. Its wood was deep brown and layered with thick grooves that branched across the deck. The vessel itself was neither large nor small and sported two robust masts. White sails hung from them, looming as clouds in the sky.

Beneath the sails stood the same teams of men from the evening prior. Their robes were gray and thick, and they fluttered in the wind as the men practiced their magic. Their hoods now hung loosely behind them, allowing the sunlight to reveal their masks. Curious things they were — William could not keep himself from staring at them. They were of an opaque gray material that resembled stone for color yet only sported the thickness of a small coin. It looked both durable and flimsy at the same time, and most surprisingly, it only covered the right half of each man's face. With such coverage, they appeared to serve poorly for the protection of life or concealment of identity. But what could their purpose be, then?

He watched as the men rotated shifts of standing beneath the sails and conjuring a steady stream of wind into them. Some held their arms out toward the sails, while others kept their hands fastened to their sides. A couple let their hands hang loosely, even using them to scratch an occasional itch as they kept the stream unbroken. There seemed no rhyme or reason to their postures, and William eventually gave up trying to figure it out.

He strode toward them, but they paid no heed as he drew close. Even after he called a greeting to them, he received nothing but a darting glance from those beneath the sails. Those in the shifts not actively channeling wind glared at him, their eyes and lips drawn tight. The halfmasks did little to hide the disdain that emanated from behind them.

William slowed to a halt and held their gaze for just a moment longer. He could see there was no use interacting with them, and he harbored no intention of rocking the boat, so to speak. Turning back around, he explored the rest of the deck. The other crew members he encountered treated him in a similar fashion, so he spent the remaining daylight hours observing silently from a distance.

It was not until the sun began to set that Brinwin emerged from the lower deck. He stood in place as he looked about the ship, searching intently until his gaze fastened on William. With colossal strides he closed the distance between them. "Ah, there you are," he said. "I'm surprised you didn't go back to rest in your room."

William shrugged as he sat upon a barrel and gazed at Brinwin as he approached. "What can I say? We Englishmen are tougher than we look."

Brinwin stopped beside William and gazed across the waters with his hands behind his back. "Let us hope so, for your sake," he said quietly.

Nervousness quivered in William's stomach, but he brushed it aside. "Is something the matter?" he asked.

Brinwin looked at the shoreline for a moment longer before turning to face him. "No, not yet anyway. I came to tell you Zála's awake and feeling much better."

"Oh, thank heavens!" William exclaimed as he rose to his feet.

The ghost of a smirk played across Brinwin's lips. "I had a feeling you'd welcome that news."

The two of them set off across the deck as the sun continued to dip closer to the horizon. Several crew members scowled at William as they passed by, and a few even dared to glower at Brinwin before he made eye contact.

"What's put a bee in their bonnet?" William asked as they descended the flight of stairs. Brinwin sighed and said nothing until they reached the bottom of the steps.

"You, Wil-yim. You're an outsider, and Yahos help me, I'm working with you. Even the blackest criminals money can buy have enough pride for their homeland to hate you Europeans."

William grimaced. "And why don't you?" he dared to ask.

Brinwin paused as he glared down at William. "Azkalah doesn't care who you are or what you've done so long as you've paid the right price. You paid the price of contract, so that's that. Hate you or not, a deal's been struck." He sighed again as his hand clasped the handle to Zala's door. "The fault is mine for naming a price you could somehow pay."

Before William could think further about the implication of these words, the door swung silently open to reveal Zala's smiling face.

She sat upright in bed, reading from a book she held in both hands. The bandages around her head had been removed, leaving her hair to hang loosely around her as she scoured the pages in front of her. The clomp of William's first step into the room drew her attention, and her eyes lit with excitement to find him standing before her. She set down the book and drew her hair back, even as a mischievous grin spread across her face. "Well, it's about time you came to visit me!" she exclaimed tongue in cheek. "I was starting to worry Brin had thrown you overboard."

William failed to laugh as Brinwin stepped behind him with a chuckle and laid a hand on his shoulder. "An excellent suggestion, Sister. If only I'd thought of it sooner."

Zala rolled her eyes and nearly threw her book at him. "You're such a jerk!" she quipped.

Brinwin responded with a bow. "As in everything, I try my hardest."

Zala shook her head, then turned her attention back to William.

"Just ignore him," she insisted as she patted a chair by the bedside. "Come and sit for a while. If you're up for it, that is."

William's grimace swelled into a smile as deep as the sea below him. With eagerness tempered by nobility, he said: "My lady, I should like nothing better."

* * *

The evening hours passed as seconds while William and Zala talked with each other. Free at last from the cares of a life-threatening situation, they shared many a laugh as they compared their experiences together. Of such quality was the fellowship they shared that even the recollections of their grimmest moments felt somehow richer. Brinwin said nothing as the evening wore on but simply watched and waited with attentiveness as sharp as the alchemy tools by Zala's bedside.

The conversation flowed in bliss until William shared his experience with the air mages and the rest of the crew. Zala's lips drew first into a tight line, then into a scowl as he recounted their demeanor toward him and Brinwin on the way down. "They aren't worthy of the masks they wear, going on like that," she huffed with a shake of her head. "Bluehelm would have never responded that way."

William paused as he threw her a questioning look. Multiple questions floated through his mind, and it frustrated him he could only ask one at a time. "Actually, Zala," he said, "I'd been meaning to ask you about those masks. They don't look suitable for safety or disguise, so what are they for? Are they a symbol of rank?"

To this, Zala pursed her lips. "Of a sort, yes," she answered. "They're worn exclusively by mages in commemoration of Komarin Bluehelm: one of Cabalia's founders and greatest mages. As the legend goes, his helmet was broken in half like that while battling with the last of the *Ezith Baal.* Ever since the founding of the Mages College, the halfmask has been worn as a tribute to him."

William's brow remained furrowed in confusion when Brinwin nudged his sister and spoke for the first time in a while. "I don't think he knows half those terms you threw at him." Stroking his chin, he then squinted at William. "In fact, I'd wager he knows hardly anything at all about Cabalia."

Curious and somewhat embarrassed, Zala raised her eyebrows. "I suppose that's something I never thought to ask. What *do* you know of us, William?"

William felt acutely uncomfortable as both Cabalians focused their stares on him. "I... well... not much, I'm afraid," he stammered. "Your people did a good job destroying our knowledge of them when they left. Most of our books were either stolen or defaced, and people too familiar with Cabalia vanished into the night. A handful of them remained, but even the most knowledgeable of us just have summaries and scraps to guide us."

A silence ensued as they continued to scrutinize him, unsatisfied with his answer. Brinwin leaned back in his chair and pursed his lips. "Such as?" he asked.

William wiped his brow of sweat as he scrambled to gather his recollections. He shared with them the history commonly known in Europe, from the appearance of the Mist to the reappearance of the trade ships. Moving then into what only loremasters knew, he said, "We know that Cabalia is ruled by five royal families: Bluehelm, Barcbane, Tropis, Hearthfell, and Shadowcrest. We know rough details of those families, like how Shadowcrest is a dark house of thieves and assassins, and how Hearthfell is an honor-bound family of rugged warriors."

At the mention of Hearthfell, the eyes of both brother and sister lit up. Zala chuckled to herself. "So that's how they view us, is it?"

William nodded. "Yes. But beyond that, we don't know much of anything."

Zala clapped her hands together in delight. "Well, I think it's time we remedy that!" Taking up the book she had been reading earlier, she held it proudly in front of her. "This will be a great place to start. Don't you worry, William! By the time we're finished, you'll have a proper understanding of Cabalia." She opened the book to its first page, but before she could begin reading, Brinwin snatched it from her hands.

"Absolutely not," he said. "You're still recovering. The last thing you need is to stress your voice this late in the evening. You've already been talking for hours as it is."

Zala's eyes narrowed. "Fine then," she said. "You can read it instead. It'll help me fall asleep anyway."

Brinwin opened his mouth in protest but received a look that silenced even him. With a shake of his head, he settled in his seat and opened the book. He skimmed it until his eyes darted back to Zala, incredulous. "You can't be serious!" he exclaimed. "These are all legends and fairy tales!"

With a shrug of her shoulders, Zala merely reclined in bed. "They're not just fairy tales," she insisted. "But if you really can't stomach it, just read the first chapter. It's my favorite story, and every child in Cabalia has heard it. William should hear it, too. You can tell him whatever else you'd like after that."

Brinwin clenched his jaw and gave an exasperated sigh. With a final mutter under his breath, he began to read thus...

* * *

Long ago, on the other side of the sea, there once lived three brothers. The names of the brothers were Eztir, Telebor, and Galadon.

Now Eztir was the eldest and wisest of the brothers. Tall and thin, he was a man who thought much and spoke little. So great was his knowledge of the stars, his eyes even began to shine like them. People came from far and wide to ask his counsel, and they never left disappointed.

Now Telebor was the middle brother. He was a mighty hunter and a man of war. None could match his skill with a blade, and none could shoot an arrow truer than he. His heart was valiant above that of his brethren, and his courage in battle surpassed all.

Now Galadon was the youngest brother. He was also a man of war. He was the smallest of the three, but what he lacked in size, he made up for in wit. A tinkerer he was, and with his inventions he won many battles. Yet he was also a stubborn man who caused much grief in his anger.

Now in the days of these brothers, the children of men rebelled against the gods. With Galadon's aid, they sought to build a tower that would reach all the way into heaven. If they could just reach heaven, they thought, they could overcome the gods. But before they could finish the tower, the gods prevailed against them and scattered them over the face of the earth.

Fearing the wrath of the gods, the brothers fled to the West with their wives, and children, and friends. They traveled over many miles through fields, forests, and mountains until they came to the edge of the sea. "Why should we settle here, where the gods can still find us?" demanded Galadon. "Surely, there must be a way to cross the sea!" Yet as hard as they tried and as long as they thought, no one could find a way to cross the sea.

The people had nearly given up hope when Eztir finally spoke. "Wait here," he said, "and in three days, I shall find a way to cross the sea." He then disappeared into a cave, and for three days none could find him. On the fourth day, he reappeared and called everyone together with exceeding joy. "Fear not," said he, "for I now know how to cross the sea!" In his wisdom, he showed Galadon how to fashion three great ships of wood, one for each brother and their companions. He also instructed Telebor which animals to hunt to make skins for the sails. When all was ready and the ships set sail, he himself guided them with the stars above. He led the way, followed next by Telebor and then Galadon.

They traveled in peace over great distance until one day, Galadon became angry that he was last. "Come now!" he said. "I see land in the distance. Why should my brothers arrive first and take the best land for themselves?" Reasoning thus with himself, he passed by the others and gave no heed to their protests. He would have reached shore first, but his greed angered Yahos, who saw lands even the other gods could not. He sent a great storm to overtake Galadon's ship and turn it back out to sea.

When Eztir perceived the storm as the work of the gods, he refused to go forward until the storm had passed. But Telebor feared the wrath of neither God nor storm and continued to sail on. The winds beat hard upon his sails but failed to tear them, for he had saved the best skins for his own ship. And even when the waves soaked his people, their courage held fast. So it was they survived the gale and became the first to land on the shores of Cabalia. For this reason, the descendants of Telebor are known as the Edecians — *the First Ones* — even to this day.

Now when all three brothers had landed their ships, they each established a kingdom in their own name. Time went by, and the kingdoms grew into mighty realms. Peace reigned throughout the land until one day, two demons appeared. One, named Zelabaal, appeared in the east, in the lands of Telebor; the other, named Obline, appeared in the south, in the lands of Galadon. Zelabaal soon left the island when he found the inhabitants of Telebor to be pure of heart and immune to his tempting. Obline, however, found fertile soil in the hearts of Galadon. She tempted them to anger and jealousy, moving them to war against the First Ones of Telebor.

The First Ones sought the aid of Eztir but found them to have vanished from the earth in a single night. So they fought alone until the corrupted realm of Galadon had been driven from the shores of Cabalia and Obline bound in a prison deep in the earth.

Now peace reigned once more for thousands of years, until one year, a great sorcerer arose. None knew where he came from, only that he called himself Kavathos — *the Divine Warrior*. He corrupted the hearts of many, and he raised an army for himself with which he killed the last king of Telebor on the fields of combat. Having done this, he freed Obline from her prison. Darkness and terror then plagued the land as none could vanquish the demon's might.

Encouraged by the freedom of Obline, Zelabaal returned to wreak havoc on the island with his special creations: the *Ezith Baal*. These monsters — the *children of Baal* — ensured no one could defeat Obline. Even when empires from across the sea came with their legions, they too failed to free Cabalia.

Now the people despaired and toiled in darkness until one day, a mighty savior appeared with a band of heroes. Haldvar was his name — *the Mighty Conqueror*. With the might of his magic and the aid of his five companions, he drove Obline back into the depths of hell and set a seal on our domain that she could never again return. The *Ezith Baal* were hunted and slain, but Zelabaal escaped west across the sea.

Seeing the land was at peace once again, Haldvar then disappeared into the heart of the mountains to learn deep secrets of the world. Before he departed, he divided Cabalia into five kingdoms, giving each of his companions the stewardship of a kingdom until he one day returns to rule a united Cabalia.

To Komarin Bluehelm, his trusted mage, he left Cabalia's center, to guard the entrance of his sanctuary and teach the practice of his magic.

To Valdric Hearthfell, his seasoned warrior, he left Cabalia's north, to guard its regions no other people could stand to inhabit.

To Cenicus Tropis, his expert navigator, he left Cabalia's east, to guard its trade and entrance to the outside world.

To Messala Barcbane, his courageous bard, he left Cabalia's south, to guard its culture and vanquish all who still worship Obline.

To the Shadowed One, his inscrutable spy, he left Cabalia's west, to guard its most mysterious regions and observe the loyalty of the other kingdoms.

For this reason, the five kingdoms rule Cabalia: Bluehelm, Hearthfell, Tropis, Barcbane, and Shadowcrest. Long shall they rule in peace until Haldvar returns for his dominion and slays the demon Zelabaal at the end of the age.

* * *

Brinwin looked up from reading the book to find Zala fast asleep. William, however, sat wide awake, attentive to every word he heard. Brinwin marveled at the amazement he saw in the Englishman's demeanor. For a brief moment, he remembered feeling the same way when his mother read the story to him as a child. He shook his head as he closed the book. The lamp by Zala's bedside cast a gleam into his eyes that danced about as he spoke in a hushed tone.

"Now Wil-yim, you understand, of course, these are simply myths and legends we tell the children for bedtime. Half of everything I read to you didn't quite happen like that. As for the other half, I can explain that much more clearly after you get some rest." He dimmed the lamp and then directed William back to his quarters.

Before they reached their destination, William suddenly remembered the question he had meant to ask Brinwin. Standing next to the imposing giant of a man made the idea of asking about his crew seem ridiculous, but William realized it would never feel like an appropriate time to ask. He may as well ask then, even if he did feel like an idiot.

"Pardon me, Brinwin," he said. "I meant to ask you earlier, but... well, you see...I really had been intending on rendezvousing with my men back in Elkreath... especially since I gave them orders to sail back to England without me if I didn't return as expected..."

With the raise of an eyebrow, Brinwin silenced the Englishman's stammering. "Let me set your mind at ease, Wil-yim," he said. "Your crew isn't going anywhere until we're ready for them."

"They're not?" William queried.

"No. They're not," affirmed Brinwin. "I could bet you every last coin I own that the Council of Inquest had already found your ship and linked it to you before our escape last night, which means they're going to be detained at port indefinitely. Even if they wanted to leave, they couldn't."

William's heart sank in his chest. He opened his mouth to speak again, but Brinwin cut him off with a dismissive wave. "Don't worry about them, Wil-yim. Once we're all set, we'll get both you and them back on your way to England. But until then, just enjoy the ride. Understood?"

William resigned himself to silence with a reluctant nod. Brinwin's tone and body language made it clear there was nothing left to discuss. As much as he hated to be delayed even further from his return to Henry, there was nothing more he could do at the moment. He parted ways with Brinwin and traveled the remaining distance to his quarters by himself.

Once back in his room, William sought to distract himself from his disappointment by writing as much as he could remember of Brinwin's story of Cabalia in his journal. Myths or not, he was confident no one in England had ever heard these stories before. Even if no one believed the authenticity of his source, he would at least have a story to share with his child before bed. As long as he made it back home alive, that is. Try as he might, he could not shake the feeling he got from Brinwin that their worst troubles had yet to begin.

He fell asleep with great difficulty, and the few hours he slept were crowded with dreams of Cabalian fairy tales. Lost kingdoms and mighty demons waged war before him. Fire and blood, darkness and steel — they rose from the tips of mountains and sank into the ocean's waves as he towered above with a bird's eye view. Three ships sailed before him, filled to the brim with men shouting and pointing to the abyss before they sailed off the edge of the world into a void darker than night.

The last of their screams woke him with a start and nearly made him tumble out of bed. He gazed about his room in shock until he realized it had all been a dream. Gradually, his panting ceased after he sat up in bed. Beads of cold sweat lined his forehead and soaked his back, but he did not mind much. He was just glad none of it had been real. Only a nightmare, that's all.

After he had taken some time to calm himself, he changed into a fresh pair of clothes and then fell back to sleep. No further nightmares haunted him, and he did not stir until the sun had already passed the horizon.

Once awake, William grabbed a quick breakfast before heading above deck. To his delight, he found Zala awake and fully active, standing next to her brother at the forefront of the ship. They seemed involved in a heated discussion, with both of them pointing into the distance and shaking their heads at each other. The sky was overcast, and a harsh breeze made it a miserable time for everyone on board, especially for the air mages as they attempted to keep a steady course.

William bundled up in his coat and drew it close as he went to join the others. Brinwin noticed his arrival first, and the conversation immediately dwindled. "Ah, good morning," he said coldly. William glanced over to Zala to find that she appeared out of sorts. She flashed him a forced smile, then turned to face her brother directly. She muttered something too low for William to pick up before storming off below deck without saying a word to him as she passed. He considered going after her, but a strong feeling in his gut warned him against it.

"Dare I ask what's going on?" he inquired.

Brinwin shook his head. "Nothing to concern yourself with," he replied. "She'll be fine in a little while." The glint in his voice warned William not to pursue the topic any further, and he took the hint.

Stepping forward to Brinwin's side, he surveyed the area ahead of them. They were closer to shore than yesterday, and he could make out a line of cliffs that towered above them. Flocks of black birds circled above the cliffs and sounded an unusual call that William found unsettling. "Where are we?" he asked at length after staring for some time.

Brinwin did not immediately answer, but gazed on in silence a few moments longer. "Beyond those cliffs are the Plains of Olwin. According to the legends, the last king of Telebor fell to Kavathos on those fields."

They stood in silence once more as ashen waves thundered against the cliffs and fell back to the sea in billows of foam. A somberness held them both spellbound until Brinwin eventually turned toward William and spoke quietly. "Which means we're on schedule to our destination."

"Which is...?" William queried.

Brinwin turned his back to the cliffs and sauntered toward the rear of the ship. "Edomear," he said. "The capital of House Barcbane." His tone and demeanor were dismissive, but William was too eager to learn more information to let that deter him.

William kept pace and followed alongside Brinwin as he went. "Is it anything like Elkreath?" he asked.

Brinwin refused to make eye contact with him as he bent over a barrel and inspected its contents. "Not quite. You'll see when we get there."

"And how long until we get there?"

Brinwin rolled his eyes in annoyance and closed the lid of the barrel. "Two days if nothing else goes wrong."

William pursed his lips. "Brinwin, could I ask you a question?"

Brinwin finally turned to look at William, his eyes sharp and ready to skewer him alive. "What a stupid question to ask!" he blurted out. "You've already asked five, and you obviously want to ask more. Get on with it if you must."

William bit his lip and struggled to keep his cool. Were Brinwin a man of average size and skill, he would have been happy to knock some civility into him. But that was clearly not an option on the table. Swallowing his urge to lash back, he said calmly, "You said last night you'd elaborate on the real history of Cabalia. I'm not sure what's got you and Zala in such a fuss, but perhaps a change of topic would help settle your mind. I know that it sometimes does for me."

Brinwin stared at William a moment longer, evaluating him. His demeanor then softened slightly, and with a grunt he muttered, "Well, I suppose I did say that. Fine...." He reluctantly motioned for William to help himself to a barrel for a seat. He ran his hand through his hair as he gathered his thoughts, then proceeded in a much calmer tone.

"Everything about the three brothers and their kingdoms is either a complete myth or heavily based on legend. There might have been early kingdoms by those names, but it's nothing we can prove. Writing from that time is non-existent, and hardly a ruin can be found of them. There *were* people living here that predated the Founders, who called themselves the First Ones. It's also likely there was a sorcerer named Kavathos who unified the island thousands of years ago. That whole bit about Obline and Zelabaal is a stretch, but the so-called First Ones really did worship a demon named Obline. There also really were monsters known as the *Ezith Baal,* though they weren't the spawn of a demon. The *Kumuzhkan* we fought was one of their remnants. The Founders really did round up and eliminate them. Or so we thought!

"What we do know for certain is that over a thousand years ago, a powerful mage called Haldvar came from the east with the five Founders and overthrew the kingdom that then ruled the island. He really did split the island into five parts and put the Founders as the heads of their respective kingdoms. Each kingdom started with a similar structure at first, but they have changed over time. They all still officially have a king who can trace his succession back to the Founding, but not all kings hold the same authority.

"In Tropis, for example, the king is but a figurehead with no real power. All of that was delegated to the royal councils over hundreds of years. Sure, he has a fancy summer palace in Elkreath, but he's really just there to look pretty, put his seal on laws, and stay out of the councils' business.

"Barcbane, on the other hand, still has a strong monarchy. They're probably the closest to the original form of government at the Founding. In between them, you have Bluehelm and Hearthfell. Bluehelm technically has two heads of state, the Archmage and the king, though the mages have practically removed themselves from governance. So long as the king doesn't touch the College's interests, the mages would rather study their arts than deal with civil politics. The king, on his part, has to share his power with the two houses of the Senate. He's not free to do *anything* he wants, but he still has far more significance than Tropis.

"Hearthfell has a king chosen from a special assembly of chieftains, of which there are many. There are different levels of chieftains, all of them ruling over the chieftains lower than them. The right to be a chieftain is hereditary, but through accomplishment and fortitude a chieftain can rise in rank."

Brinwin then paused, grimacing as if having swallowed something bitter. "And then there is Shadowcrest. Their history is a little compli-cated, because what that legend failed to mention last night is that the Shadowed One betrayed the other Founders when they fought the last *Ezith Baal*. It was a bitter struggle, but they prevailed against him and banished him to the far west. It's much too long a story to tell now, but Shadowcrest did eventually make amends with the other kingdoms. They have a king, but how they choose him is mysterious at best and disturbing at worst. Part of it involves a massive amount of bloodshed. Something like a 'last man standing gets the crown,' but there are so many rules and conditions that govern it, no one but themselves can keep it all straight."

Brinwin then shook his head in disgust and rose to his feet. "I hope that answers your questions, Englishman, for that's all I'm willing to share. If you want more stories, I suggest you go and get them from Zala. Now, if you'll excuse me, I have business to attend to." With a curt bow, he departed from William and disappeared into the midst of the crew gathered under the sails.

William pondered what he had heard before running back to his cabin to commit as much as he could remember to writing. King Henry would find this information invaluable. Then again, so would anyone else in the world.

By the time he finished scribbling his notes in his journal, his eyes had glazed over, and his wrist hurt too much to continue. He took a quick break, then glanced over his work one more time. Finding it to his satisfaction, he stowed it away as discreetly as he could.

At this point, William turned his attention back to Zala. He figured enough time had passed for her emotions to have settled at least somewhat. Wandering to her door, he gave a tentative knock. No response came back.

With another knock, he cleared his throat and called out her name. "Zala? If you're in there, it's William. I just wanted to check on you and make sure you're alright." But still, no response came. She must have gone somewhere else on the ship, he reasoned. Yet no matter where he searched for her, she was nowhere to be found. He eventually gave up his search and went once more above deck. For the rest of the day, he stayed there watching the shoreline of Cabalia drift by and wondering to himself what adventures still awaited him on those shores.

He remained on deck when evening fell and the clouds broke up to reveal the full glory of the stars and moon. The silvery light brought him comfort, together with the crisp evening air that fell so fresh on his face. His coat protected him from the nip in the air and padded his back enough to sit and lean against the barrels behind him. The noise of the crew had diminished, leaving only the steady blowing of wind into the sails and the lapping of the waves below.

He sat reveling in the ambiance, for how long he cared not to tell. Minutes, hours, seconds — all seemed the same to him under the stars. Any moments of peace he could experience in this land, he would relish with gratitude. Such was his state of mind when he felt an almost imperceptible tap on the floor behind him. A smile spread across his face as he guessed its source. His suspicions were confirmed when Zala's voice came softly from behind him: "It *is* beautiful, isn't it?"

William turned back to look at her. She wore a deep-blue tunic shrouded loosely by an outer cloak. A hood was drawn over her head, but the moonlight revealed the half of her face not covered by the golden halfmask she wore. It twinkled softly in the light, much as her eyes did.

"Aye," he said. "'Tis even more so now that you're here."

Even with her mask on, he could see a smile unfold behind it. She stepped forward with hardly a sound. "Mind if I join you, Sir Steele?"

William stroked his chin as if in thought. "On one condition," he finally said. At this, the light in Zala's eyes faded, and her smile fell to match the neutral expression of her mask. William kept his gaze on her and said softly, "You must call me William."

Her expression melted into a smile again, and light returned to her eyes brighter than before. William beckoned, and she sat down beside him. She drew her hood back, allowing her hair to fall to her side where it hung in a ponytail, the same as when they had met for the first time.

"I take it those masks are quite comfortable, then?" William said as he scrutinized it up close.

Zala gave a light gasp and removed it from her face. "I forgot I even had it on, to be honest," she replied. "I put it on when I visited with the air mages. There's a mutual respect among us mages, you see. It makes conversation much easier when they see you in one of these."

William nodded, then turned to look back at the moon. They sat in peaceful silence until William spoke up again. "I hope I'm not intruding," he said, "but I couldn't help noticing you and Brinwin were in a sour mood this morning. If it's none of my business, you need only say so."

Zala brushed back her hair and sighed. "No, it's alright. You're not intruding. It's just that Brinwin and I have caught so much disapproval for helping an outsider. We didn't expect to feel it this hard among Azkalah, and Brinwin doesn't know how to handle it. His place of honor with them means everything to him, but the same honor also binds him to help you. So he's stuck." William frowned with a nod and waited for her to continue.

"And he took some of his frustration out on me this morning for how close I've been getting to you. He changed his tune from, 'Oh, you're finally interested in a man. Behave yourself,' to 'You're an embarrassment to your people. Remember your place.' I didn't expect to hear that from him, and I didn't know what to do with it. So..."

"You hid," said William.

Zala bit her lip and nodded. "Yes. I hid." A characteristically mischievous grin then spread across her face. "Which is really quite easy to do when you're a light mage."

William shook his head. "Well... I, for one, am glad you stopped hiding." Zala gave a bashful smile, then leaned against him and rested her head on his shoulder. "Yeah... I am too." William wrapped his arm around her, and together they sat in the moonlight watching the stars move across the heavens.

In time, the serenity gave William the courage to ask the question that plagued him the most. When he spoke, his voice barely rose above a whisper. "Zala," he said. "Why do you find me interesting?"

With a pause of deliberation, she turned to look into his eyes. "Because, William, you're everything I've been looking for in a man."

William blinked as his brow furrowed in confusion. "How do you mean?"

Zala sighed and leaned her head back against his shoulder. "Since I was a little girl, I knew I wanted a man who was strong enough to protect me and good enough not to abuse me. Plenty of men are either one or the other. One who's both is so very rare." She then looked up at him with tears in her eyes. "When I fled Hearthfell for my life, any chance I had at finding such a person was gone. I was a fugitive who joined her outlaw brother as an accomplice. No good man would be able to share a life with me. Even if one somehow wanted to, I couldn't let him."

Tears began to roll down her face, beams of moonlight reflecting off them and causing them to sparkle as polished silver. "Don't you see?" she said. "You're the only one my past doesn't matter with because you're not *from* here. It doesn't matter if I'm a Cabalian fugitive when you're not a Cabalian. And I knew from the first time I laid eyes on you that you were strong enough to protect me. I've served in armies — I know what an experienced warrior looks like. The scars, the lines, the way they carry themselves. The only thing I wasn't sure about was whether you were a good man."

Zala brushed her hair away and looked down at her feet. "So I tested you. I flirted with you to see how you'd respond. A boorish man would have tried to force himself on me, and I'd have dealt with you as I did the last one who tried that. But you didn't. And when you stood up for me at the trial... no one's ever done that before. Defend my honor after I'd endangered your life?" She shook her head. "Only you."

She turned her head back up to look into his eyes. "So I'm sorry, William. I know you loathe your appearance, perhaps even your past. But that really doesn't matter to me. You're strong, and kind, and the only one I've met who can live with my past. That's why I find you interesting."

William gaped in awe at her as the waves lapped softly against the ship. "I don't know what to say," he faltered.

Zala drew her head close to his. "You don't need to," she whispered. His lips then closed the distance to hers, and the beauty of the stars above them failed to match that of the kiss they then shared.

Time slipped by as they held each other, their shared warmth protecting them from the chill of midnight. The moon continued its course toward the horizon in silence until Zala stirred in William's arms. "I have something for you," she murmured drowsily as she straightened herself up. She slipped her hands behind her head and undid the latch of the amulet that hung about her neck.

Opening William's hand, she pressed it into his palm, then closed his fingers back over it. "A very wise man once gave me this amulet and told me I'd know when the time came to give it away," she said. "Take it. Whatever happens, you'll have this to remember me by." Planting a kiss on his cheek, she then giggled playfully. "Besides, it really looks better on you than me. Now let's get you back to your room before Brinwin has a fit."

24

Course Correction

"What do you mean, our port is out of commission?" Brinwin demanded. The ship's captain stood grim before him, dressed in a sleek black coat. On the corner of his chest, the grinning skull of Azkalah lay emblazoned with a ring of black flowers that bordered its purple backdrop. The same insignia on Brinwin's chest shook as he gestured in dismay. The captain remained unflinching, his frown as fixed as when he had first told his compatriot the bad news.

"I mean exactly what I said, Brinwin. Barcbane paladins raided the haven two days ago. You know what happens when our security is breached."

Brinwin clenched his jaw and brought his fist to bear on a crate by the table. It proved no match for the force of his enormous hand and splintered into pieces. "My equipment was there!" he exclaimed with a curse. William cringed and took an instinctive step backward. Zala did the same with her hand in his.

Brinwin then sat down and lowered his head into his hands. Bringing himself back under control, he fixed his eyes on the floor in deep concentration. No one else dared to speak as he muttered aloud to himself. "I'll need to use what's already here on the ship... which will be another day at least to set up." He then shook his head and gave a rueful laugh. "Well, I guess it's a good thing Wayfollowers are hospitable." Zala's countenance stiffened, though William did not know why. He made a mental note to ask her about it later.

Brinwin sat in silent contemplation for a few moments longer before rising to address the captain. "Adjust our course for the Galfrid Docks. We'll blend in with the crowds there." The captain bowed, and Brinwin exited the cabin. Beams of sunlight fell briefly into the room before the door slammed shut behind him.

The captain whistled and shook his head. "Nothing but bad luck to be had bringing you outsiders," he grumbled. With a scornful glance at William, he then turned his attention back to the maps and documents strewn across the table before him.

Zala pulled William's hand and nudged him toward the door. "We should catch up with Brinwin," she whispered.

William raised his eyebrows. "Are you sure that's a good idea right now?" he muttered in reply. Zala merely nodded in silence. With a sigh, he offered no further protests, and he led their way to the main deck. The door shut behind them with a clink as they stepped out into the mid-morning sunlight. Thick, billowing clouds of gray and white floated across the sky, casting deep shadows on the scenery they passed over. The wind from the day before had ceased, yet a slight nip still hung in the air.

It was not hard to pick out Brinwin's frame as he paced across the deck, lost in his own world of a hundred calculations. He nearly crashed into a variety of objects and people as he went, but always managed to avoid a collision at the last second. At first glance, one might have chalked it up to luck. But by the fourth occurrence, William realized the man's reflexes were just that exceptional.

"Just don't say anything until he speaks first, and you'll be fine," said Zala as they closed the distance. "He'll eventually want to tell us his new plan." William nodded outwardly, but the doubts inside him surpassed the clouds above in number.

Brinwin came to rest at the bow of the ship, leaning his back against a mast as he stared across the waters. William and Zala drew quietly to his side and remained there until he acknowledged their presence at last.

"Well," he said. "This puts a kink in our plans. We'll need to keep a low profile when we enter Edomear, so I fear we'll need your light magic once again, Sister." Zala nodded and waited for him to continue. "I really am sorry," he said. "You've been through so much already, and I know you aren't keen on seeing Gaimis. But I think he'll be the safest refuge for us while I gather new equipment. And don't worry," he said, turning to William. "I haven't forgotten about our mission. It'll only take a few days to finish my preparations, and then we'll be off to get you that recipe."

William's head tilted with a squint. "I beg your pardon? What do you mean, recipe?"

Brinwin put his head back into his hands. "Please, Wil-yim, now is not a good time for sarcasm. This voyage has been more stressful for me than you realize."

William's mouth dropped slightly as he stood more puzzled than ever. "But I wasn't being sarcastic, Brinwin," he asserted. "I honestly have no idea what you're talking about with recipes. I'm here to get the suits of shadesteel my king ordered, not cookbooks."

Brinwin's eyebrows nearly raised to the crown of his head. Now he was the one who seemed puzzled. "That's what I'm talking about. The recipe to make shadesteel, so you can make all the suits of armor your King Stephen wants."

William's jaw almost fell to the floor. "Stephen?!" he gasped. "I'm not here for that usurper! I was sent by King Henry to get two suits of shadesteel armor. Isn't that what you've been doing this whole time? Trying to craft those suits for me?"

The blood drained from Brinwin's face, and Zala's eyes grew wide in shock. "No... I... what are you talking about, Wil-yim?" Brinwin's voice quivered.

"You're contracting for House Shadowcrest, aren't you?" William stammered. "I was told to meet a Shadowcrest agent at the Yohati Inn and give him the Danuri stone."

Zala became as pale as a ghost, and Brinwin struggled to speak. "You weren't in the Yohati Inn," Brinwin faltered. "That was the Kozheithy Tavern."

In one sickening moment, things clicked into place for William. An image of the tavern where his troubles all began loomed into view. Its sign rattled in the wind as thunder boomed in the distance. But of course! The tavern's sign was not in English — it was in Cabalian! God knew what the letters Y-O-H-A-T-I actually sounded like in Cabalian. And the yellow paint! It was still fresh. Which meant...

"It wasn't the Yohati?" he said feebly.

The blood returned to Brinwin's face in a flash of anger. "No, you imbecile! It was the Kozheithy! Where a man named William from England was supposed to give me a blue Danuri stone so I could haul his rear to Shadowcrest on a suicide mission! To discover the secret recipe those scoundrels have hidden for a thousand years!"

Brinwin's hands shook, and Zala trembled where she stood. Her conversation with William by Lake Iddeah flashed back to memory in vivid detail. *"William,"* he had said. *"He's my namesake, you see, as well as for every third man-child born under the sun back home."* It had never occurred to her that more than one man named William could be sent to Cabalia from England.

Brinwin unleashed such a string of curses that even the sailors on deck gasped in surprise. "You odds-defying moron!" he screamed. He looked ready to throw William overboard, but Zala stepped between them. White hot flames flickered above her hands as she stared down her brother.

"Brin... you need to calm yourself. Now." Reflections of Zala's flames flickered across Brinwin's eyes, yet they failed to compare with the flames that burned behind them from within. He stood taut, like a rope stretched to its breaking point. Every onlooker aboard the ship held their breath in suspense. No one dared to move.

William steeled himself for the fight of his life when slowly, imperceptibly at first, Brinwin's anger dwindled to a smolder. His muscles relaxed somewhat, and his beet-red face shifted to a lesser shade of red.

Clenched fists came to rest at his side loosely, and he exhaled with a low, hot breath. "Very well..." he growled. Breaking contact with his sister's gaze, he glared behind her once more at William. "If you know what's good for you, I'll see you both in my quarters in one hour." He then turned on his heels and strode below deck, each footstep resounding like a peal of thunder.

The sailors released a tentative sigh of relief and resumed their duties. William and Zala, however, experienced no such relief as they remained rooted in place, their hearts laden with anxiety. William stepped forward to Zala's side and stared at Brinwin's receding form. "What do we do now?" he asked. Their situation looked bleak indeed, and he could only hope Zala had at least some idea of what to do next.

Such hopes were disappointed as her eyes sank to the ground, downcast. "I don't know," she said. "All I know is we'd better be in his room in an hour. I just hope for our sake he's calmed down by then." William nodded, and with little else to do, he resigned himself to whatever fate awaited them.

The hour passed by with no small amount of anguish until they found themselves standing in front of Brinwin's door. William opened the latch with apprehension, and Zala stepped in first. The lighting was somewhat poor, but they had no difficulty in seeing Brinwin as he sat ready for them behind a large, oaken desk. Two candles stood on either end of the desk, each a foot away from the chairs that lay in front of them. Brinwin's tattoo glowed brightly as he eyed them, his expression indecipherable. "Have a seat," he said in a perfectly neutral voice. William's eyes widened as he saw the blue glimmering of the Danuri stone in Brinwin's right hand.

Once they had all taken a seat, Brinwin held the stone in front of him. He wasted no time in small talk but cut directly to his interrogation. While not harsh, his voice was nonetheless intimidating. Instead of the brute force of a smoking cannon, it more resembled an array of a thousand finely calibrated needles. "Where did you get this?" he demanded.

William's reply remained calm, even as his stomach did somersaults in panic. "My king gave it to me when I was appointed to this mission." "And where did he get it from?"

William shook his head. "I don't know. He never told me. I can only assume from somewhere in England, probably while I was still bedridden with injuries."

Brinwin's eyes narrowed in distrust. "Explain," he commanded.

William withdrew his journal from his coat and turned it over to Brinwin. "This is a private record I've kept since I was first sent here. Even if you don't believe my spoken word, I present you my written one. This is the extent of my knowledge."

Brinwin examined the book in curiosity, then peered back at William. "You seem to have forgotten, Englishman, that we don't read English here. What good would this do me?"

William shrugged. "I assumed that if you have a magic ring to let me speak Cabalian, then surely you have one that lets you read English."

Brinwin shook his head. "You assumed incorrectly."

Before William could respond, Zala cleared her throat. "Actually, Brin, we do." Their eyes fastened on her when she withdrew a ring of fine gold lined with sapphires and offered it to her brother. "When we stopped at the haven before Elkreath, I figured something like this might prove useful. I bought this off one of the vendors there."

"Now just a moment!" interjected William. "When did this happen?"

"After we left the Essari. You were still unconscious," Zala replied with a gleam of amusement in her eyes. "Where did you think we got that carriage and everything else we had on hand when you woke up?"

As William sat puzzled, Brinwin took the ring and slipped it onto his finger. He opened the journal again, saying nothing as he read its pages. He closed the book at length and returned it to William. "Your writing is sloppy," he said. "Especially where you talk of your commissioning. But at least it gets the point across. I now have all the information I need."

Brinwin then removed the ring and returned it to Zala. Straightening himself, he looked directly at William. "And now I have some bad news for you, Wil-yim. You may have come here for the business of Henry, but fate has decided a different course for you." William's heart sank in dread. Whatever Brinwin was about to say, it would surely be nothing good.

"You are, no doubt, unfamiliar with our customs here at Azkalah, so allow me to explain them to you. We are not aligned with House Shadowcrest. In fact, we are not aligned with any house. We serve whoever pays us. 'Anything is possible for the right price'- that's our maxim. When someone has a need they can't handle, they come to us no matter how difficult or illegal it is, knowing we'll never break a contract. We, in turn, reserve the right to set the price of our service. If we don't want a job, we'll just charge higher than a client can afford.

"It was nearly two weeks ago that King Stephen contacted us, wishing to obtain the recipe of Shadesteel. Now mind you, this recipe is one of the most closely guarded secrets of the most secretive kingdom in all of Cabalia. Such a mission is of the highest order, and as it so happens, I am an agent of the highest order. And so I set the price of service.

"For the life of me, I didn't think you Englishmen had enough gold to cover the cost I set. But even if you somehow did, I also named a blue Danuri stone as part of the price. I doubted you would know what one even was, let alone find one. They're incredibly rare, but something I've been longing to find for years. And somehow... somehow! You outsiders didn't just find one. You found two! A pair of twins, no less!

"I'll spare you a long story. Just suffice it to say the magic in those stones did some strange things to fate, such as drawing you to accidentally annihilate your rival king's agent and wind up in the very transaction he was supposed to serve in. It was Stephen's request that his agent accompany us for the mission — a condition you are now bound to fulfill."

William rose from his seat with a start. "What are you talking about? That makes no sense!" he nearly yelled. "Why would I be bound to a contract I never agreed to?"

Brinwin remained seated and responded impassively, as though lecturing a schoolboy on how two plus two equals four.

"Because of two things, Wil-yim. First: the policy of substitutionary assumption. When someone shows up at the right time, and the right place, and pays the right price, they're considered the subject of the contract regardless of what they may otherwise claim later. People once used to cheat us by paying for a contract, and then when things went sour, claiming there was a mix-up. So we adopted the policy. And, as it happens, you were in the right place, at the right time, and paid the right price. As far as Azkalah is concerned, you are Stephen's Wil-yim. If I cancel the contract, I'll have a target placed on my back for failing it."

Brinwin's voice then dropped low, ominous as the growl of a lion. "Second: I've already *personally* sunk too much into this mission. If you try to run away before I give you that blasted recipe and get the contract off my back, I'll gut you like a fish."

William's head spun as his world turned upside down.

With a grim frown, Brinwin proceeded to speak. "Now, here is what's going to happen. For the remainder of this mission, we will all pretend you are Stephen's Wil-yim. You will come with us into the heart of Shadowcrest, and you will help us retrieve the recipe. Once the recipe is in your hands, the contract will be fulfilled, and I will, for my sister's sake, do everything I can to get you back to England. Perhaps I can even find you a couple of suits of shadesteel for good measure. If Zala wants, she can even go with you, and you two can live happily ever after. But until we get that recipe, I'm calling the shots. Understood?"

William stared blankly and nodded. "Good," said Brinwin with a curt smile. "We'll be arriving at Edomear tomorrow. I suggest you enjoy the rest of our voyage and do whatever you must to prepare yourself for what lies ahead. I'll give you further instructions when we come to port." Having said this, he slipped the Danuri stone back into his pocket and dismissed them with a brush of his hands. William fumbled to his feet and staggered out of the room, with Zala following close behind as he ascended to the main deck.

So absorbed he was in his thoughts as he paced, it startled him when Zala took his hands and held them firmly. The resolve in her eyes was overwhelming at first, but it became a greater comfort the longer she spoke. "Listen to me, William," she said. "I know this is all a shock, but we're going to make it through this. We've already survived certain death together, and this won't be an exception. Whatever happens, I've got your back."

From anyone else, these would have sounded like hollow words, spoken by a well-meaning fool to reassure an even more gullible fool. But the certainty with which she spoke, along with a track record of actions to back them up, bolstered William's courage as little else would. He endeavored to match her resolve as he met her gaze.

"Likewise," he whispered. They then embraced, not just as lovers, but as comrades sent to war. Neither knew what to expect from the days to come, but they purposed in their hearts that whatever came their way, it would not be faced alone. They thus stayed in each other's company as their last evening aboard the ship came upon them. They could only hope the deep red of the setting sun was not an omen of evils yet to come.

25

The Wayfollower

When the sun rose the next day, a breathtaking view waited above deck. Silver-white mist billowed from the water's surface, only to dissipate below eye level to provide a clear view of the crown jewel of Cabalia: the city of Edomear. It rose in the distance, its vast spires of marble and granite towering above the horizon. The polished surfaces of innumerable stone buildings captured the first rays of dawn and cast them seaward for travelers to observe in wonder. At a distance, the city appeared to glow as golden as Heaven itself.

A great river flowed from the midst of the city and emptied itself into a bay brimming with activity. Majestic ships drifted on the waters, sails of every vibrant color unfurled and adorned with royal insignia. One could see the occupants of these ships arrayed in equal amounts of splendor as they drew closer. Courtesans frolicked about the decks with their entourages, entertaining themselves as best they saw fit.

The texture and build of the ships' frames surpassed all the trading ships William had ever seen, leaving him speechless. He then understood that the trading ships that sailed to Europe were not meant to showcase the fullest extent of Cabalian opulence. These ships were.

Not every ship in the bay was so luxurious, of course, but the grandeur of these vessels overshadowed the existence of all others: a fact Brinwin and his crew relied on heavily as they weaved a path to the Galfrid Docks.

When they reached the shipyards, they passed themselves off as a tourist boat. They disembarked without incident, for the crew members had stashed away their Azkalah clothing, and Zala had placed an enchantment on Brinwin to disguise him. Once past the docks, it was easy enough for them to blend in with the crowds that swarmed the thoroughfare. The streets were not quite as wide as in Elkreath, yet they felt less congested. Bright-gray cobblestone paved the way for all who traveled the city, remaining in immaculate condition no matter where one cast their gaze.

William could only guess how the streets remained so clean, but the answer revealed itself soon enough when he noticed the backbenders scattered throughout the crowds. Each one stood roughly the same size as those at the Essari compound, but the color of their bipedal form was lighter. They wore official uniforms with the Barcbane crest stitched on the front and back, and they carried an array of mops, brushes, buckets of water, and soap. They cleaned the roads for hours on end, yet for all their labor, they appeared to be in excellent health. They were clearly well taken care of by their masters.

The mood that governed the city was of a more wholesome tenor than Elkreath. The people, in general, were better dressed — or at the very least, better behaved. Luxury permeated the city yet did not preclude the existence of poverty. Many of poor status roamed throughout the city, but many helped alleviate their condition, also.

William took special note of men and women adorned in simple brown robes, armed with nothing but food baskets and traveling staffs as they interacted with the poor throughout the day. Passing by one such man, he could see the plain red cross sewn across the back. William turned to inquire of either Brinwin or Zala, but they kept their eyes fastened straight ahead as they went. With a shrug, William followed along as they moved toward the center of Edomear.

Shortly before noon, they reached a large plaza, its floor lined with a sea of red clay tiles and filled with a variety of fountains and statues.

In the center of the area, one of the statues towered above the rest. It commanded the attention of all who passed it, not just by its size but also by its detail.

A man of solid gold held his sword before him, pointed downward as he gazed toward the sea. He appeared to be a king, dressed in a crown and royal apparel that accentuated his herculean physique. So detailed was his visage that one could distinguish the individual hairs of his head and beard from each other. The man wore an expression of wisdom mixed with might: that of a perfect king gazing over his perfect city.

"Is that a statue of Barcbane himself?" asked William.

Brinwin chuckled to himself. "No," he replied. "Messala Barcbane may have been a comely lad, but he was nowhere near *that* strapping."

"Well, then who is he?" William pressed.

Zala smiled and said, "He *was* King Galatrix the First. He ruled as Barcbane's king over four hundred years ago. His grandson, Galatrix the Second, commissioned the statue in his honor."

"It's impressive!" William exclaimed. "I've never seen such a beautiful piece of art."

"It *is* quite impressive," Zala agreed. "It's even more so when you realize it's the only surviving structure from the old city." William raised an eyebrow and waited for further explanation. Zala laughed, clearly enjoying his curiosity and wonder at learning such things for the first time.

"There's a plaque at the base that tells the whole story. Not long after it was built, a great war decimated the city. The royal loremaster at the time was so dedicated to preserving his city's art that he used every last ounce of his magic to defend the statue, even as the whole city fell to pieces around him. His comrades at the time weren't happy with how he focused on the statue instead of the rest of the city, but everyone today is pretty grateful."

William stepped forward to investigate it further when the deep toll of a bell sounded from above. The noise startled him, causing him to glance around the square in search of the disturbance. His searching was soon satisfied when, to his right, he noticed a bell tower of rusted-red sandstone that rose above the nearby buildings. At its summit, a bronze bell twice the size of a man clanged back and forth, calling the square to attention.

The noise faded, and as he pondered the meaning of the great bell's summoning, a troupe of musicians filed into the square seemingly from nowhere. They took their positions by a fountain and began to play their instruments as small crowds gathered to hear their melodies. The garments they sported were as colorful as the instruments they played, leaving them beautiful to behold in both sight and sound.

The beginning of their tune was slow and mellow, with flutes and stringed instruments working in harmony to draw the crowds into a soothing lull. The low beating of drums then rose and filled the plaza with a deep booming. Baritone chants from the male singers rode along the peaks of each drum beat as the song progressed until there came a rise in the pitch and tempo. The drums beat faster, the flutes piped louder, and the women singers raised their voices until the square swelled into an exultant chorus of song. The crowds stood spellbound as the music reached its crescendo, then waned gracefully into the silence it had been born from.

The musicians bowed as the audience broke into a round of applause. Once the accolades had dwindled, many in the plaza dispersed into the streets. As they left, they tossed coins of various worth into a decorative drum turned upside down beside the troupe. The keeper of the drum then distributed the earnings among his companions before they also dispersed into the streets. They went in every direction, each playing their own solos as they wandered about. The result left the streets of Edomear filled with song wherever one found themselves.

William had never heard anything like it. "Does this happen every day?" he asked in amazement.

"Pretty much," replied Zala. "Every day at noon, the plazas across the city host a *domir* like that — *a glorious song*. It's where Edomear gets its name from, actually." She paused to toss a coin to the performer with a stringed instrument who passed by them. The man flashed them a smile of appreciation as he played his tune and ambled farther down the street. "They break off into solos for the next several hours until they all gather for a grand finale at sunset at the king's palace," Zala continued. "In fact, I'm sure tonight's performance would be a splendid one to catch."

Brinwin cut off his sister before she had a chance to say more. "Out of the question," he said. "We're supposed to be laying low."

Zala sniffed back in ridicule. "Coming from the one who just dared the largest city in Cabalia to a game of cat-and-mouse?"

Brinwin glared at her with a hiss. "Are you insane? Keep it down!" Zala rolled her eyes and fell silent as Brinwin led them through the streets. "This is nothing like Elkreath," he muttered loudly enough for only his companions to hear. "Much less corruption to take advantage of here."

They walked west for several miles until they reached the edge of a certain park. Grassy hills rolled past them into the distance, and a small stream wandered through its midst before feeding into a pond at the back of the area. To the side of the pond, at the far corner of the park, a stone cathedral sat nestled behind a growth of trees and holly bushes. A simple dirt path wound through the park and past the trees, all the way around the cathedral to the massive wooden doors that guarded its entrance on the other side. Brinwin led the others down the path in silence, stopping only when they reached its final destination. He motioned for Zala to put her hood up, and he refrained from knocking on the cathedral's doors until she had done so.

Carved into the archway above the doors were the words: "Knock, and the door shall be opened unto you." Such words proved accurate when the doors parted open and a woman stepped outside to meet them at the threshold. She was small, arrayed in the same style of brown robe that William had seen earlier.

"Can I help you, friends?" she asked, her voice as mild as the stream that ran behind them in the park.

"Yes," said Brinwin with such politeness that it caught William off guard. "Is the Wayfollower in at the moment?"

The woman shook her head and eyed them in curiosity. "No, I'm afraid he's not. He left almost an hour ago to make his rounds through the city." William saw her curiosity change into concern as she gazed at Zala's hooded face and then at the sword by William's side. "What business do you have with him?" she queried cautiously.

Brinwin motioned for Zala to remove her hood. "It's a very long story," he replied. "My friends and I have found ourselves in a difficult situation, and we're here to seek his counsel." The woman appeared somewhat satisfied with his reply, but traces of apprehension still lined her face. "It's going to be a while before he comes back," she said. "If you're willing to wait, you can help yourselves to a seat inside."

Brinwin bowed in gratitude. "Thank you, Miss. You have no idea how much this means to us."

He would have stepped forward to enter the church, but she still stood blocking the entrance.

"If you don't mind, might I first have your names?" she asked.

"Of course," said Brinwin. "My name is Kaldris, and my friends' names are Alana and Velkis," he said, motioning to Zala and William, respectively. "I doubt he'd remember Velkis, but he's spoken with me and Alana before."

The woman nodded and ushered them past the entryway. "I'll need you to leave your weapons with the porter if you would, please," she insisted. They obliged, and this having been done, she guided them into a broad corridor lined with benches. They sat down together while the woman excused herself to tend the grounds.

William gazed about the cathedral as he waited, taking stock of whatever entrances and exits he found. The woman had seemed a little too suspicious, he thought. If they needed to make a getaway, it would pay to be aware of their surroundings. From what he saw, the corridor wrapped around the cathedral in a semicircle, each end most likely opening to the rest of the building. From where they sat, the only clear entrance and exit was the front door from which they had come.

The stonework surrounding them proved a shield from the sun's heat, leaving them comfortably cool as they waited. Its architecture was of simple design but beautiful all the same. In some ways, the stones reminded William of the churches back in England. The longer he thought about it, the more he realized how much he would have given to be safely seated back home in a church. The monotonous drone of a priest would have been far more preferable to this nightmare of adventures he had been thrust into. Perhaps if he promised to attend a church more faithfully, it would help his chances of making it back home to one.

As he sat thinking thus, the doorway opened with a creak. "Welcome back, Brother!" he heard the porter say. The reverence in his tone seemed out of place for addressing a mere "brother." When the newcomer replied, it was easy to imagine why.

"Thank you, Valin," he said. "I see all is still well?" His voice was deep and rich, filled with all the kindness of a grandfather despite not sounding old enough to come from a grandfather. His stride was long and heavy, much the same as Brinwin's.

"Indeed!" the porter said. "There are visitors waiting for you in the corridor if you have the time for them. They seek counsel."

"There is always time for seekers in a house of Yahos," the man scolded ever so lightly. As he passed into view of the corridor, William observed the full profile of the man who lumbered into their presence. He stood several inches over six feet tall, with his gaze turned down upon them as he entered. A golden sash wrapped around his black robe and matched the color of the cross that gleamed across his chest. His eyes removed all doubt that he was a Zikennig. They were hazel, the same as Zala and Brinwin, and brimming with expression. While Brinwin's eyes were keen and Zala's full of laughter, this man's eyes were soft, filled with wisdom and peace.

He glanced over William first, then Brinwin and Zala. Brinwin's true appearance still lay masked with Zala's enchantment, and Zala had drawn her hood back up to avert his gaze. "What can I do for you, my brothers and sister?" he asked. Something in how he asked that question led William to believe he somehow knew exactly who stood before him.

"You're the Wayfollower, yes?" Brinwin responded as he feigned ignorance.

The man nodded. "Yes. For better or worse, that's what they call me. Please, though, just call me Gaimis." With a bow, he then gestured down the rightmost corridor. "I'm told you've been waiting for me for some time. May I offer you some refreshment in my chambers?"

They nodded and followed him as he led them to a door at the end of the corridor and retrieved a worn-out key from the pouch at his side. With a firm twist and shove, the door budged open to reveal a steep flight of stairs. Small torches lined the staircase and were the sole source of light as it ascended.

Once Gaimis had closed the door behind them, he laid a hand on Brinwin's shoulder. "You're taller than last we met, Brinwin," he said.

Brinwin cleared his throat awkwardly. "And you're wider," he quipped.

The dimness of the corridor hid the slight blush that came across Gaimis's face, but he responded with such grace that one would have hardly noticed anyway. "Perhaps so. The wife's been treating me well." Turning to his sister, he offered a bow. "It's good to see you, Zala. I hope you're not here under compulsion." Zala said nothing but a slight mumble and kept the hood over her eyes.

"I see," said Gaimis with a grimace. Turning to face William, he eyed him thoughtfully. "I'm quite certain I've never met you before... and I doubt your name is actually Velkis." William followed Zala's example and said nothing. Gaimis seemed little more than a kindly priest, but William was nowhere near ready to trust him with his identity. An awkward silence ensued until Gaimis cleared his throat and began to ascend the stairs. "Right then. Let's get you situated upstairs."

A small metal door awaited them at the top of the stairs, which Gaimis knocked on with a series of short raps. A voice then called from behind the door: "The first Colossian?"

"Epaphras," replied Gaimis with a smile. The sound of a latch being undone reverberated down the staircase before the door swung open to reveal the smiling face of a woman. Her eyes sparkled as she gazed at

Gaimis before widening in surprise to see the company that followed behind him.

"You didn't tell me we'd have company today, Husband," she gasped.

Gaimis lowered his voice in apology. "Yes, I'm sorry about that, Dearest. They need more privacy than downstairs can afford."

A somber look spread across her face, and she nodded. "Of course. They'll have to excuse the mess."

It was all William could do to hold back a laugh. *If she only knew what messes we've already been through,* he thought in amusement.

Gaimis drew close to his wife and whispered a few further words to her before they entered past the threshold. She stiffened for a moment, but recovered herself and welcomed them into her home. Stepping forward, they found the upper room of the cathedral to be spacious, adorned with many stained-glass windows that cast a soft glow of orange and yellow throughout it. The furnishings were of more modest means than the array of light upon them: A simple carpet covered the stone floor, and weathered furniture lay sparsely arranged on top of it. Curtains hung down to divide the various regions of the room, able to be drawn back as needed to provide additional space.

Zala gasped when the curtain directly to her right suddenly ruffled, then flung back as a small child tumbled past it and crashed into her. The impish grin on his face dissolved into a look of fear and embarrassment when he failed to recognize her. He stood frozen, unsure how to respond, when another child bounded through the curtain. This one, a girl somewhat older than the boy, failed to notice the visitors as she grabbed her brother and tackled him to the ground. "Got you!" she called in triumph as she began tickling him. Zala's face broke into a slight smile as they continued to wrestle each other before Gaimis raised his voice.

"Children!" he called. "We have company!"

On hearing the voice of their father, they immediately ceased their wrestling and scrambled to their feet. Hands behind their backs, they stared at the floor in guilt, waiting for what came next. Their mother broke the silence with a gentle voice of reassurance. "Avah, Gilwin...

meet your Uncle Brinwin and Aunt Zala." They looked up in surprise and seemed uncertain how to respond, even as they offered a deep bow.

Brinwin and Zala shifted awkwardly before offering bows of their own. "Hello there," said Brinwin in a feeble attempt at greeting. The children nodded and mumbled a reply before Gaimis moved to diffuse the tension.

"Why don't you two help your mother prepare for dinner?" he said. "Your aunt and uncle have traveled a long way to come here, and I'm sure they'll be very hungry."

The children jumped at the chance to excuse themselves and scampered off to join their mother as she withdrew behind the curtain that divided the living area from the kitchen. Gaimis sighed and shook his head after they disappeared. Turning to face Zala, he said, "You and your friend can help yourselves to the couches over there. I'd like to have a few words with Brin." Zala and William nodded and sat down together as Gaimis led his brother past several curtains to the door of a truly separate room. He withdrew a different key than the one he had used earlier and undid the door's lock.

Once seated inside the room, Gaimis's demeanor became grim, and his voice fell low. "What are you doing here?" he pressed.

Brinwin shifted in his seat and looked directly at his brother. "I need your help, Gaimis."

"No kidding? I could gather that much," remarked the priest sarcastically. He then stroked his chin as he stared at Brinwin. "You're here to use me as a safe house, aren't you? I heard about the raid on your haven."

Brinwin inhaled slowly as he weighed his words with care. "Partly, yes. I could have gone to a different haven, but I really wanted to pay you a visit. I'm trying to plant two seeds with one hand."

"That sounds about right," replied Gaimis with a sigh laden with unpleasant memories. "If this has anything to do with your profession, I want no part of it."

Brinwin nervously tapped his fingers on his lap before dropping his gaze. "I know you don't approve of my choices, Brother," he finally said. "But please believe me. This isn't what you think it is. I just need a safe space for a few days so I can complete some alchemy research completely separate from Azkalah. If you have any respect for what I was before, then please... grant me this favor. I'll be gone before you know it, and no one will ever know I was here."

Gaimis shook his head. "Except for me and my conscience," he muttered. He stared at the floor in thought before looking back up in resolve. "You can spend the night. I'll let you know what I've decided tomorrow morning." He then rose and opened the door, motioning for Brinwin to lead the way out. Brinwin bowed in gratitude, and the two brothers exited the room without another word said.

They regrouped with Zala and William in the living room area, where they passed the time until the evening sun cast shades of deep orange through the windows. Gaimis's wife then beckoned them to dinner, where they sat around a table just barely large enough to seat everyone. Gaimis prayed a blessing over the meal before they all helped themselves to a hearty serving of venison stew. Perhaps as an answer to the Wayfollower's prayer, the meal hit just the spot for William and the others. It was easy to understand what Gaimis meant about his wife taking care of him.

While they ate, Avah and Gilwin stared at their aunt and uncle, attempting to work up the courage to ask a question they were dying to have answered. Once Brinwin had wiped his mouth clean with his napkin, Avah finally piped up: "Are you really the world's best alchemist?"

Their parents frowned in embarrassment, but Brinwin assuaged their fears with a smile. "As far as I know," he said with a delighted laugh.

"Can you prove it?" Gilwin then asked, unable to hide his eagerness.

Brinwin paused in thought, then grinned knowingly. "Do you know what a Danuri stone is?" he queried. Zala shot him a stern look but said nothing as he ignored her and continued to interact with the children. When Gilwin and Avah both nodded their heads, he smiled and withdrew the Danuri stone from his pocket. "Then you know how rare something like this is, yes?"

The eyes of both the children and their parents widened to the size of their supper bowls. Brimming with confidence, Brinwin then leaned forward and dropped his voice to a hush. "In just a couple of days, I'll make it even rarer. I'm going to turn it violet."

No one spoke for several moments until the children came to themselves and nearly squealed with excitement. "How are you going to do it?" Gilwin asked.

Brinwin laughed. "Until I prove it for certain, I have to keep that a secret."

Avah then squinted at her uncle and said with the unfiltered skepticism only a child could manage, "How do we know you don't already have a purple one? Papa says you're good at tricking people."

Brinwin threw a glance toward his brother before recovering himself with a smile. "A fair question. It's good to have some healthy skepticism in cases like this." He reached for the pitcher of water beside him and held it for the view of all. "As I'm sure you'll learn in school one day, every Danuri stone is unique. Each one looks different, feels different, and *sings* different." He dropped the Danuri stone into the pitcher and waited for the water to still. Silence filled the room until a distinct humming rose from the submerged stone. It was soft in tone — melodious even — as it cycled through a peculiar rhythm.

"Each Danuri makes its own unique sound when submerged in water," he explained. "Listen well, and remember this tune. When I transform the stone to purple, it should retain the same sound and rhythm — except for a slight rise in pitch, of course, from having more energy than its previous form." Everyone listened intently as the stone's melody etched itself into their memories. At length, Brinwin removed the stone from the pitcher and returned it to his pocket. "Are there any other questions," he asked.

To his surprise, Gaimis cleared his throat and spoke up next. "And what will you do with this stone once you've transformed it?"

Brinwin pondered his words carefully before resigning himself to candor. "I suppose it would bode ill for me to lie in a house of Yahos, Brother. It would be far too great a risk to take the stone where we are going, so I intend to fashion a few needed items with it and then donate it to the Church." At this, Gaimis and his wife nearly choked on their stew. "I know that would come as a shock," Brinwin continued, "but I have no desire for wealth or power beyond what's necessary for my mission. And to be honest, I don't expect to return from this one. Perhaps this will in some small way compensate for the path I've walked these ten years."

Gaimis sat still with his head in his hands, lost in deliberation. No one else dared to speak until he looked up from his musings and motioned to his wife. She understood his meaning and led the children off to bed. Once they had disappeared behind several curtains, Gaimis then turned to address his brother.

"Brinwin," he said gravely. "If you intend to bribe Yahos with this gift, I suggest you keep it for yourself. Even a violet Danuri stone is but a drop in the sea of his infinite might. If you think such a meager drop will earn his good favor and cover a lifetime of violence and thievery, you are sorely mistaken."

Brinwin's countenance fell as he looked to the floor in grief. Zala's face flushed red with anger, and before William could urge her to hold her tongue, she lashed out at Gaimis.

"Then answer me this, oh holy Wayfollower," she blurted. "If Yahos is so powerful and wealthy, then why is this world of his so rife with evil and poverty?"

Brinwin spoke to calm his sister, but she would have none of it. "No, Brin," she insisted. "It's not fair to see you offer the world's most powerful artifact just to be turned down by some self-righteous saint who has yet to give me a good reason why his god allows worse evils than yours to exist." She eyed Gaimis sharply as she spoke, daring him to defend himself.

Gaimis sighed deeply and motioned for Brinwin to remain still. "It's alright, Brin. Our sister raises a valid question." He rose to light the lamps around the table as the last glimmers of orange faded into twilight, then seated himself in his chair again. "It's a question even the most faithful of us have wrestled with." Turning to face Brinwin, he said, "Though before the night is out, I wish to clarify what I first said to you." Brinwin nodded, and Gaimis turned his attention back to Zala and William.

"I'm sorry if I came across as self-righteous, Zala. Please believe me, that was never my intent." Gaimis paused as he organized his thoughts, and for a short while, only the crackling of the torches could be heard as they cast their light on his care-drawn face. At last, he spoke softly: "Plenty of men wiser than I have tried to answer this question of yours. If you expected one of the most difficult questions posed by man to be answered in a single phrase, I'm afraid you'll be disappointed."

A small but sincere smile then creased his lips as he leaned closer. "We Zikennigs might pretend to know everything, but between you and me, I think our knowledge is a bit overrated."

Zala said nothing as she glared at her brother, her posture making it clear she expected far more of an answer than that. After a tense pause, Gaimis sighed in resignation.

"But when has that ever stopped us from trying? Fine then. You ask why evil exists in this world? In one sense, I could tell you quite plainly: It's because of men choosing it. Show me an example of evil, and I can show you an example of someone who had the freedom to choose good instead but didn't. For every murder, someone could have spared the other's life; for every theft, someone could have respected the other's property; for every lie, someone could have told the truth; for every child that goes hungry, someone could have shared their food. How often do we choose evil over good? To shake our fists at Yahos when we're the ones who choose evil seems an unfair position to me."

At this, Zala rolled her eyes, not even attempting to hide her annoyance.

"Spare me the sermon, Gaimis," she interjected. "I don't want a flowery speech. Just tell me plainly: Why doesn't Yahos stop evil? How can you say he's good when all he does is stand by and watch us suffer?"

Gaimis shifted in discomfort and inhaled sharply as his eyes fastened on the floor. William thought he could see his lips moving faintly as if in silent prayer. When the priest looked up, he trained his gaze on Zala. While focused, it was not sharp. It was intent but soft — that's how William remembered it, just as distinctly as he remembered what Gaimis said next.

"Because he's merciful, Zala. He doesn't stop evil yet because he's merciful."

For the first time William could recall since leaving Elkreath, Zala sat speechless in confusion. He really could not blame her, either. Such a statement would have sounded more appropriate coming from a sadistic madman than a priest. Before she could recover, Gaimis took the opportunity to continue. For just a moment, William observed the same glimmer of intensity in Gaimis's eyes that he had seen in the man's siblings as they faced the *Kumuzhkan*. It suddenly seemed as if Gaimis had found his own serpent to battle.

"Forgive my boldness, Sister, but your question assumes that we're the innocent victims here," said Gaimis. "But we're not. If Yahos granted your wish right now and stopped all evil in the world, then every human in existence would go up in a puff of smoke. Because whether we like to admit it or not, *we're evil*. All of us. Look at the things we do and the things we think. Day after day, we lie, steal, curse, lust, murder, grumble, and blaspheme at the drop of a hat, and that's just what we do on the outside. The better question is, how are we still standing if Yahos really is good?"

The bluntness with which this hitherto gentle giant spoke knocked the words out of everyone around him and brought a fresh round of silence. The surrounding torches flickered against the twilight as his expression softened again, and a twinkle came to his eye.

"But we *are* still standing. And that's proof in itself that Yahos is merciful. Even after everything we've done, we still have time to turn from our evil before he deals with it."

Gaimis's eyes suddenly darted to a torch extinguished by a draft of air, and he rose from his seat to tend to it. The others waited for him to finish his work, thankful for a moment to process what they had just heard. When Gaimis returned to his seat, his gaze fell again on Zala.

"As for Yahos 'just standing by and watching us suffer,' that's simply not true. He *did* do something so we don't have to suffer. Something that involved *him* suffering, as a matter of fact — something that provides a place for us free of charge where pain no longer exists for the rest of eternity. Compared to forever, seventy or eighty years of pain is something of a moot point in the grand scheme of things, don't you think?"

Finally given the chance to speak again, Zala's eyes flared with indignation. Her brother's question may have been rhetorical, but it nonetheless provided just the opportunity for her to vent the scorn that welled within her.

"Unless, of course, a person doesn't *go* to Heaven," she suddenly quipped. "If I recall, the Church teaches that a lot of people will end up in hell, yes? The place where the pain is never ending?"

Gaimis paused as a grimace swept across his face. For a few tense breaths, it seemed he could find no words to say. If uncertainty were ever to have a face, Gaimis would have been a perfect candidate at that moment. It was what impressed William all the more when the priest suddenly rebounded.

"Yes..." said Gaimis. "Though I might point out that if people end up in hell, it's only because they've earned it by willingly choosing evil and for some foolish reason having chosen not to take Yahos up on his offer of mercy. He very graciously sent his son as a sacrifice to die in our place so no one *has* to go to hell. When he's provided the means for anyone to avoid judgment, can we really blame him if we choose not to avail ourselves of it?"

As Gaimis spoke, William remembered the times in England when he had heard of the evils of sin and the death of God's Son. He had always found the concept somewhat odd, but then again, such things of faith were supposed to be mysterious, were they not? Yet something led him to ask more of this Cabalian Wayfollower.

"Tell me more about this offer of mercy," he said. He felt Zala's shock beside him, and if he were honest, even a part of him was shocked at what he was asking. To some extent, it felt as if he watched from the outside while he inquired further. "What exactly does the death of Yahos's Son have to do with our evil?"

At this, Gaimis's eyes beamed with a sincerity that was difficult to ignore. "Well, it's pretty simple," he said. "We've all sinned against Yahos, so only Yahos himself could forgive us. And he wants to forgive us. But letting evildoers like us go free without punishment would be endorsing evil, which a good god could never do. So, to solve that predicament, he sent his son, Yeshun, to the world as a perfect human to take our punishment for us by dying the most painful death possible on a cross. The penalty we earned for ourselves was pain and death, so he suffered pain and death for us. Yeshun satisfied justice and mercy at the same time because he substituted his life for ours.

"We broke the moral law of Yahos, and Yeshun paid our fine — it's that simple. He died, so we get to live. When he rose from the dead three days later, it showed the sacrifice was sufficient and death had been defeated. Anyone who believes in him can be forgiven all their evils, reconciled to the God who made them, and rest assured they will live forever free from pain and decay. If they truly believe in him with their heart and submit to him as the Lord of creation that he already is... they will not perish but have everlasting life. Does this make sense to you?"

William stroked his chin as he pondered what he had just heard. Something inside him knew truth hung on these words, yet something else inside was deeply offended by it. His heart felt like it teetered on the edge of a fence, divided between two pastures of which he could not tell which looked greener. Whatever his response, he did not want it to be rash.

"I'm not sure," he replied at length. "I need some time to consider all of this. I've never heard it put quite like this before in... where I've been." William caught himself as he almost revealed where he came from. Beads of sweat trickled from his face and down his back. He hoped no one noticed.

Gaimis's smile held steady, even as it underwent a subtle shift from cheer to sadness. "Of course," he said with a bow. "Such things are weighty matters. However you handle it, it's your choice. I've done my duty as a Wayfollower in telling you of the Way. But if you have any questions, please don't hesitate to ask."

William met his smile with a tenuous but sincere one of his own. Gaimis then glanced across to his siblings, and his sadness deepened even further when he discerned that neither of them wished to talk any further. But there was still one thing left to address.

"Now, Brinwin," he said. "While I still counsel you not to give from ulterior motives, I was perhaps too rash in jumping to conclusions. If you truly want to offer the stone out of the goodwill of your heart, I won't reject your offer. It would be used for the good of many, should you still wish to give it away. Whatever you choose, I apologize for coming across so heavy-handed." He looked down and shook his head. "I suppose it's a curse that comes with being a Zikennig."

Brinwin nodded his appreciation and bowed with unfeigned respect. "I suppose so," he mused in agreement. Zala seemed to be at least somewhat appeased by this exchange, relaxing her shoulders for the first time since the discussion had started.

Gaimis cleared his throat and moved to pull back the living room curtain. "At any rate, I'm sure you're all quite tired. We don't have much in the way of luxury, but let me show you where your cots are."

The others followed him into the living room, where his wife had already spread makeshift mattresses for them to sleep on. They were nothing lavish, little more than thick blankets folded together. But after the long day they had all been through, even these they received with gratefulness. Gaimis brought two lamps from the dining room and set one in the middle of the sleeping area. The other he carried with him as he excused himself and disappeared behind another set of curtains.

For all their exhaustion, sleep came slowly for everyone as each pondered in silence what they had discussed with the Wayfollower of Edomear. The physical struggles they had faced up to this point were no less acute than the spiritual ones they faced in those evening hours, huddled beneath the roof of an old stone cathedral. The more he thought about it, the more William could not help but agree with Brinwin. This city really was nothing like Elkreath.

26

Dreams Come True

For the next couple of days, time passed by as a blur. Gaimis rose early the next morning and offered his guests permission to stay two more days, until Sunday. "But should the authorities ask me if you're here," he warned, "I will answer truthfully." Brinwin found the arrangement agreeable enough, and with no further delay, he set about to conduct the last of his research. He spent the entirety of the first day relocating his alchemy equipment to the cathedral, which proved no simple feat. William stayed behind as Zala and Brinwin each used their expertise to smuggle the necessary items in. Once it was safely in the upper room, William helped them unpack the equipment and set it up to Brinwin's specifications.

When William was not engaged in this, he spent his free time making the acquaintance of Gaimis's wife and children. Gaimis himself had too many duties for him to stay behind in the upper room, but he did not seem to mind leaving his family unattended. With the wisdom given him, he had apparently discerned that "Velkis" could be trusted. His wife remained wary, but the children warmed to him in short order, quicker even than to their aunt and uncle — a fact no doubt aided by the friendliness stirred up in William by Gilwin's resemblance to his own son.

He took joy in telling them stories of his past experiences in England and Cabalia, easily captivating their imaginations with his tales of adventure. He did not, of course, tell them he was from England, but merely made mention of "a far-off place."

In the meantime, Brinwin and Zala worked skillfully. By the end of the day, they had relocated all of Brinwin's equipment without raising suspicion. Zala joined William after dinner to amuse the children with her light magic, while Brinwin stayed up late into the evening to make his final calibrations. Only after everyone else had retired to bed did Brinwin permit himself a few hours of sleep. Long before anyone else awoke, he rose to complete his grand experiment.

It was in silence and solitude that Brinwin Zikennig best worked his craft, and it was thus in the early morning hours in the stillness of a church that the shimmering blue of a Danuri stone quietly and suddenly changed into violet. Had such an event transpired in legitimate circles, it would have been celebrated with pomp and fanfare, lauded by scholars and laypeople alike. Yet as fate would have it, nothing but an exultant gasp from an outlaw in hiding ushered in Cabalia's greatest advancement in alchemy in over five hundred years.

The irony was not lost on Brinwin as his face lit up with a smirk. With quivering hands, he set down his records and inspected his work. It felt as if he held the power of the sun at his fingertips as he turned it over in his hands, and the brightness of the stars outside failed to compare to the light that gleamed inside it, bristling with newfound energy eager to be used.

Visions of the possibilities now open to him flashed through his mind like a flood. In a single instant, he saw himself seated as Lord Supreme over all of Cabalia, surrounded by mountains of wealth and crowds of adoring subjects. Those who had dared humiliate and banish him as a Keeper of Alchemy were reduced to nothing but a smoking pile of ash, a perpetual monument of his triumph over them. The accolades of all surrounded him, and the mysteries of the universe unfolded before him like an open book. All this and more he now held in his grasp.

He sensed, as it were, the willingness of the stone to grant it all as a reward for advancing it above its brethren. But he felt another presence also, stronger and yet gentler than what he held before him. No words were spoken, but it impressed on him a clear understanding: *Such power and knowledge were not for mortal men.* If he went back on his word and took the stone for himself, an even deeper Power would ensure ill fortune by the end.

Brinwin set the stone back down and trembled. As clear as the dawn then rising, he knew what the will of Yahos was. He dared not cross it. *I see now what my brother meant about your power,* he mused fearfully. In the days ahead, he would speak of his encounter to no one, but rather treasured it up in his heart. To the day of his death, he could no longer deny the existence of the God his brother served. What he remained unsure of was such a God's willingness to forgive a criminal like himself.

He sat in silence for some time until the first rays of sunlight roused him from his thoughts. He heard the rustling of the others as they stirred, signaling that his time of solitude had reached an end. He tidied his research notes with a sigh and deconstructed the most volatile pieces of equipment. After pocketing the Danuri stone, he peeled back the curtain and withdrew to the sleeping area.

William and Zala had already risen, and they sat together on a couch in discussion with each other. They fell silent upon noticing Brinwin's arrival, except to offer an amiable greeting that seemed genuine enough. "Well?" Zala pressed after a brief pause. "Did you do it?" It was all Brinwin could do to refrain from smiling when he noticed his niece and nephew peering from behind a curtain, trying not to be seen and desperate to hear what his answer would be.

"When's breakfast?" he said dismissively with a feigned tone of seriousness. "I'm famished." Zala raised her eyebrows, struggling to discern the meaning of his response. She pressed him further with her eyes, even if just for a sign only she would understand. He offered no such satisfaction, however, as a mischievous streak seized upon him that relished his sister's unsatisfied curiosity.

"I think it's going to be any minute now," William replied. "Everyone else has been in the kitchen since sunrise."

As if on cue, the voice of Gaimis's wife rang out from behind the dining room curtain. "The food's ready, children! Go fetch the others for breakfast!"

Avah and Gilwin waited a few moments before racing past the curtain, hoping it was not obvious they had been eavesdropping. "Breakfast's ready!" they echoed in unison before racing back into the dining area. William, Zala, and Brinwin exchanged amused glances with themselves as they followed behind.

Upon their arrival, they all sat down to a meal of buttermilk and a pie of meats and berries topped with a sweet, light syrup of a rich green hue. William was skeptical of the dish at first, but the voracity with which his companions devoured it assured him it could not be too bad. Upon tasting it for himself, he found it the most delicious meal of his life. Try as he might afterward, he could never find one comparable to it. It would be a source of regret in later times that he failed to ask for the recipe.

Once they had all devoured their portions, every eye at the table turned to Brinwin. The air grew tense with an unvoiced question that demanded an answer. Not even his mischievous mood allowed him to postpone the topic further. With a final swig from his mug, he glanced around the table and met everyone's stare. He kept his expression in perfect formation, neither smiling nor frowning.

"I'm sure you all noticed how late I stayed up last night," he began. Everyone gave a collective nod and not-too-secretly hoped he would stop beating around the bush. "And I'm equally sure," he continued, "you are all wondering how my research fared." Avah and Gilwin nodded with excitement while the adults sat still as statues.

"Well," he said. "It would appear that after a lifetime of research and the best equipment I could procure..."

Everyone held their breath and leaned forward as Brinwin paused for dramatic effect. Like the sun breaking from behind a cloud, the smile he gave dispelled all shadows of doubt.

"I was correct."

The stone whipped from his pocket to his palm as if by magic, and the violet glow of the transformed Danuri stone suddenly shone before them. "Gilwin, if you would please fetch us a pitcher of water. All that remains is to verify its authenticity before a room of witnesses." He hardly finished his sentence before his nephew dashed from the table and disappeared in a blur of motion. He returned faster than anyone expected with a clay vessel filled to the brim with water. How he failed to slosh it onto the floor as he went, anyone could only guess, but he somehow managed to set it down without making a mess.

Brinwin laughed as he took the pitcher and poured some water into his mug to make enough room for the stone. "Everyone remembers how the blue stone sounded, yes?" he asked. After confirming they did, he dropped the stone into the pitcher with a flick of his wrist. The water splashed, then rippled with a violet glow beneath its surface. When it stilled, a humming sound began. To the onlookers' astonishment, it was the same humming they had heard the evening prior. The pitch was just slightly higher than before, which was what Brinwin had predicted would happen. Aside from that minor detail, there was no mistaking it: This was indeed the same song as before, coming from the very same stone as before.

A hush fell over the room and remained unbroken until Gaimis rose from his seat and clapped his hands. "Well done, Brinwin!" he said. The others followed his example and joined in applause, each congratulating him in their own way. Zala's eyes beamed with pride, the fullest they had been in a long while, and William offered a bow fit for a king. Brinwin blushed, and before he could react otherwise, his eyes began to tear up. Nothing he envisioned earlier with the stone could compare to the richness of the moment he then experienced. Sweeter was this praise among family than anything the outside world could offer. He would not have traded it for anything else, for this was indeed a thing meant for mortal men.

* * *

Zala looked at Gaimis with greater respect from this time onward, which helped the final day of their visit pass all the more smoothly. When evening arrived, they spent it in fellowship and goodwill over a home-cooked meal. True to his word, Brinwin presented the Danuri stone as a freewill offering to the Church of Edomear — a gift that Gaimis did not refuse. This having been done, the adults then discussed their plans of departure for the following day.

They agreed the best course of action was for them to leave after the early morning church service. While everyone else in the church was occupied with worship, they would move into position in the lower corridor. Zala would then disguise themselves as visitors when the doors opened for dismissal, and they would simply walk out the front doors and onto the streets. Most of the equipment they had smuggled into the cathedral was no longer necessary for Brinwin to keep, so he donated it to the Church, too. Everything they needed for the rest of their journey fit into a single large trunk that Gaimis would have carted to the Galfrid Docks later in the afternoon.

It would be a full day ahead of them, so they decided to retire early that evening. Brinwin and Zala offered their final farewells to their niece and nephew before their mother led them to bed. Once they departed, Gaimis lingered behind to offer a parting prayer of protection over the next stage of their journeys. The gentle confidence with which he prayed soothed them greatly, such that even Zala appreciated the gesture. Before they withdrew to bed, William had one final question to ask.

"Please sir, pardon me if this is a silly thing to ask," he said to Gaimis. "I was too embarrassed to ask it at the time, but I really have been curious ever since we arrived here. How exactly did you know it was Brinwin and Zala when you first met us? I can only assume the groundskeeper told you the false names they provided. Did those names have some special meaning to you? It seemed to me your siblings weren't even surprised when you saw through their disguises."

Gaimis smiled with a mischievous gleam in his eyes that one would have expected to come from Zala. "Actually, William, the truth is a bit more interesting than that."

William's mouth dropped slightly at hearing his real name used. He had not told his name to anyone since he arrived. How could Gaimis have known? It must have either been Brinwin or Zala who slipped up, he reasoned. He would need to have a serious talk with both of them before they left.

Gaimis continued to smile as he spoke further. "While you are right about the groundskeeper, those false names had no prior meaning to me. The only reason my siblings weren't surprised is because they're used to me knowing things I shouldn't have otherwise known, such as your real name, my fine English nobleman." Now William's mouth dropped fully. Gaimis reveled in his guests' surprise before proceeding to elaborate.

"Ever since I was a child," he said. "I've occasionally had dreams and visions from Yahos. This past Sunday, I had a most curious dream as I slept. In it, I was somehow lost in England and had to find my way back home. I had nearly given up hope of ever making it back, when I ran into *you* at a certain port in London. You introduced yourself as Lord William Steele, the advisor of a great king who had just overcome his rival. You offered me passage in your vessel and treated me kindly, bringing me all the way to Elkreath.

I saw the city stretched out before me in the moonlight when a ball of fire leaped into the sky from out of nowhere. It exploded and then formed into the shape of my brother's tattoo. The city then burst into flames when suddenly my brother and sister appeared beside me. 'Don't worry, Gaimis,' they told me. 'We'll get you both home safely.' And then the dream ended."

Even Brinwin and Zala stood in shock as they heard what their brother shared. They waited in stunned silence for him to continue.

"Not surprisingly, the dream left me shaken. I knew this was no ordinary dream, but I knew not what it meant. I fasted the next day and prayed the whole rest of the week, but Yahos provided no interpretation. And then, two days ago — the day you arrived — as I made my rounds through the city, he spoke to my spirit. He didn't speak audibly, mind you, yet he spoke so clearly. 'Go back to the church,' he told me. 'Your brother and sister are waiting for you.' I became anxious then, and I tried to protest. 'But Lord!' I said. 'If this is so, you know they're outlaws! Even if they aren't here to do me harm, they haven't spoken to me in years. What would I even say to them?' But he only insisted the more. 'Go back,' he said. 'And do not be afraid to shelter them for the night. I will have you share my word with them.' I still doubted that you had actually come to the front doorstep of my church, but when the groundskeeper told me of you and what you looked like..." Gaimis then shook his head. "I knew what I had to do."

A silence fell as the others marveled at him. When they came to themselves, they explained to Gaimis their adventures in Elkreath and the signal Brinwin had launched into the sky. William also shared his history, that he was indeed the advisor of an English king, but that his king was still at war with his rival. Gaimis listened attentively, pondering for a while what they shared.

He spoke again at length, saying, "I see now in hindsight what Yahos has revealed of things past. I can't help but wonder what he's revealed of things yet to come. I dare not predict from what remains unclear, but still, I offer you this consolation: Perhaps it wasn't to me, but to *you* that your words of safety were addressed in my dream. May Yahos protect you all until you make it back home safely."

These words comforted the others and filled them with peace as they slept their final night at the cathedral. They slept soundly, waking the next morning refreshed and in good spirits. The worship service was already underway, but they rose with enough time to gather their belongings and execute their plan.

They made their way in silence down the staircase without much difficulty. Opening the door at the bottom proved to be more of a challenge, but Zala and Brinwin were both experts in stealth. They pried the door open with care, and Zala cast her camouflage enchantment with no less mastery. They took their positions in the corridor as planned, waiting for the service to end.

While they waited, they heard brief snippets of Gaimis's voice as he preached his sermon. Words of mercy and the love of Yahos resounded off the old stones around them, amplified by the passion with which he spoke. Edomear's culture was nothing if not elegant, affecting the city's religion as equally as its architecture and music. Even if they had lacked interest in the content, they would have gladly listened longer to the eloquence of the great Wayfollower of Edomear. But as it was, they had arrived at the tail end of his speech. Before long, they heard him offer the benediction, and they prepared themselves to spring into action.

The sanctuary doors soon swung open, and the clomping of many feet filled the corridor. Zala undid their camouflage and applied a disguise to Brinwin just before they rounded the corner and joined the passing crowd. No one seemed to notice their presence, but progress to the exit came slowly. The service had been well attended that morning, and all the passageways in sight grew congested. They came to a standstill many times, unable to jostle themselves forward. At such times, they peered back into the sanctuary behind them.

Gaimis still stood by the altar at the back of the area, behind which an immense stained-glass window stretched upward and across. It depicted the crucifixion of Yeshun, with a crowd of bystanders gathered at the foot of the cross. To the far side, an empty tomb stood with the stone rolled back. William could not read the Cabalian lettering, but above the cross was a scroll drawn out horizontally, which read *It is finished*. He would not have known it, but the Sunday morning service was structured to end at the same time sunlight hit the window most directly. It thus shone in its full glory as they departed, leaving a deep impression in their memory. They pondered both its beauty and its meaning until the line in front of them moved forward at last, and they made their way to the city streets.

The sun shone clear and bright as they exited the church, with but a few passing clouds to hinder its light. They descended the flight of stairs, then peeled off from the crowd to return through the park they had entered on their arrival. Stopping beside the pond, they gazed around the rest of the park to see many people spread out across its grassy hills. The majority were families that arrived straight from church, busy setting up picnics at their favorite locations. Children raced along the river before it fed into the pond, playing tag or engaging in foot races. A number of young adults brought their musical instruments with them and practiced as they waited for food to be prepared. Others of the young men occupied themselves with some good-natured wrestling, attempting to claim the highest hill in sight. Taken all together, it made for a pleasant scene to watch as Brinwin and his companions walked onward.

Once they reached the other end of the park, William turned toward Brinwin. "I imagine it'll take some time for Gaimis to send the carter to our ship," he said. "What's the plan for now while we wait?"

Brinwin looked back out across the park and shrugged. "For now? We may as well enjoy ourselves. This could be the last day of happiness we have for a long time." He hardly finished speaking when a cloud passed overhead and darkened the sky for a few ominous moments. Something inside William shuddered, but Zala attempted to lighten the mood when the sun came back out.

"Does this mean we can catch the grand finale at the palace tonight?" she pleaded. Brinwin wavered as he stroked his chin in thought. "Please, Brin?" she continued to beg. "You know I've never been to a Sunday one."

Brinwin struggled a moment longer before relenting to his sister. "It's later than I'd like to stay," he grumbled. "But fine. We need to leave as soon as it's over, though. The longer we stay here, the greater our chances of getting caught."

Zala grabbed William's arm with a triumphant smile and nearly squealed in excitement. "This is going to be so much fun!" she said. "I've always wanted to hear a Sunday finale—they say it's the best one they have!"

Much to Zala's impatience, there was still a whole day ahead of them until sunset. They spent most of that day wandering the streets, entertaining themselves with whatever attractions they could find. They sampled the local cuisine for lunch and dinner while also visiting no small amount of tourist locations.

At one point, Brinwin could not resist taking them into the city's most eminent alchemy supply store. It was amusing to watch his reactions as he inspected its inventory, muttering under his breath about how inefficient this tool was, how overrated that tool was, and how it was robbery to be sold at that price. William could barely hold back from laughing when Zala plastered a giant frowning face on the back of Brinwin's tunic as he grumbled his way through the store. He never noticed, which made it all the more hilarious.

They busied themselves with other things after leaving the store, and time continued to slip away from them until sunset arrived at last. They attempted to beat the crowds at the palace gate but ultimately failed in their endeavors. They wound up sandwiched in the middle of a vast assembly of spectators in a plaza by the king's courtyard. The area that hosted the performance was massive, yet still too packed for them to see the performers from where they stood. Zala solved this problem by cloaking herself and climbing to the top of a statue in the plaza. She took William up with her but left her brother down below, much to his chagrin. Only after night had fallen and the performance was underway did she relax the use of her magic that concealed them.

From where they sat, they could see the line of musicians arranged at the edge of the plaza. They aligned themselves in ranks, with different performers arrayed in separate colors. The players of stringed instruments had turquoise tunics that allowed them free movement of their arms, while the players of wind instruments displayed trailing robes of deep gold. The percussionists bore cloaks of brilliant crimson, and the singers sported shirts of forest green. The dancers wore gowns of many colors that flowed about in the early evening breeze. Torches shone bright around them all and caused their garments to glitter as a sea of gemstones.

The chatter of the crowd before them was deafening, but it proved nothing in comparison to the summoning bells that commenced the festivities. They tolled in unison from a ring of spires at the top of the king's citadel, each louder than an average domir. They were overlaid in pure gold and covered in fine jewels, such that a single bell could hardly be afforded by any of Europe's kings. Overwhelming they were in sight and sound—effective, too, in quieting the masses. Most everyone had to cover their ears when the tolling began, and conversation was all but impossible while they rang.

When their sound finally ceased, a light shone upon a balcony of the citadel, where the king of Barcbane himself appeared. He raised his hands and spread out his arms to address his subjects with a booming voice to be heard by all. He congratulated them on the state of their glorious city before praising the performers for their most excellent services. His speech was the same as every week, but for those visitors who heard it for the first time, they would have never been able to tell. William and Zala sat enraptured by the spectacle, waiting with anticipation for the performance to begin.

With a final wave of his hand, the king stepped back from the balcony to sit upon a throne, and the headmasters of the Musician's Guild then rose to direct the ceremony. What followed next was nothing short of glorious. The singers raised their voices in perfect harmony to start the chorus, and they continued to sing in angelic voice as the song progressed. The dancers weaved to the beating of the drums as they spun each other around with the ease of acrobats. From slow and mellow to fast and spirited, every good facet of song and dance proceeded forth at the citadel of Edomear. For hours the performers played, and not an eye remained tearless by the end of the performance.

Zala looked as if a dream had come true. The joy in her eyes was as vibrant as the domir before her. Perhaps it was due solely to his bias, but William found her more beautiful at that moment than the finest troupe of Edomear's musicians. He reached his hand to encircle hers, only to find himself breathless when she cast her full gaze toward him. There atop a statue in the king's courtyard, they shared their second kiss.

The evening went on in mirth until a single bell tolled at midnight, which signaled for the music to cease and the crowds to disperse.

William and Zala dismounted the statue without being seen and regrouped with Brinwin at its base. They passed through the crowd as quickly as they could, but it still took several hours longer to make their way to the Galfrid Docks.

William and Zala nigh-on floated along the streets in their happiness, but Brinwin kept a keen watch, often looking over his shoulder as they wound their way through the night. Whether his vigilance was necessary or not, whatever harm he worried about did not come to pass. They arrived at their boat to find Gaimis's shipment loaded safely aboard and the crew ready to depart. In short order they set out, leaving the proud spires of Edomear behind them.

Even in the dark, the city was as glorious as when they had first seen it. Untold thousands of lamps and torches cast their glow across the city, causing its buildings to look like flaming pillars of stone crafted by the gods of old. It stood beneath the stars, ethereal, as a city on a hill whose light could not be hidden. So it remained as they sailed the Southern Sea, traveling still in the domain of House Barcbane.

William watched helplessly as time and distance pulled the light of Edomear farther away from them until it appeared as but another pinprick of starlight. Their course then adjusted and bore them northwest to the lands of another territory. The atmosphere changed in the following days, announcing without words when they reached the final stage of their journey. Thickening shadows and silence grim were their new companions, for they had now entered the lands of House Shadowcrest.

27

The Haven of Sicwood

Brinwin refused to share his plan with the others until Barcbane's realm lay behind them. Perhaps his motivation was mercy, to not burden them with cares while they traveled in happier places; or perhaps it was pragmatism, desiring to speak of it only when the surrounding darkness turned their full attention to how they would conduct themselves in it. Regardless of his reasoning *why*, the time had come to explain *what* they were to do. He summoned William and Zala to his cabin the fourth day after leaving Edomear and sat them before him.

A map of Shadowcrest lay stretched out on his desk, and by his feet stood the trunk he had packed before their departure. No one else had seen what Brinwin packed into it, but they could only assume it was what he had crafted in secret before giving the Danuri stone to the Church. They hoped this mystery would now be revealed, but as usual, Brinwin's expression was impossible to decipher. The room was lit almost exclusively by the candles that burned on his desk, which had been purchased on their last day in Edomear from a street vendor. They gave a pleasant aroma as Brinwin spoke and were intended to serve as a comfort. Given the circumstances, however, they simply clashed with the atmosphere, as perfume applied to raw garbage.

"Our journey's end is near," said Brinwin with a cough as he shoved the candles away from him. "Which means it's time to settle our course of action. As I see it, there's only one way open to us." William and Zala remained silent, giving him their full attention as he spoke. It was no exaggeration to say their lives depended on it.

"The recipe of Shadesteel," he continued, "is one of the most closely guarded secrets of House Shadowcrest. Our first problem is finding where and in what form the recipe is kept. Fortunately for us, I have access to sources no one else does. I know for certain that a physical copy exists, and I even know where it's stored."

He then leaned closer to them and dropped his voice as if in fear that the shadows themselves were spying on them. "Beneath the capital city of Everoth," he said, "there's an underground complex known as the Underwatch. Somewhere in this complex, they manufacture shadesteel in a special foundry called the Underforge. That is where the recipe is hidden."

On hearing this, Zala inhaled sharply with a hiss. "But it's impossible to get there, Brin!" she blurted out. "If it's anything like the legends say, we wouldn't even reach the front door without getting caught. How are we supposed to go in, traipse around, find this recipe, and then leave without getting captured?"

At this, William perked up and turned toward Zala. "Pardon my ignorance," he said to her, "but couldn't your magic get us in there? You've been using it to sneak us around the rest of the island. Why not there?"

Zala paused, hoping her brother would answer the question for her. When he remained silent, she replied with despondence. "Because of the Azgari, William." She shuddered as if the term left a bitter taste in her mouth. She did not want to continue, but Brinwin still refused to elaborate.

Collecting herself, she gazed back at William. "They're abominations made from dark alchemy. My brother won't even speak of them if he can help it, they're such an affront to his craft. But I guess you need to know. They were once normal people, like you and me, before Shadowcrest corrupted them into monsters. They neither eat nor sleep, and they wield all the strength of a bear robbed of her cubs. They're tall and muscular, with skin blacker than night and eyes that glow purple. And before you judge me for believing fairy tales, I've seen them myself. They're horrible and wretched, and I never want to see one again!"

Her voice broke as she said this, even as her eyes filled with tears. William put his hand on her shoulder and waited for her to gather herself again. "But beyond all that," she continued at length, "they can sense when magic's being used. Any enchantment I have to disguise us would be like screaming at the top of our lungs that we're there to rob them. They'd find us in a heartbeat."

William shuddered and turned to Brinwin. "Then how are we supposed to make it past them if we can't use magic?"

Brinwin's countenance remained impassive as he replied, "Simple. We won't use magic." Both Zala and William stared at him dumbfounded. Brinwin then rose from his chair and bent down to open the trunk. "There was a reason we visited the Essari, my friends. They're master inventors who rely on the natural world, not magic. I pulled a few strings and smuggled some of their technology with us. Such as this."

He pulled from the chest a cloak of pale green. Something about its texture seemed unusual as he put it on before them, but no one could quite place it until he suddenly vanished. The others marveled as they stepped closer, still unable to see him. Only after circling him with still no success in spotting him did he pull the cloak from his head. It was unsettling to see Brinwin's face floating above them by itself as he talked. "With these cloaks, they'll never see us coming. Or going," he assured them.

Zala ran her fingers over the material, impressed with what she could (not) see. "That's all well and good, Brin," she said. "But the Azgari aren't the only things guarding the Underwatch. What about the Night Roamers?"

"Night Roamers?" William repeated. Part of him did not even want to know.

"They're a type of thilmig," Brinwin explained. "Each of the Families pioneered their own breed. Backbenders were Barcbane's innovation; Night Roamers are Shadowcrest's. What my sister is worried about is their excellent sense of smell. To which I say: Come now. You honestly think I couldn't find a way around that?" He withdrew a vial of clear solution as he said this and gave it a satisfied shake. "I designed this concoction myself. Mix it in with a bath, and your scent will be gone for weeks. We'll soak the cloaks in it too, for good measure. They'll neither see us *nor* smell us."

Zala smirked. Her eyes lit up with mischief, even as her tongue shot forth a dare. "But what about hearing us?"

Brinwin's eyes gleamed with equal amounts of mischief, and he replied, "I think you'll like this part." He hoisted from the chest a pair of greaves, black as midnight and mingled with strains of deep blue.

"Is that what I think it is?" William gasped.

"Yes, Wil-yim," Brinwin chuckled. "This is shadesteel. I thought it would be a nice touch to infiltrate their home with their own creation. I'm not sure if your king told you, but one of its many unique features is that it silences noise. With these strapped to our feet, they will neither see nor smell nor hear us coming." His face was smug as he gazed at Zala, ready to accept her resignation from the defeated challenge. She failed to do this, however, but held out with one last question.

"And how, pray tell, will we coordinate our actions with each other if we can neither be seen nor smelt nor heard?" she asked. Brinwin's smile deepened in preparation for checkmate. Without a word, he reached into the chest and produced a headband of transparent, rubbery material. He adjusted it around his head before fitting himself with an attached earpiece. He then retrieved another band just like it and set it up over William. The material felt strange and uncomfortable at first, but the longer he wore it, the less William noticed it.

"These," said Brinwin, "will allow us to communicate silently. Observe." Brinwin stepped back from William and stared at him. As William wondered what was about to happen, he heard Brinwin's voice through his earpiece. Yet Brinwin's mouth had not moved! "The device transmits your thoughts as a voice to the other headband, Wil-yim," he heard. "If I can think it, you can hear it."

William's eyes widened with a gasp. *How was this even possible without magic*, he thought to himself.

"I'm not entirely sure," came Brinwin's reply through the earpiece. "The Essari's knowledge is far beyond me in this field." William sputtered, flabbergasted that Brinwin could hear his thoughts.

Zala stared at them in confusion, only able to see William's outward reaction. She, too, was blown away when fitted with a headband. "Does this mean both of you can hear my thoughts at the same time?" she thought.

"Indeed it does," came Brinwin's thought, coupled with a physical chuckle. His chuckling ceased when Zala let loose with a curse that caught him and William off guard.

"I don't enjoy being spied on," she reprimanded in thought. "Also, there was a good reason I dropped my mind-reading classes at the Mages College. Seeing how men *acted* was disgusting enough. Seeing how they *thought* was even more so. Keep your dirty thoughts away from me, or Yahos help me, I'll make you regret it." Both men grimaced, and everyone slipped off their headbands and turned them back over to Brinwin.

"I would imagine there's some way to manage how much we hear," William mused with an apprehensive look at Brinwin. "Being forced to listen to each others' thoughts for hours on end would be almost as bad as being captured." Zala nodded heartily in agreement.

Brinwin hesitated a moment too long for either of his companions' comfort before he replied, "Not to worry. The devices won't transmit every last thought at full volume. The less deliberate your thought, the softer it comes across to the others." Brinwin paused as he twirled the devices around his fingers. "I can't guarantee it will be a peaceful experience. But it should be tolerable."

William and Zala only gaped at Brinwin in dismay. *If worse comes to worst, I can just pull the blasted thing off*, thought William with a twinge of defiance. *No one would see me do it.*

After stashing them away again, Brinwin opened a drawer in his desk to retrieve one final item. He held it in his palm for the others to observe. It looked at first glance as nothing more than an ordinary compass, but on further inspection they saw a bead in the center that glowed a dull orange. On the inside of the compass's cover, there was another smaller compass with a needle that only pointed up or down.

"This," explained Brinwin, "is what I crafted with the Danuri stone before I gave it away. It's a special compass that points not north but toward what we seek: the recipe of shadesteel. With this, we'll know exactly where to go once we infiltrate the Underwatch. The bead in the center glows a different color based on how far we are from the target, and the vertical arrow should be pretty obvious," he said. "It won't tip off the Azgari as we use it since it works passively off the magic spent at its creation. This, along with the other items, will let us sneak our way to the Underforge. And with a boatload of luck, we'll even make it back out, too."

He tucked the compass back into the drawer before drawing their attention to the map spread out before them. "But to get there, we'll first land here at the town of Sicwood," he said, pointing to a starred location on the map. "It's about a four-day journey from the outskirts of Everoth, and it contains the only haven of Azkalah in Shadowcrest."

William squinted at Brinwin, incredulous. "Really?" he asked. "The only one?"

Brinwin shrugged. "Is it terribly surprising that the kingdom of spies and alchemists can keep out an illegal organization of spies and alchemists? The only reason they allow the one at Sicwood is because even they need our services every once in a while. Which conveniently gives us a place to land without raising too much suspicion. Even if they notice us, they'll just see us as Azkalah agents going to an Azkalah haven. Hardly something unusual."

Returning his gaze to the map, he traced his finger down a river leading to Everoth. "If we travel south along the Silent River, we can veer east at the Dusken Hollows to skirt around the city and enter by the southeast. It'll be the least guarded entry since most of their attention will be drawn to the northwest where the river enters the city. No one but us would be crazy enough and skilled enough to approach it from the Hollows. If and when we accomplish our mission, we'll trace our steps back the same way we came. We'll ship out from Sicwood to Elkreath, which by then would be no match for our stealth skills. We'll get you on your own boat back to England and call it a job well done. Fair enough?"

William stroked his chin in thought. He would not use the term "fair" to describe this turn of events, though he had little choice but to go along with it. Still, there was the matter of his original business. He would hate to survive by the skin of his teeth only to return empty-handed to Henry. "As long as I come away with the suits of shadesteel my king sent me for, then yes. Fair enough," he said.

Brinwin nodded, then turned his attention back to the map. "Now then, I'm certain neither of you have as good a memory as I do," he said. "I'll be able to guide us around well enough, but it would be helpful to have studied these maps in the event we get separated. This here is a general map of Shadowcrest, and that chart there is a detailed plan of Everoth. I suggest you spend at least some time familiarizing yourselves with them. We'll be landing at Sicwood by the end of the day. Then our adventure really begins," he said with a wink more ominous than reassuring.

As much as William hated to admit it, there was wisdom to Brinwin's advice. He spent the next several hours with Zala studying the maps, paying particular attention to the layout of Everoth. Brinwin excused himself to deal with other matters aboard the ship, returning just after nightfall when the time drew near to disembark. After helping them pack the last of their items, he led them to the main deck. They waited there until they came at last to the town of Sicwood.

The light of neither moon nor stars penetrated the clouds that night, leaving them in thick darkness when they took their first steps on Shadowcrest soil. Before long, William caught his initial glimpses of the people of Shadowcrest. Many still walked the streets, even in the dead of night, shrouded with thick cloaks to protect themselves from the evening chill. He saw their faces in the torchlight as he followed Brinwin's lead — they were pale and grim. Silver eyes glared from them, brimming with an acuity he found both mesmerizing and repulsive at the same time. He quickly learned to keep his head down as he went and to ignore the stares that seemed to surround him.

Time passed slowly as he and the others snaked their way through the town, unable to see much of their surroundings. It had been a while since Brinwin last visited the Sicwood haven, but he still remembered enough to guide the way safely, if a little slowly. They went until they reached the outskirts of the settlement, where they came to the edge of a forest. No clear paths existed to follow into its depths, but Brinwin led them on with confidence.

For everyone else but him, the way through the forest was harrowing. Everything that grew there was blighted, as if by some malignant curse. No matter where one brought the torch to bear, there always seemed to be movement in the shadows at the corner of one's vision. Worse yet, the sound of neither bird nor beast could be heard — only silence. And not the kind of silence that brings serenity and refuge. No, this silence was of that wretched type that hangs tensely in the dark and gathers behind one's back, then grows, warning of terror to come any second, until a moment too late it snaps with a scream.

Yet no harm befell them that night. Brinwin led them true until they came at length upon a clearing in the woods, where a small cabin stood. A light from within flickered through its clouded windows, dim enough to be hidden from afar but bright enough to comfort them as they approached the door. The grinning skull of Azkalah lay etched into its timbers, a most ironic symbol of solace. Brinwin knocked at the door and offered a password when prompted by a guard on the other side. The door then swung open to grant them refuge, and they lost no time moving their convoy inside.

Not until the door shut safely behind them did William take in a detailed view of the haven, which, if he were honest, left much to be desired. The interior was bare and weathered. At the far end, a single wall of half-stocked shelves stood covered in cobwebs, while barrels of supplies lay in a disorganized heap in the center of the floor. A small backroom served as a pantry, but the quality of the stores was questionable at best. Aside from the single guard with a torch who kept the door, it looked to be all but abandoned.

Brinwin, however, was not the slightest bit phased by the ramshackle appearance. Once Zala removed the disguise charm from him, he greeted the guard with a professional salute. In response, the guard snapped to attention. "An honor, sir!" he said. "How can the haven assist you?"

"We require lodging and food rations for the next stage of our mission," replied Brinwin.

Pointing to the pantry, the guard spoke but briefly. "The usual rules, sir." Brinwin nodded his acknowledgment before taking William and Zala to the backroom pantry while the remaining crew members stayed behind with the guard. Not until he closed the door behind them did he allow them to speak.

"Pardon me for saying so, Brinwin," said William with a glance around him. "But this seems a tad underwhelming, don't you think?" Brinwin merely responded with a dismissive grunt as he fumbled with the sacks of grain piled on the shelf in front of him. Before the others understood what was happening, he reached his hand behind the sacks, and there suddenly came a loud *click*. A hidden hatchway popped open beside his feet to reveal a ladder descending deep into the earth.

"Fortunately for us, not everything is as it seems," said Brinwin with a sweep of his hands. "I was half-minded to let you go first, but I think I'd rather see your reaction when you reach the bottom. You can follow me whenever you're ready."

William stepped cautiously to the edge of the ladder and peered down. The passageway was both darker and narrower than he would have cared for. At the bottom of the ladder, a light flickered in the distance. William grimaced, and Zala put her hand on his shoulder. "Don't worry, William," she said. "I'll fashion some orbs of light to follow us. We won't be climbing in the dark."

Her words offered some consolation, but not enough to rid William of his anxiety. He would once again find himself underground—a place he had very much come to hate. The temptation to climb back up would have been too great for him if he went last, so he decided to go before Zala. Practical though it was, it was a decision he regretted the moment he lowered himself past the floorboards. Even with Zala's orbs surrounding him, the climb was long and tortuous. The only thing to rival his relief at reaching the bottom was the wonder that filled him upon seeing for the first time the sprawling hub that was the true haven of Sicwood.

Spacious caverns opened before him in every direction, amply lit with a warm, robust light. Agents of Azkalah teemed about in the middle of their errands, dozens upon dozens of them. Some stood with maps and parchments, scrutinizing their targets and planning their strategies with the advice of their cohorts. Others lugged crates of supplies with them, groaning under the weight of their mysterious cargo. Still others stood at their alchemy stations crafting their potions with great care. Instruments of bronze and steel gleamed in the light alongside vials half-filled with bubbling solutions of every scent and color.

William stepped near one such station and would have investigated further had Brinwin not yanked him away. "Rule number one in a haven," he said firmly. "Never interrupt a crafting session in progress. That's how limbs get blown off. Or worse." William gulped as the agent at the station glared at him, unamused, before resuming his work.

William looked at Zala, who simply nodded back at him. "It's true," she said with a casual stroke of her hair. "Once saw a guy lose his nose that way. It didn't really diminish his appearance, though. He still looked as ugly as before."

William continued to gape at the experiment in progress until Brinwin laid a hand on his shoulder and guided him farther down a cavern. More than a few agents stopped in passing to pay homage to Azkalah's Best, and it was then that William realized how far Brinwin's fame extended within the organization. It rivaled, if not exceeded, that from without. As flattering as it was for Brinwin, it was also a burden that slowed their progress considerably. Eventually, his focus on the mission outweighed anything else, and they interacted with few others until they reached their destination.

They stopped at a reception area where a team of agents sat stationed behind a counter, armed with quills and parchments. The agent closest to them looked up from his records as they approached and eyed them intently. "What can we do for you, Mr. Zikennig?" he asked with the impeccable formality of a bureaucrat. Brinwin produced a pile of papers from his bosom, which he then slipped to the receptionist.

"I'll need these sent as covertly as possible to the Keepers of Alchemy at Ansrith," he said. "It's of the utmost importance they arrive there intact."

The agent deposited Brinwin's research notes on Danuri stone transmutation into a secure container, which he stamped with an official seal. He scribbled a list of instructions and attached it to the container, then flagged down another agent who lugged a wagon full of cargo. "Ansrith, priority five," he instructed. The carter took the package and continued steadily on his way until the life's work of Brinwin Zikennig passed out of sight.

Brinwin stared after the wagon for only a few moments before turning his attention back to the receptionist. "I'll also need eight days of food rations for a class seven stealth mission."

The receptionist dug out a folder and poured over its contents, scribbling circles and crossing off check marks as he went. He soon looked up from his work with a satisfied nod. "You'll find what you need in storeroom 46A. Take this receipt and present it to the clerk there," he said as he handed him a small scrap of paper. "Is there anything else you'll be needing?" he asked.

Brinwin nodded. "Lodging for three in one room. Ten hours, please," he said.

The receptionist crunched yet more numbers before handing them each a copper badge. Imprinted in the badges were what appeared to be a random string of letters and numbers. "You'll be staying at den number five," the clerk said. "You can turn in your badges at that sector's reception." Brinwin nodded and stepped away from the counter with a quick word of thanks. He promptly led the others aside to make room for the applicants next in line. The whole interaction happened so quickly it made William's head spin.

Brinwin noticed his companion's bewilderment, and his lips curled into a grin. "What do you think so far of our haven, Wil-yim?" he asked. "A tad underwhelming, isn't it?" William shot back a dirty look and shook his head, which only delighted his companions even more. He at least had the good sense to hold his tongue, and he continued to do so as he followed them to den number five.

With a name like that, he expected their lodging to be a dingy sort of place, but he once again found his expectations far from the mark. The "den" was a comfortably adorned suite with all the amenities one could ask for from a civilized abode. The wares of Cabalia's black market were extensive, and the very best of it lined the shelves, cabinets, and other furniture before them. Zala and William acquainted themselves with their surroundings while Brinwin left to procure the necessary items from the storeroom. By the time he returned, they had made themselves at home.

"Don't get too attached to it," Brinwin warned them. "We're just here to get a final bit of rest before we depart. The goal is to leave in the middle of the morning, so rest up." He dimmed the lights, and the plush bedding soon had them all sleeping as deep as the rocks below them. Such was spent the last night of peace they would have for a long time thereafter.

It took some effort when the time came for Brinwin to wake his companions, but he still managed to keep them on schedule. Once they had gathered their final provisions and turned in their badges, they followed Brinwin down a long, winding passage that stretched south. Few others traveled that way, and the traffic only grew sparser as they went on. In time, none but the three of them remained to travel alone in silence.

At this point, the full gravity of their mission settled into their awareness. They knew their plans would soon be put to the test, and their fates decided for either good or ill. Ready or not, the calm had now passed. All that remained for them was the storm.

They stopped at the end of the passageway, where a small rope ladder led to the surface. They donned their equipment there and wished themselves the best of fortunes. William and Zala shared a final embrace before they ascended the ladder and took their first steps into a wilderness of shadows.

28

Journey into Darkness

The sun shone drearily through a haze of clouds when William took his first glance upward. He had hoped the daytime would bolster his spirits as he set out with his companions on the final leg of their quest, but the thick curtain of gray that draped the heavens left nothing but a sense of gloom that refused to dissipate. The scenery of the ground below was only worse.

Behind them stretched the forests of Sicwood, their gnarled and leafless branches raised as thorns to the sky. Before them ran the Silent River, its gray waters as still as a graveyard. Everywhere else was a barren wasteland of scorched grass and scattered crags. Nothing alive could be seen for miles around, yet they dared not lower their guard. An unseen presence filled that land, one that felt just inches away from discovering them.

They communicated little as they set out, afraid at first to test the limits of the Essari technology. Nothing but the pressure of their hands holding each other reminded them of their company. But after miles of travel through an unchanging landscape, the need for companionship to stave off the despair proved too great. They began to share their thoughts freely, finding themselves much better off for doing so. The invisible presence did not seem to notice, so they traveled their first day as ghosts, unseen and unheard: wisps of nothingness in a land of nothingness. So passed their first day without incident.

The nighttime was mercifully uneventful, though still as nerve-wracking as one might expect. Even if it had not sunk its claws into them yet, the gloom of Shadowcrest was now palpable, no longer an abstract concept of "somewhere else" while they tried to sleep. This realization only lent strength to the convictions which nagged William's conscience since his conversation with Gaimis in Edomear.

Amid the tossing and turning that plagued him that night, the image of the priest's sad but hopeful face came into his memory's view. The priest's words stood ready to recite themselves yet again if they would be suffered just a moment longer. But William dismissed such thoughts as one would shoo a butterfly from a picnic basket. Even if the intruder meant no harm, he was still unwilling to grant it the chance to feed any further. Who knew where such things might lead? The struggle eventually subsided enough to blend with general anxiety before dropping off into an uneasy slumber somewhere along the way.

The next day began the same as the first, showing no sign of change as they went along. Only when nightfall was nearly upon them did the scenery begin to alter. Patches of wild grass appeared in haphazard formations, and small shrubs grew amid rocky outcroppings. Rivulets broke off from the main river and ended in swirling pools that rippled and bubbled softly. Beyond these pools, they heard for the first time the sounds of wildlife. Owls screeched in the distance, and other nocturnal birds mingled their calls with scavengers. Some unfamiliar sounds could be heard also, making them glad to have their scent masked by Brinwin's elixir.

They took refuge that night amid the outcroppings of rock by the river. Some were deep enough to act as a shallow cave, and in one such outcropping, they huddled together to pass the night away. Sleep came uneasily and left them in a state of half-wakefulness for most of the evening.

At one point, William stirred to find the dark form of a creature as it crouched before them. The clouds had parted enough for the waning light of the moon to fall and expose it from the shadows in which it lurked.

It stood on four legs, half the height of a man. Silken black fur with silver streaks covered it from head to toe, and its talons were the same ivory color as its teeth. A low purring growl built up from its throat, ready at any moment to break into a shrill cry. It stood sideways at the entrance of the outcropping, facing toward William's left. The one eye visible at that angle was yellow like an owl's and no less piercing. Its nose glistened and twitched in anticipation until it suddenly leaped out of view.

A second later came an awful thud of bone pounding into fur, followed by a rip of tearing muscle. A shriek rang out from the beast's prey, which turned out to be another of the same beast. A vicious fight ensued, and William watched the two forms struggle to the death as they rolled past the entrance. Fresh calls rang out in the distance, and before he knew it, five more beasts entered the fray.

By then, Brinwin and Zala had been startled into full consciousness, and all three of them watched in horror as the carnage played out before them. Fur and flesh flew about in a spray of blood amid the snapping of teeth and the slashing of claws. Were they to be discovered, they would be done for, and they knew it. They dared not move, breathe, or even think. They simply watched and hoped in their heart of hearts for deliverance.

The fight ended with three of the beasts mauled on the spot and the others limping off with serious injuries. Their pained howls rang far into the distance until they faded away and left the land in silence once more. William trembled where he sat and reached out to Zala with his thoughts. She did not reply immediately, but when she did, her "voice" was clear and solemn. "Those would be Night Roamers, William," she thought.

"In bestial form," added Brinwin. "In their other form, they're trained in the use of daggers and serve as assassins. No less deadly, just more refined than... *that*." Everyone shuddered, bemoaning the fact that at least two more days remained until they arrived at Everoth. Any hope of sleeping the rest of the night was gone, so with nothing else to do, they waited anxiously for dawn to arrive.

When at last dawn came, it rewarded them with a small boon for their troubles: The clouds were spotty enough to afford them a clear view of sunrise. Were it not for the carcasses in front of them as a reminder of the evening's horrors, it would have been a beautiful moment. The rugged landscape fit perfectly with the crisp, orange light that flooded it and the wind that blew just softly enough to rustle the grass on its hills of stone.

They tarried but shortly to enjoy the view before setting out, each of them eager to leave that place far behind them. The farther they went, the more the scenery changed before them. The Silent River flowed wider and more lively. It no longer lived up to its name, for it rushed along as any other river would, with all the sounds one would expect a river to make. The vegetation around it grew denser, too. By the middle of the morning, healthy-looking grass of full green lined the foothills, signaling they had reached the fringes of the Dusken Hollows.

They veered off to the east, where the vegetation grew lush and the first signs of population appeared. Dirt roads ran across the land, past well-kept orchards and spacious farmland. If he had not known any better, William would have guessed this to be the countryside surrounding Edomear. Compared to the wasteland they emerged from, it seemed impossible for this to be the land of House Shadowcrest. And yet it was.

"It seems beauty can be found in the most unexpected places," thought William to himself.

"Of course it can," responded Zala. "Shadowcrests are people, too, after all. They try to hide it, but their land isn't completely barren. People can't live off rocks, you know."

William did not quite know how to respond. To think back, "Thanks for the lecture, but I wasn't talking to you," would come across as rude, but it was annoying to have her butt in on his thoughts. "And here you worried we'd spy on *your* thoughts," he mentally murmured. It was everything William could do to keep his thoughts further in check. How he wished for a return to normal speech!

Before the conversation could carry any further, the bushes that lined the edge of a nearby orchard drew William's attention. Their ebony leaves were prickly like a holly bush but also flatter and more rounded. A brilliant red berry sat at the tip of each leaf, similar in appearance to a raspberry, if raspberries were but a single unified form without divisions. The berries caught the sun's light in a dazzling way, appearing translucent, with juice that swirled inside ready to burst with flavor in the mouth. He stepped nearer to investigate this strange plant and felt the tension in the others' arms lessen as they followed him.

"What are these?" thought William.

Zala refrained from answering, so Brinwin thought back in reply, "They're called blood berries."

William nearly gagged. "Blood berries?" he thought with disgust. "Please don't tell me that's actually blood in there."

"Well, not quite..." came Brinwin's hesitant response.

Now William's suspicion was piqued. "What do you mean, 'not quite?'" he shot back.

Brinwin paused before replying with as much bluntness as he thought William could handle. "It means that no, the juice itself is not blood. But the only way these bushes flower is by being soaked with blood. So, indirectly, they come from blood. The more blood they soak in, the bigger the berries become and the more nutrients they provide. Depending on the quality, a single berry can serve as a whole meal. They're said to be quite tasty."

William gaped in horror at the rows of berries that lined the hedge. Most were the size of a fingertip, but some were twice that size. Their beauty quickly transformed into revulsion, and he could not bear to look at them any longer. How much blood had been spilled to make these plants bloom? And what kind of blood? Such questions he did not care to dwell on, and he let Brinwin lead the way onward down the dirt paths.

By the middle of the afternoon, the skies had cleared enough for sunlight to fall directly into the valleys they traveled across. The light brought warmth wherever it landed, yet a chill still hung in the air. The people of Shadowcrest wore long sleeves and trousers as they traveled the roads, but they lacked head coverings for the most part. This afforded William a clear view of their hair, which came in but two varieties: raven black and silver white. They all had the same gray pallor of skin, however, which made them look all the more unusual in the daylight. Something about them seemed off. But William could not quite place it beyond their paleness. They looked like normal humans and yet, at the same time, not. He was glad none could see him as he passed through their midst.

The roads he and the others traveled were well maintained, which sped their progress considerably through the Hollows. By the end of the day, they were a fair distance into the region's heartland and well poised to enter Everoth by the end of the next day. They expected little danger to plague them that night while firmly in the confines of civilization. They thus rested in an open field by a manor house, looking forward to a peaceful night's sleep. But such did not prove to be the case.

The first hour after sunset passed quietly enough, and they had nearly fallen asleep when the muffled sound of footsteps came from behind them. They turned to find a band of ruffians gathering at the edge of the field, each brandishing spears and spiked clubs. Alongside them, human-like figures half the size of people slipped by, their daggers as sharp as they were silent. "Night Roamers!" came Zala's thought of realization to her companions. Their sable bodies blended perfectly into the shadows as they approached the manor house to which the field belonged. Had they not passed within feet of where William and the others slept, they would have neither been seen nor heard. The formation slipped by in a few moments, and all was left still yet again.

The silence lasted just a minute longer until an ear-splitting shriek rang out from the manor house. Lights flared to life from within, and all pretense of stealth dropped. The ruffians smashed down the gate to the main building without a care for the noise they produced. Their clanging mixed with the alarm bells that sounded through the property, leaving all in a state of confusion.

Brinwin alone had the keenness of sight to distinguish the Night Roamers that still scaled the sides of the manor, as well as the scowling figures in the windows above them with glowing green beakers in their hands. They smashed the beakers against the window sills, sending their contents cascading down onto the intruders. Some of the Night Roamers were lucky enough to avoid the oncoming liquid; those that were not met a painful end as their flesh dissolved in seconds, leaving them as nothing but a puddle of entrails on the manor grounds.

A fresh band of guards dodged the puddles as they streamed from the building to meet the thugs who had broken past the gate. Some held leashes with bestial Night Roamers at their ends, growling and frothing at the mouth. When the guards released their leashes, the massacre rose to new levels of violence.

Just when William and the others thought things could not get any worse, a roar rose above the chaos. The conflict paused, and a hush fell upon the area. The ground then rumbled beneath their feet, and a second roar rang out louder than the first. The attacking forces turned on their feet and ran from the battle, but it was far too late for them. From the manor's courtyard, there rose the towering form of a great beast. Its visage struck terror into the hearts of all who looked upon it as it stamped upon them in wrath. Friend and foe alike dove for cover. Most did not survive. Gruesome moments passed, and the battle appeared to have reached its end when suddenly a second beast appeared at the edge of the field with a fresh band of reinforcements.

Brinwin and the others ran for their lives, refusing to stop until the beasts' roars faded far into the distance. They ran through many fields and leaped over many fences before finally stopping to catch their breath at the edge of an apple orchard. For a time, they gave little effort to regulate their thoughts, being so wrapped up in them that they failed to notice those of their companions. They eventually calmed down enough to interact with each other, and when they did, William was the first to "speak."

"Can someone please tell me what the bloody hell we just saw?" he demanded with a curse. Had they been able to see each other, he would have seen Brinwin avert his eyes in shame.

"That's all you, Brin," came Zala's thought, unwilling to bail her brother out of an explanation.

Brinwin sighed before thinking, "That's part of how Shadowcrest chooses its leaders out here, Wil-yim. I should have known better than to sleep by a manor without checking it first. I'd bet you any money there was a Seat there."

"A what?" spat William's thought.

Brinwin wiped his brow of sweat before he responded, "A Seat. It's the basic building block of Shadowcrest politics."

"I don't follow," said William.

"Most people don't," replied Brinwin. "From what little I know of politics around here, Shadowcrest is divided into regions. The Dusken Hollows is the most populous one, aside from Everoth. Each region can have any number of Seats. If someone wants to be a leader here, they gather a following and literally plop a fancy seat down at their house. Whoever sits in a Seat rules the boundaries it claims for itself. If boundaries clash, they settle their differences like this. The last man standing becomes the ruler of a Seat. Whoever can survive ruling a Seat for at least a year gets to join the House of Seats in Everoth. From there, they get a chance to be chosen king. Don't ask me how that works. I don't know."

Brinwin then paused to collect himself before continuing. "So like I said, we probably stumbled across a contested Seat. I've heard of what they do in these conflicts but never seen it firsthand. The stories always seemed too astonishing to be true... but it turns out they weren't astonishing enough!"

The explanation appeased William somewhat, as much as a response could under the circumstances. He was still furious to have suffered such a scare through the blunder of a native who should have known better. He fumed further in his thoughts until Zala eventually managed to pacify his anger. Once their nerves had settled, they sought a new place to spend the night. They eventually settled on a deserted patch of land off the main road and spent the rest of the evening there. No further incidents befell them, and they found at least a few hours of sleep for themselves.

They set out quickly when they awoke, hoping to arrive at Everoth while sunlight remained. Progress came slower than they would have liked, however, as the orchards grew denser and the roads jammed with traffic the farther west they went. Wagons packed full of produce dominated the roads, leaving little room to navigate. Many on foot chose to pass by on either shoulder, making it difficult to avoid a collision no matter how carefully one trod. The situation away from the road was hardly an improvement. High walls and thick hedges surrounded the fields, which would have proven just as slow to navigate as the roads—if not more so. At the rate they went, it would have taken twice as long to reach their destination as they would have liked.

They nearly resigned themselves to spending another night in the Hollows when Zala spotted a trade caravan marked with the seal of Everoth heading toward the city. The procession was long, but it plowed through the congested streets with ease. The middle of the formation was lightly guarded and composed of wagons only half filled with textiles. "Quick!" thought Zala as the procession passed by them. "This is our chance! We can ditch it at the city gate!"

"Or use it to sneak in," added William. Brinwin hesitated as he calculated the risks. The grinding of the wheels was loud and distracting. Dust shot up into the air, and precious moments slipped by until the middle of the caravan nearly passed them.

"Come on, Brin!" they exclaimed. He held back a moment longer until something suddenly clicked in his brain. With mere seconds to spare, he yanked his companions forward and leaped into an exposed cart.

The wagon proved sturdy, barely jostling as they landed in its middle. The fabrics inside padded their impact and left them without even a bruise for their efforts. Their hearts, however, pounded heavily as though to compensate for the lack of a rough landing. No one could see Zala's face, but her glare was as tangible as the goods they sat upon.

"Way to drag it out to the last moment!" she scolded her brother. "If I'd known you were so scared of textiles, I wouldn't have given you that tunic for your birthday!"

Were stealth not imperative, Brinwin would have shoved her. "Not everyone can afford to be as impulsive as you, Zala!" his thoughts shouted. "Did it even occur to you we might have botched the landing? Or that this caravan might be subject to inspection? What happens when we get surrounded by customs and they start searching for contraband beneath us?"

"What do you think we'd do, you clodpoll? Sit around and wait until they start searching?" she shot back.

William's jaw clenched as his frustration mounted. To hear them bicker out loud was irritating enough in the past, but for them to trade blows inside his head was more than he could bear. "For the love of God!" his thoughts shouted back at them. "Give it a rest, the both of you! We made the jump safely, and we're already farther along than we'd have ever gotten on foot. If you want to take your headbands off and shout at each other, be my guest. But as long as I can hear you talking in my head, shut it!"

William's intensity caught the siblings off guard and silenced them for a few long moments. Nothing but the jostling of the cart could be heard as their surprise reverted to a simmering ire. "As you wish, *Lord Steele*," came Brinwin's response at last. The sarcasm in his tone almost set his sister off once again, but a fresh squeeze of William's hand on hers was enough to keep the silence unbroken for the time being.

The air remained tense as they rode the last several miles to the gates of Everoth, but they traded no further blows among themselves. By the time the sun set and the air cooled, so had their tempers. They agreed to abandon the cart before they had a chance to be discovered at customs, and so they slipped away when the first signs of the city proper rose in the distance. There was no telling if they would find a safe place to sleep once inside the city, so they pulled aside to an inn by the side of the road and sneaked their way behind it to where an empty field stood. Brinwin made sure to thoroughly scout the area this time, and he found nothing of concern. Their safety thus secured, they prepared to sleep their last night outside Everoth beneath the stars.

No one dared relax their efforts at stealth, so all were privy to each other's thoughts through the Essari headbands they continued to wear. If it was possible to receive thoughts without sending them out as well, such knowledge eluded them. Fortunately, the past few days of traveling together gave them enough time to settle an agreement on handling such a state of affairs.

It was impossible to not hear someone else's private thoughts, but it *was* possible to pretend not hearing them. Anything not addressed to a particular person was ignored as a matter of courtesy so long as no one's safety was at stake. With some practice, a consensual, pretended privacy almost felt like the actual thing. Almost.

William could not help feeling a little self-conscious as his mind wandered. Anxiety over the next day's activities prevented him from sleeping right away, exhausted though he was, and it was this anxiety of the future that drove him to examine his memories of the past. In particular, William could not shake the memories of his time in Edomear. Such a glorious time it had been, traveling through a prosperous city with music unparalleled in quality and a beautiful woman by his side who loved him despite his flaws. If he had ever come close to seeing heaven on earth, it was there in Edomear!

But such thoughts about heaven led inevitably to the enigma of Gaimis the Wayfollower. It was something that William would have been hesitant to consider, even if he could somehow have had more than just an illusion of privacy. The questions this kindly giant of a priest had raised would take him a mile if he gave them even an inch. If he dared to answer them honestly, they could change his life in a way he could not predict. And here, in the heart of Shadowcrest, was the last place he wanted to deal with something he could not predict.

But what about the predictions of Gaimis himself? There was no conceivable way the man could have known William's name and country through any natural means, to say nothing about their fiasco in Elkreath. Like it or not, his dream had been accurate about the past.

Could it also be accurate about the future? Could it be that they would actually succeed in their mission and "make it back home in safety?"

William drew himself into a sitting position as he gazed around. The exact locations of his companions were hidden by the cloaks they wore, but he knew that Zala lay next to him just a few feet to his left, as Brinwin did to his right. Either of them would know their brother better than he, and undoubtedly had heard William's thoughts of him just now. Brinwin seemed to be the more levelheaded in his relationship with Gaimis, but Zala was by far the more pleasant for him to talk to.

No sooner did he begin to address Zala than her reply came, "I don't know, William. My brother has had some uncanny dreams before, but never quite like this. Honestly, I place as much faith in his predictions as I do in the God who supposedly gave them to him. He might well exist, but he won't do what you want him to. Trusting it all to play out in your favor is just setting yourself up for disappointment, believe me."

William paused, unsure how to respond. He reached out to Brinwin next, who merely said: "If Yahos could show my brother the past, why not the future, too? I prefer to think with my head, not with my feelings..." His thoughts stopped short, but the finished sentence would clearly have been, "unlike my sister."

Had the three of them been interacting under normal circumstances, there might have been a fresh round of squabbling. But as it was, they were all weary, dreading what lay in store for them the next day. The conversation died down, and they kept their gaze to the east, away from the silhouette of the city gates that rose above them in the distance. Whatever lay within those boundaries was ominous and ever-watchful, especially in the night. They cared not to look at it, fearful of the invisible presence discovering them right on its doorstep. Daunting, too, were the battlements and spires that lined the wall, specially designed to instill fear the longer one looked upon them.

Worse yet were the gleams of darkened amethyst shining down from them—the eyes of the Azgari themselves. Hundreds of them surrounded the city, peering down with unyielding malice toward all who would enter without permission. Had William and the others given in to the temptation to stare at them through the night, they would have lost all heart. So they instead set their gaze toward the fertile fields of the Dusken Hollows until the light of day returned as a faithful ally against their fears.

The sun, for its part, proved grateful for their reliance on it, and it rose the next morning full of vigor. Scarcely a cloud impeded its progress through the heavens, allowing it to strengthen both their hearts and their vision as they set themselves to entering the city. After sharing a quick breakfast, they left the inn and its field behind them. They traveled once more along the main road, finding it lightly traveled in the early morning. Almost before they knew it, they had reached the southeast gate. Looking up, they found the Azgari still standing at their posts, unmoved from their original positions last night. They loomed as shadows high above them, formidable even in direct sunlight.

William and the others held their breath as they crept past the gate, half expecting them to leap from their perch at any moment to apprehend them. Yet the Azgari remained motionless as they took first one, then two, then five steps into the city. By their tenth step, the gate lay behind them, and the city of Everoth stretched into view. And what a view it was!

The dirt roads they had traveled up until this point transitioned into a pavement like obsidian, from which there rose immense buildings with an exterior like polished onyx. So seamless were their foundations, they appeared to have risen straight from the very roads themselves. Crimson banners hung from their roofs and windows, their colors reflecting off the roads below so that a red glow filled the streets as long as the sun shone.

A grand courtyard also sprawled before the gate. In its center, there rose a solitary figure of breathtaking craftsmanship. Of what material it was, an outsider could only guess. The subject, however, was plainly stated by the inscription at its base.

Elithora, Queen of Everoth, it read. Above these words stood a woman of fearsome beauty. Waist-length hair hung loosely behind her as she looked down in scorn at those who entered her domain, with eyes both sharp and seductive. She wore no crown, and neither did she need to.

Alluring. Haughty. Deadly. Such words proved inadequate to describe the visage of the Gray Lady who sneered over her subjects. Though but a statue, its presence evoked a sense of wonder, fear, and lust all rolled together into a single dreadful feeling. It also made clear the unusual appearance of the people of Shadowcrest. They were without doubt her progeny.

William and the others gaped at her, transfixed as if by a spell. Not until their sense returned to them did they notice the silence that set the city apart from all the others they had traveled. Crowds of people and their animals roamed the streets, conducting business as any city would, yet nothing more than faint whispers reached their ears. An unearthly paradox, it seemed: a city that bustled with life but remained as mute as death. It was enough to send chills down their spines.

William felt the others shudder alongside him, and he took a sliver of comfort in knowing he was not alone in his reaction. Even native Cabalians found this place as appalling as he did! The comfort, however, was short-lived. The fact remained that they still had to press onward into the depths of the city. No amount of dread would change that.

"Well, friends, it was nice knowing you," came Zala's thought as Brinwin stirred and led them onward. No one bothered to challenge her pessimism, for it mirrored their own. Only a fool would insult their companions' intelligence with positive thoughts at a time like this. So in silent despondence they went forth. Perhaps it was merely a trick of the nerves, but they could have sworn the queen's sneer deepened as they took their first steps past her.

Only through great exercise of will did they begin their progress, and slow it was at first. Once they exited the courtyard, however, it felt as if a burden were lifted from them. Their thinking grew clearer and their hearts bolder as the queen's effigy fell farther behind them. They noticed, too, that the scenery became less intimidating the closer they traveled to the city center.

The streets transitioned from glossy obsidian to black cobblestone, which later changed to a normal-looking gray. The buildings, too, became more average in appearance, similar to the structures William would have found back home in England. It was not what any of them expected to find, but they were more than grateful for the change in scenery. The silence surrounding them remained unbroken, but it was tolerable enough to bear as they wound their way through the crowded streets.

William and Zala's memory proved more accurate than Brinwin had given credit, making their study of his maps worthwhile. With each avenue they turned onto and every bridge they crossed, they knew exactly where they were and where they were going. By early afternoon, when the sun was still near its peak, they had reached their target.

The gates of the Underwatch were not well hidden, and upon seeing it for themselves, they knew why. An unbroken line of Azgari barred passage to a mound of stone whose entrance resembled a gaping mouth. Past their waists, one could see the beginnings of a tunnel as it descended into pitch black. A complex system of pulleys and platforms at the end of the tunnel served as a ferry that led through multiple checkpoints, each station more heavily guarded than the one above. How deep the shaft descended was impossible to tell.

"It's as I feared," thought Brinwin. "The entrance is every bit as guarded as the rumors say."

"Then how are we supposed to get through?" pressed William. "Surely you must have planned for this being the case."

"Of course I did," replied Brinwin. "I just wanted to make sure it was truly as guarded as they say before I went to my main plan."

"Which is?" asked Zala.

"Simple," he answered. "We're not going to use this entrance."

"Of course we aren't," she replied sarcastically. Both William and Zala had a sinking feeling the alternative would be no easier than what lay before them.

"Then what entrance *are* we going to use?" asked William.

There came a pause before Brinwin turned and pulled the others with him. "The secret one that lies in the king's throne room," he thought.

Zala nearly groaned, but she caught herself. "But of course!" she mocked. "That'll be much less guarded than here."

Brinwin remained strangely calm as his pace held steady. "So little faith," he chided. Nothing more he communicated until they reached the gates of the King's Palace about a mile away. The structure looked as formidable as the city wall had the night before, with a line of Azgari stretched across a barred gate of shadesteel. No sign of an opening could be seen.

Zala nearly threw her hands in the air. "Oh, look! What do you know? The palace is guarded to the brim, too," she sneered. "Dare I even ask what the backup plan is?"

Brinwin stretched his legs and gave a silent yawn. "That won't be necessary," he thought. "My main plan will be arriving any minute now."

The others turned their gaze in every direction, but no matter how hard they looked, they could not find the source of Brinwin's confidence. Zala stood ready to offer a fresh retort when William tugged on her hand. He could finally see what Brinwin had. "Look! Over there, to the northwest!" he thought to her. "Something's coming toward us!"

Zala looked, and she saw the people in the main street stepping aside to make way for an approaching procession. A blue banner rose from its midst with an insignia clear and bold even in the distance. The twin heads of a unicorn stood back to back, ready to defend themselves from whatever came their way. Wisdom and resolution they held in their eyes, and they struck an impressive figure as they blew in the wind.

"House Bluehelm?!" Zala exclaimed. "What business would they have here?"

Brinwin shrugged. "Does it really matter?" he asked. "If my intelligence is correct, they're here for an audience with the king. Those gates will be opening for us any moment now."

As the procession drew closer, William could distinguish the individuals who comprised it. At the edges of the formation were men in pale gray robes, whose halfmasks only partially covered their frowns as they guarded their leaders. In the center, two men of equal stature walked side by side. One wore a trailing cape with a crown of silver on his head. The other wore a hooded robe of many colors that glimmered in the sunlight. Neither of them looked pleased, and they conversed with themselves in low tones as they approached the gate. When the gates opened for them, their scowls only deepened.

"The king *and* the Archmage?!" Zala's thoughts exclaimed again. "This is no ordinary meeting, Brin."

"All the better to keep their attention elsewhere," he replied. "Now, let's get moving. We'll follow at the very end." He pulled them along, and they fell into line behind the entourage as it filed past the gates and into the palace. William nearly gagged at the stench from the line of Azgari they passed. They smelled of death and decay long suppressed. His nerves tightened further when the gates slammed behind them with a *clank*. He dared not look behind him, for there was no going back now.

He gripped Zala's hands tightly as they followed house Bluehelm through the halls and courts of the palace. The interior was luxurious but also unsettling. It felt as if a poisoned hook lay behind the comfort and beauty that surrounded them. No one dared fasten their eyes on anything for too long as they advanced.

"Please tell us we're almost there," William pleaded with Brinwin. "This place gives me a bad feeling."

"As if the rest of this land didn't?" Zala quipped.

"Enough, you two!" commanded Brinwin. "We're almost to the throne room, and I need to focus."

The others' thoughts fell silent as they followed Brinwin's lead to the final set of doors before the throne room. A delegation of Shadowcrest officials waited by the doors, where they exchanged formal pleasantries with Bluehelm upon their arrival. The doors then opened, and a herald announced their presence to the King of Shadowcrest. Only the King of Bluehelm and the Archmage proceeded into the room. Brinwin and the others slipped in behind them just before the doors were closed and sealed.

Free at last from having to keep pace with the leaders of Bluehelm, the three of them paused to marvel at the room in which they found themselves. Pillars of black and red marble circled the edge of a spacious area, rising from a floor of polished black stone. Azgari stood between each pillar, armed with swords and ready for action. A red carpet stretched up a flight of stairs until it ended at a platform just a few stairs below the throne. The throne itself was covered with intricate patterns of gold and precious jewels, and upon it sat the King of Shadowcrest surrounded by his closest advisors. Their eyes were sharper and their features grimmer than any of the other people of Shadowcrest. The largest and most crafty of them all was the king himself.

Rising from his seat, he spoke with a voice smoother than oil and crafty as a serpent.

"Welcome, my friends," he said. "It gladdens me greatly you both could answer my summons." He beckoned them with his arms to ascend the stairs, even as he descended toward the platform. "Come hither and join me. It isn't fitting for equals such as ourselves to stand above or below each other."

"And yet you would have us walk the greater distance to this equal footing," said the King of Bluehelm. His face remained grim as he stood motionless at the bottom of the stairs with the Archmage.

The King of Shadowcrest paused for but a moment before replying, "My deepest apologies. Sometimes a small inconvenience is necessary to rise above the others and converse with those in power." The Azgari's grip on their swords tightened ever-so-slightly, but not slightly enough to escape the notice of the Archmage. "But I can understand your misgivings," the King of Shadowcrest continued. "I assumed it would have been seen as an honor by the people of the mountains to hold council above the lowly ground."

The Archmage glanced at his companion before throwing him the slightest of nods. "Ah, but of course," replied the King of Bluehelm. "The gesture is well met. You must forgive our missing it. Many have been our cares of late, and we have traveled a fair distance to come here."

The King of Shadowcrest smiled. "Of course. That is most understandable. Ruling a kingdom has never been easy, especially in these uncertain times." He beckoned once more for them to join him, and they ascended the stairs with reluctance.

"I don't like the look of this," thought Zala. "I'd bet you anything the Archmage is just looking to hold higher ground than the Azgari if things go south."

"Which still puts him right where Shadowcrest wants him," mused Brinwin. "On second thought, this might be interesting to watch after all. I dare not look for the secret passage during a full council session." The others agreed, and the three of them crept up the steps, careful to leave plenty of room between them and the heads of state conversing with each other. They soon found the perfect position to eavesdrop and remained motionless as the proceedings continued.

They watched as the King of Shadowcrest clapped his hands on the shoulders of the leaders of Bluehelm and said, "Long and faithful has been the service of House Bluehelm to this island. You've led as first among equals, and your wisdom has only grown to match the peaks of your mountains. Haldvar would no doubt be proud of both you and your ancestors."

The Archmage and the king stiffened, unimpressed with the flattery piled on them. "Surely, the Fox of Shadowcrest has not called us here just to commend our service," said the Archmage. "Of what business does he truly wish to speak?"

The smile of the King of Shadowcrest remained unflinching, even as he withdrew his hands from their shoulders. "But of course. Bluehelm has always been more practical than Barcbane and cares less for flowing words. Here is my concern, then. I fear that while you've been leading from the heights of the mountains, you have missed the whispers of the ground below. We of Shadowcrest have ever been in tune with the stirrings and shadows preceding change. And the stirrings have grown unmistakable: The people of Cabalia are becoming dissatisfied with the ancient order. Haldvar has been gone for almost a thousand years, and the people will soon long for an overlord to unify the island."

The king and Archmage recoiled in shock. "You speak treason, Gelitar!" exclaimed the King of Bluehelm.

"Nay," replied King Gelitar. "The Great Conqueror has taken a fancy to other worlds and forgotten about us. Not even he cares for the ancient ways. Mark my words, the time will soon be ripe for a new overlord, and one of us will need to lead."

"And what is your proposal then?" demanded the King of Bluehelm. "That we forsake the oath of our ancestors and fall prostrate at your feet?"

The eyes of Gelitar narrowed. "Hardly, my dear Queterius," he said. "I propose we join our worthy families and rule with both wisdom and knowledge. You, the masters of magic, and we, the masters of alchemy —our combined assets would be superior to all others. Bluehelm has long held a dual government. Why not make it threefold in the interest of a greater good?"

The faces of both the Archmage and King Queterius lit red with fury. "Absolutely not!" yelled the King of Bluehelm. "Your words are a poison that would destroy this island and everyone in it. We reject your offer!"

The King of Shadowcrest sighed and paced back up to his throne. "I thought you would be wiser than this, my friends." The Azgari silently drew their swords and moved toward the base of the stairs.

"Has not your own proverb occurred to you?" pleaded the Archmage. "You say that a fox's tail is longer than its head. Would not the overlordship of Cabalia lessen your lifespan?"

King Gelitar sighed heavily. "It would be like Bluehelm to think they know our proverbs better than we do," he muttered.

The Archmage glanced down the flight of stairs and noticed the approaching Azgari. Turning back to face the King of Shadowcrest, he said, "Be reasonable, Gelitar. We both know how a battle between us would end. Shadowcrest would be down both a king and its palace before your wretched servants could reach the top of these stairs."

Gelitar stood beside his throne and turned back to face them. "That is a fair point, Felstis, but it still makes no difference in the long run. Another king would follow in my footsteps, and the people's hearts would still long for a new emperor. Whether in our lifetime or in that of our children, there *will* be a united Cabalia. If you care not to lead with me as the head, then you can follow as the tail." With a gesture of his hand, the Azgari stopped halfway up the stairs. He sank into his throne and gave another wave of his hand. "I care not for bloodshed tonight. You are free to leave if you wish."

The Archmage cast a worried gaze at King Queterius before turning to face the King of Shadowcrest for the final time. "We will do everything in our power to stop you. Unlike Shadowcrest, Bluehelm is no traitor to Cabalia."

Gelitar shook his head. "Have you not listened to what I've said? You fight not against me but your own people. Do what you must, but not even the heirs of Komarin Bluehelm can hold back the tides of change forever."

"We will see about that," the Archmage said before escorting his king back down the steps. "It wouldn't be the first time Shadowcrest has misjudged the other families."

The Azgari returned to their posts by the marble pillars and stood motionless as the leaders of Bluehelm exited the chamber. The doors slammed shut in anger, which sent echoes racing up to the throne of Shadowcrest. King Gelitar rubbed his temples wearily before calling to his advisors, "It appears Bluehelm's wisdom has waned further than I thought. Arrange for an accident to befall our most esteemed guests... outside our borders."

His advisors snickered with a bow. "The mountain passes are known to be quite treacherous," they said. "Especially since avalanches are quite common this time of year."

The king stroked his chin. "True enough. But unless it's strong enough to overpower an archmage, it would be best not to damage our paths of commerce."

The advisors bowed, then followed the king as he rose from his throne. "It's always wearisome dealing with fools," he said. "I'm going to refresh myself. This council is adjourned." With that, the heads of state dispersed, leaving the room empty except for the Azgari that stood around the base of the stairs.

Brinwin and the others crept the remaining distance to the foot of the throne. "I have to admit, that was quite unexpected," mused Brinwin. "What do you think, Zala? Could such a thing be possible?"

Zala did not respond immediately. When she did, her thoughts were laden with uncertainty. "I don't know, Brin. This whole kingdom leaves you not knowing what to think anymore. If you asked me that before we left Edomear, I'd have laughed in your face. But if the King of Bluehelm *and* the Archmage themselves are worried..." Her thoughts trailed off into silence.

"Agreed," thought Brinwin. "This is a most surprising turn of events. But right now we have other things to worry about." He then turned his attention to the throne before them. "Somewhere in this design, there's a way to open a hidden entrance behind the throne. William, I want you to stand behind and let us know when the passageway appears. Zala, I want you to stay in front and keep a lookout. I'm going to see if I can crack this enigma."

Brinwin stepped onto the throne and ran his fingers across the design as the others took their positions. The examination proved tedious, and what felt like hours passed by with no success. "How do you even know this passage exists?" Zala asked as her patience ran thin.

"Like I said," replied Brinwin, "I have access to sources no one else does."

Zala rolled her eyes. "No kidding, genius. But what source in particular mentions this passage?"

Brinwin shook his head. "If you really have to know, there's an obscure piece of poetry called the Song of the Underforge. It mentions a path to the Underforge from Everoth's high seat. And then it rambles on about fancy designs, which is actually just a clue on how to find a secret switch. I've followed the clues, but still nothing happens!" he thought as he jammed his thumb against a sapphire stone on the armrest.

Zala shook her head in frustration. "Poetry indeed!" she fumed. "Next thing you'll tell me is the recipe's on the back of a chamber pot."

Her murmurings suddenly paused, and she squinted into the distance. "Hey, Brin!" she thought abruptly. "How does this poem start?"

"Why do you ask?" he replied, somewhat perplexed.

"Just humor me. How does it start?"

Brinwin took a deep breath before reciting the song from memory. "Down in the shadows where caverns run deep..."

At this, Zala immediately perked up. "Down there, Brin! The song's etched into one of those marble pillars. *Down in the shadows where caverns run deep, our potions are brewing, and secrets we keep...*"

Brinwin spun in excitement and searched for the pillar. Upon finding it, his mind uttered a curse in amazement. "Of course!" he thought as he scanned its text. "This version's different. They must have changed the words when they wrote it down in books any outsiders might read. Figures it's written on the pillar with the most Azgari standing by it."

He finished reading the rest of the pillar, then wheeled around to face the throne. He traced his fingers once more along the backrest until his finger landed on an onyx stone cut in the shape of a triangle. "Got you!" he thought as he pressed the stone inward and rotated it carefully.

The faintest sound of a click reached his ears, and William's thoughts then rang out, "Whatever you did, Brinwin, it worked! I can see the entrance. It just needs to be pushed open without making too much noise."

Zala and Brinwin joined William behind the throne. Between the three of them, they managed to pry the door open without alerting the Azgari. They peered inside to find a well-lit staircase of carved stone that descended far beyond sight. "Well, friends... I guess this is it," thought Zala. "Time to get ourselves the recipe."

Brinwin entered first, followed by William and then Zala. They made sure to close the entrance as carefully as they had opened it before setting off down the stairway. The stairs were wide enough for two people to descend at a time, so William slipped back to walk alongside Zala.

Lines of bold text were inscribed on either side of them as they traveled the passage. Above the text, a stream of pictures flowed by in fine detail. The words and the paintings stretched down thousands upon thousands of steps to a mind-numbing depth.

"What are these?" gasped William.

Zala remained speechless as she traced her hands along the walls until she finally dared to whisper a reply. "I think this is history, William. A very dark history."

Her assessment proved accurate in more ways than one. The light that so generously spread at the passageway's entrance dwindled as they descended so that each new scene depicted on the ancient stonework had deeper and deeper shadows cast upon it. The first scene to attract their attention still had a fair amount of light around it, as full of life as the newborn child it portrayed. A frowning woman held the boy in her arms as he cried, her gaze centered on the dagger grasped firmly in his hand. A ring of text circled over their heads, but to the surprise of William and his companions, it was not Cabalian.

"I've never seen any script like this!" thought Brinwin with amazement as he stopped to examine it. Zala was also astonished. Neither they nor any normal Cabalian would have expected to see a foreign script in the heart of a Cabalian palace.

Their bewilderment only intensified when William thought with a sudden realization, "But *I've* seen it..." The fact that his companions were invisible made no difference — William felt their widened eyes trained on him. "There's hardly anyone in England who knows what language that is," he explained, "but I once knew a traveling scholar in my youth. It's been years since he showed me those symbols, but now that I see them again, I'm certain of it. Those letters are Greek!"

Before the others could ask the inevitable question, William hastily added: "I can't understand a word of it, though." Their disappointment was heavy but brief. Their thoughts were soon swept away in the tide of curiosity as they continued to examine the scenes below them, now titled exclusively in Cabalian.

The child grew in strength and agility, always clutching the dagger he had been born with. In just a few scenes, he was a young man of handsome build and cloaked in black. If there was any doubt before, it was now clear whose history they observed. The shadows across the wall grew longer as one by one, another target of assassination met their end at the blade of the Shadowed One. The torches on the wall were spaced such that the founder of House Shadowcrest was always lurking in the shadows just before he struck.

One of the most stunning displays showed him dropping from the roof of a palace straight into the midst of a frightened group of politicians. Most of them scattered, tripping over their togas as they went. The leader in the center, however, still fought even as the Shadowed One's dagger protruded from his chest. Just above the wound, a symbol rested on the man's tunic, smeared in blood. Once again, Brinwin and Zala's amazement was palpable.

"Impossible!" they gasped in unison. William remained in silent confusion for several long moments until the brother and sister came to their senses enough to explain the source of their amazement.

"That symbol is the seal of Haldvar, Wil-yim! The Founder himself!" Brinwin thought as he trembled.

"Do you understand what this means?" interjected Zala. "The founder of House Shadowcrest tried to assassinate the founder of Cabalia itself!"

Their shock made it apparent this was not something taught in Cabalian history. Incredible as this knowledge was, it paled in comparison to what came after.

Even William could not contain his astonishment when the very next scene showed Haldvar, his wound still fresh on his chest, sitting at a table and bargaining with the man who had almost killed him. Whatever it was they negotiated over a thousand years ago, it must have gone well. The next scene depicted something any Cabalian child would have been familiar with: a magnificent ship crossing the sea, with Haldvar poised confidently in the front with all the other Founders behind him. They gazed with one accord at the Island of Magic, even as the Shadowed One lurked behind them in the darkness as he always did.

Brinwin and Zala's excitement calmed somewhat as the story moved into more familiar territory. The original inhabitants of the island, their eyes glowing a variety of colors, tried at first to resist the conquering Founders. They inevitably failed, and the next dozen scenes showed them working with the Founders to rid the island of the *Ezith Baal*. With each passing victory, Haldvar took less and less of a prominent position until he was absent altogether at the final battle. That may have been an important detail, but something else caught William's attention instead. The monster that everyone fought was, in fact, a familiar figure.

"That's the queen from the statue!" thought William. "She's..." William stopped in shock. "You didn't tell me she was the Queen of Vampires!" his thoughts hissed.

Brinwin shrugged. "I didn't think it was necessary for you to know. Sometimes ignorance really is bliss."

"Then that means..." William gasped. He looked on with disgust as the Shadowed One, enraptured with his new queen, fought against his former allies. The text said their love was chosen willingly, but William doubted it most strongly. He felt no sorrow when the scene of Valdric Hearthfell striking Elithora with his great spear came into view. The wounded queen and her lover then fled into the West, where they founded the city of Everoth on the banks of the Silent River. Six children she bore to the Shadowed One before succumbing to her wounds and giving the city's name its meaning: *My Sorrows*.

They saw the tears of the great betrayer as they spilled deeper and deeper down the passageway until they fell into a great pool of blood at the final step. The final words of text read, "Here continues my work in the Underforge." A depiction of the veiled face of the Shadowed One stared down at them from the eaves of a simple door of shadesteel. Nothing but a weathered wooden latch kept the door shut.

Brinwin and the others took in a deep breath as they stood before the door. They all knew what they needed to do next, but none desired to do it themselves. Each waited for someone else to crack under the pressure and open the door, until finally the delay became unbearable.

"Here goes nothing," thought Brinwin as he readied his compass beneath his cloak. "On the count of three." They stared in apprehension at the doors before them as Brinwin's thoughts called out steadily.

" One…"

William's heart raced as a sick feeling rose within his stomach. Something did not feel right at all.

"Two…"

Zala's face broke into a cold sweat as she trembled. Something was definitely not right. She would have reached out to stop Brinwin but found herself paralyzed in fear.

"Three…"

Brinwin regretted his choice the moment he undid the latch, but it was too late to stop. The door swung silently open, and through it… came nothing. Nothing but darkness, the distant whooshing of bellows, and the clinking of metals being hammered into form.

Everyone released a quivering gasp and wiped the sweat from their brows. They collected themselves a few moments later and set out down the hallway they found themselves in. The center of Brinwin's compass glowed a light blue, which indicated they were but a few hundred feet from their target. They rounded the corner of a bend when William smelled a rancid odor that reeked of death and decay. It was the last thing he remembered before the fist of an Azgari brute crashed upon his head, and light he saw no more.

29

Shadowed Blood

Inquestor Raiko groaned as he raised a hand to his pounding head. The waning light of sunset gave his eyes a rest from the strain they suffered, but each fall of his steps on the streets of Elkreath only worsened his head's throbbing. The plight of his other muscles was no less comfortable, but he could not allow himself to rest yet. Not when there was so much work left to do.

The last couple of weeks had been nothing but one headache upon another as he and the remaining inquestors scrambled to restore order in the wake of Brinwin's escape. Nothing could have matched the intensity of those first few nights, where the chain of command had been all but sundered and criminals openly pillaged the streets. Those with the ability to lead under pressure soon proved themselves, and Telnis was among that number. Upon waking from the blow to his head atop headquarters, he was among the first to establish cooperation between the disparate branches of law enforcement. He used his light magic to great effect for communication across the city, proving both literally and metaphorically to be a light in their darkest hours.

He also in that time found an unexpected ally in Galfrik, who helped him rally the enforcers and recapture the city's fugitives chase by chase and fight by fight. With each criminal they caught together, his respect for his formerly aggravating colleague only deepened. So it was that when Telnis rounded the corner of a still-scorched building, he smiled to stumble upon Galfrik in the middle of his patrol.

"Ho there, Sargeant!" he called out. "How blow the winds?"

Galfrik spun his gaze around, and upon recognizing Telnis, his face broke into a wide grin. "Why, if it isn't *Captain* Raiko! It's good to see the jackrabbit still hopping!"

Telnis shook his head, laughing as he replied in jest, "Careful there! I could have you disciplined for remarks like that."

Galfrik rolled his eyes and offered a ridiculously deep bow. "Of course, sir! You'll have to forgive me. Still takes getting used to calling you the boss now." Even after he straightened from his bow, his eyes still gleamed with mirth. "I hope ya don't throw me in the stocks for sayin' so, but you're just not as, well... *terrifying* as old Tilthrir. Ya still look like a junior inquestor, if you ask me."

Telnis's eyes narrowed, but before he could offer a fitting response, Galfrik raised his hand and continued to speak. "But in all seriousness, Telnis, ya more than earned your promotion. I'm sure you'll do just fine at the helm." He clapped an arm across Telnis's back, and for the first time that Telnis could recall, it was not with an unbearable amount of force. He accepted the gesture with a small but genuine smile before his gaze wandered back to the damaged remains of the old Dungeon of Elkreath.

"I don't know, friend," he said with a shake of his head. "I thought there would be fewer reports to worry about with a higher rank, but it turns out to be quite the opposite."

"Oh yeah!" spouted Galfrik. "Aren't ya giving a speech to the King of Tropis tomorrow night?"

Telnis grimaced. He hated giving speeches. It was bad enough that he had to listen to his own voice drone on, but to have thousands of strangers listening too made his stomach turn somersaults. "Oh... yes. Thanks for reminding me," he mumbled. "I'll definitely have to discipline you for that."

"Oh, come on!" retorted Galfrik. "You'll do just fine. If you could throw a report together in time for Tilthrir, you can handle this."

Telnis shook his head as he stepped forward and brought his hand to wipe his brow. "I don't know, Galfrik. At least then I had some idea of what was going on. It's been nearly two weeks, and I still don't know how Brinwin did it or where he's gone. How can I stand there with a straight face and tell everyone it's all going to be fine when he's still running amok Yahos-knows-where?"

He leaned wearily against the side of the dungeon as he spoke and ran his fingers over the still-charred bricks as memories of the fateful evening came rushing back. Echoes of screams rising among the flames drowned out his thoughts until Galfrik spoke with a calmness that caught Telnis off guard. "Because you've done everything you can and have results to show for it. Criminals ain't pillaging the streets anymore, and we're not scramblin' like ants on a hill someone stepped on. Ya helped bring order back to these streets, Telnis, and someone has to give 'em hope it'll stay that way."

Telnis sighed as he straightened his shoulders and stepped away from the dungeon. "Small comfort that hope would be," he said. "It doesn't change how many people are dead, and it doesn't guarantee the safety of those who remain."

Galfrik frowned. He understood his boss well enough to know how pointless it would be trying to cheer him up. Still, he could not bring himself to remain silent. "I know it's the boss's job to worry about everything, sir," he said. "But maybe Brinwin was on to something. You let that worry eat you up, and we'll be down one more person able to do something about it. If you can't do it for yourself, at least try for the rest of us." He paused as he laid a hand on his shoulder. "Like it or not, people view you as a hero, Telnis. If you won't lead them in hope, then who will?" His eyes met Telnis's and held his gaze until he stepped aside with a salute and took his leave, resuming his march down the street.

Telnis stared after Galfrik until the man rounded a corner, and all was left in silence once more. With a heavy heart, he looked up at the setting sun, then back toward the looming silhouette of Headquarters directly opposite it. Hero or not, he still had to prepare his speech, which meant returning to his new office. He paused for but a moment before setting out on an all too familiar path through the city. Progress came quickly, as the streets were still lightly traveled. Many still feared to travel at night, leaving only random piles of debris to hinder travel to the Harbor District.

Telnis walked briskly, lost in thought as he went. He certainly did not feel like a hero. Not when a full third of his coworkers remained as lifeless as the charred buildings he passed, and he dared not even contemplate the civilian casualties. No amount of praise given to him could wipe the guilt from his conscience that he had survived but still could not change any of it. Half of him wished the Englishman had let him drop over the edge.

But no, he chided himself. He mustn't think that. That would have left his wife a widow and his child fatherless. But then again, all the new duties piled on him made him practically as good as dead. Something would have to change soon. He did not know how much more he and his family could take. But how could he back down now, with more need than ever to attend to?

By the time he reached the doorstep of headquarters, his head once again pounded under the pressure of his thoughts. He stared up in dread at the top of the building where his office was. Try as he might to steel himself, he could not bring himself to write his report. Not now. Not without a rest.

He looked out over Glimmerstone Bay, where the first stars in the sky beckoned him to leave his cares behind for just a little while. The breeze carried the sound of sea birds preparing for another day's end, inviting him to stroll along the waterfront. Galfrik's advice then came to him, still fresh in his memory. It only took a moment longer for him to make up his mind. The tension in his shoulders relaxed as he released a pent-up sigh. "Fine then," he said aloud to himself. "I suppose I can spare a walk."

He ambled his way down the piers, letting both his eyes and his mind wander from one sight to the next. The rise and fall of the anchored ships atop the waves brought him comfort, and he relished the sound of creaking wood and splashing surf. The longer he walked, the more the fresh air invigorated him and cleared his head of the pounding that plagued it. Even after night fell, he continued to walk beneath the stars, savoring every second of clarity he could. It felt as if he could spend the whole night doing this.

But, alas, he knew he could not actually do so. His mind was now clear enough to focus on his report. He threw a final prolonged glance at the stars before turning back to headquarters. As he did so, he noticed a passing shadow that crept along the piers. Were it not for its gait, he would have assumed it to be that of a dockworker or sailor returning to his ship. But it handled itself far too suspiciously. If years of light magic had not sharpened his sight, he probably would not have noticed it as it snaked its way toward a ship and slipped aboard.

Telnis's lips drew tight into a frown. If that wasn't a remnant of the dungeon's escapees, then he was blind. He braced himself to make yet another arrest as he approached the ship, secretly glad for the chance to postpone working on his report. This was much more of what he enjoyed doing.

He glanced at the vessel's side as he approached it and lit a dim light to see its name spread across weathered timbers in bright white letters. *The Snowbird*, it read. Telnis doused the light before slipping aboard the ship. *Well, well*, he thought. *Let's see what stowaway this bird's got in its gullet.* Ready as he felt, little could have prepared him for what he soon found.

* * *

William groaned as a drop of squalid water fell from the ceiling and splashed onto his nose. How long he had been awake, he could not quite tell. Consciousness came to him gradually as a melting fog. All he knew for certain was that the pounding in his head was relentless, and it only intensified when he reached out an aching hand to brush aside the water from his face. A dim, gloomy light diffused itself through the dungeon in which he found himself, leaving little visible from where he sat. Yet despite the light's dimness, it was still enough to overwhelm his eyes as they recovered from the blow to his head. They stung if he kept them open for too long, so he only caught glimpses of his surroundings in short bursts.

It was not until the third or fourth stint of observation that he noticed the hunched-over frames of Brinwin and Zala beside him. They, like him, had been stripped of their gear and clothed in prison garments of plain white. They both were breathing, but it was difficult to tell if either was conscious. Stealth was of little concern anymore, so William risked raising his voice for the first time in days.

"Brinwin...? Zala...? Can either of you hear me?" he croaked out.

Zala stirred beside him, and Brinwin nodded his head ever so slightly. "Yes, Wil-yim. We can," said Brinwin quietly. Even with the pain that burdened it, his voice remained calm and calculating. That was a good sign, at least.

Zala shuffled closer to William and leaned against him. She spoke with more difficulty than her brother, her voice little else than a hoarse whisper. "Hearing you is about the only good thing in this place," she said. William barely had enough time to wrap his arm around her before a voice cut through the dingy air and caused them all to shudder.

"Awww, isn't that sweet? It appears we have a pair of lovers." The light around them intensified, forcing them all to squint as a shadowy figure drew close to them with a lantern. The figure stopped at the bars of their prison cell and remained silent until their eyes adjusted enough to gaze upon the newcomer.

In time, they distinguished the slender form of a Shadowcrest man peering down at them with a crimson hood drawn over his head. His voice was as piercing as his eyes and elegant as his robes. It took but a moment for their recollections to identify him as one of the councilors who stood with the King of Shadowcrest in the throne room. To either side of him was an Azgari warrior, arms crossed and perpetually scowling. Once he made eye contact with his prisoners, the man proceeded to speak with the smooth, icy voice of a viper.

"I do hope you can pardon us for the state of your accommodations.

It's the best we could arrange for trespassers at short notice." The man hung his lantern on a hook by the cell and folded his hands behind his back. "I'm sure you're all quite exhausted, so I'll get straight to the point. I have many questions for you. The quality of what little remains of your life depends on how cooperative you are in answering them. You can either be reasonable and come clean now, or you can be stubborn, in which case you'll get to spend some quality time with me one-on-one until someone finally snaps and tells me everything. So what will it be, Brinwin Zikennig? Reason or stubbornness?"

If it was possible, it seemed the Azgari's scowls deepened as they waited for a response. William and Zala remained speechless, but Brinwin found his voice with little difficulty as he sat upright. "If you know enough to use my name, you should also know my choice. We count stubbornness a virtue in House Hearthfell." William and Zala remained silent as they braced themselves to accept the outcome of Brinwin's decision. If he would not back down, neither would they.

A sadistic sneer spread across the councilor's face as he removed the torch from its hook. "Excellent," he said softly. "I have much more fun when people are stubborn." His gaze fell upon each of them in turn, lingering on Zala for a few seconds longer than the others. "Yes..." he mused aloud. "You'll be softened up quite nicely before His Majesty comes." Raising his voice, he then said, "If you can excuse me for just a few minutes, I'll be back to fetch the first of you. Hospitality does, unfortunately, take some time to prepare." He turned and strode out of the room, pausing on the threshold for a moment longer. "Should any of you change your mind before I come back, just give a *holler*." The way he emphasized that last word sent chills down William's spine.

The Azgari withdrew to guard the entrance of the jail room, but they remained within a constant line of sight. One could only guess how well the Azgari could hear, so when William and the others spoke, it was in just the faintest of whispers.

"I sure hope you know what you're getting us into," hissed William.

Brinwin remained still, but the gleam in his eyes betrayed that he did, in fact, know something his companions did not. "How do you feel, Sister?" he asked abruptly.

Zala blinked in confusion. She would have thought the answer was obvious, but she knew her brother well enough to realize he was asking a serious question. "Well, let me see... horrible," she replied. "My head is pounding, my muscles are sore, my skin is cut and bruised, and I'm likely sitting on death row and about to be tortured." A sudden belch then escaped her. "And on top of it all, I feel as bloated as a stuffed pig." A faint smile crossed Brinwin's lips, which thoroughly confused the others. He then pulled Zala closer to him and whispered something in her ear.

William could not catch what Brinwin said, but he saw plain as day the gleam that flashed across Zala's eyes. It disappeared as quickly as it came, but it was enough for William to suspect a plan of some sort was being hatched before his eyes. He could only hope it would be enough to rescue them from certain doom.

The brother and sister conferred with each other for a little while longer until Zala shuffled away from Brinwin to recline against William. She nuzzled up against him and brought her mouth to within an inch of his ear. "Just so you know," she whispered. "I'd have done this even if it wasn't his idea." The door to the room then clinked open as the councilor returned with a set of keys jangling from his belt. Zala waited until he stepped past the threshold before leaning in to kiss William, moaning softly as she did so. The councilor's stride hesitated for a few moments before he reached the edge of the cell and ground his keys into the door's rusty lock.

"Alright, love birds, that's quite enough!" he called out. "You've had your fill of fun. Now it's my turn." The door to the cell creaked open, and Zala startled when she turned to see a pale finger pointing straight at her. "Starting with you, Zala Zikennig," the councilor said. He grabbed her wrist and held it in a grip colder than ice. His lips curled into a sneer as he yanked her away with a laugh that made William sick to his stomach. "Women are always the easiest to bend," he explained as if conversing with an imaginary colleague. "And much more satisfying.

Even with the strongest of them, their wills are like their bodies: so very weak. I'd give this one an hour at most before she's fawning at my heels."

William could not contain himself as a red mist of anger clouded his vision. He rose and flung himself at the councilor with all his might, fully intent on wringing the man's neck if he could get a good grip. His ferocity caught the councilor off guard, and for the slightest fraction of a moment, his eyes widened in fear. Such fear was short-lived, however. An Azgari lunged from his side and struck William down with the pommel of its sword. Had it not been ordered to stand down, it would have ended him on the spot.

The councilor calmly brushed away the trickle of blood William's fingernails had inflicted on him. "On second thought..." he mused. "Perhaps pain would be the best means of persuasion." He locked eyes with William, even as his teeth glimmered in a gruesome smile. "Or then again, why not both? Pain before pleasure, I think the saying goes. Yes, your reward for that little stunt will be to hear her screams first *before* I turn her affections elsewhere."

William would have thrown himself again at the councilor, but Brinwin reached forward and held him back. "Easy Wil-yim," he muttered. "Save your strength. You'll need it for later."

It was with great difficulty that William stilled himself, especially when the councilor sneered down at him with a huff. He dragged Zala behind him as he exited the room, each step he took piercing William's soul like a wooden spike. Zala cast a glance behind her as she reached the threshold. With but a second to spare, she threw William a wink and then was gone.

William sank to the ground in despair, far too entangled in his own emotions to notice Brinwin as he methodically scouted the room before them. The two Azgari warriors returned to their posts by the door, which appeared to be made only of wood. Between them and the Azgari, there stood a simple table also made of wood. On it lay all the gear confiscated from them. Brinwin's compass sat in the center, its bead glowing a dull blue.

Brinwin smiled in determination and pulled William to his feet, very much against his will. He opened his mouth to protest, but Brinwin would not suffer him to speak.

"Save it, Wil-yim. I need you to listen to me now. We'll be on the run in three minutes or less, and I need you ready for action. I'll grab my compass as soon as the guards are dealt with, and you'll gather their swords. Everything else we leave behind. I don't know how they discovered us in the first place, but apparently our gear isn't as stealthy as we thought."

William's head spun as he tried to follow Brinwin's reasoning. He failed to understand what madness could possess him to talk like this, of escaping from the bowels of the Underforge in the state they were in. He nodded blankly as he mentally repeated Brinwin's instructions to himself. Just when he thought he understood everything, Brinwin spoke up again.

"Make sure you don't let their swords touch your bare skin. They say Azgari swords are made of a special shadesteel cursed to drain away one's life essence, and frankly, I don't doubt it. Perhaps we can use the Essari cloaks as a hand wrap."

William's memory flew back to his conversation with King Henry, held long before any of his troubles had started. Was this cursed shadesteel part of what his king had sent him to gather — to act as a "Trojan Horse" against Stephen? His musings were cut short when a series of screams erupted from the torture room nearby. They were not Zala's screams.

The Azgari turned to investigate the disturbance, but Brinwin drew their attention back with a roar as he pounded against the prison bars. He shouted something incomprehensible to William's ears, but whatever it was, it more than succeeded in holding the Azgari's interest. They swept across the room in a fit of rage, their swords drawn and ready to strike Brinwin down where he stood. Brinwin stepped back at the last second to dodge the edge of their swords, even as the door to the jail room burst into flames. The Azgari turned in time to see the wrath of Zala's fire magic hurtling at them with deadly accuracy. Their howls rang out for a few seconds longer as their blackened skin disintegrated into ash and their armor fell to the ground with a crash.

Zala staggered into the room with the councilor's keys in tow, her smile weary but triumphant. "I hate to admit it," she panted as she approached the cell. "But that really was some quality time with him in there. Wouldn't trade it for anything."

Brinwin and William sprang into action as soon as the gate swung open. Brinwin grabbed his compass and tossed William a cloak, which he promptly used to gather the swords still lying amid the Azgari's smoking remains. "Now what?" asked William as he transferred one of the swords to Brinwin. "I doubt they missed the commotion."

Brinwin wrapped his hand in a cloak and swung his new sword to get a feel for its weight, then strode to the exit. "What do you think we're going to do, Wil-yim?" he said. "We're going to get ourselves the recipe and then try to escape this godforsaken place. Elkreath was the practice, and this is the real thing. Let's get moving!"

They fled from the jail room to find themselves in a broad corridor lined with dim torches. No one else but the distant figure of a patrolling Azgari at the far end could be seen. "Forget about stealth," said Brinwin. "Speed is our only hope now. Follow me!" They raced behind him as he led the way, following his compass as they weaved and ducked through one passageway after another. The alarm cries of the Azgari soon mingled with the panting of their breath and the pounding of their feet, even as the hammering of smiths at their forges clinked ever onward in the distance. They could barely find their footing in the dim light, but they rushed ahead regardless.

"A little light would be helpful here, don't you think?" William called out to Zala.

She simply shook her head as she continued to run. "I would if I could, love. They spiked me with Virilium extract before we woke up. Can't use my light magic for a while."

"Then how'd you deal with the councilor just now?" he called out before nearly tripping on a jutting pavement stone.

Brinwin saved his sister the effort of a reply, even as his focus flashed from compass to surroundings. "Because they thought she was only a light mage," he called back. "Virilium's a finicky substance you have to prepare just right. One way blocks light magic, and another way blocks fire. They only blocked her light magic since hardly anyone in Cabalia knows more than one element."

"Could they have blocked both if they'd known?" William puffed. Zala yanked his hand as they rounded a corner to prevent him from smashing into the wall.

"Sure," said Brinwin. "But the more it blocks, the more damage it causes. Pure virilium would block all magic *and* leave permanent brain damage. Not so useful for interrogating someone." Brinwin's eyes narrowed as the corridor they rushed along sloped downward at a steep angle. The side corridors quickly filled with more Azgari than he cared to count.

"Do you know any other elements?" William asked Zala, bracing himself for the hordes descending on them.

"No, not really!" she yelled louder than necessary. An Azgari leaped out of the shadows at William, but it soon found its head sundered from its body when William swung his sword with his full might. He marveled at the ease with which the shadesteel weapon vanquished his foe, understanding even more fully why King Stephen would want the recipe for it.

Zala's flames kept the monsters at bay behind them while Brinwin and William continued to hack at whatever brute obstructed their progress forward. By the time Brinwin's compass shone a deep violet, they had gathered an impressive amount of momentum. "We're almost there!" yelled Brinwin with a slice of his sword. "Get ready!"

At the bottom of the sloping corridor, they saw the opening of a small room rushing toward them. The door was sturdy but left wide open. Brinwin could hardly believe their luck. "Grab the handle and close it!" he shouted to Zala. They all braced themselves as they doubled their efforts for a final dash to the door. The Azgari's stench was hot on their backs, pressing ever closer until they whizzed past the door and

Zala shot out a hand to grasp the outstretched handle. She could only hope it was as sturdy as the door it belonged to.

* * *

All three of them tumbled to the floor as the door swung shut and locked itself with a resounding *clang*. The Azgari collided hard against the door, unable to stop themselves from peppering it at full speed. Their impacts reached the other side as a series of thumps, much like a hailstorm would make in an open field. Their subsequent attempts to break down the door were terrifying but unsuccessful. For the time being, the pursuit was over.

Brinwin regained his bearings first and glanced at the compass in his hand. Its bead glowed a brilliant violet, even as its arrows pointed ahead of him. His face broke into a smile. They had found the recipe at last. Not even the eerie green light flooding the room from the lanterns along the walls spoiled his joy at that moment. He rose to his feet, and the others followed suit.

They found themselves in a simple but comfortably adorned room with a row of pedestals at its far side. A glass case surrounded each pedestal as it sported one kind of relic or another, with the grandest pedestal of all at the very center. The inscription above it was clear for Brinwin and Zala to read.

Recipes, it said simply. Rather than bringing joy or relief, the display filled their hearts with dismay, for it was empty inside.

Brinwin checked his compass again in a panic, only to realize it pointed not straight ahead to the display case but farther off to the right. He whipped his gaze to follow the compass, and as he did so, there came the most unwelcome sound they could have imagined: a laugh.

In the shadows between lanterns, they saw a stone table. And from it, there suddenly rose a man who until then had been sitting in silence. He stepped into the pale green light, and the others' hearts filled with dread. A codex of great size he held in his hand, which he waved about in a taunt.

"Looking for this?" asked the King of Shadowcrest. His smile was calm and commanding, to say nothing of his voice as he strode into their midst. "What? Did you honestly think we wouldn't inspect your items once we captured you?" he queried smugly. "Your compass's purpose was easy to discern. I knew that even if you escaped your prison cell, you'd come running back to your doom. Why else would I leave the door wide open for you?" He set the book on the table and gave it a contented pat. Brinwin and the others squirmed where they stood, knowing their chance of escape had been reduced to nothing. All that remained for them was to listen and see how their fate unfolded.

"I must admit," the king continued, "I'm torn between admiration and anger toward you. No one else has ever ventured this far into our realm without getting caught before, and as a Shadowcrest, I find that *most* impressive. But then again, you also reduced my Grand Inquisitor to a pile of ash. It will be difficult for me to find a replacement as effective as he was." A silence followed as he gazed each of them over, then turned to stroll toward the pedestals. "But," he said, "as irksome as it is, you have traveled a long way into our lands. That makes you our guests. I can't do much to satisfy your hunger for food, but perhaps knowledge would be more to your fancy? Go on, Brinwin: Ask what you'd like of me. You've at least earned that much for your skill in the sacred arts of stealth and alchemy."

Brinwin and the others remained spellbound as the king wandered past the pedestals as if on tour at a museum. Only when he paused to glare at the empty display case did Brinwin's sense return to him. "How did you find us?" he finally asked. "And when?"

The king gave a small chuckle. "Ah, well, technically speaking, we knew *where* you were the moment you set foot in our lands. But we didn't realize *who* you were or the threat you posed until you entered the passage beneath my throne."

"But how?" Brinwin's voice trembled. The king brought his hands behind his back as he still gazed at the empty pedestal. Brinwin alone detected the faint convulsion that rippled across the king's frame. The others, however, could clearly distinguish the change that came over the king's voice. It no longer sounded smooth and elegant but had become deep and otherworldly. It held in its rasp an echo within an echo they had heard neither before nor since.

"My blood," the king said. He turned to face them, and Zala shrieked when she saw his face. Instead of the bright silver eyes of Gelitar, the figure now before them held purple eyes that blazed as a flame. Where the pupils had been, there was a depth that seemed to reach into hell itself. William stood petrified in fear, unable to bear the horror of it yet unable to turn himself away.

"I know where all my blood is, even that which resides in shadesteel. For it is that which makes shadesteel what it is: my very own *shadowed blood*." The king glared at them as they all fell to their knees in terror. There was little doubt who now spoke with them while possessing the king. It should not have been possible, but it was.

"But how?" Brinwin stammered. "The Shadowed One lived a thousand years ago!"

"As I still live beneath this forge, if you can call it 'life,'" echoed the Shadowed One through Gelitar. "Such was the power I claimed when I joined in union with my Queen. It was either I or my offspring that could inherit the lion's share of her characteristics, and I chose it for myself. There was much more power to be had that way." The flame in his eyes dwindled to a sickly soothing ember, and his voice took on a far more natural sound.

"But it won't do to keep you scared out of your minds while I talk with you. Get on your feet, all of you." As quickly as they could, they obeyed. The king's frown slipped into a neutral expression, perhaps the closest thing to a smile possible for him. "I've noticed you, Brinwin, for some time now," he said. "Your skill with alchemy reminds me of a good friend I once knew a long time ago. A fine successor to Tanwin Hamul you would have been."

Never in his wildest dreams would Brinwin have expected to receive such coveted praise in as loathsome a manner as this. Whatever glimmer of pride he felt was far outweighed by the revulsion that gripped him. If Tanwin Xhamul had truly been a "good friend" of this fiend, he was ready to recant all the admiration he previously held for his hero. But who could tell with how much truth the old betrayer spoke? Such were Brinwin's thoughts when the Shadowed One continued to speak.

"Despite the fact that your forebearer slew my wife, I find myself filled with admiration for you. And thus I offer you this favor: Go on and complete your final mission. Fulfill the meaning of your name, Brinwin, and end with success. Give the Englishman my recipe."

Beside himself in fear, William spoke up in a stupor. "Will you let us go, then?" he asked.

The Shadowed One retained the same unchanging neutral expression. "No child, I'm afraid not. You know too much already, and to let your bodies go to waste would be unacceptable. No, I have other plans in store for you. But first, complete your mission, Brinwin. Give the foreigner my recipe, and thus fulfill your end of the bargain. Read it, even, if you would like. I won't prevent you."

Even if it was given as a handout, what little remained of Brinwin's pride led him to do just that. His contract, after all, had to be fulfilled. He strode as firmly as he could to the table and picked up the codex of recipes. It took just a minute of thumbing through it to find the entry on shadesteel. Brinwin gazed long at it, and his mouth moved slightly as he processed what he read. The brilliance of its crafting amazed him, but he also realized that even with this knowledge, he could never have brought himself to craft shadesteel. The chief ingredient was all but impossible to obtain on his own terms. And even if he somehow could, he certainly did not want to.

His curiosity got the better of him, and he turned the page to find a recipe that drew the color from his face. He glanced at the Shadowed One, who nodded at him as if he could read his thoughts. It was then that Brinwin realized he and his companions were marked for a fate worse than death. With trembling fingers, he quickly turned the page on Azgari transformation back over to the pages on shadesteel. It was with great dread that he closed the book and set his gaze on William. His countenance then changed as he resolved within himself that whatever would follow afterward, the completion of his final mission would not be lacking in decorum.

He strode to William with his face held high and offered the book to the trembling Englishman. "Lord Steele," he said with all calmness. "Our contract is now complete. I offer what is yours, as you have offered what is mine." Brinwin then beat his hand to his chest, clenched it, and brought it to his tattoo as he closed his eyes. "Our debts are now finished."

Zala wept as she witnessed the interaction. She only saw Brinwin's face as a blur when he turned to face her. "Not that it matters anymore, Sister, but as far as I am concerned, you have more than earned a life of your choosing. It appears our partnership has run its course." Brushing away her tears, his voice dropped to nearly a whisper. "And a good run it was." Never before had his sister heard him express such tenderness as in those final words.

Zala turned to face the Shadowed One and fell to her knees once more. "Please, oh Mighty Founder!" she begged. "Please, have mercy!"

The Shadowed One's eyes looked on her, unblinking. When he spoke, it was only with a quiet echo, as if remnants of the first winds of the world rustled on through caves eternal. "I'm sorry, child. I have none to give." His eyes then flared with a great flash of light, and the others fell to the ground in shock as the door opened at the far end of the room to allow the ranks of the Azgari to swarm in.

* * *

Brinwin, Zala, and William remained beside themselves in terror as their belongings were gathered and they were dragged through the Underforge back up to the city of Everoth. With each checkpoint they passed along the elaborate system of pulleys and platforms leading to the surface, their panic gradually subsided enough for them to notice their surroundings. William was the first to discern the roughly dozen Azgari that surrounded them on a platform no larger than a horse's wagon. They handled him roughly as they transferred him to a new checkpoint, almost making him glad his companions were still too numb with shock to feel the full impact. Not until they reached the last five checkpoints did Brinwin and Zala fully return to their senses.

The lighting was poor, but it was still enough for William to see the expressions of his companions beside him. He hoped against hope as the Azgari herded them onward that there would be a spark of confidence in Brinwin's eyes, some sign of yet another plan ready to defy the impossible. But no such confidence did either he or his sister hold.

Brinwin languished as he went, the light in his eyes dampened as a candle tossed into the sea. Zala was all but consumed with fear as she clung trembling to William. For her sake, William composed himself as best he knew how. He felt neither bold nor peaceful, but to have his loved one face death without any semblance of support, without a single token of reassurance or stability, was more than he could allow. The final barriers that hindered his affection crumbled under the weight of their impending doom.

Gently but firmly, he took her hand. "Come now, love," he said as they approached the open entrance to the city. "We've not made it this far just to cower at the jaws of death. A princess of Hearthfell you are, and try as they might, they can never take from you your dignity. You've shown nothing but boldness since the day I met you, and there's no reason for that to stop now."

Even as he spoke to her, a fire kindled in him that only grew. The pale light of an overcast sky filtered down to the entrance of the tunnel ahead, contrasting sharply with the conviction that now lined his voice. "If nothing else, we can spite them here at the end. They may kill us, but we won't give them the satisfaction of seeing us whimper like cornered mice. Let's face this cursed city — together."

Zala looked down as they stumbled their way to the entrance. Uncertainty clouded her countenance, and her lips drew tight until she suddenly broke into a smile. When she looked up at William, a proud fire once more blazed in her eyes. "Have I ever mentioned how much I love you?" she said. "This is twice now you've defended my honor."

William's eyes beamed back at her. "Not bad for a horse dancer, eh?" he laughed.

Zala shook her head with a laugh of her own, ignoring the shove she received from the Azgari beside her. "No... Not bad at all. Shall we go together then, dearest?"

William took her arm with all the grace of a nobleman as the line of Azgari at the entrance stepped aside to make way for them. "Together," he nodded. Brinwin followed behind as they took their first steps above ground, shaking his head as he kept silent. He knew too much of what awaited them to believe their newfound courage would last long. But who was he to rob his fellows of their last few moments of comfort? He, too, lifted his head and set himself to match their boldness, at least on the outside.

The three of them took in their surroundings after they emerged from the main entrance to the Underforge they had first spied on when they entered the city. A crowd had already gathered in the streets, watching silently as the Azgari led them in a procession down the thoroughfare. There were no shouts or jeers, but the intensity of their stares was powerful enough on its own. Countless pairs of silvery eyes gleamed at them as a heavenly host of malicious stars, gloating over them as they were led to their doom. Whether the bystanders frowned or smiled, it felt as if each breathed down their captives' necks, eager to see them buckle under the pressure and give in to despair.

William and the others held firm nonetheless as they traveled northwest through Everoth. Even when the scenery changed from natural stone and wood to the infernal black onyx they remembered from the southeast entrance, they kept their heads aloft with pride. Only when they reached the city limits did their resolve falter, for there they passed another statue of Elithora, the Vampire Queen of Shadowcrest.

She sneered down at them as when they first entered, but her eyes held greater malice than they recalled seeing before. The moment they passed beneath her, it felt like a cloud of darkness passed over their hearts, unbearably cold and wickedly seductive. Each one suddenly felt pressured as if by enchantment to prostrate themselves before her feet and pledge their souls to the conquering queen. Indeed, the procession paused at the feet of the statue as though their captors expected them to do this very thing.

Lesser men would have given in to the impulse, but Brinwin and the others rejected the queen's advance on their hearts, and it soon became clear to the people of Shadowcrest that they would get no such reaction from their prisoners. The Azgari jabbed them forward to resume the march, and within minutes they reached the northwest gate. Whatever vigor they held before passing the statue was all but spent, leaving them each in a melancholy mood.

The assurances of Gaimis's dream all but taunted them as they took their final steps out of the city, daring them to hope for deliverance, only to fade into the hopelessness of their fate. No matter how pleasantly the priest had suggested otherwise, Yahos would not be protecting them after all. There would be no "making it back home in safety."

They followed the banks of the Silent River with their heads bowed in defeat until they reached a hill less than a mile away from the city limits. Three great poles jutted out from the peak, standing as silhouettes in the distance. The dark forms of men and women milled about at the base, appearing as little more than ants.

The overcast sky broke momentarily to allow some rays of sunlight to fall on the hill as it loomed closer. Brinwin's memory then flashed back to the stained-glass window that graced the Cathedral of Edomear so many miles away. He saw in his mind's eye the crucifixion of Yeshun and the banner spread above his cross, reading, "It is finished." And so it appeared their lives were about to be finished, too. Even as he contemplated this grim reality, something inside Brinwin's heart gave way, and he turned his attention back to the struggle he had never fully resolved in Edomear. He could postpone it no longer.

Only vaguely was he aware of his surroundings when he and the others were led to the base of the poles and stripped down to nothing but the plainest of undergarments. A team of alchemists attended to them as a crowd gathered around the hill, culminating at last with the arrival of King Gelitar and his entourage. Before this happened, the alchemists wiped down their skin with a sickly green solution and forced them to drink a preparatory concoction that, thankfully, was tasteless. William and Zala grimaced as they overheard the alchemists talking to each other.

"The orders say to treat the woman with a second dose of Virilium extract... for both fire and light magic," murmured one.

"A rogue mage of multiple elements?!" exclaimed the other in a low tone. "Should we treat her with the full package, just to be safe?"

"No," replied the first, who seemed the most experienced. "The King wishes her to have enough awareness to experience maximum suffering. Only the Archmage knows more than two elements, and this is no archmage. She hardly looks to be above her thirties, at most."

Zala resisted the second dosage as much as she dared but soon found herself with the worst stomachache of her life when the extract took effect. The pain, however, remained purely physical. The previous solutions administered to her preserved her mental faculties enough to experience clearly whatever horror was in store for them.

They were soon bound to the poles by shadesteel manacles, William and Zala side by side, and Brinwin in front facing toward them. Behind Brinwin sat King Gelitar at the forefront of the gathering. Once all had gathered, the king rose to his feet and addressed his prisoners. "Brinwin Zikennig," he called. "You and your accomplices have trespassed in our lands with the intent of grand theft. The laws of our ancestors call for your death."

At this, a murmur of approval rose from the crowd, eerily similar to the hissing of a viper's den. "But, as the king of these lands," he continued, "I have the authority to offer leniency. It would be ill-fitting to treat one as skilled as yourself to the punishment of a commoner. No, for all your accomplishments in that which we most highly value, we instead offer you and your friends a more worthy form of recompense. You shall join our ranks in everlasting servitude as members of the Azgari."

Brinwin winced as the king said these words, knowing full well the terror that would rise in his companions. His assessment was accurate. William and Zala blanched as pale as their captors, and they would have fallen to the ground if not for their restraints. They had expected death by execution, not transformation into an everlasting abomination. Whatever pride or courage remained in them fled, and they begged with tears for death instead.

The king held up his hand and silenced them sharply. "The matter is closed. All that remains for you is this: Will you join us willingly or unwillingly?" None of them spoke but only shook their heads as they trembled. The king's smile deepened, and he called to the team of alchemists, "Very well! Prepare the apparatus to administer the elixir."

In a matter of minutes, an appalling contraption was set up over each of them. A tangled mass of hoses and clamps stretched over them, with a great glass beaker that pried their jaws open to receive the elixir of the Azgari. At the top of the apparatus, the alchemists affixed a vial of the most putrid-looking concoction any of them, Brinwin included, had ever seen. To call the solution "black" would have been an understatement. It looked darker than death itself, with nothing but small streaks of coagulated blood — Shadowed Blood — to offer any other color.

In the time it took to set up the device, William and Zala availed themselves of the most natural response to unavoidable doom: They bargained desperately with their Creator.

Even as he pleaded, a firm conviction settled on William that he had been wrong to wait this long to make things right with God. But still, he pleaded. "Please God, anything but this!" his thoughts screamed. "Let us die in any other way."

Or live, came a sudden thought. Whether it was his own thought or not, he neither knew nor cared.

"Yes, or let us live! I promise to serve you the rest of my life, Lord, if you will let us live!"

Zala, meanwhile, dealt with more anger toward Yahos than William did and reasoned thus: "I knew that dream of Gaimis's was a farce! But if you're really as merciful as my brother says, Yahos, then save us now! I'll even drop the grudge against you if you'll rescue us! Please!"

She looked to the heavens as she pleaded for help from above. But no matter how intensely she begged, there came no salvation from the sky. When her gaze returned to the ground, however, she found a sight that shocked her.

Standing in the middle of the crowd, a familiar figure stood gazing at her. His gray robes blew softly in the wind, along with his beard of white. A staff of almond wood he gripped in his right hand, and his left hand hung loosely at his side. His body was aged, but behind his brown eyes shone a youth that still defied the grasp of time. Zala's heart skipped a beat as she paused, breathless.

"Toff?" she gasped in a whisper. The face of her old teacher gazed back at her silent but keen. His eyes probed her, waiting for her with sorrowful patience to understand what she must do. In a single moment, two realizations flickered through her mind. First, she recognized the ethereal transparency of Toff's visage. No one else seemed to notice the man, and it became all too apparent that her teacher had not physically come to rescue her. *But of course he hadn't*, she chided herself. She knew all too well that he could not leave the shores of his sacred lake. All she saw now was a projection of him meant solely for her.

Secondly, she realized the purpose behind his appearance. She shook her head in protest. "No! No, I can't... I won't!" she moaned as tears fell from her eyes. Not even now, on the brink of tragedy, could she bring herself to apply his last teachings.

Toff's visage continued to stare at her as he leaned wearily on his staff. She knew what she must do. Whatever followed thereafter would only be magnified by her hesitance. But Zala could not find the will to overcome her fears. What was required of her was far too unpredictable, and she would never forgive herself if she lived at the expense of everyone else's death. When Zala looked back up, Toff had vanished. He had served his purpose. She alone could do anything more, if she dared.

The contraptions were now fully fitted around them, and their doom stood at the threshold. The elixir would be administered to Brinwin first and then to William and Zala after they witnessed the horror of his transformation. All that remained was for Gelitar to give the signal.

While William and Zala extended their last desperate offers to God, Brinwin did not bargain. He alone saw the bigger picture, including the futility of anything he had to offer. "Yeshun," he gasped as best he could with the contraption lodged in his mouth. "I know my brother is right about you. If you still want to show mercy to the likes of me, then please, Lord... save me."

A sudden wave of peace flooded through him, even as the king gave the signal and the murky liquid traveled down the transparent hose toward his open mouth. His eyes followed the cursed liquid as it flowed closer through the contraption's kinks and loops. Time slowed to a crawl, and a reassurance flashed across his consciousness: *Do not fear, child. It will be over soon.*

One further understanding came to him, and he turned to look at Zala first, then William one last time. He pointed toward Zala, and William understood Brinwin's meaning without words.

"Promise me you'll take care of her," he meant, clear as day. How exactly he could carry out this last wish, William stood at a loss. But however he could in these last moments, he would. He nodded back his promise to keep Brinwin's request. Had his hands been free, he would have clasped the amulet Zala had given him and sworn on that. Nevertheless, the promise satisfied Brinwin. He looked toward heaven and fastened his eyes on the clouds as the first drops of the elixir washed across his tongue and dripped down his throat.

Convulsions shook his body as the reeking stench of the elixir refused to dissipate in his mouth but rather grew to envelop him in pain. The transformation that followed was rapid. His already massive frame swelled further, even as his hair and skin darkened in color until it resembled ash. His eyes contracted before his pupils expanded to fill his entire eye sockets. A purple flame then lit from their depths and spread to engulf the eyes' entirety until nothing remained but that wicked flame. From start to finish, the whole process occurred in less than ten seconds.

Brinwin remained fully conscious as this happened and looked on in horror at what his body became before his eyes. Whatever pain he felt in those moments paled in comparison to what happened next as his mind was reconfigured and subsumed into the collective Azgari consciousness. It felt as if the very fabric of his thoughts and memory were torn apart by the hands of a million demons, only to be stitched back together into something completely foreign to the natural mind.

In the waning moments of his private consciousness, there flashed before him all the secrets known by House Shadowcrest: thousands upon thousands of books' worth of forbidden knowledge, overwhelming him and sweeping him away into the depths of mindless servitude. Within five seconds or less, the mental entity known as Brinwin was no more. Last of all, his spirit departed to happier shores.

The cry that began as the scream of a man in agony ended in the roar of an infernal beast. William turned his head away in horror, unable to bear the sight. Zala could not bring herself to avert her gaze, and she thus felt the full impact of her brother's transformation. The fear and sorrow that welled within her at the beginning of his scream transformed and erupted into something far more potent: *fury*.

She cursed the Shadowed One and his ilk with the vilest of language before throwing herself entirely into executing Toff's final lesson. Though she had claimed to lack knowledge of other elements besides fire and light, that was not entirely true. In the last of her time spent with Toff, he had reluctantly taught her the most dangerous of all elements. So it was that she knew chaos magic. Partly.

She had been right to shun its use in all her previous run-ins with death, but now she no longer cared for reason. Even if its most likely outcome was a fate worse than death, it could not possibly match the horror of what she had just seen. With a fearsome scream, she closed her eyes and channeled her wrath toward summoning destruction from the Eldanu.

A bolt of lightning struck the ground beside her, knocking the crowd from its feet. A storm of purple beams then sprang from nothingness and whizzed about in random directions, vaporizing anything they collided with. The shadesteel manacles holding her and William in place were no match for the intensity she brought to bear on them. Within moments, they had freed themselves from their restraints.

All was chaos as the Azgari sprang into action and fought to subdue their enemy. Some were flung back while others were disintegrated as William and Zala dodged the swinging of fists and slicing of swords. William ripped the garb off a fallen Azgari and used it as a hand wrap to wield its sword to great effect. He and Zala held their ground for a time, but the intensity of Zala's magic dwindled as her anger was spent. It soon became clear they could not hold off their foes indefinitely.

A brief pause in the onslaught gave her all the opportunity necessary to execute the last of her chaos magic. A circular portal suddenly crackled into being a dozen paces beyond them. Purple sparks flew into the air from its depths as pure energy swirled in the portal's midst. "It's time to go, William!" she called as she grabbed his hand.

They dashed for the portal with all their might, but before they could reach it, the Azgari formerly known as Brinwin broke free from its restraints and came barreling upon them in full fury. It was the largest of all the Azgari they had seen, and it proved impervious to the stray bolts of energy that peppered its chest as it charged on. Zala stopped to face the beast, and she faltered. Could she bring herself to end what remained of her brother? Did she even have enough magic left to do so?

The delay was disastrous, giving the Azgari all the time it needed to fall upon its former sister. It stabbed her through the leg with a sword it retrieved from the ground, and it would have proceeded to pierce her heart, too, had William not yanked her through the portal at the last moment. The amulet around his neck flashed white as they entered, blinding them as they tumbled into its midst.

The Azgari's roar combined with the tumult of the Void between space to surround them with chaos. So great was the chaos that it should have been impossible for William to notice when Zala's grip slipped from his hand and she vanished into oblivion. But notice he did, and with a scream of dismay, he tumbled onward through the Void, alone.

30

The Second Escape

William remembered little of his journey through the Void. Nothing but a constant tempest of motion and energy bombarded him, such that all sense of time and space was uncertain. There was no up or down in that place. No near or far. No short time ago or long time ago. Only forward and ever onward.

He despaired that such would be his fate for all eternity when he was suddenly flung back into the world with great force. Sunlight overwhelmed his eyes as he flew through the air in a somersault and slammed into a pile of neatly stacked barrels. The sound of splintering wood merged with the crack of his back and the whoosh of the portal closing to create the last jumble of chaos that assaulted his senses.

He lay on the ground for some time, dazed and moaning, until his senses returned to him with a start. "Zala!" he exclaimed. He tried scrambling to his feet, but a surge of pain sent him straight back to the ground. Once the pain subsided, he attempted more cautiously to rise again. Resting on his arms and stomach, he glanced around desperately, hoping to find Zala nearby. But Zala was nowhere to be found. Nor was anyone else, for that matter.

At first glance, he appeared to be in the middle of a city. He lay on the edge of a broad street lined intermittently with barrels like the one he had just crashed into. It was not until his second glance that he recognized the dull emerald line running down the center of the stone pavement. On the other side of the road, he could barely make out the faint glowing lines of blue, green, and purple that stretched across the wooden buildings in front of him. It was then that he realized where he was.

"Why... I'm in Elkreath!" he gasped. Whatever relief he felt at once more being in a place he knew quickly evaporated when he realized his danger. *"Surely they're still looking for me!"* he thought. *"If they find me, I'm as good as dead."* He rolled off the main road as quickly as he could into an alleyway behind the barrels he had smashed. How no one saw him yet, he could only guess. The Elkreath he had left behind was always packed full of people. Now, there was not a soul in sight.

It was indeed fortunate for him that the King of Tropis stood at that very moment some ten miles away, addressing the city in a speech all civilians were mandated to attend. Even as the king spoke of the dangers they had overcome and the honor it would be to hear next evening from the Hero of Elkreath, the unwitting catalyst of their woes crept away unnoticed through their alleyways.

To his dismay, William found that the barrels he had pulverized were filled with flour, and he now left a white trail behind him as he went. Even after brushing off as much as he could, he remained anxious it would lead to his capture.

Once more or less secluded safely in the alleyways, he pondered his next move. He tried at first to fend off the obvious but was soon forced to admit that his chance of finding Zala was practically none. She could be anywhere in Cabalia, or in the world, or even outside the world for all he knew, and he was in no position to find her. His emotions swelled and threatened to overwhelm him, but he forced them further inside.

He could not afford to sit weeping now. He was a fugitive on either end of the island, clothed in nothing but his undergarments, a hand wrap, and some stray flour. He still had the Azgari's sword, but little good would that do him against a whole city bent on bringing him to justice. Fighting was not even close to being an option. The only places he could flee were either farther into the depths of Cabalia to remain a hermit forever searching for his lost love or to the docks where he could perhaps somehow find a way back to England. It took little time for him to make up his mind.

He looked up to find the afternoon sun bearing toward the west, and he knew that Glimmerstone Bay lay to the east of the city. So it was that he reluctantly turned his back on the sun and made his way as stealthily as he could to the docks of Elkreath. He could not shake from his mind how ridiculous he must have looked as he went. If anyone did apprehend him, perhaps they would die of laughter before they could cart him off. *Fat chance of that*, he thought with a shake of his head. *But where are all the people?*

It was not until he came within a mile of the docks that he found the first signs of life. Guards on patrol still covered the area in a vigilant watch, and visitors not subject to the king's decree attended to their ships. Even with fewer people than usual crowding the ports, escaping from Cabalia would be every bit as difficult as he thought.

He paused to consider his options further but could think of no good way forward. It was only at his wit's end that an unexpected chance provided itself in the lone guard who came marching up the main road toward the alleyway he lurked in. Even a casual glance told William this guard was nothing but an inexperienced youth pressed into service by great need. The forces of Elkreath must have suffered a grievous loss indeed for them to rely on recruits such as this! He hated having to assail such a young one, but it was his best chance at survival. The guard even walked on the side of the road closest to the alley.

No sooner had the lad come within arm's length than William snatched him aside and muffled his startled cry with a firm hand. The Azgari sword proved enough to render the young man unconscious without too much of a struggle, and William made quick work of fitting himself into the guard's vesture. It was somewhat tight on him, but at least it was better than nothing. He was grateful for the helmet to cover at least some of his head, even if it was a size too big. He hung the Azgari sword by his side and hoped no one would recognize its origins as he set off down the main road in the same direction the guard had been traveling. He kept his gait as steady as possible but held his breath as he came within view of the docks. Would this simple disguise really be enough to fool them, he wondered.

Apparently, it was. At least for the time being. No one accosted William as he marched to the docks and scoured its piers in search of his ship. He could only imagine what had happened to his crew since he went missing that first night in Elkreath. More likely than not, they had already been released from custody and departed for home. Such seemed to be the case as he searched the shipyards in vain. Pier after pier of unfamiliar ships passed him by, and his heart sank lower with each passing step. People were returning from the king's speech, but he was still no closer to escaping from Cabalia.

He had nearly given up his search when he tripped on an uneven plank and almost bumped into a dockworker returning to his duties. The man's eyes opened wide, their copper-brown color similar to that of the freshly setting sun. To his great surprise, William recognized the man as Valdwin, the bard-turned-dockworker he met on his arrival to Cabalia. Doing his best to disguise his voice, he offered a hasty apology and tried to withdraw as quickly as possible before the man might recognize him. But it was too late.

Valdwin's eyes narrowed in thought before a look of amazement and concern spread across his face. He opened his mouth to say something, but William drew him aside and pleaded with him in a hushed voice not to turn him in. "Yes, Valdwin, it's me," he said. "I'll tell you anything you want to know, but please... don't say anything. My life is in your hands now, and you have no idea what I've been through. Please, I beg of you, at least hear me out!"

The Cabalian's eyes filled with doubt, teetering on the brink of distrust. One wrong move to startle the man would result in disaster, and William dared not move except to plea with his eyes. Valdwin's brow furrowed while he wavered. "They say you're a murderer, William," he murmured. "And I lost some very dear friends when you and Zikennig escaped. Give me one good reason why I shouldn't turn you in."

William's mind spun. He felt as one listening in from the outside when the words finally came from his mouth: "Because you said it yourself, that duty's call is a hard master, but most necessary for us all. I only came here to fulfill the duties of my king, and that didn't involve anyone dying." With unfeigned grief, he averted his gaze. "I didn't intend for anyone to die that night or any other night. I wouldn't blame you for doubting me, but if you let me explain, I swear to Yahos to speak nothing but the truth. Please, Valdwin, don't turn me in." He saw that no further good would come of more words, so he rested his plea and resigned himself to whatever outcome would follow.

Valdwin hesitated as the sun continued to sink past the horizon. A debate raged through his mind, and William could see it in his face. The man had been uncommonly kind to him before. But would he be so again?

Valdwin spoke at last with a shake of his head. "I suppose there's no harm in listening. If I sense you to be anything but honest, I'll turn you in then."

William sighed in relief and motioned for them to step aside from the flow of traffic. Only when he could be heard, but not *overheard*, did he recount to Valdwin everything that had befallen him, starting with his assignment by King Henry and ending with his exit from Zala's portal. He left out the detail of knocking the guard unconscious and stealing his clothes, but by that point, Valdwin had heard plenty enough to consider. He remained silent as he listened and paid especially close attention when William mentioned his stay with Gaimis in Edomear and the dream the Wayfollower had shared with them.

When nothing was left to hear, Valdwin stared at William intently as he stroked his chin. "They don't think us dockworkers pay attention to people while we work," he said. "But we do. I can tell an honest man from a crooked one the longer I listen to him. I think you're an honest one... at least for the most part." William dared give only the faintest of smiles. He said nothing as Valdwin sighed and continued to speak.

"It truly is a smaller world than we think, William. I'm very familiar with this Wayfollower you spoke of. Though, he wasn't a Wayfollower when I first knew him. No, he had but freshly entered the Church when I first met Gaimis Zikennig. But he was the only one there to treat my family fairly when my father fell from the Church's favor."

Valdwin paused as he stared out into the twilight. "I know for sure that Gaimis is a good man. If he truly had this dream you spoke of, then I can see it's the will of Yahos for you to leave this place safely." A shadow of pain then fell across his face, and it was with some difficulty that he continued, "I will help you for duty's sake... as hard of a master as it is."

He held up his hand when William began to thank him. "Don't misunderstand me, William. I personally still want to see you brought to justice, regardless of whether you intended for all the carnage or not. But I trust Yahos will deal out his own justice in due time."

William merely nodded as he waited for Valdwin to continue. Rather than speak, Valdwin motioned for him to follow as the sun set below the horizon. Only when they were walking briskly along the main pier did he speak again. "Your ship and crew are still at port here, but you cannot go to them. They have been guarded since you became a fugitive, and the security around them has only increased since your escape. You will have to find another way back to England."

Valdwin paused at the base of a platform and peered across the harbor. He then pointed to a ship in the distance, the white of its sails still visible in the early evening. "I dare not accompany you any farther," he said, "but that ship over there is a trading vessel due for England later tonight. It's called the *Snowbird*, and I've dealt with its captain long enough to know how foolish and corrupt he is. He and all his men are out enjoying themselves before they set sail, and they've bribed us dockworkers to keep an eye on the ship while they're gone. But I also know the dockworkers they bribed tonight are just as crooked as he is. They're also occupying themselves elsewhere, if but for a shorter time. If you hurry, you could stow yourself away before they come back."

A gleam then came into his eyes, accompanied with a sardonic grin. "And before you thank me, I believe their primary wares for this trade run are raw fish. Perhaps even now, the justice of Yahos comes upon you." He then looked at William only briefly before departing without a farewell.

Such would have been the reaction William expected when he first arrived in Cabalia, but the rejection still stung. He nonetheless owed the man a debt of gratitude. It was doubtful he would ever be able to repay it, though.

With a shake of his head, he set out to reach the *Snowbird*. How his crew from England would escape Cabalia was anyone's guess; the best he could hope for at this point was to smuggle himself out by the skin of his teeth.

The night was now well underway, and William trusted more in stealth than disguise as he went. He could only assume the guard he knocked unconscious had woken by now, and the city would be searching for a man in the guard's uniform. He probably should have just killed the man, but he already felt guilty for the death he had brought to Elkreath. He would not add further to that number if he could help it. Such a decision made his conscience feel better, at any rate. His nerves, however, were a different story.

Time slowed to a crawl as William closed the distance to the *Snowbird*. Each step on the wooden walkways sounded like thunder to him, even when he did his best to tread lightly. The darkness was thick with a new moon overhead, but he still could not shake the sense he was being watched. Nothing good ever came on the heels of that sense, but he had come too far to turn back now. Whatever was bound to happen would just have to happen. As quickly as he dared, he reached the vessel and slipped aboard.

* * *

The timbers below him creaked softly as he crept his way forward. Nothing else could be heard except the rustling of the sails above him and the pounding of his own heart within him. Lights flickered from lamps and torches around the ship's deck as if the vessel were occupied, but it appeared Valdwin had spoken the truth. At present, the ship was abandoned. Such fortune seemed too good to be true.

Any stray voice that floated from shore set William on edge and stirred the worst of his imagination. Every drunken laugh was from a dockworker returning to his watch, and each order called out in the distance was the captain sending his men back to the ship. He dared not linger to discover the accuracy of his predictions. Even as the reek of raw fish grew strong in his nostrils, he made his way below deck with as much speed as his attempt at stealth would allow.

Once below deck, he found it likewise abandoned — except for the fish, whose stench only intensified. It made sense now why the crew was so lax in guarding their ship. None but the starving would find anything of value there. William had never been one to enjoy seafood, and it was all he could do to avoid gagging as he scouted for a place to stow away. There were other commodities besides fish, but nothing strong enough to overpower the smell.

The Cabalians evidently found a way to preserve their goods for the journey since most of their wares lay exposed to the open air with little to none of the preservatives the rest of the world used. Crates and barrels lay open, filled to the brim with food, but nothing was spoiled. Vague memories of Cabalian merchants unloading their wares at a crowded market came back to William, and he recalled the surprise of the local merchants at how unspoiled Cabalian food was. If he could just make it back to England in as good a condition, it would be enough for him!

The more he searched, however, the more precarious he found his position. There was little room to hide behind the cargo without spending precious time unstacking it, and he could only fit into the containers themselves if he emptied their contents elsewhere. He could not afford to waste time. Not when it was unclear how much of it he even had left.

Dare he continue his search and hope to stumble across a suitable spot, or should he start immediately to *make* a spot suitable?

As he pondered these two choices, there suddenly came the sound of footsteps from above. The steps were faint and only belonged to one person, but they were still enough to fill William with alarm. Ready or not, his mind had been made up for him.

He darted further into the recesses of the ship, hoping to find an adequate refuge in time. The footsteps faded, but that fact brought little comfort as he passed row after row of cargo without finding a suitable hiding spot. The footsteps then grew louder, and to his dismay, they passed down the stairs to the lower level. The degree of intent behind those steps threw William into a panic, and he fled to the very edges of the ship.

He found a small crevice between two stacks of crates, which he squeezed between as best he could. For good measure, he dowsed the torch closest to him, hoping the darkness would be enough to shroud his half-exposed frame. He then held his breath as the footsteps reached the bottom of the stairs and paused.

For a few tense moments, there was nothing but silence. The timbers then creaked as the steps resumed — toward him. The pace they held was brisk and resolute. There was no doubt in William's mind he had somehow been discovered. He breathed in deeply and tightened the grip on his sword as the steps drew near. There was nowhere left for him to flee; all he could do now was fight. If either of them perished, so be it. He would not face capture willingly.

He waited until the steps were nearly upon him before leaping from the crevice. His sword swung through the air, but a flash of light blinded him before it could reach its target. He staggered backward, even as his sword crashed against the steel of his opponent's sword. A quick cut from his adversary knocked his sword from his grasp, and the blow of a fist sent him to the ground. The force of his landing dislodged his oversized helmet and sent it rolling away with a clatter. At the same instant, the torch he had extinguished earlier flared back to life at twice its original brightness.

In its light, he saw none other than the inquestor he had saved from falling to death, standing with his sword pointed at William's throat. The surprise he felt in that moment was clearly mirrored by his opponent.

"You?!" exclaimed Telnis in disbelief. He held his sword steady even as his expression clouded with indecision. This was not what he expected at all. William responded with nothing but shocked panting as the inquestor continued to examine him.

Telnis saw in the fugitive's eyes the same fear he had felt within himself when their positions had been reversed — when he was the one filled with terror at the prospect of losing his life. The memories came flooding back in full strength, and it felt for a split second as if he were now looking at himself.

William slumped in defeat as Telnis continued to stare. "If you're going to kill me, just get it over with," he panted. "Better to finish it now than waste time with a trial and execution."

At this, Telnis's mind snapped back into focus. He kept his sword pointed at William, but drew the tip a little farther from his neck. "We're not savages here, Englishman," he responded. "I don't plan on killing you. Not when you chose to save my life."

William sat up weakly but dared not to hope. "Then what *are* you planning to do?" he asked.

"I suppose that depends," said Telnis cautiously. "I have some questions for you. Answer honestly, and I'll make up my mind."

William shrugged. It was not as if he had many other options. "Ask what you will, then. It appears I'm at your disposal, sir."

Telnis sheathed his sword and quickly warmed to interrogating his prisoner. It was the best possible situation for an inquestor to find himself in, a key witness in his custody and ready to cooperate. His magic would discern the truthfulness of the answers he received.

"Why did you save me?" he began. "You had every opportunity to let me drop, and by all accounts you should have. Why did you spare my life?" The question was personal, one that would give insight into the true nature of this foreigner now before him.

The Englishman looked up at him from where he sat. There was a knowing in his gaze that was difficult even for an inquestor to explain. "How many children do you have, sir?" he asked. "A single boy, yes?"

The inquestor's startled pause was all the confirmation William needed. "So do I," he continued. "I know all too well what it's like to be on the brink of death — to be on the verge of leaving my only son an orphan. I saw it in your eyes up there on the rooftop. Believe it or not, I didn't come here to kill anyone. The bloodshed that night was more than I asked for... and I suppose I just pitied someone I saw a little bit of myself in."

Telnis's emotions were shaken, but his intellect still gleaned a fair deal of information from William's answer. His outward composure remained fixed, and he fired away his next question. "Which king do you serve: Henry or Stephen?"

William clenched his jaw at the mention of Stephen. "I serve Henry, the rightful king of England," he replied before adding: "I must say, it's refreshing not to have someone assume from the start I work for the usurper."

"And what did Henry send you here to do?"

William sighed. "I was supposed to conduct a trade with House Shadowcrest at the Yohati Inn. A blue Danuri stone for a couple of sets of shadesteel armor. A single evening to complete." He then looked down and shook his head. "But things went wrong."

Telnis's lips drew tight. "The man on the bridge?"

"Yes. I swear I didn't intend for that to happen. I was just as surprised as the bystanders. I ran to what I thought was the Yohati Inn, only to get mixed up with..." his voice dropped as a host of sorrowful memories pounded into him.

"...with Brinwin Zikennig?" Telnis finished his sentence.

William nodded. "He thought I worked for Stephen, and I thought he was an agent of Shadowcrest. The price of his service was also a blue Danuri stone, so when I offered it, he took me along for the contract he'd negotiated with Stephen. Neither of us realized the mix-up until it was far too late."

Telnis could now ask the question most relevant to him — one he would have paid dearly to have answered. "And where is Brinwin now?"

William shuddered. "Dead," he replied. "Brinwin is dead."

Telnis blinked and remained silent for some time. He sensed the Englishman was not lying. "You're certain of this?" he asked at length.

William nodded with no small amount of sorrow. "I saw it with my own eyes."

"And what of his other accomplice?" Telnis probed.

William bit his lip and fought back tears. He could not bring himself to answer. Telnis tilted his head as he read William's emotions and thoughts. "You believe her to be dead also," he posed, not as a question but as a statement of fact.

William barely had the strength to nod. Since their separation in the Void, he had recalled the wound she received from the Azgari sword just moments before they entered the portal. If Brinwin was right about the cursed nature of such weapons, what reason did he have to think she would survive it, even if she somehow survived the Void?

"I see," said Telnis as he folded his arms. Now came the part he dreaded. He was confident he knew everything relevant to the case at hand. Now he must make a choice. Would he turn a blind eye and let the Englishman return home? Or would he bring him to justice, where he would surely be tried and executed?

The man had been honest in his interrogation, the results of which painted him as a hapless innocent swept along by the most unfortunate of fates. He had even saved Telnis's life out of sheer goodwill and pity. How could it be just to repay such a deed with what would surely be a death sentence? But at the same time, his arrest was called for by Cabalian justice, which Telnis had sworn to uphold. If he, a captain of the Council of Inquest, let him go free, would he not become the very kind of corrupt hypocrite he despised before all this had happened? The successful capture of Brinwin's accomplice would only increase his honor, too. Perhaps even enough to land him a position that didn't require handling as much paperwork and speeches as a mid-level captain.

Telnis stood frozen in contemplation. Nothing in his training had ever prepared him for a scenario like this. Reason and emotion tugged heavily at him on either side, each option laden with both duty and empathy. Even if he had a lifetime to decide, he doubted it would have been enough time to settle his mind. But such time he did not have. The scales hung in the balance, and a decision was needed *now*.

At that moment, his mind's eye flashed forward to him presenting his speech to the King of Tropis the following evening. Crowds of people surrounded him, cheering him as the hero of Elkreath. Men, women, and children looked upon him in admiration, and coworkers saluted him in honor. For the rest of his lifetime, people would hold him up as an example — but as an example of what? The vision then faded.

He looked down once more at William and made his choice. Reaching toward him, he offered his hand to the Englishman. He could have never lived with himself to be hailed as a hero when it came at the expense of repaying mercy with death. A higher justice than Cabalian law lay written on his conscience, something he could not bring himself to cross even for all the honor in the world.

"Well then, William of England," he said. "If Brinwin Zikennig is truly dead, I don't deem you a threat to my people. Back to your own land will you go." William stared incredulously at Telnis, even as he rose to his feet. Once he was fully upright, Telnis then added, "But should you ever be found in our lands again, I cannot spare you from the judgments of my superiors. Consider your kindness to me repaid."

William nodded, still numb with disbelief. He stooped to retrieve the Azgari sword, but Telnis planted his boot firmly across the blade. "I cannot allow you to take our weapons with you," he said firmly.

William straightened himself but refused to step away from the blade. "I apologize, sir," he said with a bow. "I dare not cross one who has shown me such mercy, but I cannot return to my king empty-handed. You may as well turn me over to your people if such is to be the case. My king sent me to obtain shadesteel, and shadesteel I must obtain. You have respected my virtue thus far; please respect my duty in this also. I swear not to use it on your people if that is what you fear."

Telnis frowned, but he lifted his boot after a moment's pause. "Fine then," he said. "But now you're in my debt. If so much as a drop of Cabalian blood is spilled from that blade, may you suffer the same fate as Brinwin."

William shuddered before bending down to retrieve the sword. Once he had fastened the weapon to his side, he faced the inquestor. "Before we go any further, I just have to know. How did you find me so quickly? You hardly missed a stride between entering the ship and finding me."

A passing gleam flashed across Telnis's eyes. With the faintest of smiles, he replied, "I'm an inquestor, William. It's my job to be attentive. I saw you when you sneaked aboard the ship, and it was easy to guess where you went by the time I made it here myself. No stowaway is going to hide above deck in the open." He then turned and pointed at the torch closest to William. "But your biggest mistake was extinguishing the torch. It was the only one dark when I reached the bottom of the stairs. You may as well have planted a sign with a giant arrow pointing at you."

"Oh... right," William mumbled. "Perhaps we should return it to its normal light, then?"

Telnis glanced over at the torch. With a flick of his eyes, its light dimmed until it matched the rest of the torches. Once satisfied with this, he turned and paced toward the center of the ship to a barrel the size of William. It was one of the few containers covered by a lid, and when opened, it was easy to see why. It held a variety of Cabalian fish that stank even worse than the others on board.

Telnis smirked as he patted the barrel. "This looks like a good fit for you. Help me empty it." William did not argue with the man, even when the odor reached his nostrils. He had survived so much already — what was one final stench to deal with?

With just a few minutes of labor, the fish sat piled in a heap at the corner of the ship. "Now, how are we going to hide this?" asked William. "I hope you aren't expecting me to eat all this before I go."

"Why?" Telnis laughed. "Are you not feeling hungry at the moment?"

William remained silent as Telnis stepped closer to the pile. The inquestor cracked his knuckles, then trained his gaze on the fish while he began muttering to himself. "Ages since I tried this... blasted Illusion magic... never liked it in school," William barely caught him saying.

Nothing happened at first until the fish vanished with a sudden ripple into thin air. On closer look, William could distinguish slight variations in the area where the fish still lay. If one looked close enough, small bulges rose where the grain and color of the wood did not quite align with its surroundings. Telnis simply shrugged. "It's close enough. They won't be looking that hard, and by the time they trip on it, you should be safely ashore."

They returned to the empty barrel, where they exchanged their parting words.

"I suppose this is farewell, then," said William.

Telnis bowed slightly in response. "I suppose so."

Not knowing what else to do, William offered a bow and hoped it was not received as awkwardly as it was given. "I am sorry for the blow to your head," he apologized.

Telnis quickly waved his hand. "Ah... think nothing of it. It's the best sleep I've had in a long time." A silence followed until Telnis cleared his throat. "*Sitallas*, William," he said curtly. When the Englishman only tilted his head, Telnis offered the translation William's ring apparently could not. "It means goodbye. Forever."

"Oh..." mumbled William. "*Sitallas*, Inquestor."

He clambered into the barrel with a final nod, and Telnis shut the lid. As he did so, he brought it to bear with such force that William slumped unconscious. Telnis paused to listen against the side of the barrel, then gave a contented sigh as he ascended the stairs to the main deck.

"Sorry about that, William. Our debts are now even again."

* * *

Telnis breathed deeply of the crisp evening air as he disembarked from the ship. He reached the piers in time to brush elbows with the first dockworkers returning to keep watch on the *Snowbird*. They eyed him in suspicion but said nothing as he sauntered back to the Council of Inquest's headquarters. He cast little more than a glance back toward the *Snowbird*, now small in the distance, while he pondered the fate of the stowaway in its depths.

It was certainly a strange tale that wove their fates together — a pity indeed no one would ever know of it! Whatever disappointment he felt at keeping such a tale to himself, however, was quickly overshadowed by the joy that welled within him with each step he took. It felt as if a burden were lifted from his shoulders, knowing that Elkreath was now safe from the mischief of Brinwin. He smiled at the thought and began to whistle an old Cabalian folk tune as he strode beneath the stars.

As much as he still hated having to give his speech the following evening, he could at least offer it wholeheartedly since he now believed it to be true. Elkreath was safe, free to rebuild in peace. Whatever criminals would still haunt its streets, none would compare to that of Brinwin Zikennig. He was sure of it.

He paused at the doorstep of headquarters and looked up to the heavens one final time. He could not help but marvel at the stars shining so brightly, like diamonds scattered across a plain of coal. The words of Brinwin came to mind, as fresh as when he had first uttered them: "Keep up the good work, Telnis... I can already see you'll become an important person. Just don't forget to rest when you can."

Did Brinwin know just how true those words would be? Could he have foreseen how it would all play out? Telnis shook his head. "Sorry, Brinwin," he murmured. He was not about to rest now — not when there was still more work left to do. He stepped through the door, and with a *clink* it shut behind him.

* * *

The *Snowbird* departed for England half past the stroke of midnight, an hour past its scheduled departure. William woke sometime after that to find himself cramped in the darkness of a reeking fish barrel. He rubbed his aching head and silently cursed the inquestor who gave him such a thoughtful parting gift.

At least the man had the decency to cut an air hole in the back of the barrel, for which William was thankful. He breathed a sigh of relief to feel the Azgari sword still hanging by his side, having feared at first the Cabalian might have stolen it while he was unconscious. Now, all that remained was to make the journey back to England. How long that would be, he could not tell. But at least his task going forward was pretty simple. He just needed to sit still... alone, with his thoughts.

He realized then his last trial was to be the sorest of them all. There was nothing left to distract himself with, no immediate objective to divert the flow of his memories from flooding their bounds and making him relive his whole adventure from beginning to end. The voices of the drunken crew above reminded him that whatever he had to suffer, it would have to be in silence. And suffer he did.

Any pleasant memory was a reminder of what he would never see again; most other memories were of the horrors he had but barely survived. Of all the afflictions suffered thus far, the loss of Zala stung the worst. He had not counted on falling in love with a Cabalian noblewoman when he left the shores of his homeland, and yet he had — just in time for her to be yanked from him as suddenly as she had appeared in his life. Her similarities to the last woman he had loved intensified the loss, making it twice as painful. No sum of riches would he have spared if only he could have her by his side on the home stretch of his journey.

What kind of life could they have built together in England? And what kind of happiness could they have known? Such questions were now futile, for she was gone.

He clutched at her amulet still hanging around his neck, given to him the night they had shared their first kiss. "Whatever happens, you'll have this to remember me by," she had said. Such remembrance seemed now a curse rather than a comfort as he wept most bitterly.

Untold hours passed, and his confusion only grew as his tears subsided. How could God have allowed this to happen to him, he wondered. Why had he been spared, but not Zala? Why had Gaimis been given that stupid dream of assurance, just for it to have proven false?

Unbidden for, the memory of the dream played before him, more vivid than any of his other recollections. It was then he realized how they had all misinterpreted it.

Brinwin and Zala had promised Gaimis that *he and William* would make it home safely. And so they had. Gaimis was, in all likelihood, sitting safely in his cathedral while William was bound for England, hurting but safe for the moment. The revelation struck him as sunlight after drawing back a curtain: Henry *would* be king of England, just as the dream stated. And William would make it back home to complete his mission. He was meant to survive.

Confusion gave way to clarity, and William's heart hung at that moment on a precipice. There had been a purpose to all of this. That much was clear. But how to feel toward the One who purposed? Anger? Or trust?

He remembered Gaimis's elaborations on the problem of pain and suffering, but such things felt far too inadequate in the thick of his own struggles. His emotions were raging, yet he still had a choice to make. He had postponed since Edomear the call his soul felt, and now it could wait no longer. He remembered his promise to serve God if he had lived. And lived he had. Would he make good on his word, or would he run further?

The tension was unbearable, and he gripped his head in his hands. Questions yanked at his heart, even as a certain presence came alongside his soul. How could he serve a god who had treated him so poorly?

"*William,*" came the call to his spirit. William ignored it in his despair and let fly with more questions. If God really is love, then why doesn't he treat his creation better? What did anyone do to deserve this?

"*William,*" came the call again. It could not be ignored this time, so William directly poured his cries of anguish to the One who called him.

"Why did you let this all happen, God? Did you not notice, or do you just not care?" A silence fell, but it lasted for just a moment.

"*William,*" came the final call. "*If you desire peace, then you must stop fighting me.*"

As quickly as the exchange began, something inside his heart gave way. An assurance unsought for came knocking at the door, and exhausted from the struggle, William undid the latch. He slumped within the barrel and trembled, his words pouring out through a stream of tears and whispers. "I'm sorry, Lord. I'm done fighting... I promise I'm done fighting you."

31

A New Plan

It was with no small amount of surprise when, three days later, the merchants of the *Snowbird* saw a man spring from their barrel of fish with a sword in hand and flee into the depths of London. He moved too quickly to identify and was too familiar with the area to catch. The "fish man" remained a topic of their discussion for a long time thereafter, even past their return home from the voyage. William, on his part, gave little thought to the *Snowbird* as he set himself wholly on making it to his master's courts as soon as possible.

At the time, Henry had returned to his holdings in Normandy, and it thus required a final journey to France to reach him. William's connections allowed him to arrange the trip faster than most, and he stopped only for the most necessary of reasons along the way, such as drink and winter clothing. He was thoroughly exhausted when he finally reached the doors of Henry's court, but he dared not delay in his mission.

It was the early morning of a winter day, much the same as when he had first been summoned, that he presented the passwords and credentials necessary to gain access to the king. He wound his way through a labyrinth of halls and stairs until he reached the secret council room

Henry was known to frequent. In the room stood Henry, conversing with Geoffrey of Blois — his second most valuable asset.

While William was the man of action, Geoffrey was the man of knowledge. An accomplished spy he was, so cunning a double agent that he had worked his way into service as Stephen's spymaster, too. He had always made William uncomfortable. A man that crafty could not be trusted. But Henry believed otherwise, so William often had to tolerate his presence in the court.

William overheard their conversation as he approached, and he could not help but smirk to himself.

"It's been over three weeks, Geoffrey," said Henry. "He should have been gone only a week and a half at the most. Have you heard nothing about him on Stephen's end?"

"I'm afraid not, sire," replied Geoffrey. "But I do know Stephen's agent hasn't returned either."

William saw nothing but Henry's back, yet he still sensed the frown that spread across the king's face.

"I fear this bodes ill, then," said Henry. "Perhaps I acted too rashly in sending him to the shores of that accursed land."

It was at this point that William strode forward, relishing the shock on Geoffrey's face. "Fear not, sire!" he called out. "I may have been delayed, but I return now at last."

Henry spun around as his consternation turned quickly into joy. "William!" he gasped. "You live!" He closed the distance between them and clasped an arm on his shoulder. He would have embraced him further, but his nose wrinkled in disgust. "And good heavens, you *reek*! Of fish, no less... " He looked William over in confusion. "I thought you cared not for seafood?"

It was all William could do to keep his composure as he fought back the annoyance of Geoffrey's ever-so-subtle snickering.

"Believe me, my lord, I care for it less than ever. But that is beside the point. I've come to report on my mission."

"Ahh, yes, but of course!" exclaimed Henry. "You have it, then? You have the shadesteel armor?"

William stammered as he considered how to respond to this direct a question. "Ah... well, not exactly, my lord. There were a few mishaps."

Henry's brow furrowed as his expression darkened. "What mean you by this, Lord Steele? Surely you did not interrupt a council session while smelling like raw fish to bring us naught but ill news?"

Geoffrey did little to hide his smile from William. It was no secret he delighted to see William in a position of less favor than he. The last time William had failed his king, Geoffrey was among the first to step into the vacuum of influence left behind. He was clearly delighted to have the scenario repeat itself.

"No, sire, of course not," William replied. "While I was unable to procure the armor—"

"So you failed, then," cut in Henry. His frown was as ominous as the flurries of snow blowing in from the east. If things did not improve quickly, William's position might well be in jeopardy. Before he could explain himself, Geoffrey took the opportunity to capitalize on the situation.

"This is twice now you've failed to live up to your reputation, Lord Steele," he chimed in. "How are we to defeat Stephen with performances like this?"

William glared at Geoffrey as the snow fell thickly outside. He then looked down at the Azgari sword fastened by his waist and smiled. His mind grew clear, and when he spoke, it was no longer with a stammer. He stepped forward to the table and retrieved the sword from his side. The shadesteel gleamed in the light as it came forth silently, drawing to itself the eyes of all as he laid it on the table.

"Actually, my dear Geoffrey, I have an excellent idea how."

Epilogue

A Fate Revealed

So it was that in the end, neither king received what they wanted from Cabalia. One, however, received what he needed. With great skill did William explain the nature of the Azgari sword and convince his king to use it in place of the Trojan Horse he had first intended. Geoffrey then arranged for the sword to be given to Stephen as a token of peace and goodwill.

Stephen was all too eager to receive the sword on the heels of his failure to obtain the recipe of shadesteel. He hoped in vain to find for himself the secret of its composition, and toward that end he spent much time in seclusion at St. Matthew's Cathedral, ostensibly for prayer vigils seeking the blessing of God on his kingdom. But no such blessing did his endeavors there bring.

The effects of the cursed shadesteel he handled began slowly at first but progressed with use. What began as confidence plodded forward into frustration. And from frustration, there arose a sense of foreboding gloom. And amid the foreboding gloom, there lingered paranoia. And paranoia, when it grew stronger, brought on weariness. And weariness, when it matured, fostered infirmity. And so it was that in October of AD 1154, King Stephen of Blois succumbed to a stomach illness of "natural causes."

History then tells us that Henry II ascended to the throne, where he ruled as the king of England for over thirty years. He went on to father sons both famous and infamous: King Richard the Lionheart and King John of the Magna Carta, for example. But of these men, one will have little difficulty finding more to read. What is much less known is what became of the prime agent behind this turn of English history — Lord William Steele.

It is difficult indeed to verify these facts, but what can be said with certainty is now presented here. By all accounts, Lord Steele remained a faithful servant of King Henry for years after his return from Cabalia. He was careful, however, to keep himself hidden from public view. He would avoid spending time at any port, especially when a Cabalian trade vessel lodged there. More so than the ports, he regarded any place belowground with extreme aversion — even basements.

Yet for all his eccentric and reclusive ways, he was regarded by those who knew him to be a man of piety. He talked little of his experiences, but to the end of his days, he never forgot his adventures in Cabalia; neither yet did his adventures forget him.

Brinwin and Zala will return in *The Children of Kennig...*

Acknowledgments

Nothing worthwhile is possible without the help of friends and family, so my heartfelt thanks go out to the following people who helped make this work a reality:

* My brothers and sisters at Calvary Chapel of the Berkshires, whose love of reading is surpassed only by their love for the Lord. To call your input "invaluable" would be an understatement. Missy Corbett, Andrea White, Bill and Anne-Marie Webster, Justin Lottey, Stephen Jensen, Emily Winters, Amelia Corbett, Emma Isenhart, Bella Corbett, Jay and Miranda Tracy, and anyone else I may have missed, "I thank my God through Jesus Christ for all of you."

* The Griffith Family and Adam Barham, for the hours around a campfire listening to my ramblings of Cabalia and inspiring me to develop it further. You had every opportunity to lynch me for the cliffhangers, but you didn't. For that I am most grateful.

* Stephen Larson, my experienced beta reader, for humoring his friend's insanity with some constructive feedback. It may still be insanity, but at least it's more polished insanity, thanks to you.

* My Cous, for the early encouragement and reminding me about sound.

* Lisa and Patrick McColgan, my dear mother and father, for being at the vanguard of listening to new chapters.

* Ben McColgan, for the timely, if not blunt, advice his knucklehead of a brother needed to hear.

* Bernie Klem, for the final round of proofreading. I would smirk if I could, but...

* Ashton Ritter, for the wisdom of her advice and generosity of her spirit that brought this creation all the closer to its "ideal completion."

* Melanie "Zeragii" Griffith, for all the truly wonderful artwork. No matter what people say, they totally judge a book by its cover. Thanks to you, that initial judgment isn't a poor one.

* And lastly, my two other musketeers. You know who you are.

Anti-Acknowledgments

For every up, there is a down. And for every person who aided in this endeavor, there was something else that hindered it. Here I'd like to sincerely thumb my nose at the following thorns in my side, who IN SPITE OF YOU, I somehow managed to finish this story:

First, **The Wasps Upstairs.** Your tenacity was admirable, but also terrifying. I do not mourn your demise.

Second, **COVID-19.** While I'm grateful for the time off you provided to write a few chapters, the havoc you wreaked in my life far outweighed those gains. I wish you the same fate as smallpox and rinderpest.

Third, **Insomnia.** Many are the curses I have for you, my ancient foe. But for the sake of my well being, I think I'll need to sleep on it first.

Fourth, **Laziness and Procrastination.** You're as repulsive in me as you are in others. Would to God you'd die a painful death! But knowing you, I'm sure you'd put that off for another few centuries, too.

Fifth, **The Busyness of Life.** [I was planning to write something witty about you, but my goodness! How time slips away...]

Last, but certainly not least, **That Which Shall Not Be Named.** Through all my miseries, you smiled on, and works greater than this have you desecrated. James 5:1-5.

A Final Note

The astute reader may have noticed that the Essari's style of speech seems inconsistent in certain places — in some sections using the verb-last construction of "Old Speak," and in others using standard English word order. Rest assured, these inconsistencies were intentional. A closer look at the text will reveal that the standard English order was used only when commands or instructions were given. This was done in adherence to the grammar rules of "Old Speak," where word order changes in the imperative mood from a verb-last construction to a verb-first one.

Printed in the USA
CPSIA information can be obtained
at www.ICGtesting.com
LVHW021310140524
779690LV00018B/909